Alice in Welfareland

Christopher Gilmore's
New Age Novel Faction

Alice in Welfareland

Christopher Gilmore

ROBIN BOOKS · LIVERPOOL

ISBN-: 978-1-904843-32-8

Robin Books Limited
First floor, Mission Hall, 36 Windsor Street
Liverpool L8 1XF.

2 4 6 8 10 9 7 5 3 1

Additional copies of this book can be ordered from:
Website: www.robinbooks.co.uk
E-mail: readers@robinbooks.co.uk
or
Freepost: RLXA-BZTZ-XXKC
Robin Books Limited
3, The Boundary Lane
Lancashire, L40 5XT, UK.
Tel: 0800 45 85 397
Fax: 0800 45 84 913

A CIP catalogue of this book is available from the British Library

Typeset in 9½/15pt Helvetica
by Derek Doyle & Associates, Shaw Heath
Printed in and bound in Great Britain
by St Edmundsbury Press Bury St Edmunds, Suffolk

About
Christopher Gilmore

Telly addicts might have seen him in *Dixon of Dock Green* or in Michael Winner's early nudist film *Some Like It Cool*. He also acted with Glenda Jackson, Dame Maggie Smith and, briefly, with '*Awesome*' Wells. At Bembridge school his theatrical talent was, significantly, inspired by the works of Lewis Carroll. Aged eight he played Humpty Dumpty in *Alice Through the Looking-Glass*.

Christopher's three Talking Books are used as 'edutainment' for teaching philosophy to +4-year-olds at Saturday Schools. Hence his new CD, '*Early Learners Know Lots*'. These children, like feisty Alice in Welfareland challenging the strange but familiar characters in her epic adventures, are also seeking more fun, truth and love. Encouraging sparky learners of all ages, Christopher writes in many modes including *DOVETALES*, D.I.Y. pictorial guide-books to kick-start personal creativity. This series of 10 titles includes *Holistic History, Arts Within, Godly Geography* as well as *Mighty Mathematics, More Fun, Less Fear*. All titles are listed.

When Director of The Holistic Education Foundation he facilitated varied Self-Development 'Playshops' in four continents. But carved upon his gravestone no www.christophergilmore.com will be inscribed. Instead, he sees cartoons to illustrate his light-hearted stories celebrating death, ALIVE-ALIVE-O!- How to Die Laughing and Survive! The last caption to read:

'There's always a creative alternative!'

DEDICATIONS

Alice in Welfareland is dedicated to three ladies. First, to Elspeth Cochrane, my keen literary agent, for her patient and unselfish faith in this new novel 'faction'. Second, is Daphne Evens, my cherished editor for her sustained concentration on every detail. Thirdly, to the Muse herself, the Spirit of Alice.

Not to be sexist, I also dedicate this book to two men. Firstly, John Crowe who published my book *Soul-Centred Education*, a modest healer of distant friends. Now I send warmest thanks to another unsung hero, founder of the School Children's Song for Europe, Geoffrey Jackson. With his customary good-heart, between jobs, he generously applied his skills in carpentry to teaching me, not how to escape from a rabbit hole, but from the weeks I spent framed by the puzzling constraints of PDF!

With Alice, may we all enjoy our own inner adventures, even relish the unexpected in all of life's magical lessons.

CONTENTS

PROLOGUE

So she sat on, with closed eyes, and half believed herself in Wonderland, though she knew she had but to open them again, and all would change to dull reality – the grass would be rustling in the wind, and the pool rippling to the waving reeds – the rattling teacups would change to tinkling sheep-bells, and the Queen's shrill cries to the voice of the shepherd boy – and the sneeze of the baby, the shriek of the Gryphon, and all the other queer noises would change (she knew) to the confused clamour of the busy farm-yard – while the lowing of the cattle in the distance would take the place of the Mock Turtle's heavy sobs.

Lastly, she pictured to herself how this same little sister of hers would, in the after-time, be herself a grown woman: and how she would keep, through all her riper years, the simple and loving heart of childhood.

Taken from the last page of *Alice in Wonderland*
by Lewis Carroll.

**Until the day he died, he did not admit to being the mathematician,
and Oxford Don, Charles Lutwidge Dodgson.**

CHAPTER ONE

THE RIDDLED WOOD

'Reeling and writing, of course, to begin with,'
the Mock Turtle replies;
'and then the different branches of Arithmetic -
Ambition, Distraction, Uglification, and Derision.'

Before the sleeping nun awoke for her early morning pee, Alice needed to flee. And yet . . . and yet, wouldn't it be more fun to share Sister Margaret's embarrassment with her other convent girl conspirators?

Alice listened like an owl for rustlings under their bedclothes. Although already dressed and ready to run none of the other girls seemed even awake. The whole dormitory was gently heaving with the sleepy harmonies of combined heavy breathing. Not one snore punctuated the peaceful atmosphere. Only one distant owl called as if enticing dangers outside the convent walls were far more exciting than spiking a teacher's chamber pot.

To save water, on the stroke of seven promptly, Sister Margaret always enthroned her queenly posterior. But Alice and her rebellious classmates having prepared a prank, that morning their dormitory Sister was sure to be shocked into retaliation.

Alice, always brimming over with tricky questions, was a pain in the bum, especially to Sister Margaret. Marking LET'S HELP AN ACCIDENT was the clincher. Though Alice wrote her essay on the dangers of nuclear power, the nun felt the child's approach too subversive to earn high marks. Getting the lowest grade in the class had again kick-started Alice into yet more daring. In answer to her deluge of restless questions dammed by Sister Margaret's fear of facing floods of heresies, Alice had arranged a fizzy wake-up call. Never again, would she be ordered to empty the nun's potty slops by way of a punishment for so often asking in her primmest tones, 'Sister, why do boys, like us, have two tits too?'

Lying low inside the plain white nun's chamber pot was a thick layer of Epsom salts sneaked in by a day pupil from Boots the chemist. When heated with night-warmed pee Alice and rebels hoped to overhear the nun's pot bubble over and the nun herself to squeak. Yes, instead of the usual genteel flow of holy water, they visualised a veritable Vesuvius of effervescent froth erupting all over the Sister Margaret's immaculate floorboards.

Should Alice wait long enough to be discovered as ringleader or run into the wood before dawn? Hurriedly, she stuffed a spare pair of knickers into her satchel as, more loudly, the owl again cackled its warning. Feeling unsupported by her sleeping teenage chums, Alice tried not to stay brave. Hadn't her dad, before going abroad again for the Diplomatic Corps, cuddling her that last night joked, 'Sleep tight, darling. Mind the nuns don't bite'? And there was Alice trembling outside Sister Margaret's cubicle door, teeth chattering loud enough to frighten off the dormitory mouse Alice loved feeding illicit cheese crackers.

Yet . . . yet philosophical to a fault, Alice still lingered. Should she stay or go? Oh, it would be such fun to overhear the fizz of holy urine overflowing polished floorboards; hear the bum-wet nun's saintly swearwords; relish the absent handy mop being cursed, maybe in Latin.

Alice had often been threatened with expulsion, but never in Latin. For example, just before her parents went abroad, for shaving the naked legs of her best buddies in the showers, it was nearly excommunication. So, in contrast, the threat of being a lost runaway in the nearby wood was almost enticing. Alice always wanted to experience everything. That's why when carpeted by Sister Margaret about the girls' shaven legs, Alice with her best cherubic grin had asked, 'Have angels hairy legs?' As a result, in the next Religious Studies class, Sister Margaret refused to let Alice leave the room no matter how often the girl insisted she was dripping and not just from her eyes. Instead, the Teaching Sister, with a bellow, had instructed Alice to pray for better obedience.

'Pray to who Sister?'

'Whom, child.'

'Saint Martin?'

'Martin?'

'Luther!' The exploding nun's tone brooked no indulgence.

Funny, thought Alice, the more firm people's beliefs are the more they take offence. To run away or face the fanatical Sister? Soon the nun's bursting bladder alarm clock would stir her chubby body from sleep. With that thought Alice ran back to her bed. Then emboldened by the owl, she reconsidered. Humming Handle's Water Music like a funeral march, she crept back between the curtained rows of snoring girls to the nun's cubicle door.

Then she remembered. That morning, on her forbidden radio, she had heard the weather forecast. Rain was due. Perhaps a deluge. The thought of getting soaked as well as lost in the wood was not very philosophical. Or healthy. As it was the family doctor liked tapping her chest while intoning, '999!' as if Alice was a disaster waiting to happen, a daily walkie-talkie emergency.

Then Alice heard a voice. *'Oh to escape all adults and feel safe!'* But that thought wasn't her doctor's or even her own voice. Hearing it again in her head she guessed it was a croaky boy's voice. Though it was uninvited Alice felt strangely curious. Wonder if he's got two tits like me, thought Alice as she strained to hear any exciting messages that might lead her further astray in a hurry.

By then her so-called girl friends were snoring too loudly. Obviously they were pretending to be still asleep in order not to be accused of spiking Sister Margaret's potty with Epsom salts. That is even though they had agreed with Alice on the dose. Since no nun is expected to be pregnant or breastfeeding the potty was given a safe and healthy big dose of salts.

Holding her breath outside the nun's door, Alice asked for a firm decision to arrive like a delightful surprise birthday present. That boy's voice obliged. '*Trust M-mother Nature m-more than M-mother Superior.*'

'Meaning what?' she wondered. 'Oh I see. If by five to seven it really IS raining outside, stay innocently in bed as if fast asleep.' This Alice pictured; lying low in her dormitory cubicle, a sheet stuffed in her mouth to stop herself laughing aloud as the nun's blessed trickle became more than a damp squib. Hopefully by then, the saturated Sister would be too wet to barge straight out of her cubicle as was her way every time she thought she heard the girls swearing, talking about boys, or both at once.

But wait. Alice spotted a flaw in the boy's suggestion to trust the English weather. What if by five to seven there was no rain? All dry outside? All right, instead of facing the music of trickle rising into high tide, Alice would fling her satchel over the convent wall. Then urgently, helped by the apple orchard's stepladder, follow her few worldly goods into the wood. Such would satisfy her growing quest for uncertain adventures.

Reaching the large bay window, the one nearest to Sister Margaret's door, Alice listened. Thankfully, the nun was snoring tunes that even the charitable Hildegard von Bingam would have found unmusical.

But Alice still couldn't make up her mind what outcome to pray for. Chanting prayers by rote had always seemed such a chore. Like cleaning her teeth before bedtime. But her mother, holding Alice warmly round the waist as she flashed her own bright white teeth in the bathroom mirror, had already cured that. Alice, risking her own well-brushed smile, bared her teeth. In the dormitory window her reflection smiled back like the Cheshire Cat. Surely that signalled it was time. Yet as she peered at the courtyard clock, still no sign of rain. So should she stay dry and run for cover under the trees in case. . . ?

Five to seven came. And the weather? Outside it was neither wet nor dry. Darn it, it was DRIZZLING. Oh dear. But as the nuns always advised, 'When in doubt girls, listen out for God to speak up.'

Still in doubt Alice listened not out, not up, but in.

Suddenly, an upsurge of virgin snores shook the dormitory. It sounded suspiciously orchestrated. But no word from God. Or from the rude boy who had chatted her up earlier. Worse, no clear wet tadpoles slithering down windowpanes. She longed to watch lots of such weaving raindrops in pairs wobble into hugs making each couple twice as big. 'Why does Sister Margaret never hug me?' grieved Alice. 'Or even hug Father Murphy?'

'I know. It's because she's afraid of getting bigger. Horrid the way he eats too many hot dogs. And his frisky sideburns might singe her dimples. Gosh though. If I do stay here Sister might, just might say, 'Clever girl for thinking up such a prank. Go top of the science class.' Then I'd let her off if she never wanted to hug me.

In her hot head the clock outside ticked ever more loudly.

Four minutes to go.

Alice breathed hard on the windowpane and rubbed it with her elbow. With all her might she was willing raindrops to dramatically splatter the windowpane. But no, on the dark glass, not one trickle, rivulet, or flash flood. And below in the courtyard, not one friendly overflowing drainpipe chuckling away down the drain. With three minutes to go, just misty grey drizzle everywhere she looked.

God, she decided, was speaking in silent riddles.

Two minutes left. Alice forgot Mother Nature, forgot the Mother Superior, forgot Sister Margaret, forgot all she'd learnt about droughts and monsoons. 'No more pissing about, girl,' Alice said almost aloud just after five to seven, 'Make up your own mind and go with the flow. . . .'

As the convent girls corporate snoring reached a crescendo, a downstairs toilet was heard to flush. The girls' snoring mid-note stopped. The oaken dormitory door burst open. Through it Sister Margaret sailed like an embattled galleon in a gale guided by God to a safe harbour or, better still, to a dry dock.

Alice gasped. She knew it. One of her so-called chums had snitched on her. In shock she felt more alone than ever before.

Until . . . the owl's hoot was calling her . . . Alice still blushing.

From the floor below another familiar sound shook her further; a toilet flushing. Downstairs in the blue toilet bowl in Mother Superior's chamber. Before the flush had subsided – but not in either of her hot burning cheeks – Alice fled.

The day her doctor no longer charged for medicines there was a queue all round his block. Patients demanding free cotton wool. What a way to encourage earache.

Lost in the forest Alice remembered those demands for cotton wool. Probably because she was anxious to disentangle her own woolly thoughts. Being lost in the Garden of Eden, she mused, could not have been much fun for Eve either. Like being unemployed; with no housework to do, no fig-leaves to wash, nor apples to cook: just God's own ever-growing open larder, divine optimism beaming everywhere at once, and for ever, the whole blooming garden brimming over with the joys of generosity. How boring!

Surely Alice could earn the right to find her own way out of the forest without intervention, celestial or otherwise. The fireflies were starting to wink in the twilight, dizzy clusters of them under the trees. An insect with too many legs seemed intent on ignoring her plight. Still, this reminded Alice of a verse attributed to that ageless bald Master, Sri Yaubl Sacabi who works marvels from the high Himalayas. To comfort her aloneness, she recited it aloud:

'The centipede was happy, while the frog in fun said:
'Which leg, please, comes after which?'
This raised her doubts to such a pitch,
she fell confounded in the ditch,
not knowing how to run. . . .'

Yet Alice dared to keep running, to leave behind her old life of silver Apostle teaspoons and parents more often abroad than at home. Even the darkness about to descend would not undermine her wish to explore life outside her convent school walls. Yet she felt bad. Maybe because so often in the past being in the right had always made others seem in the wrong. Especially nuns. Worse than that even, the more often adults had found Alice to be correct, the more often they wished to kick her. That hurt. Now she wished to kick herself. Only she was afraid of missing.

That really WOULD make her feel a fool.

Twitching its way through giant glass-blades, she watched a second centipede undulating in the opposite way to the first. 'Really,' thought Alice, 'why can't portents point the same way like signposts? How intriguing!' She looked closer, imploring guidance from the timid little insect seeking a hole in the undergrowth. 'What's it all for, all those legs and no clear direction? Such mathematical incompetence doesn't add up.'

The old Owl above her chortled, invitingly. Creatures lost in mental turmoil were his juiciest kills. One stir in the darkest undergrowth, one second's muddled thinking and the owl cast his deathly shadow over them like a black blanket – too late. 'On the first split infinitive, I STRIKE!' warned the Owl with relish. 'But I never kill with my mouth full, not kids.' Clearing his throat, he then purred out this wisdom: 'God's all grammar. Life's all predators. And Death, delicious girl, is all P-R-E-Y!'

'Oh God, help me predicate!' gulped Alice, eyes tight as clams. 'Save me from strong verbs, indefinite articles in the dark and all compound fractures before I stumble over them!' With that, she fell. To her knees, humble but not humiliated. Not YET!

'It stands to reason, It sits to sense.'

'What does?' asked Alice scanning the tree above her for danger. 'Maybe putting the horse before the cart, perhaps.'

'Descartes before the 'orse,' quiped Owl, his French accent making the word 'orse sound like a fat tasty frog.

'Sorry, but sense to me seems rather COMMON. I think . . . there-fore. . . .'

'There you are!' proclaimed the Owl, beaming.

'Where's THERE, sir? I'm lost.' At this, the unblinking Owl ruffling his feathers chortled. 'Please Mr. Owl, show me the way. Only don't expect me to take it. I hate crowds.'

'That won't save your Francis Bacon. Lost is only looking in the wrong places. Think again, little lady. Philosophy isn't just cotton-wool to stuff in both ears to stop your brains from overflowing.'

'No?'

'Oh dear me, no. Think again.'

'But what exactly IS philosophy?' pleaded Alice.

'EXACTLY!' said the Owl, then laughed.

Alice did not like this. Owls were meant to be know-alls, not clowns. In any case, he might be laughing at her and that wasn't comforting. Still laughing, the Owl said, 'I'll tell you what philosophy ISN'T, if you like. . . !'

'Isn't?' sniffed Alice. 'Just because I'm lost in this wood and the dark is falling, there's no need to be nice to me with negatives.'

Mr Owl stopped laughing. Scowled. Then for three hours and four minutes, he told Alice what philosophy ISN'T. Most of that time he glared at her Ban-the-Bomb badge, as Alice, suffering from bladder-bursting boredom, struggled to stay respectfully attentive. Eventually, he ended the grammatically accurate sermon with a resounding 'AMEN!'

'T-h-a-n-k G-O-D!' hissed Alice, thanking God instead of the Owl. Mistake. Obviously the learned Mr Owl thought he WAS God. 'But I'm lost,' complained Alice, wriggling. 'And now it's really dark, and what's worse, I know what philosophy isn't but I still don't know what it IS.'

Owl regurgitated a field mouse or, rather, that's what Alice hoped it was since she adored dormice and didn't like to think of them feeding a philosophic old Owl who laughed at her. 'Would you agree,' crooned Owl, 'that this, my oak tree, is not knotted, too?'

'Actually, I'd rather un-knot myself, thank you.'

'Exactly what my oak tree did,' added Owl. 'That's why there are holes in it.'

'Like logic!' offered Alice with her raffish grin.

'No, madam, not like in gruyere cheese either,' countered Owl pretending not to be flustered. 'We speak of higher mathematics. How many holes pray, in my oak tree? – COUNT!'

Without looking, since it was too dark to see, Alice announced, 'Three thousand.'

'Couldn't be more correct!' crowed Owl, 'Three holes. I call them windows. Look through them, if you care to.'

'No, I never look into noughts, Mr Owl. I'm afraid of finding nothing there.'

'From God to gravity, girl, and nothing in between!' observed the Owl with new gravitas, peering at her Ban-the-Bomb badge. 'For one apparently just starting her second 12-year cycle, some advice. Fear hell on earth and you'll never become a high-flier like me. So now I urge you to trot off back to your school before I regurgitate.'

'That's what most teachers at both my schools did. That's why I escaped. They burped and we yawned. Then WE burped and THEY yawned. For them, that's learning. They don't like me, the teachers.'

'How unexpected!' Owl's yellow eyes became two narrow glints of irony.

'I ask too many questions. They prefer answers.'

'An appetite for learning, have we?' nodded Owl, head heavy with mortarboard, the top branches creaking with his weighty thoughts. 'And in my wood, what words will you eat, girl?'

'For you, my DIET OF WORMS. Would you care for a quick taster, Mr Owl?'

'A snack?' Owl scowled, 'Any minute now you'll be asking, 'WHICH CAME FIRST. . . ?'

'I don't eat chicken.'

'Then why did the chicken cross the road?' he asked, crossly. He hated interruptions.

'Easy-peasy, that!' gloated Alice. 'That's like dying. To get to the OTHER SIDE. I do it daily. By Astral Travel!'

'Really, you are quite impossible,' snorted the Owl.

'That must be because, like Descartes, I'M POSSIBLE,' chirruped Alice. 'Be-cause that's what the very word means. BeCAUSE – not effect!'

The effect of this was to make Owl want to fly off to catch a rat in the moonlight and shake it by the scruff of its neck until it is dumb enough to admit it is dead. All rats should be modest, especially dead ones.

'What about GHOSTS?' probed Alice, wide-eyed with wonder. 'I'm haunted by a wonderful boy. Is he hiding in your wood? I do hope so, sir. His ghost told me to find him!'

GHOSTS? Too much! Such superstitious variables! In his highest dudgeon, Owl challenged again, saying 'What's logical about walking through classroom walls, let alone through looking-glasses. . . ?' Then, starting to screech, Mr Owl persisted with, 'All men are MORTAL. Socrates is a man. Socrates is mortal!'

'Bad algebra!'

'It's not MATHS, you silly, stupid, smug little madam. It's ENGLISH!'

'But Socrates was Greek. So no IS. He's a WAS. He's DEAD. Got it?' her full bladder making her feel frisky, Alice added, 'It might just as well be

Japanese, Owly dear.'

'Was.' cooed Owl, not turning a feather. 'Was, was, W-A-S a man. There, that's better!'

'Why?'

'Because I say so.'

'That's how I know when grown-ups don't really know. They always say, **"Because I say so – so there!"** and fluff up their feathers to look even bigger fools than they already are.'

'It's YOU who are lost in my wood – without my permission too – young Alice, NOT your boyfriend. Not even your teachers.'

'They're not curious enough to lose their way. Now will you please listen to this: ALL MEN ARE IMMORTAL. SOCRATES WAS ALSO HU-MAN. SOCRATES!'

There was a silence in the wood. Even the crickets stopped chirping.

'WHAT?' demanded Mr Owl like some nuclear scientist finding a dainty dead girl on a slab winking at him.

'A Haiku,' exploded Alice.

For a moment Owl thought that Alice had sneezed. Before he could decide not to bless her, she continued. 'Japanese, you see. A Haiku is more generous than logic. It leaves room for one's own contribution.' She grinned, experimentally. Flogging her ideas, she felt like the Cheshire Cat, uncertain that its nine lives wouldn't suddenly turn into a cat-o'-nine tails for her own back. 'Heads down, you ignorant lot,' shout the schoolteachers above as they lob at us their bombs marked KNOWLEDGE. But I won't duck. I say, "Get knotted!" '

As if being introduced to a new mix of mouse gravy, the Owl sagely nodded. 'Next stop – Humpty Dumpty! For more knowledge, he'll soon whet your girlish appetite. Unless, that is,' he added salaciously, 'you wish to fall off his wall, commit kamikaze and meet up with your ghost boyfriend in your frilly camiknickers for a quick. . . .'

Only having heard words 'wet' and 'girlish appetite', more than her ardour was dampened. Crossing her legs, Alice blurted out her next plea. 'If kind teachers only assumed that I was wise already,' she said, 'I would not need to become wicked. Then, as friends, they would welcome my questions. If Truth is All, then surely, I also must be a large part of it.'

'Such arrogance! After Mr Dumpty with his appetite for thick twits beneath him has spat you out,' hissed Owl with greedy intensity,' he will leave some tit-bits for me to digest. . . .'

'Socrates didn't ever squash his students,' defied Alice. 'So sir, please, what word, please, should follow the second SOCRATES? Yours?'

'**YOURS**, girl. You started this one!'

'But you must finish it, Mr Owl, It is YOUR truth, not mine.'

'Then return to the original formula,' insisted Owl as if settling the argument.

'Curiouser and curiouser,' thought Alice as Owl ranted on. 'What a dead-end logic is. There just has to be something better than being told we're always wrong. But what. . . ?'

At that second, Alice seemed to jump out of her head, as if with a fright. What if Humpty Dumpty had squashed her boyfriend and that was why he was now only a ghost? On cue, as if by way of an instant answer, Alice suddenly found herself able to even out-hector Helen of Troy. But it was in a husky, stuttering voice, sounding like a lost boy in a confusing forest. As her ghostly words echoed through the dark trees, Owl almost puked. With the assumed daring of a Direct Voice Medium, Alice was also astonished to hear her new self stammering out, '*If m-matter cannot be destroyed, as m-most scientists now seem to believe, and if Socrates was m-made up of m-m-matter, then the answer to our riddle is plain – **SOCRATES!** An affirmation if not an explanation. Experience does not need proof. Experience IS, not was. It m-may be in a different form, but it still lives, invisibly, on one level or another. Are not Owls m-messengers from the Underworld?'*

As if to widen the spooky distance between them, the Owl hopped onto a higher branch, shrieking, 'Bombs away!' An owl egg dropped. Alice, alert as ever, was able to catch it as, in post puberty boyish tones, she heard herself declaring, '*Mr Owl we m-may not know which came first, the chicken or The Diet of Worms, but energy cannot be created or destroyed. It only changes form. TRANSforms. If in chemistry this can be accepted, why not in philosophy? Science is now starting from space; from gasses, to liquids, to solids. Philosophy still ends with gas!*'

By way of relief, Owl released a plume of vermin-flavoured exhaust fumes.

'We try to support itself on a solid foundation of logic with language. But language is too alive to keep still. It wriggles all over the place. Just like Alice now, lost in this wood but can't find a tree quick enough to pee behind!'

Hearing the use of her own name in the first person as Alice herself boomed out more boyish tones, Owl observed, 'There does seem to be more to you, girl, than meets the ear. Indeed, it is so eerie, I demand this demonic burble cease forthwith! Has not your ghost boy the wit to woo you in the flesh and blood. . . ?'

But Alice seemingly possessed of such ethereal and passionate chan-nelling was unstoppable. *'Even grammatical, language will not be bewitched by logic,'* she stressed, scratching her invisible scrotum with-out crushing the owl egg in her hand. *'What's more, in m-modern physics, the notion of a solid is daft since all life is m-made up of atoms as they m-m-m-m-move about just as surely as moon m-mist, or as a ghost boy through me and the unseen sun which, without visible proof, we know to be only in hiding tonight, not dead. Like God, like dogma. Like grammar. Education forces us into straight-jackets, into uniforms, not to serve life but to do detention in the mental wing, rows and rows of cloned robots m-mouthing off parrot platitudes as we try to fly, lop-sided, to escape from our prison classroom. . . ! What a long sentence!'* So long the peckish Owl was glar-ing at her moonlit eyes.

'You looked trapped, Owl!' blurted Alice, refocusing with clairvoyant eyesight but returning to her own voice. 'Like a parrot in prison.'

'PARROT!' exploded Mr Owl with over-pronounced apoplexy. 'Your impoliteness is too . . . too . . . provocative!' said Owl giving his right temple a good scratch. 'Such psycho-babble. I'll have to think that one out. . . .'

'Sleep on it.' advised Alice, soothingly.

'Never do sleep in the dark,' said Owl getting ratty. 'Far too dangerous, fasting!'

'I dreamt of a Black Dog last night. Chasing me. So I ran away. From my old life. From the convent school, looking for better dreams . . . for better lessons . . . my mission. . . .'

'Me, I can't think when I dream. I think.'

'**WOW!**' cried Alice, clapping one hand. 'That's when the machine works best, when its ghost is free to kiss and cuddle. When he's not rusted up with logic, yes, but lubricated with rest!'

From whence had come all her new found confidence? Such clarity was scary! She'd no friends left apart from her ghost boy so why frighten off the chatty Owl as well? But like some fanatical demon, the boy's voice returned, saying, '*Mr Owl, may we agree that Socrates is IMmortal because, being atomic chemistry, he has changed? Not died so m-much as shed his earthly space suit. So now he walks free through all the prison walls of logic and knowledge – EUREKA!*'

'But **HOW** can you **KNOW** all this?' challenged Owl, his laser-like bloodshot pupils piercing the dark like pistons.

'How? Because I have my Dream Dog!' claimed Alice in her usual voice. 'Because my boyfriend visits my mind like it's his bedroom and I'm his. . . .'

'Shaggy-dog fairytale, happy ever after doggy sex. I KNEW it!'

'Now the Queen of Spades says that dogs are dirty but mine can hear things I can't hear, even though he never washes behind his ears. Also, he can SEE things I can't see, like GHOSTS. His hair all stands up on end and he growls and backs away. What am I meant to tell Rover my psychic cleverstick? "STOP that, silly dog, you're only IMAGINING IT!?" '

'Exactly,' clucked the owl, clapping one wing, soundlessly. 'Like your phantom boyfriend!'

'Oh dear. That's what grown-ups always say when they can't see the very point in front of them. How can even earthly dogs have imagination if they don't have minds? Where's your precious logic now? Unless, that is, you think that dogs are backward gods.'

'I'm glad to report,' retorted Owl, 'that since Sunday school, I do not believe in Mister God.'

'Sad. But I do, Mr Owl, I DO! And I even manage to believe in ME. M-most times, that is. Especially when He comes calling. . . .'

'Calling you what – POTTY?' Owl spat out his last word as if to puncture her aching bladder. Then, with a burst of derisive laughter, he asked,

'What is the sound of ONE wing FLAPPING?' Another guffaw. 'Bet you have no Japanese answer to THAT! No, no, NOH!' added Owl, puffing out his pun with his proud feathers.

Frowning, Alice stated that when she had asked a Zen Master that very trick question, he had beckoned her before him. 'I went in, closer,' she continued. 'Again, he gestured me to stand within a foot of his wise, old face repeating in a whisper: *What's the sound of one hand clapping. . . ?*'

Under deep darkness, gossiping crickets silenced and still, awaited glimmers of wisdom.

'Then the old Master, with his upraised right hand, hit me hard with his left hand. Smack across my right cheek. I heard the SOUND?'

Except for faint bell ringing in a few inner ears, silence. On this, Alice declared, 'It was my lover boy calling me home.'

'Death, sweet Deathbed! What next – turn the other cheek?'

But before Alice could answer Mr Owl, all the crickets, and the mice and rats, started to laugh. Alice felt punished. Just as the Queen of Tarts made her feel when she took Cookery Class, saying that good sense was common, like the cold, and therefore should be seen and not heard. Though this lack of formal logic appealed to Alice, chopping off the heads of sheep did not, especially when they were dressed up to look like lamb. Is it wrong, she often wondered, to wish for the lion to lie down with the lamb chop with foot and mouth? Only if you can't cook your own miracles, thought Alice. If so, perhaps one day the lion will change into a god-eater; that is, eat only atoms and change into a Queen of the Inner Kingdoms instead of the jungle.

Aiming the owl egg at the inattentive bird, Alice said, 'Mr Owl, kindly praise me. I'm being provocative again.' This request startled Owl out of his reverie. From her school satchel she extracted a long computer print-out. 'As I say in this, my DIET OF WORMS, Isn't Darwin's ladder of evolution always leading to Jacob's ladder . . . with no real bad luck under them...while all life forms wish to CLIMB. . . !'

'To the top of their tree, like me, girl,' agreed Owl readjusting the mortarboard on his big head. Raising both frilly ends of his Oxbridge United scarf, he rotated them like a pair of football rattles, victoriously.

Changing to post-pubic mellow tones, Alice continued, boyishly. Not quite herself, she again found her voice deepening with such passionate persuasiveness that Owl was re-animated by her more macho approach. Was she changing sex before his very eyes? So far, as the Owl glared down on her, Alice looked like some born-again ventriloquist's dummy.

'Mr Owl, I like to stay open. Yep! To everything. Everyone. Not closing up m-myself in narrow systems that lock in instinct and lock out intuition. YEP!' Clearing her throat of a frog seeking a prince to turn into, she continued in even deeper tones, saying, 'M-maybe this is the joyful optimism of the anarchist. It can lead us to the essence, atomic and SUPER-atomic, which unites all again in one Big Bang; an essence that, singing inside, will guide us back to the Black Hole through which we all slipped down. Why? To woo old lessons like old friends! Alice, when we meet, let's both have the wit to woo. Just call m-me to your side, my-my love-kissed pussy. . . !'

'The wit to woo? Who – WHO?'

Alice, girlishly, found herself flushing, 'Actually, Owl, that was mostly my ghost boy just talking through me again, not. . . .'

'POSSESSION!' grimaced Mr Owl with a ghoulish shudder, his tree trembling in deep fright. 'It's Humpty Dumpty you need now, girl. As Boss of E.M.B.E.R.S., he'll soon demolish your Diet of Worms! Give him that egg to fry. Then he'll know I sent you. He'll unscramble your hot virgin fantasies before breakfast.'

'But not with this owl's egg. My boy voice tells me to keep it. That it brings healing in the Underworld.' But before Alice could confess to Owl that she hadn't yet met the owner of her inner voice, or yet knew what exactly was meant by the Underworld, the bird was poised for flight. At the centre of the tree's crown was a hole. Spontaneously, as if to use the theology of the thermals, the Owl was aiming himself towards it, about to fly off skywards. . . .

'Off to the hole at the North Pole, Mr Owl?' asked Alice already feeling left far below. 'Earth's ozone hole's not closed up.' Crossing her legs with a wince, hoping for a bush to squat behind, she added, 'I feel like a monsoon about to burst. . . .'

'Exorcise that randy ghost. Inside you without permission, Alice Widdle-Liddle. That's psychic RAPE!'

'But Owl, for high-flyers, for further giddy adventures, that's what Black

Holes are for. I'm up for it all, I am. . . !'

The White Rabbit popped up out of the earth. Though blind, he accurately jabbed Alice with a firm paw saying, 'Quick! Be safe! Follow me before the next Big B . . . Into the WHITE hole at the North Pole, Miss Alice, **WHITE!**'

Suddenly at the other side of Alice, a blind Black Rabbit popped up from another hole.

'**BLACK**, Miss Alice,' said this other intruder, sharply. 'A BLACK hole! Dodgy, except for us daring ones. Alice, you're chosen. Quick! Join us! Down to the Rainbow Survivalists before. . . .'

'Follow ME!' sang out the Rabbits in unison. Both bunnies rubbing the Ban-the-Bomb logo on their brows, ran off in opposite directions as if being chased by separate shampoo bottles.

Alice was in a quandary, which rabbit to follow. 'Mr Owl, please be my umpire, before you. . . .'

Having bumped into each other, both Rabbits were flexing front paws like two mad March Hares shadow boxing. Their joint struggle continued into the deepest darkness, White Rabbit against Black Rabbit, until Alice and Owl heard a yell. At least one of the bunnies had fallen screaming down through the earth.

'Even the ground's not solid enough to fight over,' sighed Alice. 'Poor Rabbits. Both wanted to rescue me. But Owl, if you're not into the rat race but hunting Wisdom like me, see what we kids cooked up in maths. Nuns don't count. Not when asked, How many blood oranges vampires on heat eat? So now. Diet of Worms!'

'You kids have worms, child? Send for a vet!'

'We crave your indulgence, sir. But it's free. May I please read it out before. . . ?'

Repeatedly, Owl regurgitated a loud and noisy 'NO!'

'Oh, how polite! Well now, with no "please" or "thank you", how can you call yourself educated? Let alone a high-flier?'

Scowled Mr Owl with a menacing twinkle, 'Before I murder my first Martian mouse, be warned. Humpty Dumpty is no pushover. You'll remember me as the sweetest of pussycats once you've met that fierce fat pedant on his high wall waiting to torture Alice Liddle-Widdle, chipped old piss-pot on his egghead like a crown of thorns. Better relieve your Diet of Worms on him, girl, than under any prickly holly bush hiding snakes alive! He has ways of making you learn!'

'Egghead Humpty Dumpty? I'll crack him!' boasted Alice, so bravely that she nearly crushed the owl egg still in her hand. 'He'll welcome my DIET OF WORMS – you watch!'

'No wait, girl. First, submit to Humpty Dumpty's strict potty training. He'll swear that's your next best lesson! Like me, he loves ogling his bedroom victims. I see you now, smugly sitting on his china potty listening to his lecherous lectures, you yawning impolitely at both ends. Seduce you he will, sure as eggs is eggs!'

Though uncertain about prophecies, especially alarming ones, Alice felt that Humpty Dumpty's potty might suit her better than any nearby holly bush squatting in a shadow. The nearest Alice had ever been to the countryside was through the radio's soap opera, The Archers, so even a male holly bush was an eerie unknown, no matter how alluring its brightest berries. And as for lectures, Alice felt she'd hold her own with any egghead.

'Well, no more metaphysics for me. Before the next Big Bang I'm off to explore astrophysics. . . .' With that, Mr Owl flew off towards Mars.

Left alone Alice asked herself, Is Mars a dead wet planet with big red mice ready to eat? No reply. So she tried to console herself, let alone control herself, like a well-behaved convent girl should. 'At least we got Owl out of his knotted old tree,' she said aloud by way of cheering herself up. Or was it her ghost boy, processing even her thoughts? As if to confirm his intimate presence, inside her head Alice heard further bright boyish tones: *'Alice look up. See! Owl's oak tree is less bowed down since he's removed his top-heavy brain from its topmost branches. Yep, he's flown off into other areas he was afraid to explore before in case he found anything that didn't fit in with his pre-digested crop of knowledge. Amazing! Extra clever, MY GIRL, M-MY M-MY ALICE!'*

Oh boy! Oh joyous M-MY MY! But why the last ditch stutter?

All the same, feeling a little less alone, she managed to tip-toe away.

Stll strangely insecure, Alice carefully picked her way through many rabbit holes peppered with little black pellets like incontinent grapeshot. So many black holes made the topsoil in the moonlight look strangely sinister; intimating a ghostly minefield in no-man's-land. Meanwhile, Mars slipped behind a red cloud as if afraid Owl would soon solve all its nuclear mysteries. Throughout the ether a silent urgency seemed to be screaming that night, dim stars in the Milky Way weeping, all sleepless birds and bees attentive as if already alarmed by some strange cosmic alert.

What next?

'To stay safe, all I have to do,' thought Alice encouraging a lighter mood, 'is to find my own way of out the wood. That's all!'

As if trying to enchant the creepy forest, Alice sang out again and again more boldly,

'I WONDER WHERE WE'RE GOING, YOU AND I, YOU AND I.
I WONDER WHO'S GOING WITH ME, TILL I DIE, TILL I DIE.
I WONDER, I WONDER, BEFORE I BURST
WHICH CAME FIRST, THE LIGHTNING OR THE THUNDER?
BUT BEFORE TEACHERS GO OFF THEIR HEAD,
LET'S INVITE AUTONOMY INSTEAD.
MUCH LESS STATE CONTROL, MORE LISTENING TO SOUL.
MUCH LESS STODGY CAKE, MORE HOMEMADE BREAD!'

This ditty she sang all the way until the dawning of the next day offering unknown delights and unknown dangers.

'Fat as a Bishop!' blurted Alice, scrutinising him critically, her legs crossed. 'Are you Mr Owl's Curate's egg?'

'Guess again, little chick.'

Alice prickled at the world 'little' but the portly gentleman above her looked too self-important to notice such childish trivialities. 'Why sit on the wall instead of on that potty on your head? And why does your wall go straight into that church?'

'Tradition,' replied Humpty Dumpty, beaming. 'If you look to my left you will see the wall there goes straight into a bank.'

'Of roses?'

'Gold, silly child, GOLD. There's glory for you!' Continuing to ogle her over the business section of his Sunday paper, his hands sweating, a page slipped down to Alice's feet. A timeless bookworm, Alice retrieved the escaping page and read aloud, *'The I CHING, the Book of Changes . . . It indicates this: very important new ideas are coming forward from 1984 onwards. These will continue to challenge existing systems, greatly upsetting the Church of England. . . .'*

'But not the Bingo! All the queen's horses and all the queen's men may not be Christian now but they are still paid by the queen, Head of the Church. As for me, unlike Adam, Lucifer, Wall Street, or the City of London, I shall never EVER fall. . . !'

Looking as robust as John Bull, Alice reckoned it would take more than a crash to make him even crack a joke, let alone a yolk. 'You must be Master Pot Head of the Egg Marketing Board.'

'Guess again,' said Humpty Dumpty now sharpening a large silver axe.

'Are you Colonel Goldilegs, the battery-hen butcher who crams chickens into cages, into correct pecking orders, then kills them with kindness, calling it welfare instead of warfare?'

Humpty Dumpty spat on his axe-blade, rubbed it dry with a silk handkerchief stained with egg white, adjusted his smile in its reflection, smirking, 'Warmer still, little chick.'

Much warmer and he'll be hard-boiled, thought Alice, offering him a wave by way of renewed warning that a war of words was brewing too fast for him to worm his way into her heart or knickers.

'Become not cocky, child. I am boss of **E.M.B.E.R.S.**, **E**ducation's **M**ortar-**B**oard **E**ggzamination **R**emarking **S**ystem.'

'Guess how I choose to spell mortar-"bored", superior sir!'

'Splendid! We specialise in rude remarks on the creative efforts of others beneath us. That way the silly mutts learn to eat their words. Very popular we are, a big employer. Go to work on an eggzam, we say. Yes, little chick, but for me laying down the rules, all the eggheads hatched out would become de-regulated. All as anarchists and scrambled EGO-centric omelettes.'

She wanted to dislodge a brick from his wall and lob it at his chamber-pot hat. 'We don't want to make the grade,' raved Alice. 'I'm not going to get boxed up into anybody's pet standard size. Smash the system!' Alice slipped off her satchel and banged it down on the ground. It sprang open and out jumped a choir of multi-coloured kids, all singing and clapping:

'WE DON'T WANT NO EDUCATION. . . !'

Humpty Dumpty, boss of E.M.B.E.R.S., was heard to groan between beats, his hands playing three monkeys. Well, at least TWO monkeys. State servant that he was, he didn't want to look or listen. And certainly not at any proposals which contained a double negative, like:

'WE DON'T WANT NO THOUGHT CONTROL.'

As they squirted graffiti under Humpty Dumpty's dangling feet, they sang:

'ALL IN ALL, YOU'RE JUST ANOTHER BRICK IN THE WALL.'

'Correct all spelling errors, in RED!' pleaded the egghead. 'I've not seen my feet since 1926 when Mr Hadow, bless him, founded our present system of education.'

Alice checked the writing on the wall. 'Not one mistake, mister,' she was proud to admit.

'Then EGGalitarian education thrives!' said Humpty Dumpty a rancid-looking leer linking invisible ear with invisible ear. 'Ask Pink Floyd. Haven't they all got comprehensive degrees. . . ?'

On that word DEGREES, all the kids screamed '**TORTURE!**' and ran off into the wood, hiding among the shivering trees.

'Kids wish to protest.'

'So do I,' snapped back Humpty Dumpty. 'Where's your school uniform?'

'Burst out of it, like, didn't I?' answered she in tough Cockney tones.

'Don't effin' treat me like Alice whatsit, that Victorian freak. Me, I'm a mod punk, ain't I? A welfare brat wot gets heveryfink for noffink wiffowt asking, so like, heveryfink's like wot we're not worf noffink, see – RIGHT?'

'Enough to make the real Alice turn in her rabbit-hole,' sighed Humpty Dumpty, straightening his Union Jack bow-tie. 'Obviously, free milk went to your head, child. Thank God our Parliament's Queen of Iron Rations has curbed the kindness of leaking school canteens. Let them eat cake, I say. Of their own make. To rise, cakes must stand on their own feet.'

'OK for you, like, too fat to see yer own effin' feet. But wot about the workers? The miners an' that. Don't they get a voice in this bleeding democratic society of ours, eh? EH?'

Like a soul in torment, some distance away, an owl shrieked.

'A raucous one,' said Humpty Dumpty, a lover of Wagner covering his ears again. 'Do you represent anybody? Or note, that is?'

'Middle 'C', mate. Cynical majority wot ave forgot 'ow to sing proper. Them wot you calls sub-standard, like their 'ousing. Right Guv, 'ere's yer card..' So saying, she tried to hand him the ace of spades.

Another owl's shriek, followed by a gunshot.

Tummy curdling, he declined her offer. 'I only eat union cards,' said he. 'And I do wish you'd drop that horrid Cockney accent, talking like a Shop Steward. Hypocritical, pretending to be one of the deprived. Ignorance may be in your favour, child, but don't FLAUNT it!' Then changing tactics, he leaned forward. In ogling her owlishly, he nearly fell off his high wall.

'Hand it over,' he insisted.

'I'll do most fings wot you ASKS, right,' replied Alice, hands on hips, 'but I ain't doing no effin' fing wot I'm TOLD to, right!'

'How provoking,' said Humpty Dumpty, bottom lip in a pro-nounced sulk. 'Hard not to be hurt by the hoi-poloi's notion of wit. However, no hard feelings, I'm ready to bury the hatchet. . . .'

'Not in my neck yer won't, yer bloated old bantam's egg! Only fear wot needs to defend itself. Wot we got to smash first, eh? You, the wall, or the bomb?'

'My hat! You're a red radical!'

'It's Cardinals wot wears red 'ats, Mr Bishop, not us in God's Red

Brigade.' Then suddenly adjusting her accent to its usual prissy primness, Alice announced, 'To the Elders of E.M.B.E.R.S., Education's Mortar-Board Eggzamination Remarking System.' Unfolding her White Paper taken from her satchel, she read aloud. 'Old Souls are here again looking for. . . .'

'External qualifications,' interjected Humpty Dumpty.

'Internal examinations,' corrected Alice. 'They're looking for eternal liberation. Noah's Next Children will get education to go all inter-dimensional. The next Aquarian Age watch out; they'll break out from battery-hen cramming; they won't thank you for pre-packed pellets of boring factory facts sitting down. So let 'em choose their own free-range adventures . . . scratch out their own early morning worms, lugworms, bookworms, whatever. . . .'

Humpty Dumpty, squirming, brandished his axe. 'Remarkable,' announced he with pronounced perpendicularity, 'how worms . . . after a series of painful cutbacks, even the little bits left at the cutting-edge . . . still wriggle. . . .' He spat on the axe-blade.

Lit up further by this implicit threat, Alice waved her White Paper like a red flag before a Papal Bull. Her aim was to get the fat old fogy to at least blush. Prompted if necessary by her unseen but trusted lover boy, who surely had learnt her tract by heart, (oh big warm heart in a big warm handsome boy, she hoped), Alice was about to present the schoolgirls' version of THE DIET OF WORMS.

But would he refuse to fall for it?

If not, it was high time to knock Humpty Dumpty off his lofty perch.

CHAPTER TWO

DIET OF WORMS

'I said it very loud and clear; I went and shouted in his ear.'

'Kindly leave your remarks, even your marks, until the very end,' said Alice. Then, on behalf of all colours of hurt kids everywhere, she cleared her throat to read aloud like a Town Crier. But no matter how hard she stared at the page before her, the whole paper remained blank. And alarmingly, so did her mind.

Prompt, please. Declaring herself an open channel, she invited her ghost boy's voice to come through. A shiver of anticipation and another surprise. As she started to read aloud in her boyish voice to Humpty Dumpty, the words she uttered actually appeared on the page, whole sentences as she spoke them, paragraphs filling the no longer blank computer print-out. So, placing the owl egg where she could throw it in case Humpty Dumpty lost concentration, she confidently announced:

'DIET OF WORMS'

'1. *For Students of Life, better a little humble ignorance than a lot of false facts. Truth and beauty are already innate in each of us, and universal. Trust the child within. Our futures are ever m-more uncertain so don't whet the appetite for learning with unnecessary degrees. Dead chicken may taste better wrapped in paper, but LIFE doesn't. Save the trees for human lungs, not flatten foreign forests to graze cattle for fat-cat beef burgers, bigger profits. Let teachers gain a broader EXPERIENCE of LIFE in general, outside educational establishments, especially in industry. Too m-many don't get off the academic production-line before, as programmed teachers, they are back in the ranks with regimented kids, pushing the same examination-folder, kids doing exactly the same home-work as the factory fathers did to death, 20 years earlier in the sixties.'*

Alice checked. Yes, the words were showing up on her paper.

Humpty Dumpty was still rolling around like an egg in a spoon at the start of a wobbly race. His balance uncertain, he was fanning his face with the ace of spades.

So far so good!

'2. Kids want real warm PEOPLE, not slick performers. Tamed teachers ham up the Role of Instructor, wearing their career prospects like some all-purpose straightjacket instead of a generous, liberating lifeline to help survival in stormy seas ahead. During these winds of change, the best midwife for any new age is the rough and flexible individualist. How many college degrees did Noah, Moses or Jesus m-merit? YET THEY HEARD THE INNER WHISPER OF THEIR LIFE'S MISSION AND ACTED ACCORD-INGLY. Those of any age who step out of line are the true pathfinders, the pioneers. Allow them to contribute to all necessary social changes, not reject school phobics, like Alice, because of our refusal to comply to out-dated strategies and value systems, anaesthetising individuality in the name of education instead of innovation.'

A second check. Printed words still showing but not, curiously, the stammers as before, for example, the word 'm-merit'. Humpty Dumpty was nibbling the ace of spades. Not concentrating and bored, had he stopped listening? Like a teacher, she raised her voice.

'3. Church-going was once compulsory, now education is. And atten-dance is declining. Force-feeding the mind will prove as empty as force-feeding the Soul in earlier times. Force is against the Divine Will and never succeeds in the long term. Though it often seems to, especially in the long summer term for examinations. But how short-sighted is it to build all our

futures on the early fears of public failures? Already, 40% of the total child population is said to gain but little benefit from schools, except diminishing state benefits when unemployed. Truancy, even in a Sixth Form, can run at 8%. If we don't want a slave society, let's consult the kids more, not insult them. Education seen as an open invitation, not as a closed-minded imperative. Perhaps, one day, chosen survivors will become the masters; decide on pensions, force the already poor to trim their diet, to cut their gruel, to curb their fuel costs. Heartlessness can start in the classroom. But a happy childhood lasts a lifetime.'

Alice, pausing for breath, checked again. Word perfect on the printout. Speechless with rage, Humpty Dumpty was now eating the ace of spades. He had again spotted Alice's nuclear disarmament badge. Her atomic smile made him worse. He was also gulping down neat mouthfuls of vodka. Odd fish, thought Alice. Fancy hoping the Cold War was all but over while still playing Russian roulette with your own heartbeats through heavy drinking! His complexion already looked like an addled egg.

How to distract herself until his next burp signalled he was open enough for more of the same? If she didn't DO something radical soon, she feared she might start trembling, showing all the hidden insecurities of one of society's outsiders. Only the night before, wasn't it, an alarming black dog had jumped onto her lap? Its unearthly eyes had frightened her to death even as she slept. What did the nightmare bode for her? For others, too, maybe. . . ? Shuddering, she took out a jack-knife. Whistling as Humpty Dumpty, Big Boss of E.M.B.E.R.S. sozzled more vodka, she started to whittle a fallen ash tree branch. Soon she found herself carving a boomerang. That felt right.

But WHY. . . ?

BURP!

'Calling Alice! M-m-may I offer warnings? That black m-mongrel m-might seriously m-m-mean. . . .'

BURP!

'Proceed, little chick,' said Humpty Dumpty, surprising her suddenly with his permission. Something must be wrong. Yes, he had just blocked out her nameless lover's seductive whispers. Was not the unheard boy calling Alice to her date with destiny? The thought made her m-melt with anticipation. Would he also m-melt in the heat of the moment when they met in the flesh? How could she call him to her side more quickly? He had not introduced himself properly. So was he some nameless orphan? Then, she knew it! The reason she was still bottling her need to urinate. It was this: her handsome lover boy might WATCH unseen 'Widdle-Liddle' relieve herself. No matter how painful her bladder felt, she felt she MUST stoically contain herself, from any astral Peeping Tom. A sort of competition really. Which bladder, she or the pickled egghead above her, would first BURST. . . ?

'4. Freedom does not exist in physical terms – SO WHY ARE WE SO AFRAID OF IT? Self-survival instincts in humans are strong enough to ensure that most children will stop short of breaking any bounds that make them feel unsafe. Confine the kid and it will never find its own feet, only follow abjectly in the shallow footsteps of others, fearing to make its own decisions, its own imprint or even take initiative. Education should not be just about passive input for captive victims. It should encourage OUTput from all pro-active creative partners, parents, teachers and students with less distinction between them all, all as inter-dependent learners. They should explore all self-chosen areas and activities – everything from meditation to mountain climbing.'

'5.Let's now recognise that making FREE CHOICES is the highest of all mental processes. So many adults try to break the will – i.e. high SPIRITS of the child, then wonder why school windows get smashed, doors get wrenched off their hinges. Granting 'freedom' to children offers more open-ended teaching modes, complementing traditional 'mental' methods. Risk. Allowing 'freedom', children soon responsibly determine our own limits, if these are not already negotiated. Spoon-fed schooling is not a helpful preparation for the larger classrooms of life.'

'6. African proverb: COPYING EVERYBODY ELSE ALL THE TIME, THE MONKEY ONE DAY CUT HIS OWN THROAT.

'More recognition that the transition from junior schools to the hot Henhouse Eggzamination Complex is too abrupt. Many students never recover a feeling of self-worth. If this production-line was judged on purely *commercial values, pupils as pre-packed up-market products, the factory ethos and ethics would have been changed long ago. DEMOCRATIC COMPETITION CAN KILL THE HUMAN SPIRIT. We import enough nuclear waste from Japan without also importing imitations of their kamikaze kids of eggzamination time. Expressing the true Self is never depressing!'*

The mention of the word SPIRIT had got Humpty Dumpty back on his vodka bottle.

Back whittling her wooden boomerang, Alice again whistled. She called up THE VOICE, whoever he was. If it really had been him who inspired her DIET OF WORMS, he deserved a m-mighty big kiss. Astonished, she listened. Suddenly they were both speaking in unison. Yes, as in overtone chanting and keeping their syncopated stammer together, the boy's voice through her urgently announced, 'M-m-men in Black. Nuclear terrorists. On 'Inspections'. Brittany Coast, I think,' declared their staccato duet. 'After uranium . . . Fail-Safe . . . or . . . Fall-out secrets. M-MUST GO, Alice, Don't delay. GO NOW! Go to Warren Row!'

BURP!

Breaking her inner connection again, Humpty Dumpty let out another vodka-flavoured belch. 'Luther, chick, farted in the face of clever devils. Myself, I despise all Contrary Marys who don't KNOW their history. 'Twas the scholar and humanist Erasmus who laid the egg. Luther only hatched it, his can of earthworms. He was, after all, the son of a miner. So be warned. I'll spare you just four more minutes. There's indulgence for you!'

Aggrieved, Alice impulsively threw the owl egg, aiming it for his prim face. Amazingly, though sozzled, Humpty Dumpty caught it, just as if he was a skilful cricketer on the playing fields of Eton College. But in her temper, had she surrendered the talisman, the good luck charm that would keep her safe from all hidden dangers, in every world, seen and unseen, over and UNDER the earth. . . ?

Hands shaking, Alice again picked up her White Paper. Though still lost in this world, she dreaded also losing what she took to be guidance from on High. Meaning, of course, that she hoped Lover Boy was as tall and elegant as the stud stallion she used to feed lumps of sugar. Yet what about those underground-type warnings? And the spooky voice of that sepulchral boy's voice stuttering somewhere deep inside her? That was enough to unnerve any Soviet ghost on a day-trip to, say Cellafield's nuclear power station. Yet Alice stayed determined to whip Humpty Dumpty into a fury, before he became a Big Bang pickled-egg stink bomb way beyond redemption. Full of fervour, hoping to convert the Boss of EMBERS to radical reforms, she tried to continue their crazy crusade in her lover boy's crackly voice.

'You surely don't expect me to accept all this selfish New Age rubbish, child?'

'Why not? You accept nuclear waste. Import it, even. Bury it like poisoned dog bones. Who said Japan lost the war? Oh, I could go on for hours. . . .'

To prevent this, Humpty Dumpty yawned so loudly that Alice couldn't hear herself preach. But, like all reformers who get ignored on their own doorstep, and keep on knocking anyway, Alice rabbited on. To complete the seventh section of her Diet of Worms, she intoned:

'7. Let all help us to build our vision of a better life-style. Globally, at grass-roots, let's all establish kind, fulfilling Campus Learning Communities, People's Own Olympics, personal power.

'In an age of increasing electronic leisure, more personal creativity should be encouraged, not less. Instead of only objective IQ tests as required by the old Protestant work ethic, we need subjective pleasure-centred aptitude tests. As blondes are insulted to be rated for the size of their boobs, so it's restricting to rate a child by the size of her/his brains. Graduates need to become more versatile. It's now estimated that knowledge doubles every 15 years. Learnt skills are moribund within three years. In or out of work, for a fruitful life, flexibility is all.'

'8. 'Every Soul has its own individual spiritual path.' – Steiner. A word of protection for the daydreamer, the dyslexic, all the so-called disadvantaged learners. The Rudolph Steiner Schools have for generations been the leaders in awareness of the inner levels of mankind. Any 'A level' pass is quite a lowly cosmic achievement. The m-mind is but a computer, a servant of consciousness, and not its true m-master. (M-more stutters at

last! Like inner blessings? Surely secure fundamentalists never need to stutter!) State education has little interest in such spiritual scruples, being mostly a m-matter of serving m-m-materialistic ends.

'Yet the Prince of Faith and a past Education Secretary have both suggested meditation as an aid to relieve stress in the high seas of these turbulent times of change. But why make the stress in the first place? Is it some secret weapon of state control? M-meanwhile, the disenfranchised withdraw into their inner worlds for protection. Into drugs. For illumination? Demonstrating their withdrawal symptoms? Rejecting state-imposed mental stress?'

Double-glazed as a hard-boiled Easter Egg dyed red, Humpty Dumpty was protected by his stupor. Perhaps in there somewhere he was dimly hoping to find liquid en-Light-enment!

'Einstein, entranced by a sunbeam, his daydream produced a 'knowing' – the Theory of Relativity. 'Imagination is the true reality,' writes Paul Twitchell in his book THE SPIRITUAL NOTEBOOK. 'Not the imagination mortal man thinks about, but true imagination in the other worlds.' That is, the ability to re-image what already IS. Entranced, advancing pupils can be learning far greater lessons in the private classrooms of their daydreams than earthly classrooms usually provide. Such dreams, anyway, are already shaping all of our tomorrows. As do, indeed, nuclear nightmares subscribed to by millions sharing the same thought-forms. Therein lies the ever-present Cold War or Civil War in the human heart that split the atom in the first place. . . .'

FART!

By accident or design, it sounded as if Humpty Dumpty's pants had just split. Alice, gulping down some unpolluted air, crossed her legs more tightly and sallied forth.

'Glue-sniffing, drunkenness and granny-bashing are but individuals' poor attempts to break through into more meaningful experiences. Yet, fearing being more gloriously alive, we instead take progressive risks with the agencies of death. To the emotionally desperate, agony and ecstasy are almost interchangeable, both being affirmations of personalised existence, instead of zombified anonymity. Yes, education is not just looking

backwards into yesterday's piggy-bank, all Caesar and no God. It's re-searching, finding Soul's present purpose in our good-natured service IN Mother Earth's womb as well. . . .'

IN? What a strange mistake. Cocking her right ear, she heard him chuckle. *'No m-m-mistakes in the universe,'* said he, her inside guide. These contentious words, delivered with an engaging uncertainty, did not get printed onto her paper. In case of repercussions later? Shrugging off all residual apprehensions, Alice continued to recite as instructed.

'9. Freed from state control we'd hatch more Free-Range schools. We wish to open hearts before heads, to put intuition before intellect. Let self-awareness lead to self-control. Thus what often follows is healthy self-esteem. At all levels, parental participation will be encouraged.

'Throughout Welfareland too many adults are curtailed by cabals of specialists, isolating themselves from other vital areas of expertise. Secret formulas, like sources of free energy, remain suppressed. But as old concepts are replaced by a m-m-more holistic approach, what we want are more amateurs, LOVERS, in every department of learning. Yes, life-enhancers, not life-explainers. So let's take learning fun back into the first learning environment, the home. How often do we hear, "Thank God it's school next week and I can get 'em off my hands" Loving and learning can be the same. Don't let adults kill them both as the old age m-moralists crushed the life-force by calling all that was pleasurable – SIN.'

'Let me OUT!' squawked Humpty Dumpty; a puffed-up drunken para-keet wearied and bored by persistent plucking of his own ruffled chest feathers. But Alice persevered. He was far too fat to move, too fanatical to be funny and therefore great fun to tease.

'Unfrock the high-priests of learning, all high-grade graduates who condemn classroom 'failures' to homelessness and worse yet to take bloody revenge on bad teachers; shop-door sleepers, drop-outs, dossers, those who become hypnotised by ever newer forms of SELF-DESTRUCT in these our own avaricious eighties. Yet like life itself, death is a belief system, open to m-mental imaging, thoughts being things, M-M-MIND'S BLACK MAGIC CAN KILL US ALL! Too m-much loss of the nation's natural goodness and "knowing", and we're all doomed to be ruled by a

damnable epidemic of eggheads.'

'Diet of Worms?' exploded Humpty Dumpty. '**URGH!** And again – **U-R-G-H!** I'd rather have the runs. Reformations, sad to say, were never helped by bloody swearing, even on the Bible. . . .'

'Especially in a Court of Law,' nodded Alice amazed at how the vodka never seemed to reach the floral piss-pot covering his oval bald head like some ornate ceramic egg-cosy.

'Yes, there may be some minor abuses,' conceded Humpty Dumpty between swigs of vodka with no Ban-the-Bomb logo on the Russian bottle, 'but, cripes, you surely haven't 95 of 'em, like that lunatic Luther. Chronic constipation! Pot-bound, he was, deluded, self-punishing. Punk monk's poor arguements didn't hold water!'

Pot-bound? Encouraging distraction from her aching bladder, in a lighter voice she asked, 'How many pupils tell teachers their own name with any real confidence these days, 35 to a class?'

'*Anthea,* believe me. . . .'

'No *won't*. I believe in ME – or trying to. And I'm ALICE, actually.'

'Alice Actually? Fancy name! **Ss**uits you, **Ss**yrup-chops!' he continued, getting so sozzled that he was sizzing his 'S' sounds like over-oiled hot frying chips. 'Now cla**sss sss**tructures, like con**ss**erve**ss**, keep things **sss**weetly in their place, Anthea. Just you try teaching at my giddy heights using a ladder without rung**sss**. . . !'

'Virtues don't get vertigo, Mr Bishop, only vices do. But we're not suggesting anything that has not been tried before. At Summerhill School, A.S. Neill said, "The prude is the libertine without the courage to face his naked Soul".'

'**NAKED!**' Excited beyond well-bred decorum, Humpty Dumpty suddenly spat out, 'Then **ss**trip! **SSSS**TRIP off all of your **SSSSSSSEVEN** veil**sssssss**, **sss**exy, **SS**UPER**SS**ONICALLY **FAST** . . . let's **sss**ee your frilly cami-knicker**sss** . . . lovely lady!'

No longer 'little', or a 'chick' but suddenly a 'LADY'! For how much longer could this sozzled Herod flirt with her Salome? Or was his flattery just to flatten her budding idealism?

'In your eye**s**, I'm already a be**sss**otted **sss**ad old **ss**ex-pot, but. . . .'

'Please, refrain from the use of that word.'

'**SSSEX!**' ogled he, hopefully, in another sizzle of spittle.

'No, pot. It's a bit painful to me at present. . . .'

'Wait till pot's legalised, like under-age **SSSEX! Ss**o, little lady, turn me into a pathetic Peeping-Tom pederast if you will,' hi**sssss**ed Humpty Dumpty, getting maudlin. 'I may be a china egghead . . . and hard-boiled . . . but I do have feelings, too, you know. **Ss**o arou**sss**e 'em, do. Uplift me! If your god is one of love, **ss**peak to me of unspeakable LOVE, madam. . . .'

'Madam now? I AM growing up fast,' thought Alice. If only he was not so – slushy!

'Wriggle! Giggle! Bare your toe**sss** for me! A flamenco fling! DANCE! I'd really relish that, **ss**weet honeypop**sss**! Erotic fandango**s** too, rabbit-thumping all over the joint. . . !'

Rabbit-thumping? Why the heck hadn't she asked Lover Boy or even the Rabbits where to find Warren Row? The right to roam freely, the right to take risks she'd already gladly accepted for herself. But to that befud-dled old sot on his high wall, dare Alice admit that she was still lost? And that, for both of them maybe, time was running out. . . ?

'*We're also on our Astral Timetable.*' That was helpful Lover Boy Ghost. Was he playing Orpheus to her Euridice, seeking in the shades of Hades for his future bride? '*If Eggheads can be helped by you, the Angels this side m-m-might prevent the next global hu-man pride-before-a-fall "ACCI-DENT!"* '

CLICK! Lover Boy disconnected, so Alice challenged Humpty Dumpty. 'How can kids fit comfortably into any adult system unless we can help them fit comfortably into themselves first?' 'Arcadias, please. Please help us liberate academia from the dark and dangerous prisons and poisons of the hu-man intellect. . . .'

'Depose me, eh? Fat chance! Off the wall, ALL such cranky ideas are,' boasted he, all jowls a-wobble. 'Come clo**ss**er, you **ss**exy little fire-cracker. . . .' Lurching and burping, his blandishments were hardly entic-ing. Nonetheless, Alice took two bold steps nearer to him.

'Good egg, good egg!' he gloated with lip-smacking glee. '**Ss**it close.

Let's both hatch out your sad spitefulness, little pu**ss**y. Cuddle up! **Ss**wig **sss**ome delicious vodka. . . !'

'You're not my voice from the underworld. I m-must go to him, find my true path. . . .'

'Linger longer, honeypop**s**. **S**how us how prec**oc**ious you can be, eh. . . .'

'NO! Too late!'

'Continue. Please! While I **s**ooth your **s**avage brea**sstss**. . . .'

His unromantic randy passes being rejected, Humpty Dumpty needed a snooze. Reformers, she knew, always rattled people's routines. But in one respect Alice had always agreed with Snow White, the Prime Minister. Sporting her killer handbag she always rallied her poorest troops with, '**IF AT FIRST YOU DON'T SUCCEED, SOCK IT TO 'EM, ANYWAY!**'

But for Alice, suddenly, there was only timelessness. Human tragedies, she speculated, nibble like mites within the Wings of Time, playing their vital part in evolution. And don't protesters with their nuclear disarmament badges sitting peacefully on volcanoes, only help to hatch them out? Yet couldn't all disasters get diluted, or even, diverted? On this she listened again for her siren lover's guidance, tempting him into being her Guardian Angel.

But, again, he's not there.

Inexplicably, she felt in no hurry, with eternity so un-impatient. Unfolding her printout, she checked that all the words she had heard in her head were recorded on paper. Silently, she read. Noisily, he snored.

An agreeable truce, albeit brief.

Brief? Barely four minutes, in fact.

After that spell of snoring, Humpty Dumpty woke from a bad dream with a start; such a bad start Alice thought if it was his end, that he'd seen his inevitable fall. Well, psychic predictions being as unreliable as English weather, maybe they're best ignored, especially vodka-soaked voices, let alone stam-m-ering spirit voices needing speech therapy. 'I was being eaten alive by worms!' simpered Humpty Dumpty, dabbing his face. 'All of those worms were called Alice...' Finding the next demand in her DIET OF

WORMS, Alice prepared him for further protests. 'Say it's you on a squat, trying not to get busted by the fuzz for smoking pot. It's Berlin Wall you're on because, believe me, both will fall. Now as an introduction to Number 10. . . .'

'No 10 Downing Street for YOU!' he leered with a wince as he wobbled on his wall, all cheeks and double chins. 'Expect you follow hippy Marxists! Hang out your expansionist blue stockings and burnt bras like dirty washing and then smoke 'em! Expect you share sex and socialism, listening to The Grateful Dead! Dear girl, streaking as protest is a much prettier way for us oldies to watch than the bugging and busting of student revolutionaries on the television. Mind you, more mirrors around the cabinet table now since Snow White's premiership. But, I fear me, no looking-glass would be large enough for your priggish conceit, young Anthea.'

The snooze had obviously done him proud. Sparky exchanges she relished. Thus, with an irritating lack of fluster Alice, on behalf of Anthea, retorted, 'Meat-eaters might like the cane since tough steak has to be beaten, but we vegetarians prefer carrots to any raw rump. . . .'

Raw rump? He'd make her roar all right! Humpty Dumpty badly wished to swipe her one when God wasn't looking. More badly, he longed to take a schoolboy peek at her raw rump, if only she'd urinate. So rejuvenating, young flesh! So soothing, the sound of trickling! Sweating with the prospect of giving 'Anthea' a good roasting, with assumed good grace, he invited her to continue. 'Do continue little madam do, with the usual aplomb in your shapely mouth. Sock it to me, straight between the eyes!' Again, showing his bottle, he primed himself with another slug of vodka, a stiff one to remind him of earlier more virile exploits. Undeniably, the feisty girl's relentless passion reminded him of his own more upright youthful peccadilloes.

Ignoring her waterworks, with suggestive though unselfconscious wriggles and squirms, Alice returned to the Diet of Worms.

'10. Let the teachers be glad not to be in charge. They're not, anyway, since neither the biggest carrot nor the biggest cane can m-make a child remember one irrelevant fact one second after a SUCCESSFUL exam result. So help children to set their own agenda, boundaries, goals.

Limitations always entice rebellion. Better to stress the need for all kids to take charge of themselves as soon as possible than to cause stress through the fear of not passing tests. And for the sake of surviving erratic earth changes, see that between abandoned babies of 10 months old and cats 10 months old, unaided, only kittens might survive. . . .'

Not feeling too well, Humpty Dumpty tried not to dwell too much on pussy.

'11. More Pupil Power. Let them discuss their own rules, agree to them; then punishment not only becomes less necessary as Neill's school Summerhill still shows but that, when it IS necessary, it's seen to be just and FAIR and is therefore not resented.'

People Power, and other such childish dreams, always made Humpty Dumpty pout even as he dozed off, no doubt dreaming of 'Anthea' being basted in hot dripping on some barbecue spit. Thus pouting, he slept all through her demands, dictated inwardly, as if she was being prompted by an astral auto-cue.

'We know one girl who refused to become egg-bound. When asked why, like a good broody hen, she'd not hatch out a standard grade or two, know what she said? **'I'M HAPPY!'** *she said. 'Doing your friggin' exams, man, will make me UNhappy'* **– Simple.'**

'Or is it?'

'Doesn't an unhappy childhood last a lifetime? Yet HAPPINESS is the constitutional right of citizens in the United States. Does that include the child, too? Does anyone ever ask little Jake his permission before they give him a toy gun and his sister Janet a doll? As stated before, the best exam is internal, eternal, a private spiritual matter.' How could he relate to happy references of OPEN HEART SCHOOLS, THE AQUARIAN AGE, and even, hint-hint and horror-horror, to ALICE'S FURTHER ADVENTURES UNDER GROUND, the tall story she might yet inspire Charles Dodgson before he was born. . . ?

Seeing Mr Bishop's Olympian axe, Alice treated WORMS 12 to 25 as an appendix, like a treasure-hunt, hopefully buried in compost for seekers who love young bookworms to wriggle with excitement, not worry. Before that, she would read aloud her last Declaration. Humpty Dumpty's own snoring woke him just in time, or had Lover Boy prodded him in the privates? Anyway, he was alert enough for Alice to introduce her present conclusion.

'*26. The right of a child to refuse constipating egg-zams. . . .*' she brazenly announced.

Too much! Immediately, he simulated more snoring. As with an alarm-call, this induced more real sleep. Humpty Dumpty slept as sound as a fat foghorn as Alice continued. The spoken words were still appearing on the computer paper before she heard them aloud.

'*And if that sounds too High Church for atheist eggheads, listen to those indigenous 'pagans' shot to pieces by early Wild West settlers. How do those uprooted 'Red Indians' see the United States? As the New Age Atlantis? The Hopi Tribe has clear prophecies right up to the end of this century. What did they say for the next decade or so? For 1995, they say this:* '**The new race of humans will begin to design their new reality of life on this planet as they intended it to be when they came from the stars.**'

'*We kids don't want an arms race put first, but the hu-man race, the seedcake of a healthy future. Proust's book 'A la Recherché du Tempts Perdue' was all about a cake. One, like our world's resources, that have not yet been equally shared. Remember Marie Antoinette, ego all over her face? Before we all fall down like Humpty Dumpty, let kids declare the right for fair shares for all, NOW, not tomorrow. Before we have too few options left. Before this world is taken by firestorms, floods. In the name of the Firearm, Gun, and the Holy Ghost. Ah men.*'

To secure her manifesto on the church door later, Alice hammered in a nail. The knocking, like the start of Beethoven's fifth symphony, woke Humpty Dumpty who asked, 'Is it school Assembly?'

'No!' cried out Alice, roundly. 'They're changing, too! Now we devise our own concerts instead. Last one we did was called The Teacher-Eating Machine.'

'Do we have to?' groaned Humpty Dumpty.

'Free choice, gift of Divine Will,' was Alice's glib reply. Then she slipped into Lover Boy's voice with, '*Which Angry Brigade thinks KNOWLEDGE is*

Godly, intuition devilish arrogance, commoners' ignorance exploitable apathy? Yes, we're all slaves of m-matter, m-materialism, m-money and the m-manacles of m-mind. Which'll blow up first, our brain-box or our planet? Human anger's just inverted idealism. So what would you like to do about THAT, M-miser M-minder of E.M.B.E.R.S? If God is all love, how can we kindly include you, too?'

OUCH! Dare he tell the alluring little minx his titillating truth?

'M-m-minx! He just called you a m-MINX!' protested Alice, ALOUD!

Double OUCH! Lover boy inside her was eavesdropping on their private conversation. Humpty Dumpty, alarmed, did not wish to think that ghosts could telepathise with him. Better to whisk Anthea away somewhere safe from prying eyes. Unperturbed, Alice continued. *'With global warming world-wide, we young caring ones will RAISE all levels of kindness soon. . . !'*

ITCH! In his groin. He knew what he wished to raise with her. And not just cane. If only he was able! Yet he believed in bodily resurrection. Like a sleeping dog with one open eye half cocked, hope still lay dormant between his legs. But since the girl's obviously haunted by nuclear night-mares, make her feel all safe and secure first. 'We VIPs have hidden shel-ters,' soothed he, enticingly. 'Safe for dear treasured ones. Like a bunk up, would you, dear. . . ?'

'Top or bottom, Mr Bishop?'

Double ITCH! Bottom? She on top? Gulp! Then the crunch. 'With your weight, Mr Bishop, I'd advise even Mr Noah to leave you like a beached whale. You fat old plonker, you'd sink the Ark!'

Such rudeness, so titillating! 'But it's not all rotten in the state of Denmark, Anthea dear. Welfare gives you FREE education. Fills you with physics. . . .'

'Noah rejected his schooling for carpentry. He was a craftsman, not a don.'

'Not the first carpenter to fail to save the world, neither will he be the last, child.'

'It's the ever-optimistic child in Soul that can save us, not dead so-called Saviours. Beware of grown-ups, sir. First they want to kill the child in themselves; then they want to kill the kid in the kids under their control. Why do rich clerics and dons wear black while poor people stay in daily mourning?'

'Poor clergymen known to me, Anthea, are not bad eggs. They're in mourning for their mortgages. No church union. Or unity. Yet I say, Keep our Protestant landowners in charge of their god-given peacocks. Provide good secure jobs, for lifetimes of labour-intensive grafting. Good eggs, all.'

'For underpaid workers? No wonder you're an atheist, Mr Bishop? Like Darwin!' Aping an inelegant monkey, Alice scratched under her armpits in a most unladylike manner. Jigging up and down, chewing an invisible flea, and circumcising an invisible banana, she recited:

'SPACE GAS FIRES OUR START AND OUR END
EACH BIG BANG BURNS OUT EVERY BEND.
GOOD-BYE EACH BAKED BEAN,
FLASHPANS MAKE SANDS GREEN
AS APES AND ANGELS ALL ASCEND!'

Laughing and clapping sweaty hands, Humpty Dumpty chortled, 'Yes, fear of hell's everlasting EMBERS is a great motivator. Must be why more and more silly muttonheads are now taking up the study of theology!'

'Second-hand bookworms!'

'Enough of worms, pretty princess. Or I'll turn you into a pumpkin. . . .'

'Can you do magic?' asked Alice, eagerly. 'Russia spends mints of its defence budget on ESP, 'cos of Uri Geller's spoon-bending. Can nuclear missiles be bent, mid-air, turned into boomerangs by secret powers? But before more big bangs I'll blow!' Like a Trident warhead eight times better than Hiroshima, she popped the boomerang into her bag.

'DON'T GO! Streak for me do. No? Then why don't you put on your nice school uniform, Anthea?' he wheedled, winningly, 'And DANCE!'

'Has it started already, Mr Bishop?'

'What?'

'The Third World War Dance?' asked Alice as she watched Humpty

Dumpty open a mushroom-shaped see-through umbrella above his portly frame. 'Or are you declaring it now?'

'I'm declaring a trousseau,' taunted he, aiming his tease at her ghost lover boy. Denied a sex kitten to purr in his lap, was his late libido expanding into faint-hearted charity at last? 'Let's advertise for some dumb playboy to carry you over the nuclear threshold,' he leered with barely disguised envy. Then with a spurt of lechery, he added, 'Bedding down, that's what you need – humpy-pumpy, you precocious, pubescent, pullet-brained BRAT, lots of hefty bouncy Bouncy Castle humpy-pumpy!'

Unflapped by flattery, Alice continued, *'Is compulsory education conscription charges in disguise? Like indulgences of old? Do the dead look less identifiable in uniform? The tears easier to control in crocodile lines? The rows of desks like armoured tanks in deserts of unknowing? Back from Vietnam. It's time you education bods got off your high wall and came down to kids' own eye-level, came clean about cancers, the bomb, fall-out, nuclear waste. Also all the wisdom's known to the Ancients but suppressed through all ages, but now bursting with light, ready to uplift those who seek. And soon please, before the next cosmic FLASH of insight kills us all, king and coolie alike. That could happen in less time than it takes to boil an egg!'*

On cue, defiantly he let off a bad egg stink bomb. After a deep sniff of smelling salts, he yawned like a basking shark snapping at some passing shrimp that tickled its fancy. 'A bargain,' he pronounced with pride. 'I'll still listen to this adolescent tripe since you both seem to think I need doing good to, so long as you agree that every time I **YAWN**, you remove another article of CLOTHING!'

'You mean STRIP? – ME?' Was this a price worth paying?

'Well, you want to bare your Soul, don't you? So, reveal ALL, will we? Even seal our new deal with an egg-cosy kiss or two, eh? How's that for a jolly hockey-sticks' basement bargain?'

With all the prudery of a challenged libertine, Alice resisted. So, experimentally, as he **YAWNED**, to their joint amazement, Alice flung off her left shoe. At this, Humpty Dumpty clapped. 'Naked! – NAKED TOES NEXT!' he cried, cheering her on.

51

The astral boy's voice was pumping yet another aria out through her over-active mouth. '*We've doctors we can consult about our heart, womb, nerves, head, bones, blood and toenails.*' said Alice dancing around, '*but not one of them can diagnose the sickness within. It's as if we've pulled the toy apart, while the robotic patient keeps blind faith with Doctor God in a white coat. In so doing, we hope to find out how it all works. Only it DOESN'T! The toy's been broken on the rack by drugs; fags, booze, barbiturates, schooling, free sex. . . .*'

Sex? Ear trumpet cocked to a more alert angle, excitedly, he let out a **YAWN**.

In response, Alice flung off her right shoe while saying, '*The running repairs on offer, the Band-Aids on cancer, will all fall short of the miracle cures we all crave for, until with commitment, we embrace at all levels of learning, old -fashioned WHOLESOMENESS!*'

'Embrace – EMBRACE! Now for number three.' His podgy arms opened wide as he bellowed out his next simulated and cavernous **YAWN**.

'*Before a new order, DISorder!*' She started to unroll her left stocking. '*It's entrenched resistance to change which makes it look dangerous! See change as necessary pleasure!*'

'Pleasure? I'm open, girl. Are YOU. . . ?' Ever hopeful, another inviting **YAWN**. Immediately, Alice rolled down her right stocking. Anything to keep him dribbling so intently.

'*Evolution requires changes, whether by nuclear fission, earthquakes, unemployment, Haley's Comet, UFOs, aliens, or all of them working together towards the same end, TRANSCENDENCE. . . !*'

Humpty Dumpty felt himself – yes, at his end he too was rising! Endangering his balance and his position of authority above, he tried to catch her flailing arms waving her two stockings, as, deliciously, she danced around like a dizzy Isadora Duncan.

'*Whatever we God-fearing possess will be wrested from us.*' panted Alice. More ardently, the voice of her invisible lover took over her whole body, '*. . . be it air, earth, fire or water. Secret vibrations are calling us through the etheric to rise into the Age of Aquarius, just as the sea-scoured corpse of Atlantis will arise to replace our own poisoned lands.*

Soils, like Souls, need decarbonising in the mighty oceans. Thus the prophecies of Nostradamus will. . . .'

'RUBBISH!' interrupted Humpty Dumpty, exasperated beyond belief. 'He got the date of his own death quite wrong, crying wolf once too often – STRIP!' Leaning forward he shaped another large wolfish **YAWN**, this one aimed at her innocent young lips. Yet the word STRIP, uttered by him had, amazingly, been in her astral lover's voice. Shudder-shudder. Was the wretched boy watching as well as listening – but from inside her own body somehow? What was the ghostly chap after? Yet Alice, more daring than little Red Riding Hood, had much more to learn about dirty old men crying wolf. 'What shall I strip off next? It's in our hands, Mr Bishop, not just our Maker's.'

'If only sermons were this risqué,' chuckled Humpty Dumpty, with renewed drink-driven adulation, 'I'd join any religion you care to reveal, fill up your pretty front pew, I would! Oh, indulgences I adore!'

'Yes, let's choose to cure ourselves of our own self-selected agonies. SO! Decision time. The cross is bare, the agony NAKED and NOW! I desperately need to PEE!'

Mr Bishop suddenly found himself shocked by such a revelation from a convent trained virgin. As she uncrossed her legs, he crossed himself and, as if in pious prayer, placed his hands together in front of his crutch.

Taking the hint, Alice announced, 'Our text is taken from THE AQUARIAN GOSPEL OF JESUS THE CHRIST. It tells of the sacred word, the Word of Power.'

'EDUCATION!' he declared roundly.

Alice, taking a turn, let out her first **YAWN**.

Reversal? That wasn't in the rules! So she regaled him with a defiant second **YAWN.**

Humpty Dumpty hoped these yawns were sexual come-ons. Was he now meant to rip off his Union Jack bow-tie and fling it away over his shoulder with manly abandon? In egging him on, was Anthea now willing to whisk him into an egg white froth of bliss? From in front his crutch he unlaced his podgy praying hands and flipped a quick 'thank you' kiss in to his god, Cupid.

Her own bladder aching, Alice wondered would the randy old egg-timer, after suckling so much vodka, be the first to bottle out, no matter how embarrassing, pee his pants. Meanwhile, she valiantly tried to persevere with her mission. Even though, at that moment, old toss-pot's well-bred tones commandeered attention as loudly he intoned, 'Enticing, your hints of wicked wildness! And the wilderness to follow. Yet I fear apathy, like poverty, will always be with us.' With more depth than usual, he added, 'But it's peaceful apathy. It's agony without aggression. Easy to sell to the masses. It's masochism that's too passive to march in protest. . . .'

'Not until YOU ORDER it to WAR! But Mr Bishop, those who scour the deserts for the Key Master Sound, they will render your wall unsafe. Also your banks, churches, all havens of refuge, no securities left. All Wall Streets will fall, from New York to Tokyo, just like Jericho. When? Well, today's kids are the custodians of tomorrow. If we only rely on adults' hard-boiled bombs to over-egg national security we won't make any omelettes worth scrambling. Spiritually Mr Bishop, we are NOT saved . . . not YET awhile. . . .'

'Such unadulterated callousness in one so young makes me want to spank you. You and your creepy boy seriously imply, do you, that there's no lasting tragedies, not even remotely. . . ?'

'Not in the eye of God. But in mankind, well, suffering is the LAST hobby most of us want to give up.'

'HOBBY! Damn it who dictates all this . . . this devilish drivel?'

Without thinking, she blurted out, 'HUMPHREY!' Stunned Alice still in her own voice now asked her inner self this: 'Is that right?' she pleaded. 'Is Humphrey your real name?' Finding her head nodding, she was aware of a warm drip trickling down her left leg. 'Then, if you're my boyfriend, why aren't you getting all hot and jealous, please tell me that, sweet Humphrey, before I. . . ?'

Humpty Dumpty snorted. 'Said there was more to you than meets the eye! So STRIP, you kinky little kitten, S-T-R-I-P, strip right down to your buffers! Reveal your frisky bush and buttocks!'

Temptation. If she was as attractive as a m-magnet, what m-might her boyfriend do to save her from flattery? As Humpty Dumpty's next artificial YAWN resonated through the forest, she took that as a signal. With mock sensuality, Alice slowly undid her top blouse button. As if a spy engaged in some undercover political act, she felt deliciously shocking. She had not realised that even a par-boiled father figure could make her feel so impor-tant. Probing eyes boring into her's, even those at the back of his fat head, she happily recited by heart her next chosen text from The Aquarian Gospel. **'The secret things that I have told you that may be told to all the world, you shall make known to faithful men who shall in turn reveal them unto the faithful men**. . . .'

'MORE!' yelped the old egg timer leering at her gleaming thighs, getting so excited he forgot to **yawn**. 'Gym-slip off, tits and teeth, flash 'em, girlie! Get 'em both bobbing bouncy-bouncy!'

'My teeth don't bounce, mister – they BITE!' Mistake. He nearly swooned at the prospect of his leg being bitten. Ignoring his sweltering imagination, she recited, **'Until the time shall come when all the world may hear and comprehend the words of the truth and power.'**

Pausing for effect, Alice then roundly declared in Humphrey's worried voice, *'And that time is nigh, Alice, nigh, nigh, NIGH!'*

Imagining herself and the handsome Humphrey suffused in moonlight, Alice slowly undid the next button down her heaving blouse. In his voice, she intoned, *'And as the Hopi Indian prophecy states, the teachers of the new secrets of liberation will not be successful in the material sense. No, they'll be the humble, the invisible, the nobodies; labourers on organic farms, those at bus-stops, the awakened ones, as inner powers return to the people.'*

The word 'powers' used by such an underling even with elegant legs, did not impress Humpty Dumpty. He always disliked things that pretended to be old, like temple ruins rising from the deep to warn of Armageddon yet again. 'Redundant or not, my retirement nest egg awaits me!' announced he in a smug portly voice. 'Far too late for me to change, thank God.'

Abruptly, Alice quoted, 'MY HUMAN FLESH WAS CHANGED TO HIGHER FORM BY LOVE DIVINE,' says The Aquarian Gospel, 'AND I CAN

MANIFEST IN FLESH, OR IN THE HIGHER PLANES OF LIFE, AT WILL. . . .'

'By Peter Pan Airways?' scoffed Mr Bishop as he spat out his favourite swearword, 'KNICKERS!'

Irritated, Alice whizzed her right stocking round her head like a helicopter-blade, and threw it at the old egg's moonstruck face. Defiantly, she related, 'WHAT I CAN DO **ALL MEN CAN DO**. GO PREACH THE GOSPEL OF THE OMNIPOTENCE OF MAN. THEN JESUS DISAPPEARED BUT ALL THE NATIONS **HEARD**.'

'Sounds like Dr Who on loan to the wireless!' jested Humpty Dumpty. 'Nice ankles, though. Even better than Snow White's!' **YAWN**. Alice flashing her atomic smile reached for the last button – on her blouse. *'Yes, there's m-more spiritual awareness in Dr Who and in the comics Marvel and Miracle Man,'* she said in Humphrey's voice, *'than in any church sermon we ever did yawn through. . . .'*

Alice's use of the word 'YAWN' triggered action. Like a two-eyed potato wanted to jump from the fat-pan into the fire, Humpty Dumpty unclasped his cummerbund and threw it over the wall, he gloating with glee like a naughty little boy caught scrumping.

His expression soon changed though. Alice, using the head of his axe to make her point more firmly, was hammering in a second nail into the Gothic-style church door, a diminutive imitation, perhaps, of the towering 12th-century Cathedral in Erfurt, Germany, where Martin Luther had studied scripture. On the church door between both nails Alice proudly displayed the start of her own DIET OF WORMS.

That made Humpty Dumpty roll about with derisive merriment. 'But this church, Anthea, St Jude's, patron saint of lost causes,' he chuckled, 'it's now a Bingo Hall! Pity. Handouts so sap initiative!'

The second nail might stop her manifesto from being ripped off by matrons in a mood for gambling with fate. Throwing her hair-band to the wind and hands on hips, like Luther in a loincloth, renouncing all lost causes, Alice announced, 'Here I stand! I cannot do otherwise.'

'And here I sit!'

Should she push him off, or just push off. . . ?

Defiantly, restating his upright position, he insisted, 'As a boss of

E.M.B.E.R.S., I shall not fall! Decision m-m-made.' That stammer? WOW! Was it catching? As if her protection from dark forces beyond the ken of his contemplation was too much to take, sad and shell-shocked, and clutching the owl egg more tightly as if the chick inside it was constipated, Humpty Dumpty shrank under his see-through umbrella, gibbering.

Collecting up her belongings, Alice said, 'Should you drop off the wall, and your dentures fall out Humpty dear, sure as eggs is eggs, and not all in the same basket, you'll hatch out on earth another body with, eventually, new teeth. Similar bite, maybe, similar impacted wisdom teeth maybe, but same toothache till you learn to develop a more honest and sincere smile. Au revoir. No escaping 'a tooth for a tooth'. We reincarnate.' On that, she dropped him a deep curtsy. 'So, send my love to your next dentist!'

'Contrariwise!' hissed he through gritted teeth. Raging inside like a rogue elephant, Humpty Dumpty, recalling only painful regrets, muttered, 'Such eloquent ankles!' Then added, 'Try Night School, Anthea!' On that he lobbed her the owl egg as if a shy at the fairground. It fell down her open blouse front and settled neatly into the warm cup of her young cleavage. Humpty Dumpty nearly sobbed. He'd longed to see the egg white all down her chest!

Rising from her curtsy, she winked at Humpty Dumpty, then skipped off through the trees.

'Of all the bantam-brained brats I EVER met. Notions completely off the wall yet so obnoxiously bright!' mumbled Humpty Dumpty, behind clenched dentures. 'Positive C minus!'

Nostradamus prophesied that telepathy would increase in this New Age of Aquarius. Thus it was that Alice and Humphrey 'heard' the last comment. To Humpty Dumpty Alice beamed back to him her reply. 'Contrariwise,' she agreed. 'So intoxicatingly dim! Positive C minus!'

Giving him not one parting wave or even the flapping print-out on the church door, Alice left the dark heart and noisy sarcasm of the classroom. Underneath her holy tract she'd left lashings of room for written comments from passers-by. . . .

. . . or from Mr Bishop, Big Boss of E.M.B.E.R.S. . . .

. . . should he surprise himself. . . .

. . . recant . . . before his next big stink bomb. . . .

*

Alice continued to research the forest dripping with acid rain. She was desperate to help all the other children before they believed they were lost forever.

Prompted by the inner Humphrey, she soon found herself at Warren Row. An owl above gave an eerie bugle-call. This was so soon followed by another gunshot aimed at White Rabbit.

After quick and urgent cuddles, White Rabbit asked for the secret password for underground access. Humphrey whispered it silently to her, allowing Alice to descend the dark rabbit-hole at Warren Row.

In Welfareland underground warrens were not built for the kids of *tomorrow*. Such pre-emptive bunkers were built for the presiding educated Top People. They had chosen to save themselves, democratically of course. Maybe because on earth they still had most to learn. They would safeguard their own future, without changing themselves first. But as Alice had started to appreciate, maybe that's the job each individual can do best for himself with less schoolteachers, less priests, less politicians, and without state interference. In fact, had not Alice herself tried to FORCE Humpty Dumpty to change, to convert? And had not her hotly held convictions only cemented his resistance? Basically, were they both but mirror images of each other, both deserving their come-uppance? But before the balloon goes up, will obsolete self-righteous windbags, boasting Victorian 'strength of character', voluntarily burst through and beyond their own gold-plated banks before. . . ?

A flashing camera click.

A stunning crack . . . an obliterating blast . . . petrifying forests . . . animals . . . eyeballs all bleached blind . . . all stout walls flattened . . . in one cosmic instant . . . every mortal thing . . . atomised.

'And the kids have no shelter,' thought Alice still spinning down her own safe rabbit hole while sadly aware that the owl's egg had burst open between what felt like sticky leaking breasts. 'Could have tried harder. . . .'

With that thought, Alice vanished.

In a flash.

Of inspiration.

CHAPTER THREE

UP AND DOWN THE RABBIT HOLE

'Everything's got a moral. If only you can find it.'
'And yet you incessantly stand things on their head.'

Yep, what a flash of insight!

What illumination! What an explosive idea!

And such out-reach! Each local atom splitting open like peas in all pods at picking time!

Humphrey watching her, Alice fell from she-knew-not-why to she-knew-not-where, as the forest above became a cosmic microwave-oven, ablaze with searing white heat, stunned creatures everywhere fried alive in their own juice.

'That's what m-mancruel does best.' Her Lover Boy was trying to soothe her heaving, owl egg-nesting breast. Picking his words carefully like Nostradamus when disguising one of his most damning predictions, he whispered, *'When lost in a forest, m-mancruel lights a beacon in order to see m-m-more clearly. So see every cataclysm, even today's, as kick-starts inviting us all to the next spiral of spiritual uplifts. . . .'*

'But I'm . . . I'm falling . . . FALLING. . . !'

'Yep, to the Cities of the Gods, to the pre-diluvian patriarchs, to a mega-lithic metropolis in Star Chambers of the Deep. Safe from despair enjoy flight Alice! For long before darkest deluges mancruel desperately flirts in

all ways with fiercer and fiercer military toys: a flint, a candle, a firework; a pea-shooter, a tank, a spitfire, a jet-fighter . . . any blasted contraption that can unlock the view, extend horizons, defend progress. The fell result being? To flatten all profitable trees, to destroy earth's top prize oxygen-makers. Until there's no wood left for fire or furniture, for fruit or shelter, for boats or birds. M-mancruel wants to control the whole forest, not just his own cowpats. No wonder he gets lost. The m-more forest he finds to conquer the m-more he fears being trapped by the trees themselves, just as if they were people. The m-more he fears, the m-more he fights. The m-more he fights, the m-more trees fall. As his ingenuity increases even more corpses crash to the ground until, though he can't even make a little apple pip squeak, he can push buttons that can evaporate every apple tree on earth, every Adam, every Eve and every Alice. Except you! And me! And the Survivalists below with an extraterrestrial hi-tech culture way beyond the grasp of mancruel.'

'And M-M-ME?' gasped Alice with a stammer. Although still falling, she wanted to show she still belonged to mankind.

As if drowning, more pictures flashing before her eyes, Alice saw herself selling PEACE NEWS outside nuclear bunkers. Some protesters had printed a fake Government Health Warning on bog paper using the Ban-the-Bomb logo. Rolls and rolls had been left in brown piles outside nuclear plants. Fearing arrest, many rebels had fled to France where nuclear power is even more prevalent and accidents, statistically, more likely than in Britain. Arrests followed. Brutal arrests were popular with politicians as their combined police forces over-reacted. They were given the wink from on high to cope with such 'hot subversives' who, it was believed, were disturbing the prospects of the Cold War protecting World Peace. Subsequently, the Top People defended their right to use state force, in and out of police uniforms, against all noisy peaceniks – who were 'disturbing the peace'.

'Force to protect peace?' was Alice's breathless question as still falling, her hair like seaweed swishing around above her, she spiralled down-wards towards Australasia.

'Such ironies were appreciated more by schizophrenics in M-mental

Institutions,' responded the silent Humphrey, '*than by paranoid puppets in the corridors of power.*'

Though the politically 'unthinkable' had, it seemed, already happened, Alice sensed something even more shocking. All her life she could have sent inner White Light as a blessing, instead of visualizing white light as devastating disaster, silencing all skylarks, airbrushing all rainbows, white-washing as it were, all prison walls, even Humpty Dumpty's.

Thoughts as daydreams? Or thoughts as catalysts? Either way, Alice was feeling as if that arid and banal desert above ground had happened BECAUSE of her long-nursed FEARS, because of her visionary faculties. Had not every prophesying protester actually FED the thought-form of nuclear disasters? Hateful to consider, but maybe such landlocked protesters had mentally hatched its actuality; indeed helped the very Jesuitical Hell on Earth they had tried too hard to resist. If so, what alter-natives could have prevented such alleged accidents. . . ?

Let's help an accident – or nurture a different mind-set? The film THE CHINA SYNDROME had caused right-wing critics to react with scorn saying such an eventuality was impossible. Alas, that fictitious scenario pre-dated a near catastrophic nuclear accident at Three Mile Island, Pennsylvania by only a few days of grace.

Trembling as Humphrey again whispered in her Third Ear, Alice felt her red-hot buttocks were as boldly blushworthy as a baboon's. '*So stop seeing a white light as a global killer,*' advised her ghost Lover Boy, '*Instead, to all nuclear reactors, to warheads, even to domestic power-stations or to any other m-m-monsters m-m-mankind m-makes, send White Light in the name* **M** *as a blessing, for global protection. . . .*'

'**M**?'

'Yep, in a flash, everyone can help raise the consciousness of all life!'

'**WOW!**' whooped Alice aloud in the dark wishing-well of void, hair still streaming above her in the up-draught. 'So much to learn. Please let me learn it ALL before I land!' pleaded Alice aloud, 'My mind's so restless, all over the place, like my seaweed hair. . . .'

'*Yep, THAT'S HOW m-mancruel frees himself when desperate enough*', obliged he. '*By confronting the most inconvenient truths fully, without prej-*

udice, without flinching. And now we're not falling you and I, but flying free! Not just frightened but fascinated! Not just limited but liberated, all killings like insights no longer slow, as with the bow-and-arrow in days of yore, but instant death delivered not with muskets or with lead-shot alone. Not with machine-gun or with buried mines. Neither by blitz nor by doodle-bugs, or by pox, MOX nor disease. Not even by m-missiles and rational m-madness. Not even by drugs or m-m-mind-blowing saints, BUT by. . . .'
Here Alice gulped again to steady her juddering body, upturned skirt tickling her nose. *'. . . by the Ultimate! With instant desert for afters and fall-out to follow that; a cataclysmic eclipse hu-mans obliterating all seven heavens in the twinkling of an eye. This then, is the final deception. The final temptation. This then, is the final intoxication. As with the First Blessing. As in the Beginning . . . when All of **IT** hid in the One Soundless Sound . . . the unspoken Word . . . the first void bliss . . . the first blast-off . . . the first ever-exploding, unbounded . . . big . . . bigger . . . BIGGEST . . . **COSMIC B-A-N-G!**'*

That did it! Better than on her pony Moonlight galloping downhill in the forest Alice, her skirt swinging wildly, felt such a tingle between her legs. And as if she was desperate to relieve the drought in Australia's Great Sandy Desert, her whole bladder emptied. Praying she would not drown any rabbits, moles or worms, it was as if there was a tiger in her tank burning so bright that it needed to burst free. At last, vast relief. . . !

Through the blasted tree-stumps of the burnt-out forest, Top People blundered blindly. Bent as beggars on dusty-grey beaches no longer dwarfed by the unlamented trees, they coughed through sulpherous vapours, desperately trying to cope with cosmic simplicity, their three dimensional desert. Nothing lay in their way now, except melted corpses. Winning Top People's grey power was taking control over Mother Nature's godly green goodness.

Above them pulsated the omnivorous mushroom cloud. Its reddish brown fumes came from 90 tons of acrid nitric oxides synthesized in the atomic temperatures, in heat waves of throbbing radiation. Under that opaque umbrella, blundering creatures were protected from sunstroke by the pulverising mantle of nuclear waste, no forests left for refuge or for refunding either. Long before, 95% of UK's woodlands had already been decimated.

Earlier, the Top People had been busy as usual. The White Queen had been inside her Counting House counting all her crowns. Her least favourite Prime Minister, Snow White, had been in her ivory tower counting the cost of her cut-backs, a defence policy based on Warfare before Welfare; with 300,000 people in London and the South-East working in the arms industries. Yet only three snow-ploughs allowed, weather warnings all ignored. That was a worry. Well, at least three were enough for the top politicians to pave a corridor through dust dunes caused by blizzards of lethal fall-out fumes. It was essential, after all, that the Top People got safely to the underground bunkers, their power-base and their baked beans, unruffled. In time. In tiptop secret. No leaks. No moles. No wets. No holes.

Or so 'they' had thought. But little did Snow White realise that despised wets become best at leaks; that secret underground shelters at Warren Row, High Wycombe and the like were not much safer than bunkers under the Houses of Parliament. A flash, and Snow White saw a glimpse of her brave new world as it really was . . . and it was gone.

All gone.

Gone too, were Snow White's dwarves. Clamping down their bowler-like helmets, grabbing their briefcases like personal anti-nuke survival tool-kits, they had fled from Whitehall. Not one civil servant gave a single thought to the White Queen, to her consort or dogs, to her children, or to their respective palatial kennels by then all flattened by the great leveller. Nor did any one running minister think of Snow White herself. Or of Idle Jack still gripping his bottle as if there was a genie inside it instead of gin. Through the famous front door they had all dashed, ladies first, the door being the only upstanding part left of Number Ten, instantly unprotected by their vaporised sentry policemen. The blast had turned the black paint green and the brass fittings under thermal stress, had become dark sticky toffee. Leaving ten green bottles with a sigh, Idle Jack followed his famous wife, Snow White. She held high her transparent umbrella, setting off as if to find a suitable Hairdresser's. Her husband, trying to catch up, chipped away at his handicap by potting the head of one of his wife's critics into a nearby brain drain.

The remaining dwarves peered down fisuress of fuming cinders. Choking, they were clawing the sour, powered earth, clamouring for protection inside the pre-prepared upholstered shelters underground. Being highly trained yes-men to a wimp (or wet), they lacked spontaneous combustion. Even a nuclear explosion – let alone the thought of it – could not ignite one original idea between them. Grocery Store greed and grammar school obedience often does that to those who seek social ascendancy as a top priority.

Clasping their eye sockets like St Paul after he'd seen God's Inner Light, survivors were stumbling, hither and thither, lacking a voice, a touch, a blind leader they could identify. Wailing was everywhere, no one knowing which way to blunder forth, finding all palpable reality removed. This ultimate in blind-man's buff was fast spiralling itself into giddy hysteria. Nail-less fingertips trembled over signposts scorching in the ruins. Fallen street nameplates were scalded ash-grey and blank. The only surviving cat's-eye had its sparkle fatally blinded.

Yes, in the biblical twinkling of an eye the wind of change had carried stocks and shares, bank notes of all currencies, swirling down the streets of rubble, each bank having burst; each safe as houses blown to smithereens, everything incinerated in a millisecond.

Surrounding the highly paid new homeless, pirouettes of multicoloured worthlessness,not nourishing enough to make compost fit to grow even an apple-pip. In the area most contaminated, not one apple tree was left upright; not one Adam; not even the stray lost ghost of some ambitious Eva Peron.

Fail-safe had not even worked for pet poisonous snakes. The glass cases which had safely housed such reptiles had all congealed into green jellied sludge. The snakes themselves, eyeless and unskinned, were already on the hunt for nearby sprightly cockroaches, their natural terrain now riddled with ravenous rats. The most adventurous serpent, known to her late keeper as Kali, was already on the prowl as if to entice the next Adam and Eve like aliens, to appear in protective space suits, from underground garages.

According to legend, beneath earth's oceans and the mountains, reside cavernous sanctuaries, sub-celestial cities that nurture the next New Race. Patiently they wait, some say, for the dire times when they shall be called upon to rescue Earth from Man and his Mrs. Unblinkingly Kali, the blind snake, lay in wait.

At the first flash, like grouse for a Royal Prince in the open season, jet-planes fell from the skies. Sewers belched forth, their bilious contents swirling before them a mottled swill of rubble, scree, rocks, diamonds, even chalices encrusted with jewels; expensive watches by the thousand; war-medals by the million, pearls and swine bubbling through the sludge, all equally dead, all equally equal. In the tangle of lovers' clasped hands, hungry sewer-rats sharpened teeth on sixteen-carat gold eternity-rings.

Further off, a skeleton tugboat hooted, hauntingly, the repeating sound stuck on autopilot. Cargo ships had become liquidised but not the military arms they carried, only the warm embracing arms, which had placed them there for safe keeping. Guns for God, released from crates, sank down into the blazing seas to lie there undisturbed. Until that seabed re-emerges, maybe, centuries later and offers itself as the next battlefield above the waves under leaden clouds.

Screeching through the fogs of fall-out, two tatty herring gulls were fighting over bits of human shrapnel, a bonanza, bags of fried testicles a rare and hairless delicacy, in sulphurous vapours, not be be sniffed at.

On motorways, frozen in a time warp like epic assembly-lines, sweaty cars stood with x-rayed corpses at their wheels, caught in motionless road rage. Rows and rows of panting cars, empty mile after empty mile, going no-where now, the next weekend trip postponed, unexpectedly. Smaller livestock inside the cars still thrived. Weevils appeared in picnic biscuits, maggots in human meat, lice in pubic hair, nits in soiled nappies, all changing their diet, experimentally, to fit the new circumstances, all intent at survival at any cost, just like their host corpses had been. Microbes, thanks to man's poisoned planet, had already learnt how to digest contaminated food. Termites, too, were growing fat – tiny jaws champing fast amonst scuttling crispy cockcroaches.

And fieldmice since the corn had developed nuclear mildew had turned carnivorous. Fighting rats were snatching motorists' remaining bits, stoically chewing tough safety-belts too, and washing all down with dainty sips of super-smooth engine-oil.

The dormouse, later to meet Alice, dozed in a teapot through these events, quite unaware it had no wholesome food to wake up to after long snoozes, like fresh berries and hedgerow nuts. What a wonderful Welfare State it was! What a wonderland of waste!

'Curious,' mused Alice Above-It-All, sitting in an invisible tree in her Spirit Body, 'I'd no idea an idea could be so devastating. In future, I must watch what I think – I think!'

A 'Miaow' interrupted such musings. Sitting there, in another transparent tree, was the unsmiling Cheshire Cat. Depressed enough already, Alice invited it to smile, saying, 'Please say cheese, Cheshire Cat – CHEESE, please!'

'MANCUNIAN Cat,' corrected the affable animal. 'My part of Cheshire got swallowed up. What by luv? Boundary changes. Be another name for the bomb, that. Shouldn't worry yer clever curls over it, pet. Not now you've gone up in the worlds . . . not down. . . .'

Alice remained distressed and puzzled. 'I did yoga so as to stand other people's ideas on their head but now you're asking me to be a yo-yo as well. . . .'

'A yogi yo-yo, aye. Spirit Travel, for the initiated, ain't got no no-go areas. Ever open, you might say. Before exploring underground, don't fret about them Top People left, fried alive pet, too afraid of future tests to survive intact,' explained the Cat. 'Deep thoughts with strong emotions, see, such like produces knee-jerk reflexes. . . .'

'You mean, like boomerangs? No escape EVER, from boom to dusty bust. . . ?'

'Nay, your bust not ready for dust yet awhile, pet. Not now you've learnt how to atomize bad pictures, shatter two-way looking glasses, travel through em, go God-like! Whatever we imagine, see, will manifest on one level or another. Luv, we're God's own image-makers, us. That's why my lot got worshipped, see, in Egypt. Any broken bones lass? Stroke me and my purring will heal all fractures, see . . . like, say, the Great Pyramid sarcophagus be in tune with the hu-man heart beat, see.'

'RUBBISH!' Cat sounded like the late Humpty Dumpty defying a defiant little madam too big for her booties.

'UNADULTERATED RUBBISH!' countered Mancunian Cat mildly, using gentle tact and yards of oral elastic, 'One man's rubbish is another's jumble-sale!'

'But shouldn't I blame myself for thinking the unthinkable? I've helped cause what's happened! Survivors suffering now. On scorched earth! Why aren't I, dear Cat, WHY? Yes, my knickers are soaked but not with TEARS or blood. I must take my share blame for all of this that isn't any more . . . I REALLY MUST!'

With a shrug the Cat replied, 'All shares have guilt edges, pet. Like dark clouds.'

On that, Mancunian Cat leaped into Alice's invisible tree, pushing her from her bough. During their slow-motion fall, the Cat continued explaining, 'See, as decay sets in luv, price of human tripes, they'll skyrocket in the dung beetles' market! Have a butchers. . . .'

'Too . . . vegetarian!' shuddered Alice, closing her eyes. The powdery depth of the dust dune muffled their landing. Before climbing out of her self-created crater, she asked, 'You mean whatever I think . . . here and now . . . whatever I picture, whatever I imagine and store away like stills in a movie-camera . . . that one day . . . those very thoughts will pop up into view, fully printed . . . and physically appear . . . ready for me to trip over them. . . ? But it was such a long question that Mancunian Cat had fallen asleep before landing right way up in their shared crater.

'Dormouse and Cat asleep,' Alice muttered to herself like a ghost in a morgue looking for new friends to play with, 'I feel sort of left out. There must be an end to this nightmare of my own making, to this grotty hole I'm in. . . .'

'There IS!' said a hollow voice. Recognising it as that of the Mancunian Cat, Alice looked about her. Nothing but stagnant whirlpools of glutonous ash. The feline creature had vanished. Yet its voice continued. 'Ultimately, them things what last, them which are imperishable, they're really the

INVISIBLE things, pet. Like me, you might say. Visible or not, believe it or not, I'm always with you. Like love, luv.'

Like Humphrey? Was Humphrey, after all, only a cat? Like a witch's familiar?

For all that, the thought of Humphrey purring on her lap gave her a feeling of such comfort. Whenever such warmth percolated every cell of her body, Alice felt accepted, a valuable part of the Master Plan. Hidden or not, it was as if her secret mission was getting reaffirmed. Yet she couldn't help wondering if a real flesh and blood cuddle would warm her even more. Though her ultimate destiny was still a mystery, she listened contentedly to the purring deep within her innermost ear as the cat's voice suggested, 'Go within each day. There, all those who are saved can be found, safe and sound. Enter by the eye of **M**. . . .'

'**M** for **M**other?'

'Nope'

'**M** for **M**ancunian Cat?'

'Nope'

'**M** for **M**e, maybe . . . or **M**irror?

'Getting warmer, chuck. WATCH!'

As if in answer, beneath her, up from the ashes rose a smoky blue figure in the shape of an **M**. Stretching like a **M**anx cat after a long sleep, it yawned and flexed its front paws. Then with a meaningful 'miaow', it jumped onto the nearby fallen wall, Humpty Dumpty no-where in sight, the wall's charred bricks having suffered third degree burns.

Following the feline **M**, Alice took a flying leap from the top of her crater into a pile of crumbling bricks, roasted scabs of lichen there, flaking off. Alice alighted safely only just in time as the Cat vanished into misty sand dunes, melting there maybe through an unseen metal door, a top-secret portal now set in a fenceless field of broiled slurry which, seconds after the last strike and the last handicap, the Top People's Golf Course had evaporated.

Although convinced all magic lay within her, Alice lacked confidence. Should she follow **M** inside the good earth? Or were her best good works to be with the poor survivors above ground?

'Like me, go for BOTH, chuck!' advised the flexible but invisible feline.

Alice, not sure whether she was on her head or out of it; on the earth or in it; in the air or above it; out-of-body or in a glove-puppet named Alice she, or something that sometimes felt like herself, thought she heard a knock on the metal trap-door in the ground. Yes, it was her own ghostly knuckles, knocking.

No answer.

She knocked again.

No sound. No answer. No guidance.

Knocking yet again, Alice uncovered a spy-hole a third of the way from the top (given Alice really was at the bottom). Someone or something seemed to be watching her impassively from the other side, through the spy-hole in the metal trap-door.

If she was really in her ghost body, why could she not glide through to the other side of the iron door...without the password . . . without a key . . . and join that astral cat . . . or best of all, Humphrey?

But help was at hand. Not so much for herself, Alice realized, but for those more substantial others stuck above ground. Perhaps she could help them somehow. Given that is, they wouldn't ignore her because she was just a child and therefore of no consequence. Or worse, patronise her.

Behind Alice came squeals of well-bred irritation, the remains of the Bowler Hat Brigade. It was led by the White Queen, a half-baked corgi and Snow White. Not having been given a four minute warning, both ladies were late and irate. The fail-safe had not worked in their favour. In fact, it had not worked at all. And now Warren Row's secret bunker, their desired refuge, was sealed up on the inside and guarded by homeless squatters. Dreadful!

Through swirling fogs, hairless human figures stumbled in and out of each other's path, a quadrille on hot clinkers, all hoping to find the hatch which led to safer baked beans and coke, their thickened air already tasting of carcinogenic corpses.

To such Top Persons, since a child was a statistic and not a person in its own right, Alice was invisible. She knew that adults only see what they want to see. Otherwise no doubt, she'd get prodded out of the way with pointed insults and barbed brollies and, maybe, bopped on the head by the golden sceptre now being pulled at both ends like a party cracker by the White Queen and Snow White, neither wishing to let go.

The access password was required, that Alice knew. She racked her brains to remember the word that would open sesame into the inner worlds, away from that plantless desert, away from that putrid wilderness. Choking dust fumes were already making Snow White cough up so much that only SUPA might afford to service her with private medicare. In such emergencies, common folk had already been designated as expendable. So maybe better that it WAS SUPA, which had survived and had not been bleached out of existence, unlike the poor people's National Health Service. After all, in such conditions, even the local St John's Ambulance volunteers had just turned a congealed green, and not with envy.

Like a mantra, Alice crooned out key words, experimentally. 'Love?' (Pause). 'Hope?' (Pause). 'Charity?' (Pause).

No, not one of those popular words, no matter how beautifully enunciated, would open the iron door in the ground. By then sweating, Alice was desperate to recall the access word to save the Top People before they expired. She tried again with other words that spell magic for many people. **M** for 'Money!', the cure-all for all unsolved questions?

No reaction.

'Power?' Again silence.

'Sex?'

Through the trap door, the watching eye winked. Was it handsome Humphrey?

Apart from the lingering groans from the bowler-hatted dwarfs, no further reaction in the watchful eye behind the spy-hole, the hatch staying shut, locking out all nightmarish screams as nuclear-powered earthlings continued to fall out with each other.

Round all victims above ground, closing in like the acidic stinging fumes of radiation, time and death were pressing. But to open the hatch door, Alice refused to use force, despite being snapped at by the half-cooked clairvoyant royal corgi. Yapping endlessly, and suffering its own brand of fall-out, the last little dog was getting balder (and bolder) by the second. Two bleeding eyes glaring. it growled at the ghost body of Alice. Stricken though it was, the White Queen was too preoccupied to notice such as she struggled to regain her obstinately smoking ceptre as gold flakes fluttered down, falling into the sterlised debris below.

Denis, Snow White's less better half, was rubbing up his genie the wrong way, the bottle now empty of liquor. As usual, the bossy Snow White was conducting a fire drill for the dying Bowler Hat Brigade with the immortal words, 'Never say die, chaps. What the Handsworth rioters could do with their burning streets we can jolly well beat 'em!'

'Prayer?' (Pause) 'Church?' (Pause) 'God?' (Pause). Even these more elevated code words failed to open the metal door in the sticky dust, Alice near to despair. 'Let them in, please,' she pleaded. 'They only ever wanted to be good, to serve mankind, not mancruel. To tell the truth and take the consequences.' Undoing her nuclear-free zone button, she tried to add the usual excuse, 'But like everyone else, like me, we're all only hu. . . .'

On that, it happened. Though the door seemed to swing open, it in fact stayed rigidly fixed. Nonetheless, the ghost body of Alice spun down through the hatch's iron hole . . . like mist through a cobweb sieve. . . .

Alice and her five psychic bodies telescoped back into one. In the hollow earth below she became joined-up again with all her selves. 'Hi dears, oh most Mighty ME UNITED!' greeted she, arriving.

Above ground, the two Top Ladies were left, unaware of what had just happened. Alice promised herself to return, to help them once she herself had consciously rediscovered the secret password. Surely, in the days of so much pain, do-gooding should never end.

But first, Alice had to adjust. Hidden beneath the earth's desiccated surface, her new environment was not just palatial but puzzling. Having spat out her silver christening spoon, did she deserve such privileges?

A corgi lapdog growling at her ghost body was one thing, but how long before Alice forgot her dark thoughts, those that fuelled her own fears of being found to be inadequate? That black howling hound of her convent night dreams, the slavering mastiff with the eye of an alien, still haunted her head. And the word mastiff starts with the letter **M**.

Yet Humphrey and the Mancunian Cat, if not both together, were her constant inner companions. Could they be enough comfort, or was she still craving something else, something way beyond what she had experienced in her physical body?

So far, not nearly enough excitement. Or challenge!

Alice, getting ready to face her future underground, was already on the way to discovering many new m-magic doors that she hoped might lead to a higher type of human.

Waking up, as it were, seconds later, Alice saw two wide open eyes, two staring saucers in a broad black face. 'Welcome to Warren Row! I'm the White Rabbit.'

Rubbing her rump bruised by ghost bumps from her abrupt landing, then rubbing her ever-alert eyes, Alice said, 'I must be colour blind!'

'Not none, hereabouts, man.'

'No nuns, you mean, with black habits. Or blackheads?'

'Ma skin might be black, man, but ma Soul ... well look at dees TEETH!' With that, his grin opened as wide as those white pearly gates saints dream about.

'And I'm Peter,' said the large girl next to him, her creamy complexion shining through the Rastafarian ringlets so popular in Victorian England.

'Peter?' blinked Alice, testing her hearing.

'Spelt P-I-T-T-A,' came the helpful reply. 'Like the bread of heaven, all flat. Like my tits!' On that, remarkably, she handed Alice a large handkerchief.

'But honey sweet!' winked White Rabbit. 'Pitta bread we can fill dat wit' whatever we fancy, right, bunny crumpet?' Gleefully, as he was stamping the ground like a Spanish Flopsy Bunny, Alice wiped away some of the cracking owl egg's white by now dripping down between both of her nubile nipples. Watching, White Rabbit and Pitta exploded into rapturous chuckling, both cascading down the musical scale in mutual laughter, two lovers of levity and light. Alice also felt included. Even if her head did not understand why, she also rocked with laughter. She was noticing a feeling of relief, as if she'd suddenly glimpsed the forest path that leads to home. And as if to confirm this, the owl egg having nestled safely in her breasts, the hatched chick emerged from her blouse front and flew off with a happy chortle. Her new found friends did not even gasp.

Pitta, Alice soon learned, had been to the Blue Star Open Heart School in the most deprived part of the city where she had been raised. This warmth she had missed so much when she left, that Pitta had longed to get back to that family feeling again, somewhere soon. 'That's why I come here,' she explained. 'All my best mates were homeless, like me. Jobless, OK, but no jerks. Harassed and hopeless. Schemes for the unemployed were a rip-off. Workshops the most expensive of the lot. The system legislates for failure by laying down the law that 55% will fail their exams, so that only 45% are allowed to get O Level passes. I'd of become a Primary teacher but you can't beat the system before it breaks you. With my mate Jenny, I went to our local Comp. . . .'

'Comprehensive school?' asked Alice, still grieving over the children above who didn't make it, the ones no one ever listened to in lessons with enough love.

'Big factory where they learns you less and less about less and less in boring lessons,' prompted friendly White Rabbit, '35 pigs to a pen. Pens thrown out classroom windows!'

'Well, sat at the back of Jenny's class, it were one whole hour and the teacher didn't ask one question. Didn't even know I shouldn't of been there.'

Agreeing how bad things were, White Rabbit added, 'That's why I split, man. This be the first 'ome I've 'ad like, since Remand Centre, all boots, swearing an' foot drill. I'm one of dem 45,000 claimants what were been told to get an f-in' job or move on, or no dole. Again. Was thousands of us nomads, know what I mean, man? 'Ere, in dat poxy city alone, all the best squats full up with piss-artists, druggies, refuse . . . get the picture. . . ?'

Alice got the picture. What she didn't always get were many of the jigsaw pieces, even though she wondered if the whole picture was in every piece, anyway, hidden from human eyes. But so far, so heart-warming.

Pitta continued, 'Having had the advantage of a free-style education, of course I had initiative. Could organise myself. . . .'

'And OTHERS. . . !' grinned her partner.

'Yeah man, we wasn't going to sit on dustbin-lids and wait for cockroaches to get us,' continued Pitta, slipping her arm through White Rabbit's.

'All dem crummy bed-sits,' said he, 'all dem hostels, all dem barons of the bed and breakfast bonanza. Man, I bet all that be left now of their racket, is dem dear old cockroaches jumpin' for joy now the world belongs to dem again.'

'Excuse me if I seem ignorant,' said Alice gaining confidence, 'but why didn't all those hordes of homeless barge into the nearest police station, demand to be arrested? And before they became a disturbance. They should have upset the peace of placid, middle-class householders. Say the bankrupt DHSS sent them!'

To her delight, they both hugged her. She felt like a ham sandwich in a toaster. As one, they said, 'Welcome to Costa del Dole!'

Welcome . . . WELCOME . . . **W-E-L-C-O-M-E!** The word rippled up and down the cavernous corridors as if it was the whole world singing its own true song.

'So we masterminded THIS. . . .' said Pitta, giving a graceful, generous gesture which included all. 'We're the Rainbow Survivalists, the Homeless what refused to give up hope. Now the Top People are desert nomads. Right? No-where cool to squat, but on their own hot cinders of civilization, us safe in nuclear bunkers.'

Asked Alice, 'Excluding your herb teas, but including your Decontamination Chambers, the baked beans, were these only reserved for you now, the Upper Crust Ruling class. . . ?'

Heads of all colours nodded as more folks flooded through the cavernous chambers from hidden levels below.

'That's why it was classified info. . . .' said Pitta almost smugly. 'Even the builders, the layers of concrete, weren't meant to ask questions. Most of 'em had been stuck in State Schools, like, so DIDN'T. True to form.'

'The SIXTH Form!' joked a college drop-out in hippy gear.

Down the vast corridors of sparkling murals still came a dancing sea of multicoloured friends, holding hands, chanting, singing and smiling. The cavern filled up with energies of all kinds, all ages, all backgrounds, all genders ALL, Alice assumed, who had somehow found the magic code-word, perhaps like herself, without actually being totally sure what it was or what it meant. But at least SHE was determined to find out, not just the

Word, but everything else associated with wisdom. Scrutinizing them, she looked for handsome Humphrey.

Instead of bunkers for Top People in power, a hidden HQ for control with or without an active nuclear button, Alice found herself staring at an underground garden peopled with the most beautiful 'weeds' and 'wimps' and 'wets' – these last being those who had leaked out valuable secret information about such subterranean sanctuaries. The first shall be the last and the last, first. The meek were inheriting, if not the topsoil, then at least the underworld wonderlands of the welfare state and not its dregs.

Alice marvelled how, without an outside crisis like an alien attack, the Rainbow Survivalists could all speak with one mind, yet cherish such distinct individuality, without petty rivalries and noisy egos getting in the way.

Surely there HAD to be some dissenters somewhere. Like Humphrey, if that was his real name; he a bonny boy not just a cat. Wouldn't he be too weird to fit in? Alice had always preferred the loners, the outsiders, herself being the prototype of one. She made a note to seek out and to interview the loners later. She longed to learn all about life as it could or should be lived in the love of all that is, or ever will be. A tall order but, three days out of four, Alice had felt up to it. How long before gaining the total clarity that only a once-in-a-lifetime flash of insight can illuminate forever the true seeker. . . ? Alice, as usual, was impatient to thrust forward and find total clarity for herself.

Yet, again, she delayed self-development in the name of helping others. Perhaps the Top Ladies would be easier on her solicitations than were Owl and Humpty Dumpty. Using another astral projection, compassion zoomed her above ground like a flying movie camera with a roving multi-dimensional lens. . . .

Scene 1 – Warren Row, Exterior. Nuclear night, or day

IN ANOTHER PART OF THE FOREST THAT WAS, SOME STILTED TOP PEOPLE, ON WALKABOUT, ARE STILL JUST ABOUT UPRIGHT. SNOW WHITE IS ONE OF THEM. SHE WALKS AMONG THE BLASTED TREE STUMPS WITH MUCH ROUND-SHOULDERED CONCERN. EVEN WITH-

OUT THE OXYGEN OF PUBLICITY. PRE-RECORDED WARNINGS OF NUCLEAR ACCIDENTS SOMEHOW NEVER GOT TRANSMITTED IN TIME, 'FAIL-SAFE' BEING NO MORE SAFE THAN HOUSES.

SNOW WHITE LAYS HER GLOVED HANDS ON INVISIBLE DEAD VOTERS, THOUSANDS OF THEM. THROUGH MILES OF RUBBLE, DUST AND SLURRY, SHE WANDERS, NOT ONE CABINET COCKROACH FOR COMPANY. AT LAST, SHE RETURNS TO HER ONLY HUMAN COMPANION LEFT. THIS IS THE WHITE QUEEN WHO, TIRED OUT FROM KNOCKING ON THE IRON DOOR TO AN UNDERGROUND SANCTUARY, NOW SITS WITH HER PEELING CORGI. BOTH VERY DROWSY AND DOWNCAST.

SNOW WHITE IS ALSO WEARY AND WORN, YET UNDEFEATED BY THE ARDOURS OF PUBLICLY DEFENDING THE FREEDOMS OF THE UNDENIABLY DEAD. AFTER ALL, SHE'D ALWAYS CLAIMED THAT SOCIETY DOESN'T EXIST, A SELF-FULFILLING PROPHECY.

SNOW WHITE	My own dear bunker gone bust.
WHITE QUEEN	Ah, poor poor Wasteminster.
SNOW WHITE	(*Surveying scene*) It's like the Black Country.
WHITE QUEEN	After the revolution . . . yes.
SNOW WHITE	French? Yes, I'd still blame the Frogs.
WHITE QUEEN	Your pit closures, Prime Minister. A pre--emptive strike in revenge, maybe?
SNOW WHITE	Those miners, undermined at last!
WHITE QUEEN	LOOK! Contaminated wastelands . . . not one working factory left . . . for mile upon mile. One must ask – whose fault. You promised them the earth.
SNOW WHITE	(*Respectfully*) And the sale of cemeteries. You know, survivors who could not speak, I just laid my hand on. I wanted them to know I was there . . . (*holding her killer handbag, peering through the fog at a compact mirror*). Where there's a desert, there's always an oasis. (*She sighs.*)
WHITE QUEEN	(*She sighs*) All the weeping in the world will not bring back your wets now.

SNOW WHITE   Nor all the Queen's horses, and all the Queen's men. (*She sighs.*)

BOTH   (*Together*) Couldn't put Humpty Dumpty together again. . . . (*Together they both sigh.*)

THEY CHOKE, DISCREETLY, A TIMID DUET OF POSH COUGHS.

SNOW WHITE   (*At last, bravely*) But you see, over a working break-fast, one finds there is always a way to win. . . .

WHITE QUEEN   Not the Falklands again?

SNOW WHITE   Oh, yes. Goose is very good for one.

WHITE QUEEN   Well, we have certainly cooked ours. Your pearls, they're dripping. (*She dabs Snow White's blouse front.*) Rather like goose-droppings. (*Chuckles.*)

SNOW WHITE   Plenty of birds on our own Falklands, so we won't starve. Good fertiliser, penguins. Once you get through the rocks. That's why we used rockets.

WHITE QUEEN   We have never liked rocks. So heavy to wear. (*Sighing*) Still, duty dictates that we go on . . . and on . . . and on . . . and. . . .

SNOW WHITE   Our theme song, ma'am. The unbroken record. . . .

WHITE QUEEN   God Save the Queen? Charles asks, how do they stand for it. . . .

SNOW WHITE   I don't! Nor for philosophy, Oxford or trains.

PAUSE AS WHITE QUEEN REMEMBERS TO BE GRACIOUS AGAIN. SNOW WHITE, IMPATIENT, WALKS UP AND DOWN, DISTURBING DUST. SHE KNOCKS AT THE DOOR SET IN THE SLIMY FOUL-SMELLING BLACK SAND.

SNOW WHITE   Open! (*Knocking louder*) Open in the name of the Queen!

WHITE QUEEN   (*After a moment*) They must be deaf.

SNOW WHITE   Or communists. Must tell Ronnie Raygun.

WHITE QUEEN	What did that Dean say? Was it, 'Better a dead Jesus than a red Marxist'?
SNOW WHITE	(*Apologetically*) Some mole must have let them in. Given them shelter and baked beans in preference to ourselves. Terrible, terrible, absolutely terrible. Some commoner. Will you ever honour me now? That's to say will you accept an abject apology, Your Majesty? (Pause) May I still call you Ma'am? (Pause) Or Liz. . . ?

FROM THE QUEEN THE FAINTEST POSSIBLE NOD.

WHITE QUEEN	Why not? None of my family ever did.

On thinking how humiliating for them both, Alice snapped back into her fleshly body below ground. There, she blurted out the name '**MAGGIE!**'. Instantly, another **M** word sprang to her lips. Or was it the same word, '**MONEY!**'? Both of those **M** words exclaimed aloud had the effect of making the folks around hurry off as if she was an outcast, not casting one backward glance, like Nu-Age Antlanteans looking for past Soul Mates. Missing Humphrey, plaintively, she called '**Mum**phrey!' The 'mum' sound offered by mistake provided for her a brief moment of comfort.

She wanted to stop the dear departed, to enquire if they knew who **M** was, or what, since she was determined to find that out before she tracked down Humphrey. Wasn't it too wearying to devote all her young life into chasing ghosts? But obstinately, Alice sensed that she and Humphrey had a future, as well as a past. Should she risk exploring that before her scheduled date with the Oxford Don? That was a doubt too big for her to dabble with too often.

And yet . . . and YET . . . no, not yet. Alice had so enjoyed the Rainbow Survivalists, their on-going chorus of voices, the medley of accents, the dialects, the different body languages but all, ALL conveying the same messianic message, 'Welcome to the New Age of Peace, Harmony and Spiritual Unfoldment . . . **WELCOME!**'

Not that they were expressing some totalitarian ideal. Over fresh raw snacks, individualists emerged. As others gathered to introduce them-selves, Alice watched out for those whom she might trust as a friend, especially any young man who stuttered over the letter M.

Assorted voices continued, expressing their community conscious-ness, snatches caught on the wind like multi-coloured autumn leaves.

'. . . they've ruined their topsoil . . . so them Top People fought they'd won, beaten us . . . prevented little folk . . . other than the chosen few . . . from making big bombs . . . we so-called poor no longer need the rich. We went one better. Left 'em to their own nuclear devices . . . left the exclu-sive Nuclear Club . . . let them blow each other up, maybe . . . we survive, us redundant rebels . . . we underlings . . . us apathetic Annies . . . we Moaning Minnies (IRONIC LAUGHTER). Now make bread not bombs . . . generous folks, not profits . . . of DOOM! Now we've hydraulic lake water, godly statues the size of the Valley of the Nile, not one pain-in-the-arse *denial.*' Even the puniest pun had become a friend, like a family joke. Thus this last crack got its expected chortle. Voices continued, symphonically, Alice still watching out for Humphrey.

'Welfare or warfare? We can't afford BOTH, nor assumptions of our uselessness, feudally enforced like the head-fodder forced into us in the name of schooling. We reject their slave mentally, their Protestant work ethic . . . selling our whole lifestyle for money . . . instead we get to feel good through personal enthusiasm (coming from the Greek meaning the god within) and from personal growth, not from wages packets see, since we use our energies for the whole community here, not just for our own nuclear family what could never afford its own shelter, so here we're into self-help, yeah mutual support . . . co-operation not competition . . . we was told to stand on our own feet by them wot stood on ours . . . well, by God we 'ave mate! We HAVE helped ourselves . . . we've helped ourselves to their baked beans (LAUGHTER) and bully beef before their tins turn radio-active!'

Laughter everywhere, non-sexist men and women letting off fart noises back and front, legs lifted like dogs at invisible lamp-posts.

Alice flushed, not so much in embarrassment, as at the memory of that slavering Black Dog pouncing onto her sleeping crotch the night before she decided to run away from her safe and predictable life. Maybe a rottweiler lapping up menstrual flooding...and imminent death. HERS? In dream symbolism, which end of life did it signify, back or front? Given that is, that Alice could discern which way her present time was travelling, backwards or forwards. Either way, she'd certainly never let herself stand still for long.

The rich medley of voices still explained themselves to their newly recruited Survivalist.

'Alice, we helped ourselves . . . to this, their fallback, fail-safe underground palace . . . extended our families . . . no longer do we squat in squalor on pot, peanuts and pee-stained mattresses . . . we've given the world up as a lost cause . . . anyway, what's the point of TWO homes if they both get blown up sky-high?'

Laughter and applause rippled through them like spring water.

'We give their shelter a spring clean . . . feed the spiders . . . grow mushrooms in underground bomb shelters . . . grow wheat-sprouts and trout . . . orange trees under sunray-lamps . . . recycle all waste . . . hold playshops . . . for free . . . on finding our true selves . . . at last. . . .'

Alice was giddy with anticipation, drinking it all in.

'. . . seminars, concerts, teach-ins, initiations, enlightenment from Buddha, not the bomb . . . secular societies don't last . . . so we rate each new Messiah more than bigger and better missiles . . . we keeps all life sacred, not just Sundays . . . give alms for Allah, not armaments . . . the right means of livelihood being necessary for Buddhahood. We reject sterile, repressive, nerve-racking work . . . the 5-day week . . . waste of natural resources . . . and pretence that we'll all be saved without personal effort . . . without due gratitude . . . or total surrender . . . to the greatest good . . . and without spontaneous joy'. A sudden kiss-in!

Never had Alice been touched by so many different kinds of people at once, swamped with warmth, celebrated effusively, as they supplied details of their life-style. Daily, many write their own bibles, like biographies; not study the dead who couldn't even save themselves from suffering, preferring now company of those who are looking how to live for ever, those who believe in age and death not as inevitable and ugly disasters, but as the next adventure. They claimed that their corporate 'bible' is built not with cant but with kindness, considered empathy and with general agreement. 'For us Survivalists, unsloppy love, that's our cement . . . yeah, cement that welcomes the weeds what break through it and thrive,' expressed one disciple with a relaxed certainty. 'Every weed and every wet is a miracle . . . unemployment the greatest adventure . . . wiffout the need for bleedin' leaders, right,' clarified another Survivalist, '. . . since yesterday, when them upper crusty freaks, they blew it. But not for us. So a four-minute silence, please, to remember them, especially those not yet dead. And let's remind ourselves that, even if we relent and let them in amongst us, tomorrow's world is OURS . . . not THEIRS!'

Alice, after that aria of joyful unity, expected to join rousing applause, not meditation. Enthusiasticlly she clapped. Then she saw she was on her own, though still being bathed in a glow of non-judgemental love and acceptance. In their meditation.

For how much longer, she wondered. Wait till they saw her cussed side. Wasn't she really a bit like a smaller version of Snow White? On that thought, back in her ghost body, Alice was immediately transported to above ground just in time to watch the White Queen scan the vast feature-less horizons. . . .

Scene 2 – Warren Row. Exterior. Nuclear Winter or Summer?

WHITE QUEEN	(*After a moment*) Charles does not seem to be coming. That means no dog food.
SNOW WHITE	I'd venture to suggest, that corgi is too contaminated to eat. Such a waste!
WHITE QUEEN	Oneself has never eaten like a horse.
SNOW WHITE	Better to nibble carrots, like racehorses, ma'am. Like you, ship-shape. One educates them out of being fat milksops. My husband and I, we always did learn from my subjects. (*Knocking at the iron door.*) Open in the name of the Queen!
WHITE QUEEN	(*Bridling*) Subjects?

SNOW WHITE	(*Unblinkingly*) Yes, ma'am. Maths, History, Law, Chemistry. Even I might say, Good Housekeeping.
WHITE QUEEN	But, Margaret, we're now homeless. Face it.
SNOW WHITE	Personally, I have never feared being overtaken by hippies. Not even the big 'C'.
WHITE QUEEN	Charles?
SNOW WHITE	Cancer. Passive smoking. A bit of fall-out never harmed even wimps. We only allowed the odd leak from the nuclear Power Stations to build up people's immunity to radiation.
WHITE QUEEN	Ah, yes. Homeopathy.

TOGETHER, THEY BREATHE IN AND OUT, CHOKING PRETTILY.

	(*Blandly*) Didn't work.
SNOW WHITE	(*Defensively*) No, too bone-idle. Protesters never produce solutions. Terminal cases are the worst. Take it, I say. No time for funks, have we Liz? (*Avoiding a reply*.) I agree with everything you say. Ready for exercises, ma'am? Must keep up appearances, you know.

SINCE THE WHITE QUEEN LOOKS DUBIOUS, SNOW WHITE HELP-FULLY ILLUSTRATES THE ROUTINE FOR HER. SHE STARTS WAVING HER RIGHT HAND AS IF TO CROWDS AND CROWDS OF HAPPY, GRATEFUL SURVIVING SUBJECTS.

SNOW WHITE	Practise makes perfect. . . .

HER HAND, THUS EXPOSED TO RADIATION, SWELLS. IT TURNS INTO AN OILY BLACKNESS, FINGER-NAILS DROPPING OUT.

	Arthritis can so easily set in.
WHITE QUEEN	(*Acidly*) As God gets a grip, Prime Minister.
SNOW WHITE	So accurate, Liz. Call me Maggie.

In her mind's eye Alice still gazed with pity upon the VIP victims, civil servants way beyond the vision of both the White Queen and Snow White. No group hysteria seethed under their battered bowler hats. Instead, a calm and tacit realisation was at last percolating. Idealism is not fine speeches, empty promises, emotional manipulations, strutting egos and image making. Idealism needs long-term planning and sustainable life-styles, not short-term patching for personal profit and prestige.

Below ground, everybody respected the four-minute silence for those alive and dead. Alice, of course, not being all there, was on autopilot. Almost as a robot she asked for the bedraggled few above ground, those presently dying in rich rags, those wretched survivors seeking shelter, also to be remembered.

'How long before lepers think like Llamas?' asked one of the bearded weirdoes.

To the underground Survivalists, idealism was obviously a quiet, modest, practical matter, a method of tuning into the greatest good, of enjoying unpretentious camaraderie, without fear or favour. It was such a friendly atmosphere that Pitta pulled one man from the crowd, one that Alice had already spotted in case it was Humphrey. 'Meet Guy,' she said, 'Guy Dauncey.'

Before her stood an energetic but unsmiling man of about 35, his hair and beard an ambiguous ginger.

Presenting him, Pitta said, 'He wrote THE UNEMPLOYMENT HAND-BOOK. Talks about turning all bank notes into humus!'

Firmly jolted back into her physical body, Alice left the visions of appalling devastation and suffering. Clearing her earthly eyes, she asked, 'Is that your bible?'

'Accountability, eh? What do YOU understand by accountable eonomy. . . ?' asked Guy.

A QUESTION! And so soon! Alice had been wondering when they would notice that she was not going to be a convert just because they seemed to like her excessively. Refusing to be accepted on trust, Alice preferred to prove herself, even if, as usually happened, she got rejected for being too forthright. Yes, whatever trials and tribulations lay ahead of her, Alice herself would continue to test the Rainbow Survivalists' sunny optimism.

If Humphrey was hiding amongst them, she had to check they were sincere enough to reveal him soon. To heal her sore and aching heart, she needed to nourish her strong hope of a true love nearby, one who would enjoy being among her sunny Survivalsits as one of God's own Chosen Ones.

CHOSEN? If so, for what next. . . ?

. . . for more exciting underground tests. . . .

. . . what else . . . and WHY. . . ?

CHAPTER FOUR

Halls of the Homeless

'You could not see a cloud, because
No cloud was in the sky:
No birds were flying overhead -
There were no birds to fly.'

Brashly, Alice answered Guy's question. 'Economics has to play a central role in creating new patterns of work,' she said.

With a look of quizzical intensity, Guy handed her the Newsletter, GLOBAL GOODWILL. What she read amazed her. Coincidence? Telepathy? Humphrey prompting her, inaudibly? Yes, there in bold print were the very words she had just spoken.

So, hoping they'd something more important to attend to than her own one-a-minute marvels she asked everybody, 'Haven't you all work to get on with?'

Laughter, like sparklers in the dark, lit up the gathering.

Despite her apparent coyness, she found the courage to read aloud, *'True wealth is created from moment to moment by what we all most need to learn. What's the point of being rich if your work is unfulfilling? DEAD-LINES CAN KILL!'*

Nods all round helped Alice to relax. Her own form of boarded-up good breeding had often irked her. Too often, she'd bitten back more than her listeners could chew before, spitefully, they snapped at her. 'Too much kindness can also kill,' she said and for the Survivalists, added, 'Social workers having nervous breakdowns for their clients. And for what?' she asked, rhetorically. 'Aren't a few bright exceptions better than many dull rules? Disobedience is surely the first step towards creativity.'

Abruptly, cutting short their applause before she blushed, Alice ducked behind the Newsletter and read out, *'We've reduced economics to the financially measurable, whereas I think it includes the whole range of exchange. There are 5 levels in which exchange takes place. The first is spiritual. . . .'*

SPIRITUAL? Not at the bottom of the shopping-list as usual. WOW! Many multi-coloured heads nodded with Alice their chuckling approval. Such grins and winks soon encouraged her to read on. But being perverse, she tested them first. Alice dropped the Newsletter, feigning no further interest in its contents.

Shrugging with goodwill, the crowd started to drift into intimate knots of togetherness, each discussing life's latest lessons. So she read on further without the fear of being cornered into becoming a 'convert'. *'Those who bring inspiration to their work will yield far greater economic value.'*

Spying a prim-looking man catch the world 'economic', Alice accosted him. Some yuppie defected from the city? Or maybe, Humphrey! A trim figure. Probably, a Libran. To see if the prim-looking accountant stammered, her chosen way was to keep talking fast, filling him full of admiration until she popped her mighty question, 'Do you believe in the BIG BANG?'

Big Bang? What could she be meaning. . . ?

'I m-mean, didn't all life come from one self-exploding giant dandelion seed-head?' The prim-looking man folded his hands in front of his privates. 'We and the Milky Way, the galaxies, all that is now or will ever be, exploded into being in one biblical twinkling of an eye?' The young man dared not smile. Seeing his fear of catching her excitement, like sunstroke, Alice, with much over-gesticulated eloquence, expanded her vision. 'Enough sea for trillions of fish; enough air for trillions of lungs;

enough sky for acres of eagles; enough space for aeons of angels, enough love for each to find her own freedom through correct choices! So let's all enjoy the Big Bang – yes, mate?' The prim-looking young man had shrunk. 'Well, say yes! No? Then M-MAYBE . . . YES . . . M-M-M-MATE?'

Was he nervous in case she was about to say KISS ME QUICK? To help, Alice stated, bluntly, 'We can't m-mortgage the earth. Good economy m-may m-m-m-make us a living but only good global housekeeping will keep us alive, m-mais oui?'

'Depends on the ifs and buts,' said the tight-arsed young man, not one M deployed, even as a m-mistake. For Alice, after her cosmic aria, obviously channelled, was that all he could offer her?

'M-m-meaning. . . ?' she asked with an over-articulated stutter.

'Ec-ec-ecology.'

He stuttered! He stammered! How long till the tell-tale M-words revealed her pre-destined Soul M-m-mate? Even if at first sight he did look rather m-miserly and m-malnourished.

Unresponsive to her volcanic visions, the prim-looking man explained himself in his own way. 'How the ec-ec-excentric ones like to ec-ec-ec . . . to ec-ec-ec. . . .'

'ExCUSE . . . themselves. . . ?' offered Alice.

'ExHORT,' chided he, 'Ec-extending ec-ec-ectasy with, for ec-ec-ec-example, OM.'

'Short for OMlette? Like Humpty Dumpty after his fall?'

'Ec-ec-stremely ec-ec-ecumenical ex-exercises!'

'Extraordinary! Excelling all existential explanations!' He didn't know what she was talking about either. But m-maybe he m-might just reveal a m-moment of m-mad m-manliness, so for good m-measure she added one m-more passionate ec-ec-spletive, her favourite M-word. 'M-M-MAGIC!'

'Like ecs-ecsitotal, aren't we all ex-EXCEPTIONAL?'

'He means the Man-God, Quetzacoatal,' prompted a Mexican bystander, 'who prepared us all who were with him then for the end of time around now, some say. . . .'

'Mere ec-ec-ec-zaggeration!' scoffed the young man. On that, he made a quick prim-looking exit.

Disappointed no other candidate was lining up to audition for the role of Humphrey, Alice returned to the Newsletter. In Guy Dauncey's article she read, '*The second level is between humans.*' What levels? As if reading her thoughts, a colourful couple somewhere between hippies and Mohicans, chimed together, 'Levels of exchange, Alice!'

With that, they kissed each other sharing the same piece of purple chewing-gum. Since they were both wearing the same mauve lipstick, unisex was not insulted. They even smoked the same joint and sucked on the same baby's dummy, that being dipped into . . . Too nasty to watch. So Alice continued reading, '*We clearly know about economic exchange among humans. . . .*'

Alice stayed unconvinced. The purple-lipped smokers had made her feel sick. Empathising with her, a chubby-cheeked Indian appeared, excusing himself humbly. 'Actually, ve are not saying unemployed should not grow own pots. Other vords, ve ARE saying they vill never not vant to grow own alfalfas, insteads. Also, many very healthy other affirmations, actually. Upstairs, they give millet, von of nature's finest foods actually, to budgie-birds. They gives alfalfa, one of best herbs to cattle. Not only to Sacred Cows, actually. So much for world's exchanges with animal kingdoms and vith fourth von, plant kingdoms. Actually, vhen ve love more of our best selves, drugs becomes quite not necessary. . . .'

Alice reeling, was still trying to untangle the Hindu's syntax as, hands together, he bowed low to Alice and, turning, did the same to the purple-lipped lovers. They waved back to the Indian, saying in unison, 'Potty-training. . . !' whereupon they collapsed on the floor in a giggling heap.

Determined that no more distraction would stop her self-chosen task, Alice continued with the Newsletter, her voice rising to two words she'd spotted at the end of the next paragraph, namely 'sky' and 'clear'. '*The next level is that of elemental energies. Air, fire, earth and water. In the past, we have been able to neglect the natural worlds, and discount them from economic calculations. The SKY remained CLEAR. . . .*'

Brushing aside a pricking tear for the Top People choking above ground unhelped by her Alice in some relief watched Guy, ritualistically, draw back two rippling green curtains.

Unveiled were 7 silk-screens in an arc on which were projected movie pictures of different cloud formations and, on the centre screen, like an unbounded pool of blue, a cloudless sky. Alice's voice was encouraged to continue, she acting as if she was a pre-recorded travelogue. *'And earth's water remained sweet. Today, this is no longer so, and we have to pay to get clean air and pure water.'* On that, Alice lowered the Newsletter. 'Yes, and what have we down here? Natural springs and seas, or what?'

Looking like a pre-diluvian patriarch, a man as wrinkled as Methuselah, answering her, said, 'To an alchemist, every so-called disaster has its anti-dote. Smog can be turned into oxygen, wine into water. Meantime, we tap the frozen lake under Antarctica, and call it Europa. For those who don't fall foul of the laws of M, everything becomes possible.'

M again. For multiple mysteries of manifest miracles? Not knowing why, Alice felt afraid. Then, wondering if the Mancunian Cat got pure milk from unhappy Astral cows, in her head she heard the Cat's quick answer, spoken in purry tones, 'Urns and urns, chuck, for aeons and aeons!'

'What a smug puss!' thought Alice, gently upbraiding her perennial pet. 'Someone has to pay for harps and g-strings, so how can Heaven possibly be a Welfare State?'

Quick as an unzipped smile, a reply was zapped into her brain, the Cat insisting that a human's free-will is just that, FREE. 'It's a gift, a daily Christmas present,' said the Cat, 'through the Consciousness of M, bless him. With all that god-given trust in dust, what could ever be too much for mankind to give back? See, luv, God has left us all free to get on with IT. . . .'

Alice DID just that, reading, *'Then there is the method of the gift.'* The printed words were timely. *'For instance, our spiritual nature is given to us from childhood onwards and, at the ultimate level, we all live within the gift economy of the sun.'*

On to the centre of the middle screen, a hologram of a middle-aged cinder appeared. It was the underground sun.

Shades were lowered over eyes, some folks seemingly toasting their upraised hands. Others fell to the floor and made strange sounds. Looking around, Alice could see that everyone present was grateful for the gift of inner sunshine, the biggest free energy gift of all.

And no one was using money. Not that money of itself isn't neutral. They all accepted that real wealth is the merit we carry through death's doors, not the tangible riches left behind. Watching the mauve lipstick, reefer and rubber-dummy pass from the Mohican Hippies and their cluster to a puce-cloaked couple with silver hair, Alice realised that some sort of barter was in progress, some mysterious osmosis, a communion of complimentary gift tokens. And these exchanges were not based on debt and desperation but on the trust that each individual inwardly knows what is needed and can attract it to themselves. That is, without the fears of poverty, hard-hearted market values, headaches, or the hard-sell advertising of chemical 'cures'. As the Survivalists had long pointed out to the few who cared to listen, life is given on a donation basis. Our body is leased to us, but Soul being everlasting, is priceless.

Chanting voices wove all assembled into an accepted fellowship, an open celebration of each unique individual within the wholeness of their symphonic incantations.

Alice the outsider, hawk-eyed as ever, watched for further flaws and signs of hollowness beneath their underground camaraderie. She had not yet sensed that she herself would be sorely tested before being allowed anywhere near the secrets of the inner earth, into the treasure trove of Rainbow Mountain, let alone into the presence of handsome Humphrey.

A cynic like every sincere seeker after total awareness, Alice wondered how many there present wished to win £20,000 rather than earn it. As if in agreement, the next few printed words leaped off the page of the newsletter. They read, '*And the fourth method is theft, theft between humans and theft by humans against nature.*' Still keenly effected by the despair caused by her privileged visit to the above ground devastation, Alice cried out aloud, 'Are the greedy here also? Are there thieves, muggers, destroyers amongst us even here? Fundamentalists are no fun. Just deadly boring!'

Heads nodded, many fingers pointing to themselves with glee. 'At least those blaming themselves won't be politicians!' thought Alice with affable accuracy. She had never been enamoured of manipulators, like some nuns she had known, in either sacred or in secular dealings.

Mancunian Cat, omnipresent, added further answers by whispering inwardly, 'With Survivalists here luv, each is willing to balance out their best accounts, through, like, giving – UP!'

Alice racked her brains. What could she best give them all? Oh yes, her best gift would be her own candour. 'I'd rather you honestly didn't like me,' she announced, 'rather than pretend to love me because of some law.' Shame-faced, she blushed. 'Once . . . I remember taking a dormouse away from Kitty, my cat. And, yes, I heard voices inside my head. One of them is here somewhere. Well, think me crazy but excuse me while I ask: 'Mancunian Cat, what do you think about me because I deprived Kitty of her furry toy meal, the dormouse. . . ?" '

The crowd waited for an answer.

Becoming a ventriloquist doll for her feline mentor, Alice spoke. 'About that dormouse, eh? Well chuck, consider kindness and cruelty. Why take a mouse away from a cat? When, promoted to the atoms of a superior life form, it can learn how to catch mice itself. See, luv, mice have nine lives, too. . . .'

A loudspeaker interrupted.

Like that of a Town Crier, its rolling resonance over-articulated the words, ROLL UP, ROLL UP! PLAY YOUR PART! THIS WAY FOR ROLE-PLAY RE-PLAY!

A stir rippling through the crowd made Alice wonder what she might be missing. Encouraging punters to the next playshop, the loudspeaker blared out, 'LEARN WHERE IT'S ALL AT BEFORE IT AIN'T NO MORE!'

Wishing to conclude their interior dialogue, Alice promised the Mancunian Cat this: 'The next time, I'll buy tinned mouse for Kitty my pet, and avoid some nasty catty karma – maybe!'

Suddenly feeling peckish herself, Alice quickly finished reading GLOBAL GOODWILL. To the sun-baskers before her, she read the final sentence with a wilting spirit. *'Accountants and politicians have methods for measuring the value of cutting down a forest, but we have no economic means of measuring the value of leaving the forest standing.'* Alice wanted to howl. A gust of cosmic grief raged through her at the memory of the desert above ground where once had stood fine fresh trees in their thousands. But as she finished her recitations from GLOBAL GOODWILL, Alice received a standing ovation. Whereupon – Alice fainted.

In her unconscious state, Alice travelled. She floated through the earth's crust to above the devastated forest. Below her, she watched the last few Top People, crawling like ants over an over-baked cake, floundering in their own fatal kitchen fumes, choking for lack of a window to open.

None of the famished Top People wept over the loss of deer, grouse or green-fly; woodpeckers, owls, or bluebells, frogs or princes, or over any of the other life-forms which had been vaporised; all those invisible victims, from bats to badgers (no longer endangered species being extinct); all those cats and canaries; all those donkey sanctuaries and dung-beetles rolling their balls of shit down the long curling corridors of human colons, the corpses encased in rotting cars, all, ALL had vanished. VANISHED! Why?

Was all not well in Welfareland?

The Survivalists wished to prove that life-enhancing lifestyles rather than death-defying fears were the true path. Yes, Saint Peter, the founding Rock of Ages, said that the world would end in fire, not floods. Predictions, like political protests against human suffering, never go away. Neither does the bewilderment of unexplained pain. '*Still,*' thought Alice, '*what's the point of awareness in action, if such personal values don't reflect universal values?* – Thanks Humph, good one!'

Above it all, the spirit of Alice was freed. She felt free not just from physical restrictions but free from even the best of political manifestos demanding social justice. Strangely, Alice felt impervious to all she beheld. Well, better neutral than mad with hate, better red than dead. Rather than weep, she danced.

Using her see-through body, her astral form danced a minuet with the Mancunian Cat. Together they made a cat's-cradle with blue wool both dancing through each other, and out the other side. Reversing and then dancing through each other in the opposite direction, again and again, the blue wool never once getting tangled. And this despite the now bald corgi dog, barking soundlessly, as it tried to catch the ball of blue wool for its supper. Animals, as Alice had often observed, can be seen chasing astral food-forms, even in their sleep.

For Alice then, timeless bliss had briefly uplifted her, despite her aware-ness that, in the circumstances, despair might be judged as being more seemly. Yet Alice was sensing that everyone was in his or her chosen time and place according to some mysterious System of JUSTICE. Yet to be fully understood . . . as in a swirl of mist . . . her head . . . damp . . . cloth . . . soothing motions . . . cool . . . wiping brow . . . wiping brow . . . scent . . . herbs . . . comforting . . . cool . . . moist lotion . . . eyelashes fluttering . . . pupils unpeeling to see . . . to see where she now was . . . IS . . . HERE and NOW as ALICE!

Feeling fully back down again in her physical body, Alice slowly related to the pair of eyes peering into her own. A hospital Sister was skimming pearls of perspiration from the girl's brow. Smiling encouragement, the Sister was delirious to be of use again, even though a mere fainting-fit would hardly tax her skills.

'It's the cutbacks on kindness that hurt most. Not our tea breaks, no. But when the heart is made redundant. . . .' blurted the rotund Sister, unasked. 'Not that we shouldn't all stand on our own two feet but, dear me, not if they cut the ground from under our feet first. That's what their policy was leading to, quite clearly. SUPA, Medicare for the best, the rest to the wall. That's why I joined the Survivalists. They had some vision for we little folk, some worthwhile future. I wasn't going to sit on the scrap-heap at fifty, twiddling my thumbs till it was too late, trusting "them" to safeguard my fate from their Big Boy bombs till 'twas too late. . . .' She shuddered, then having expressing emotional release, smiled.

'Did you say L-A-T-E?' asked Alice, suddenly alarmed. 'I'm late for a most important date! July the Fourth. . . .'

'Now isn't that strange? You don't sounds American, dear.'

'Must make the date of my next birth!' As Alice sprang up from the medical couch, the Sister betrayed a fractured smile, really wishing to hold onto her new mental patient. 'Mind, that's our date, too. July the fourth.' Fiercely, she polished her half-glazed spectacles, the half without glass.

'The Survivalists' birthday, God bless us, is also July the Fourth. Known, alternatively, as the Alternatives. Either way, we love the ASU. Glad you've joined us, dear, are you I expect. . . ?'

'ASU – that's USA backwards. . . .'

'Yes dear, they ARE, aren't they. . . .' agreed the sister still squinting at her spectacles. 'But we in Alternative Survivors United, we don't think a bomb in the hand's worth three in the bush. Our happiness is not in splits, atomic or otherwise. It's splintered and hard-headed hearts all the time with those well-heeled Top People. So stay here with us, dear. The next millennium needs magic medicine. Invisible energy healings. . . .'

'You think I'll make it to the 21st century, all grown up . . . not BLOWN up? Me? With . . . with Humphrey. . . ?'

'Lie down here, darling. I'll train you in vibrational. . . .'

'No, I have to leave. Somehow. Dean Dodgson, he's expecting me. If I'm late, the stars will be wrong and I'll have to wait another millennium for them to be right for both of us again. Oh dear, and I DO so like it here, ill or alive. Please ask me, Who's Humphrey?'

'Such a long time since I've had a patient,' sighed the Sister. 'When my hospital wing was amputated I felt as if my oxygen had been cut clean off . . . OFF!'

'Staying alive to love, that's the real job. Tricky, though.'

'Indeed, not just making a living. I know that, yet . . . but . . . well, I'm delaying you. Sorry. I'm much better now, dear. Thanks.'

Whisking away a tear, the Sister waddled away to wash her face.

What a labyrinth of corridors, caverns, cupboards, chambers and cata-combs. Despite the bright paint everywhere, virtual reality sunlight, phos-phorescent murals expressing the different stages of man's evolution through mineral, vegetable and animal forms, Alice longed to find the door again, the way out. But where to? And why? Alice had no clue as to the time of year, nuclear winter seeming like a never-never land somewhere beyond the reach of healing hands, while around her, inside the good earth, the trees seemed evergreen fakes without substance or shadows, despite a gargantuan statue of ancient Cabalistic Tree of Life.

Everywhere she wandered through the Halls of the Homeless, folk were engaged in tasks they found self-fulfilling without the burden of disappointing payment. Yet surely there had to be some rate of exchange. So which workshop – MONEY AS A MANTRA in the Blue Dome? Or the enticing one called ROLE-PLAY RE-PLAY? No, unless it was a Playshop on TIME TRAVELLING, she did not want to spend the time on any of them. Not yet awhile.

Hurrying off to her next appointment in Oxford if it still existed, Alice could not help asking a merry worker who caught her eye, 'Why are you sewing the roots onto those plastic evergreens, Mr Taylor?' She had read his name on the beautifully printed notice above his organic mud hut.

His feet were planted in a bucket of steaming hot water. His scarlet toes were writhing, both feet like live lobster twins being boiled to death, his face screwed up as he sat there, cheerfully scalding himself. 'Knows 'ow many Christmas-trees wot I cut down, miss, to be decorated for 12 days then destroyed, their roots boiled useless, like, before'ands. . . ?'

Obligingly, Alice shook her ringlets.

'That were, like, my last lifetime, see. Afore I 'eard the Sound and saw sense. 'Ow many Christmas trees, eh, miss. . . ?'

Mathematics not being her strongest point, Alice was reminded yet again of her promised mentor, Charles Dodgson. 'Which way to the future, please?' she requested, breathlessly. 'I think I'm meant to meet a don on July the fourth 1862 and, if it's not too much trouble, please face me in the wrong direction. Adventures I love, and I like feeling lost, just so long as you're sure such lessons won't make me too late for my most important date.'

'Wif Fate? We're inter free-love 'ere, miss, so 'ere goes. . . .'

Placing his needle and thread and the rubberised tree-root on the floor, Mr Taylor wiped his nose in both directions. Then, he pointed, at the same time, both inwards and upwards.

'Are you sending me up?' enquired Alice, somewhat crossly.

'Same things, miss, past and Christmas present. Don't matter a blue monkey's,' grinned he toothlessly, 'which way we goes, mate . . . we all meets up again. . . .'

'Do you know Humphrey – someone? I've lost him. I think.'

A good-natured shrug and Mr Taylor promptly fell asleep, snoring like a forest hog in a bog.

By then, not really feeling at home under ground, with no Humphrey, no clear path and all that un-pushy friendliness everywhere but no real human anchor, Alice forced herself to ask the question no-one seemed to want. Closing her eyes in case Mancunian Cat wanted to answer it for her, she whispered, 'So now we've all been saved . . . what do we do . . . NOW. . . ?' Suddenly, even the man's snoring went silent.

Which way next. . . ?

It was like being lost in the tubes of one's own intestines, all labyrinthine tunnels mysteriously inter-linked. But where was the mouth for fresh-air? Where the eyes for real daylight? As in Yoga classes forbidden by the nuns, she had heard the anxious blood in her veins, a closed circuit of throbbing pulses and pumps, blood turgidly getting no-where different . . . not even when she was bursting at the seams to understand her self more fully.

How, without help, could she unlock more of herself?

Exploring down each tunnel Alice longed for darkness at the end, her fibre-optic eyes as in endoscopy, peering down every shiny orifice for possible illumination. Escape? Or more darkness?

Another cavern. Another level. Was she about to reach the legendary civilisation of Star Walkers rumoured to be in the Hollow Earth, even the city of Plutonium itself, all waiting for the dust to settle before they returned earth to Heaven? More sadly, might she again be forging her physical body towards above ground's thick night of nuclear winter, its acid smog now lethally radioactive?

Yet as she searched for a way out, or for a better out-of-body adventure, she soon sensed that one solution was to sit Guru-still; not to meander but to meditate; not to hurry on like Jesus in the hidden years impatient for the Cross but, in centred stillness, to trust Creation. Herself now to unfold, like a flower, its inner nectar.

*

Another cross-roads.

Alice could recall choosing that one. Sometimes she could remember before breakfast every choice she ever met face to face. But what now? Left? Right? Left, right, left right . . . she found herself taking the middle way . . . but in which direction she had yet to find out.

Passing friendly faces, couples, groups, the jolly and the solitary, all the folks seemed engrossed in their different individual activities. All debts dutifully paid up, all Survivalists had given up the dubious privilege of helping to keep nuclear superiority to themselves. Some reading the mislaid secret words of Enoch, aimed to travel 'beyond the Great Eye of Orion', to achieve interior Nirvana.

For Alice, Nirvana was too negative, too passive, not practical enough. Like the Dean of Christ Church she was on the way to meet, Alice was fascinated by loopholes in logic. In other words, in other meanings, in eternal alternatives, both above and below, inwardly and outwardly, a sort of black dog perversity set against all preachers, profane and profound. Before his forest had been destroyed, the Owl had admonished her for such mental slackness, and Humpty Dumpty had lampooned her intensely held ideals. Before Mr Dumpty too, blitzed into invisibility, had fallen back into the cold grey mists of infinity.

Alice, though, did not long to regiment all reality like the deadly lead soldiers so beloved by the Victorians. The Mathematics of unmarked war-graves, for instance, made her yearn to catch numbers out, to prove land-locked calculations as fallible. By using intuition, rather than logic, Alice hoped when it was time to meet her Oxford mentor that by telepathic prowess, she could rescue Dean Dodgson from the darkest long night of his logic and, perhaps, lighten his head-heavy load with some laughter. Thus she really hoped to balance him out into a fuller, and less-machine-like pedant pumping into others long lectures. Without loving 'Relationships', what lasting merit has Reason or Religion? If only Humphrey would materialise, lead her to Charles Dodgson, she'd show them both. But WHAT, exactly?

97

'*M-m-m-MAGIC!*'

It was him! Inside her, eavesdropping! 'Meet me! Please. M-m-meet m-me m-me soon, DO!'

Dreaming of his guiding arms around her, Alice again drifted above it all.

Scene 3 – <u>Warren Row. Exterior</u>. Nuclear Night or Day

WHITE QUEEN	(*Thoughtfully*) Charles, the poor boy, says there's a word he uses that opens all doors. . . .
SNOW WHITE	(*Still waving, smiling*) We agree – ROYALTY!
WHITE QUEEN	(Shocked) No, indeed not. We never use that word. Not at home.
SNOW WHITE	Oh, we do. In Dulwich. (*With a sigh.*) Oh, how I wish I was there now. (*Aside.*) How I wish IT was there now.
WHITE QUEEN	Denis?
SNOW WHITE	Dulwich. (*Reflectively.*) You know, people used to think me a stuffed shirt but, really, there was nothing stuffed about me. Ask Denis. How this Iron Lady faithfully ironed party frocks for her only daughter. What's fame, anti-rooms, and aides? All I ever craved was flowers everywhere, a lovely kitchen leading on to a patio for breakfast in the sun. Feet up on the red despatch-boxes, reading one's autobiography.
WHITE QUEEN	I, too, always prefer novels. Where HAS our helicopter got to?
SNOW WHITE	The last two, trying to escape in time, crashed into each other. I shall raise the matter in the house. In fact, I'll raise the roof. If I can find it.
WHITE QUEEN	(*Getting despondent*) Not a council house anywhere left to buy, even if I had the readies. Is that what they're called these days? What one might dub as my late green calling cards. Dear me, no. Not for ever homeless. . . .

SNOW WHITE   Balmoral?

WHITE QUEEN   **IM**moral, says Charles. No more comes than is due to one, he says.

SNOW WHITE   The rent?

WHITE QUEEN   Earthquakes. Look here, read this. . . .

FROM A POUNDSAVER CARRIER-BAG, SHE TAKES OUT A COPY OF PROPHECIES BY NOSTRADAMUS.

SNOW WHITE   (*Gladdened*) Ah, I always knew History would never say it was all my fault!

WHITE QUEEN   Even though, Prime Minister, all our defence strategy was planned in secret. In a blue funk, round a coffin-shaped table. . . .

SNOW WHITE   Even that has now been cremated. Serves them right, those gravediggers who went on strike under the other lot. (*She sighs*.) If only you'd used your veto, ma'am.

WHITE QUEEN   Poor Margaret . . . can't go round the bend now, can we? None left.

SNOW WHITE   I'll make political history, do a U-turn. WATCH OUT, you lot! Cold War be blowed, this lady's not for burning!

Using intuition – or guidance – at the next cross-roads, Alice turned right. She soon found herself in the HALL OF HOLOGRAMS. Plain frames were everywhere, frames that showed what appeared to be three-dimensional pictures . . . like outstanding technicolour sculptures inviting engagement, ethereal astronauts, not couch potatoes.

First, was an apple on an outstretched hand, the fruit round and ripe, ready to be eaten. Move to grab it though, and it goes, the hand still stationary and apparently solid. Except, Alice noticed the two fingers next to the thumb. Those two, fully extended, were showing the V-sign. Alice moved closer as if to shake the hand. The screen immediately went grey again and blank.

Back to her first position and the apple, irritatingly, re-appeared, looking as solid as ever.

'It must be a warning of some kind, not to smash the glass, not to bite open the fruit.' Thought Alice. 'Maybe the original apple was radioactive and that's why Adam and Eve were forbidden to eat it.' Yet stepping again towards the glass frame, she heard herself say, 'But I still want to know – EVERYTHING – NOW!' Then she had the grace to chuckle at herself.

'Is that all luv. . . ?' responded Mancunian Cat also chuckling. 'Eat that apple, then. Raw apples get orgasms, luv, every time they go in't deep throats through human mouths. So chuck, EAT UP. . . !'

'Don't you mean DOWN?'

'Depends, does that. Like Merlin, you might want to disappear up the arse of an apple tree in Avalon vowing to return with the secrets of immortality, eh. That your style? Not mine, pet. Too many Celtic cats get stuck up trees, like. Can't get down again.'

Refusing to stay stuck, every time Alice leant in to hold the mystic apple, it turned into a baked apple too hot to handle. By then the cat had lapsed into loud imitation snores. It sounded like teasing laughter.

A globe of violet mist appeared and then, as if it were morning, soon started to clear. Hanging there in space, was a sparkling glass table on top of which was a glowing honey-golden key. Enoch's Key to all Higher Wisdom? Alice gasped. She worried that this also . . . was some secret sign . . . a symbolic signpost which, when approached, slaps the seeker down. Why? For not having risked more daring and dangerous options in earlier times. . . ?

With reluctant caution she stepped towards the glass table. Staring down at it, as it hovered mid-air, its appearance changed. Its three-dimensions seemed to become two. As she stared, astonished, its remaining size then started shrinking like a pond in hot midday sunshine. Like Narcissus, Alice watched her face shrinking inside the glass tabletop, shrinking. . . .

Yet in the centre of her reflected forehead, the image of the golden key still glowed. Move a millimetre either way and the key, she knew, would vanish. Closing her eyes, she tried to keep the vision of the key alive, there, halfway between both of her temples, just above the bridge of her nose, 'keyhole' and golden key in alignment.

Even as her lids stayed closed, Alice watched a new apparition. Through the glass table, from its other side, bathed in a haze of simmering violet, the gentle face of an old Chinaman loomed into view. His eyes were deep, calm and kind, smiling inwardly. Alice had the urge to call his name but the name that came to her seemed too earthbound for such a personage. In any case, maybe he was the legendary **M**.

In answer, the ancient Chinaman closed his own eyes. As if nodding off, he seemed to hum like a hive full of healing honeybees. Whoops! Was he sweetly snoring? 'What a pest they must all find me.' frowned Alice. Then, with a sigh, she asked out aloud, 'Why do I make them all fall asleep, snore – then VANISH?'

She opened her eyes. Yes, the Chinaman had vanished. Nothing remained of his presence but a lingering perfume. Reaching forward, Alice on tiptoe went to pick up the golden key. Nothing. Nothing but a fistful of air. And in her head, the single note of a high flute-like sound, singing in her innermost ear. 'What a funny key,' thought Alice.

Marvellously, flashing onto the central blank screen was a neat white-bearded face. The all-seeing eyes seemed to pierce her Soul. She gasped. Showing in the centre of his brow was a large M. Astonished, she blinked and blinked again. On each glance, another face, mostly male, all cultures, all colours, all ages. The screen came to rest on the most beautiful boyish face she had ever seen. 'HUMPHREY!' she called, 'I'm HERE. . . !'

As romantic music played, on her impulsive desperate thrust towards the screen, the table expanded beyond its original size, lowering itself to the floor. Appearing the other side of the table now grounded, Alice was sad to see the Mad Hatter. Sitting there, his greedy grin showed uneven jutting teeth near a large open book as if his dribbling mouth was about to gobble it all up, raw.

Closing her eyes against all ugliness, Alice quietly asked herself, 'Will I never be able to handle my own golden key . . . with no help from Guardian Angel Cat or from even handsome Humph. . . ?'

'What's the mutter?' asked the Mad Hatter interrupting. Rising to greet her, his spotted bow tie riding up and down on his Adam's apple, he hissed. 'Eyes closed for a k-k-Kiss, eh. . . ?'

Another stutterer! Humphrey incarnate? Surely not with those dark shark's teeth?

'You know what a mutter is, don't you? A mumbled utter, silly mutt!' The Mad Hatter, obviously exhilarated by her wriggling with apparent ignorant coyness, pressed himself a little closer, hot pants of breath tickling her wrinkled brow. Humphrey or not, her eyes shot open like peas in a pod about to be plucked. Squinting over the book at her long hair, he exclaimed, 'Your pretty locks require no keys. It's a HAT you need, PicK one. PICK!'

The repeated **K** in the words pic**K**, exploded two sprin**K**les of spittle on the boo**K** he held as he tried to re**K**indle her interest. 'As I flic**K** through its thic**K** pages, pee**K** at these **K**in**K**y **K**uddly pictures as they ripple quic**K**ly past your **K**indly **K**issable eyes. . . .' As if drowning, his hot breath smelling of mothballs, Alice wanted to faint again.

Yet he persisted. Pictures of hats, pages and pages of headpieces of all periods, flickered before her faltering eyes.

'Where am I?' she asked in a daze. 'Who are you, sir? Who am I. . . ?'

'The hat will tell you.'

She held up a Dunce's cap. 'Naughty! Select a nicer one. Quic**K**, chic**K**, PICK!'

So spluttering, the Mad Hatter took off his own top-hat, placed it on the glass table, made a magic pass with his hands, both of which, in the process, managed to brush deftly against her precocious breasts, his teeth glinting with extra bubbly saliva. Sucking dry his protruding teeth, he plunged his right hand deep down and, like a conjurer producing a white rabbit from inside his own hat, instead produced a hat; then another, another, and another, with a running-commentary as he placed each hat in turn on her cringing head.

'Boudoir caps, Dutch caps, leghorn hats,' he gushed, 'Blac**K** felt cloche with brim lic**K**ing both **K**ute ears . . . pin**K** hats with top flaps as **K**osmic solar-panels . . . even a red-hot hot hat from **K**in**K**y Bangko**K**!'

'Wish he'd stop,' thought Alice trying not to wince too obviously. On the final **K** of BangkoK, three more specKs of spittle had hit her face. But before she could even catch her breath, the Mad Hatter was trying out another bonnet for size, his hooked nose perilously near, whiskers inside his nostrils all quivering.

'And very popular with those Puritans, this stiff hat, with its hard tall thrusting peaK!'

Though she'd successfully dodged the wet flaK from his explosive **K** that time, Alice now wished to give offence. No wonder the March Hare had run off. Presumably to get a raincoat. But how could she be rude enough without provoKing another sprinKling. . . ?

The Mad Hatter continued to jiggle the peaKed hat about her head as Alice closed her eyes for protection from his over-flexible and be-specKled wet lips. Sweating the while and spitting, he said, 'To ventilate, after wigs came in, the entire blacK brim, like this, was turned up in the Monmouth cocK!'

That last **K** strucK home! Two large flecKs of spittle strucK her left cheeK. Before she could turn the other one, he playfully tickled her nose with a feather, saying, 'Try this toque, covered with a beautiful pheasant's head and plumage but not to be worn out in the shooting-season.' Then, steering her to the table-top, using it as a mirror, triumphantly, he pronounced, 'See for your scrumptious self. Pretty damsel, for your cute self – OBSERVE!'

In distress, she thought, 'Thank goodness he didn't use the word '*looK!*'

'A picture to be sure! Would you say these pheasant feathers come from the hen-bird, or from the coc. . . ?'

But before he could spit out the final **K**, Alice blurted, 'Taking the miK?' Bullseye! Her nose still tickling from the feathers, in a most unlady-like manner, she followed up with a dazzling juicy sneeze, splattered all over his fob-watch.

With the shocK of that slicK, well-aimed sprinKling, the Mad Hatter gaped, held his heart and sagged, wheezing, 'Why do that?' You've stopped my ticKer. You've stopped my ticKer. Wait till I tell Uri Geller. I only wanted to salve the sicK. Oh, my hat! Such a **K**ute chicK, for hunKy-spunKy boys, not a plain pig in a poKe. Oh, my palpitations! – The k-k-

Kiss of life – quic**K**, chic**K**, QUIC**K**!'

As he tried to suck a kiss from Alice, over the tannoy came an announcement, 'TODAY'S MIRACLE PLAYSHOP, WALKING ON WATER.'

Had they seen Alice surrounded by puddles of spittle? Anyway, Alice abruptly swivelled that hat on her head. Instead of its front, the Mad Hatter was then confronted, not with the girl's nubile lips only, but with the rear-end of that pheasant coc**K**. Enjoying the **K**-tric**K** herself, using it as a repeated expletive, Alice confronted her over-solicitous admirer with, 'Listen, sil**K**y dic**K**head till my next remar**K** sinks in. **K**inky **K**lown quic**K**, pass a **K**leenex, then **K**arry on up the cree**K**!'

His hands, rippling like a pianist's warming up for five-finger exercises, flickered past her cherry ripe nipples.

'Quic**K**! Thin**K**! Wal**K**!' Hissed Alice, 'See**K** some other frea**K** while I turn the other chee**K** and pu**K**e!' With such well aimed sprays on his face, the Mad Hatter skidaddled away as if he was late for an omnibus. And as if Luton was still there making mad hats.

After such theatricals from a lecher feigning a heart attack, Alice continued. Who would define her next? Would any encounter, romantic or esoteric, satisfy her many longings? Well, she still hoped that someone in the underworld would remind her of something she couldn't quite remember. But what. . . ? Or who. . . ?

'OO. . . ? OOO. . . ?'

That question had come from inside the nearest sparkling cavern. Alice cautiously entered it. From behind one of the hundreds of spangled costumes hanging on rails and racks, Alice again heard the high-pitched voice ask, 'OO . . . OO are you ?'

'Not sure. Are you-OO. . . ?'

'You are OO. . .' insisted the invisible voice, somewhere between question and statement in a French accent.

Alice searched for the owner of the androgynous voice. 'An' OO, mon darling, ze last time around, were YOU. . . ?' Alice tried to trace the foreign voice as it continued to cross-examine her. 'King or coolie? Queen or tart? Junkie or judge. . . ?'

Alice's head spinning, she saw a notice which read ROLE-CALL NOW. 'Can't the French spell English properly, either. . . ?' she enquired of the rows and rows of period costumes, all of them apparently unoccupied. Perhaps some reveille or ROLL-call was expected. Or for Alice herself, a change of dress and knickers. . . ?

Meanwhile, the **M**-sound reverberated, disconcertingly. It was as if the unseen voices from the legendary Blue Dome were radiating the power of **M**. In some mysterious way, had not that unbroken line of **M**asters' faces mysteriously asked Alice to reflect upon the multiple relationships between **M**irror . . . **M**ist and **M**irage. . . ?

Reflecting further on this, with a cold gush of loneliness Alice wondered if, after all, she needed neither the Mancunian Cat as guide nor even, God help her, Humphrey.

To the vast echoes of her loneliness, she yelled out, 'If so, where is the way OUT, from all of you-oo. . . ?'

'OOOOOH!' came the rapid reply from the unseen French accent.

Not wishing to appear mean to any invisible helper, Alice resolutely announced over-loudly 'ALL! I want you all to help me. Please! I've changed my. . . .'

'Fast as farts from quick-change artiste! Like myself, a theosophical thespian. . . ?'

Was a thespian as rude as a lesbian, she wondered. Not that Alice was prejudiced, just fascinated.

The unseen voice continued, 'Memory often is negative. And most zinking, she go backwards, no forwards. BUT. . . .' An histrionic pause was held; 'BUT . . . I expect most of us were lesbian one lifetime or anozzer. Be'ind seven sexy veils!'

Crawling out from under cassocks hanging on a high costume-rail came the owner of the voice. Fully materialised before Alice, the creature could pass as male or female or, in any casting agency down on its luck, as BOTH. 'Ze 'at catalogue, mon darlink, was to clear your 'ead of past-life traumas. Especially of ze be'eadings!'

'Not the French Revolution? ME, on the guillotine. . . ?'

Nodding with glee, the androgynous creature with silver hair explained,

'You, one of Maria Antoinette's lovers. Zat why, mon darlink, all ze bits of cake you see about ze place, zey all 'ave labels saying. . . .'

'EAT ME! EAT ME!' said Alice. 'I see. . .' Not sure whether to call the friendly rosy-cheeked hermaphrodite before her Madam or Monsieur, she used neither. But like a Hostess at a cocktail-party she could not relax until she knew whether she was being addressed by a Duchess or possibly 'undressed' by some nouveau-riche French dustman, one who would cart her off in a gold-plated Cadillac for perfumed French kisses.

'Ze Mad 'Atter, 'e it was oo chopped off your 'ead, mon darlink. Zat why 'e so crazy to find an 'at which fit you. Wiz zose 'e be'eaded in uprising Paris, like you, 'is 'ats never do fit now.'

'He did, though. He DID have a fit. Wet . . . all over me . . . he was. . . .'

'Such 'orny frustrations! Zis witty adjustment he pick for 'imself zis life-time. Just as you, mon darlink, you may choose for yourself your next life-time on earth to fit your karma. . . .'

'Earth? Is there one left worth living for. . . ?' asked Alice, adding a polite but experimental, 'Miss', short for both 'Mister' and 'Mistake' being, as it were, three for the price of one. It was hateful not being certain about people. In a passable French accent, she added, 'Oo say I wish to return to ze earth, miss?'

An ominous silence. Fearing she had caused offence, Alice quickly added a 'TER' to the 'MISS'. Either way, no response from her, or his, bonny bright face before her. At length, and in a less frivolous manner, what might such a creature reveal to her. . . ?

'Earthlings, mon darlink, are not ze only ones to play bat-an'-ball wiz ze planets. Some of ze wildest aliens play golf, putting whole planets down black 'oles. Zey zink zey improve zeir 'andicap. Fear not child, zere are SIX ozer earth-like planets to blow up, still 'atching in the incubators of unseen Milky Ways . . . after ze next End of Time. . . .'

Alice was not listening.

It was almost as if Alice, Captain of her own Polaris submarine, had silently said to her sailing Soul, 'UP PERISCOPE!' Why? Because above ground the sight she briefly beheld had to be put on hold until she could summon up enough personal strength to survey it with love. But before withdrawing like a snail head into its shell, to her own amazement, she glimpsed enough to reawaken in her heart real optimism.

Optimism? Despite earth being besmirched with bilges of dirty-grey tidal 'airwaves'? Despite too, the few remaining half-baked Top Ladies, wandering ghoulishly over mangled motorways, bleached handbags at the ready as they peered at scalded road-signs, picnic areas in lay-bys rendered into a ghastly, inedible goulash. These were the daunting images she surveyed now.

Scene 4 – Warren Row. Exterior. Nuclear Winter or Summer?

NOT A PAIR OF SPECTACLES BETWEEN THEM (EXCEPT THEMSELVES AS WORTHY TOURIST ATTRACTIONS – HAD ANY TOURISTS SURVIVED), THE REMAINING TWO TOP LADIES ARE TRYING TO DECIPHER NOSTRADAMUS (IX, 55) IN FRENCH. AS IF REHEARSING A PRESS CONFERENCE FOR TV PARIS, THE WHITE QUEEN TESTS HER FRENCH ACCENT, AS SNOW WHITE PRESENTS HER USUAL SOFTER RIGHT SIDE TO THE IMAGINARY PRESS-GANG OF PHOTOGRAPHERS.

WHITE QUEEN (*In schoolgirl French accent*) L'horrible guerre qu'en l'occident s'apreste L'an ensuivant viendra la pestilence. Si fort horrible, que jeune, vieux ne beste. Sang, feu, Mecure, Mars, Jupiter en France.

SNOW WHITE, WHO HAD BEEN COVERING HER RIGHT HAND (NOW TURNED BLACK WITH RADIATION) WITH SUNTAN LOTION, THUMPS THE BOTTLE DOWN ON THE IRON DOOR AND CLAPS DISTURBING FOLLICLES AND UPROOTING CLUMPS OF HER HAIR.

SNOW WHITE Though, you know, it sounds so much more telling in English. Listen (*squinting at the text*) '*Dreadful war is being prepared in the West.*' Myself, I was always more interested in policies than in poetry. OURS, not theirs.

WHITE QUEEN Look what Nostradamus says comes later (*squinting at the text*) '*The following year will be followed by pestilence. . . .*'

SNOW WHITE Striking miners? And their strident unions? (*consolingly*) No, surely, it's a word for the idle unemployed – pestilence.

WHITE QUEEN (*Reading*) '*So horrible that young, nor old, nor animal will survive. . . .*' Without one mate left. My last corgi. GAWN? Oh, NO!

SNOW WHITE Do try some of my suntan lotion.

BOTH LADIES, LURING THE FLESH-FLAKING CORGI TOWARDS THEM, ARE STAGGERED TO SEE A BLACK DOG, A SLAVERING ROTWEILER WITH ERECT WET PINK PENIS, CHASE IT. AS BOTH DOGS RUN HOWLING IN THE BLEAK AND BLISTERING TERRAIN, REMAINING FUR FLIES OFF THEM IN JELLIFIED TUFTS. THEIR SKINS PEAL BACK LIKE BLEACHED CONDOMS OFF HOTDOGS, WILD EYEBALLS FRYING LIKE POACHED-EGGS, TWO MECHANO-SETS OF POWDERY BARE BONES, AS IF NEVER TO BE DOOMED, BOTH OF THESE SKIN-STRIPPED SKELETONS RACE INTO BLEAK DUSTY DUNES. THERE IN THAT ALL-CONSUMING SWEATY HAZE, FUCKING AS IF THERE WAS WAS NO TOMORROW, BOTH CANINES RATTLE THEIR CAGES IN JOINT RHYTHM, SKELETAL SEX SOUNDING LIKE CASTANETS.

SNOW WHITE Someone has to give the lead, otherwise we all have a dog's life. Neither was a sterling thoroughbred, notice. Nor self-reliant. Here's to survival of the fittest. Except for foreign mongrels, of course. Capital!

IN MEMORY OF HER LATE DENIS, WITH THE OPEN BOTTLE OF SUNTAN LOTION, SHE TOASTS THE UNSEEN SKY.

SNOW WHITE To all thoroughbreds. To our undiminished dear sun. . . .

WHITE QUEEN	Not Charles?
SNOW WHITE	Long may it reign over us.
WHITE QUEEN	Oh, that ghastly tabloid. Quite horrid!
SNOW WHITE	Always given me a fair spread. Except on page 3, I'm glad to say. And look at their HOP OFF, YOU FROGS campaign. Yes, I gave them 'MISS MAGGIE!' Beware. A Catholic Jew, Nostradamus. Aberration. Don't trust him. Not even an Anglican. . . .

GENTLY, THEY TAKE TURNS IN CATCHING EACH OTHER'S FALLING HAIR AND TEARS. BUT NOT FOR LONG.

By some wizardry, safely delivered from her weeping over the wilderness above and finding her feet again below ground, something else, down below, distracted Alice; word-play. She now saw herself back staring at the same two sexy, yet genderless, eyes. Such ambiguity begged the question, Should HERmaphrodite, just like the word HIStory, be considered sexist? Although still confused by the colourful character in charge of costumes, Alice made her decision. When grown-up, she would consider writing the HERstory of the HISmaphrodite! 'Ready for Role-Call?' asked the ambivalent creature leading Alice into another cavern of costumes. That one displayed row upon row of bodywear all the way back to the sarong, lioncloths and to one shrivelled fig-leaf, not TWO. So intriguing!

'COME AS YOU WERE Reincarnation Party!' announced this attractive genderless creature. 'Ere find outfits to suit every body zo, to zine own selves be true. Even Ishtar, ze Queen of 'Eaven, she 'ave to visit ze Underworld to face 'er tragedy, So, tout mes aimis, ze whole world is WELCOME!'

To Alice, whatever the desired result, this creature's dubious invitation certainly felt like her next best option.

CHAPTER FIVE

ROLE PLAY RE-PLAY

'. . . and jumped lightly down into the looking-glass room. . . .'
'I've cut several slices . . . but they always join on again.'
'It's as large as life, and twice as natural.'

'But what shall I call you?' asked Alice, still determined to identify the actor's real gender.

'Zuit yourself!' came the saucy reply. 'Choose – choose your role and play wiz me!'

Alice was not certain whether she should address IT with some safe name like PAT. Certainly, Alice was being invited to dress-up in one of the period costumes on display. But she did not relish disrobing in front of a Patric**K** or being fussed over by Patricia. Or even the other way round.

What colourful costumes! Every possible flounce and frill, farthingale, together with wonderous collections of historical ball gowns, capes, swords and cami-bockers. Still perplexed by the sex of the costumier in charge, Alice tried out another test question. Dunce or not, Alice felt almost smug as, looking deeply into both eyes of the person before her, she asked, 'Pray, what kinds of PERIODS do you have. . . ?'

'Bloody ones,' came the instant reply. 'Wars come in every age, mon darling. Zey prefers sheeps for ze arms factories, for ze battlefields. And now, female politicians, pah! Like cardboard men, whatever their reincar-nation party. . . .'

Dismissing again pictures of Snow White the Premier with the eyes of Caligula fighting for clean air above ground, Alice felt she was being teased by the flirt in front of her with gleaming lips like those of Marilyn Monroe, be they on a man or a woman.

'Now yourself, mon darling, YOU are villainess or villain? Victim, vanquished or victorious? Ze more traumas you tame, ze less mess you take back to earth next time. Question. . . ?'

Yes, and it was burning an ozone hole at the top of her head. A deep gulp of air for courage and Alice asked, 'Are you a. . . ?'

'Mandala?' came the quick counter question. 'Meditation means medication, mon darling. Necessary for psychic 'ealth. Like ILL, short for illusion. Like ART, short for artificial. 'Ere we perform psychodramas. It 'elp us prepare for ze real thing. Like coca-cola karma. . . !'

During all that, the chief speaker had been streaking its face with black greasepaint. 'I now play ze raging baddie. . . .'

Alice slapped her thighs like a cowboy in a B movie. 'You, as Demon – er – KING. . . ?

'QUEEN!' retorted the personage in high dudgeon. 'Come. Your turn. Nudity is next to naughty knowledge. . . .'

Why was it never Humphrey who wanted to play strip poker with her? Before Alice could undress in front of that hands-on Wardrobe Mister, Mistress or Ms, she stayed determined to ascertain its gender. Trying to probe the vanity of her companion, Alice announced, 'I think, actually, I saw your Macbeth. . . .'

She dreaded an unmanageable reply. Like her uncle who had been a professional actor.

Once he had met a fan in a toilet. Standing next to her uncle after a performance of Hobson's Choice, the gay fan grinned up at the actor saying, 'I've just seen your Willie. A long part, eh!' Perhaps Willie Mossop was not such a wet after all. And perhaps gender, like the sexual act itself, is often a matter of Hobson's Choice. Even maybe, BEFORE each person's birth.

111

While theatrical make-up was being applied to her face, Alice tried another tack. 'I DID SO LOVE your Macbeth!'

'Which?'

'Lord Macbeth.' And then, as the pause grew uneasy, she quickly added, 'I mean, Lady – oh, Lord, WHICH?'

In the mirror she had already seen her companion as both Lord and Lady Macbeth, albeit only in a flash of each. Then, in another flash, the creature's black face in the mirror turned into that of a haggard and par-boiled haggis, a toothless old Halloween hag. 'OF COURSE!' said Alice, as if clicking her fingers. 'A witch!'

'Which? First, Second or Zird?'

'The one who cried out, I COME!'

'Aye, an' 'aving wee orgasms of ectoplasm e'er I see yon big Willie in 'is kilt. . . !' Like a wicked cockatoo on hot charcoal, she screeched out expletives until, still in the Highland accent, out cackled the words, 'An' I'm tellin' ye hen, that there witch can as well be played by a BLOKE as by any BIDDY! By Butch, Bitch or by any wee body, aye-aye, in between both. . . !'

Guts reeling with Highland Flings of uncertainty, all Alice could think of saying was, 'Marvellous actor – actress – which ever you are – were.' Then added, in obvious desperation, 'Oh God, WHICH WITCH?'

On that, the hag vanished. As the blackened face reappeared in the make-up mirror, French accent intact, Alice was told, 'All Souls play all genders. To ze plebs, zis versatility it seem so un-chic. But I, mon darling, I store up all my worst and best perfs on video.'

'Perfs?'

A white finger pointed to the black forehead in the make-up mirror. 'My 'ead. My cinema. Inside zis I sit, watching rolls and rolls of roles and roles, for reels and reels, me as projectionist, me as actors, directors and as ze Continuity. . . .'

'GIRL!' blurted Alice, hopefully. Squirming into a white night-gown, she added with a trifle more trust, 'I, too, only feel real when I make-believe!'

'Self-realisation require, mon darling, zat we play every role under God's good sun. Some for long run, some for short. But most, zey are for many many times. Till we learns to write our own scripts. Till wiz God's own laws, we makes no mistakes no more . . . true to script . . . making no more. . . .'

'Miss Takes?' Alice with a sense of growing certainty, over articulated the question before declaring, victoriously, 'That means that you really ARE a. . . .'

A hand shot out to be shaken. 'Call me VIV!'

'Short for Vivian?' asked Alice. Was the proffered hand needing a quick kiss?

'No, short for Vive lá difference!'

Well, that left Alice even more determined to find out the creature's real identities present, past and to come. . . .

'*It is the cause, it is the cause, my Soul,*' groans Othello, beating his chest like a bad Catholic before a good confession.

As Desdemona, Alice lies on an ornate four-poster, biting crocheted rosebuds on a silk-covered pillow. In terror, she listens to the heavy breathing of her murderous husband. His black face and blazing eyes hover in the chilly moonlight beyond the jet bead curtain hanging silently between them.

In the shadows he intones, '*Let me not name it to you, you chaste stars. It is the CAUSE.*' Jet beads rattle imminent alarm.

The pillow is snatched away. Two ebony hands lower it over the face of Desdemona.

Inside with mounting suffocation, Alice struggles to understand why she should be killed; why she as Desdemona and Viv as Othello should be re-enacting such a brutal scene together. As she writhes around before being stilled, Desdemona listens to dark tones emoting in the choking darkness. It's not just a raging African Moor. It is Viv's own voice that declaims, 'Obey zis law of action and reaction. Remember being a Carmen in Moorish Spain. Mon darling, I vas ze baby vich you vere paid to feed. But, being wicked, you stifled me wiz a pillow and fled away. Now you pay zis back wiz your own pretend death by fatal suffocation.'

'Why PRETEND?' Alice out of role cried out, telepathically.

113

' 'Cos death only pretend to exist! So 'ow can she ever be in a dead-end?'

'She?'

'Includes he, does S/HE, mon darling! IT is always bigger zan both!"

'IT?'

'All reality's in reverse, eh? Like zis ceiling mirror watching all our scenes. So by role-reversals, it's possible to – 'ow you say? – to balance out karma, ze perfect law of ad-JUST-ment. To image ze experience is OK, too. IMAGINATION, in Spirit Travel, is ze quickest LEAP and PLUNGE into. . . .'

As Othello, Viv suddenly raises high a bejewelled dagger towards the stars. Blaming fate, he rants, 'It is the cause, my Soul, it is the cause. . . .' The dagger lunges downwards into the Moor's black-sabled gut. Alice is conscious of the silk pillow. Slowly it slips down on to the opulent Persian carpet under the canopied four-poster bed.

And there was Viv. Comfortable. Rosy-cheeked and smiling. 'Each moment of every lifetime, eizer it is Cause or Effect,' came the clarification. 'We eizer work wiz Cause, or it will work against us. As suffering victim, we stay sad. Never in charge of any good cause, even of ourselves. OK, mon amie. . . ?'

'I've played Dungeons and Dragons, but I never . . . well yes . . . I feel I HAVE been in Desdemona's shoes. Also in Othello's and even in YOURS Viv, though I'm not sure they were high-heels! One Soul, so many shoes. Is that what is meant by old Souls?' she joked.

'Apply now to leave earth to ze worms?' Alice nodded. 'So, what's our next role. . . ?' asked Viv as the remaining black grease-paint was cleared from the shiny face streaked with liquid parafin.

'My next role is to inspire some stuffy Don. In Oxford's Victorian's Christ Church meadows. With cows and buttercups. On summer picnics, I think. With an Anglican Dean.'

'Anglican? You English, Alice, you copyright God?'

'Do not all religions?' Giggling she added, 'Imagine, a God of Rome! A God of England, of France, of Wales. God in bits! As if God gives a toss about any of our holy wars since, eventually, every one of us is a winner.

Anyway Viv, I'm to help Dodgson. To help him turn facts into faction, figures into fun. Though why under ground, I'm not sure yet. Humphrey called me here, I think. To meet him, I suppose, or . . . I'm so afraid he's only a ghost and me only imagining him to be my boyfriend . . . so far, but. . . .' She left her longing dangling in the air until a sudden awful but comic thought struck her. 'Oh gosh and golliwogs! What if Humphrey's only a naughty little garden gnome or elf, teasing me. . . ?'

'Cow dung in a cow horn, it stimulate underground gnomes,' said Viv, enigmatically.

Dismissing her last thought, Alice summoned up a worse one. 'What if Humphrey's only a ghost left over from the fourth Root Culture. . . .'

'IMAGINATION, mon darling, in ze 'uman machine, she is ze only real ghost, OK. . . ?'

'Not real at all? How really very sad. I won't believe I won't meet Humphrey before . . . Oh please, do tell me I'm going the right way about all of this, please. . . .'

'Oui, oui, for sure, OK! You, me, we've just shared much love, such generosity and, darling girl, so much much JOY!'

Alice and Viv, as in a reunion party, found themselves in a dancing hug. 'But the deepest secrets underground, zese you must find for yourself, Alice. After, of course, first finding more safety from evil, from ze sly Saff monks in Magic Mountain. Monastery monsters which you will 'elp to defeat!'

As they again bounced up and down, a band of black-leathered boys entered with shiny steel guns. From the other direction, a band of red-leathered boys entered, also with shiny steel guns. Viv steered Alice to one side in order to watch battle commence.

Yet how could such behaviour be happening in an underground paradise? Soon Alice saw that each of the 'corpses', red or black, got up after the ritual command, 'Bang-bang, you're DEAD!' and continued to fight with their water-pistols.

Was Humphrey amongst them, Alice wondered, eyes searching the boyish combatants.

'Istory, she keep repeating 'erself,' prompted Viv. ' 'Til we square all debts. Attitudes are more important zan facts. Feel ze pain of Othello and Desdemona and you can be eizer in imagination. Feel no pain, be neutral through all roles, voila! No need to repeat such pains, or such roles, ever again. ALL FREE. . . !'

Black and red boys hugged each other and immediately started to jump into the clothes of little girls. Alice was curious to see what sort of a battle they would next express.

'Children are natural re-incarnationists,' said Viv. 'Such optimism, such refusals to die down for long. Time is meaningless. Zey can move mountains. . . .'

'Even Magic Mountains, like . . . like Rainbow Mountain. . . ?'

Viv's face darkened. 'Evil! King Kal's abode! You blurt too much. How you know zis thing? Too much knowledge can kill, even down here. SPEAK! Who tell you such secret names. . . ?'

No answer. But suddenly through the make-up mirror, they both projected themselves swirling through giddy mountain mists . . . swirling under high slowly somersaulting pink clouds. . . .

Two climbers scaling Himalayan rocks, flowers glowing, insects buzzing, large butterflies dazzling onlookers. Ever climbing upwards, Alice now is a boy acolyte with an olive complexion and in a goatskin smock. Above the boy, a Tibetan Monk, his wild hair and beard blowing in gusty breezes, a Merlin or Moses. Or both. This ageless holy man, a knapsack over his sackcloth, speaks in a strange tongue. Yet Alice as slant-eyed lad, keeps on listening, intently.

In vibrant voice, he instructs the boy; also the birds, bees and other entities which are always hovering around words of wisdom, ever eavesdropping, like a Mancunian Cat. And, perhaps, Humphrey.

'The thought of being an elephant, a tree, or even a telephone,' says he, 'is not ridiculous to the young in heart and the old in Soul. Like love, like true magic, Soul knows no limits. Find what is to be human. . . !'

With that, two mighty hands are raised high, an uplifting gesture to include within it every atom, every bi-locating electron in the whole of Creation. 'Welfareland is tired out with the drudgery of so-called do-good-ing. Too many social workers crucifying themselves. Now take

116

Oxfordshire, whose city of spires, dear boy, will one day inspire Alice to inspire others. There, hundreds of jaded teachers, probation workers, police, home-helps, prison officers, weekly meet.'

The sound of the last word reminded the lad of his growling empty stomach. 'Meat?' he asked twice between gasped breaths as the mountain air grew ever thinner.

'Aye, a meeting. At the end of their working week.'

'Like a Feast Day after harvesting?'

'Ruined crops. They get sick, sick of caring overmuch for society's invalids. Feeling 'invalid', the hapless victims of welfare are always on the take, not the make. So their Social Workers seek new ways to keep sane before a sick society weakens its healthy helpers also. Witness the current high rate of suicide among doctors.'

'Your cure, sire?'

'Theirs, young master, THEIRS.'

'The Hunza valley diet? No gold, no oil. I remember, sire. Every child has a useful place in society. No-one succeeds unless EVERYONE succeeds on apricots and . . . and almonds . . . and. . . .'

'Such a long memory in such a young face. As you may well know, if many bindweeds choke the Rose Garden, is not careful pruning required? For new growth on old rootstocks? Maybe. But isn't it best to tell all garden weeds that they're really HERBS?' He laughs and laughs.

'Tell me about Oxford, sire,' says the acolyte. 'Any yak there to eat. . . ?'

'Only yakety-yak, college after college of academic yackers!' Another gust of guffaws before he subsided and got himself back on track. 'There, as I say, jaded professionals in the service of others, once a week, meet up to discuss case histories. Disputing dialectical materialism? Dissecting the theories of Freud? The long term global dangers of nuclear power? No, none of these, lad. . . .'

He points to a ragged flock of vultures as they tear apart the carcass of the human corpse lovingly prepared and left there for their supper. 'You vultures, how long till you learn to kill, not just scavenge?' asks the Monk. 'Maybe, as long as the Chinese learnt to use gunpowder to kill instead of just illuminate star-less night skies. See son, from those radioactive rocks,

yon bird of Soul has already left her sun-varnished human cage of bones.'
Seeing the boy's alarm, he plucked a radioactive lily. 'The virgin queen of
flowers. Inhale her fragrance. We are to become more radioactive, silicon
hu-man beings ready for the next evolutionary leap. . . .'

'Those Oxford serfs, sire? Not schoolteachers, also?'

'Kiddies' games! That's what those Social Workers meet for now!' He
roared with more liberating laughter, louder than the nearby waterfalls. 'As
in drama workshops, they release the child within. Warm-up games untie
the workaday tensions, anxieties, angst, and angers. Yes boy, teachers
also! Otherwise, they'd catch the worst cancers of society. Understand
this: Spirit is always outraged when imprisoned by others, when we permit
freewill to be taken from us by any means, fair or foul. Servile Warders of
the Welfare State are also its prisoners. Some even lower themselves sufficiently to encourage nervous breakdowns on behalf of their clients on the
dole. . . !'

Impishly, the boy held out their begging-bowl. After all, he was feeling
hungry.

'Weekly pay-cheques can sustain apathy and ignorance.'

Then a nod towards the vultures, 'Watch the scroungers feeding in
rapacious haste on old rags of human flesh. . . .'

'Supper, sire?' he asked in a small aching voice. 'Capitalism is the
rotting body, socialists its vampires.'

The boy threw the begging-bowl over a cliff edge, its clattering not
rattling the birds' feeding frenzy or his need to sulk. 'With breakdowns,
prisoners can choose to break THROUGH . . . and out, OUT into their own
creative universe!'

'Break OUT, sire? Like plagues, diseases and . . . and hunger
strikes. . . ?' He hugged his stomach, angry eyes pleading for food.

'Yea, like famines, droughts, wars; and also world-wide floods. Mother
Gaia's defensive reflexes, her sad hu-man stewards, crazed with various
states of spiritual dis-ease. . . .'

They approach a hidden cave, the entrance to a mountainside Golden
Temple. In hope of food soon, the boy sniffs.

The massive rock face surrounding the cave mouth pulsates and glows with absorbed sunbeams. On baking boulders nearby, mosaics of lizards still as clay statuettes, pose, motionless, as if listening to the heartbeats of the radioactive rocks. Not a speck of sweat on his brow, the Monk waves the lad into the cathedral-like coolness inside the darkened cave.

Nervously, the boy hesitates.

Says the Tibetan through billowing beard, 'In our endless spirals, we too have been rock, raindrop, fish, lizard, seagull, leopard, sacred cow, cat, caveman, peasant, princess, beggar, beautiful. . . .'

The word 'beautiful' was suddenly in the teenage cracked voice of Humphrey! HOW?

Yet the open sky still seems to expand with every syllable spoken by the Monk. 'We used telepathy before the telephone; changed colours like the chameleon long before we painted our bare bodies for battles. And before stealing the skins of beasts we grew our own clothes. Soul's overview helped primitive peasants long before spy-satellites. All life is bugged by the secret agents of God. Spiritually, there are no state secrets, divine or demonic. Everything is already visualised. Everything awaits re-appearances in ever-evolving living forms, all learning ever more godly love.'

The Sage beams to the boy the greatest warmth, the kind that has no need to exploit the good nature of others less advanced and, by it own good nature, nourishes all present. Even the hungry.

Accepting the Monk's encouragement, the boy tries out his own version of truth knowing he will be given a gracious hearing. 'I know we've all been elephants, blinded by fire ants. Otherwise we wouldn't all have such long memories. We've all been birds. Otherwise parents wouldn't want to hold on to our feet to stop us from flying too high, too soon. In the Hunza valley every child feels it belongs, because it is trusted, because it carries a responsibility that feeds the whole. . . .' Feeds the hole? Seeing his grimace, the Monk laughs so kindly that the lad forgets to gripe. Instead, he continues, with, 'Yes sire, we've all been trees. Otherwise we wouldn't all let the drama teacher encourage us to. . . .'

'Today, we'll all be TREES! Think, boy. FEEL!' Commands the Sage, his whiskers sparkling even in shadows. 'The Method School uses recall. All actions, they claim, have conscious motives. WELL. . . ?'

'What KIND of tree, sire?'

'Excellent! Reject our adult generalities. Treat all teachers as learners.'

'And, sire, as in a mixed forest, we can all co-operate as well as compete for, say, carbon. . . .'

'Our free present, our current energy currency . . . YES!'

With that, arm in arm, four feet off the ground, they both float into the mouth of the cave. . . .

Music. Fade.

Scene 5 – Warren Row. Exterior. Nuclear Day or night

WHITE QUEEN	What does Nostradamus mean? (*reading*) The dreadful war is being prepared for in the West?
SNOW WHITE	I told them. We are unbeatable. Great Britain, plc. Others using bombs like my handbag, unthinkable. That's why we stockpiled them. In case we had to use them.
WHITE QUEEN	But that is just why THEY stockpiled them.
SNOW WHITE	Those over-dressed Frogs, far too flamboyant. OUR bombs are bigger and BETTER. Told them.
WHITE QUEEN	Still, no reputation is unsinkable. Look at the Titanic.
SNOW WHITE	It wasn't just the Belgrano one sunk. Oh no, the real achievement was to get the Frogs to sink Greenpeace. Imagine the fuss if we'd done that ourselves, Liz. Yes, our boys in the Security Services, rightly so, have been better rivals to the French Security Forces than ever they were best friends.
WHITE QUEEN	Margaret, your face has been saved many times, but not I fear, this time. Your peach blusher is turning black. Poor dear, like runny tar. Do look into your mirror. . . .

SNOW WHITE SEES BALDNESS AS A RISING TIDE. LIKE SOME QUEEN CANUTE, SHE ORDERS HER WAVES OF HAIR TO OBEY.

SNOW BLACK	Receding hairline, white as snow – desist!
WHITE QUEEN	(*Wryly sweet*) You always swore black was white.
SNOW BLACK	Not in South Africa, I did not.
WHITE QUEEN	Apartheid? Not even against Barclays' bank I take it.
SNOW BLACK	In Africa they call it diplomacy. In France they call it imagination. In England, we call it common sense. Like stockpiling bombs for overkill, and our best butter for over-eat. What's the use of power if one spreads it about too thickly?
WHITE QUEEN	Like nuclear power?
SNOW BLACK	Shh! Don't let the foreign press get too close to state secrets. Explosive.
WHITE QUEEN	Is that why France has more than enough to spare us? Only they didn't spare us, did they?
SNOW BLACK	Nostradamus was right about one thing. He called Napoleon the first anti-Christ. Now seems his beloved Paris is not so gay, thanks to Aids. Maybe as flat as a pancake, like Warren Row here. An eye for an eye, etc., if you follow me, Liz. . . ?
WHITE QUEEN	Let not one blacken your character, like your teeth but having yours crowned, certainly seems to have gawn to your head. And Margaret, your right thumbnail. It has dropped orf.

SCRATCHING IN THE GOOEY GRIT WHICH COVERS THE IRON DOOR, THEY BOTH SEARCH AROUND FOR THE MISSING FINGERNAIL.

Back inside their present day bodies, Viv and Alice once more consider each other in their movie make-up mirror. 'Mas oui, mon darling. Truly, it's separation from ze dramatist in ze sky which pain us most, when we forgets ze right words, lose faith zat every small part is important to ze whole cast of all creatures alive.'

'Like my uncle said about Willie Mossop? No small parts, only small actors.'

'For most lifetimes we are, so to say, just walk-on parts, raging wiz 'umiliations and envy. No fun. No progress, till – to thine own SELVES be true. . . !'

'That's why I ran away from my private school. To find all of my selves. . . .'

'So now, down to business, mon ami. . . .'

'I thought there was no money here.'

'Business 'ere, mon darling, means making a life for yourself, not just a living.'

'Don't I have to earn my keep – somehow. . . ?'

'Many ways to earn. What ways do YOU like to give of yourselves, darling. . . ?'

'No limits!' boasted Alice, hoping to sound as generous as God.

'Ah, like me, versatile. You British prefer doves in pigeon-'oles, parrots in plain plumage, players of football to players of Shakespeare. You read ze classics, of course.'

'Not if I can help it.'

'Like everyone else. Pretend!'

'Actually, I'd rather write them than read them, Viv. Only they'd become exam fodder for robots.'

'Look at the Bible.'

'Never do.'

'Look at Revelation,' said Viv, hotting up her gospel.

'Look at the time!' said Alice. 'How it flies. . . !'

'Doesn't exist, mon darling. See Tim about zat. 'E do zis weird playshop on Time Travel. It might get you there sooner. . . .'

'Where?'

'Everywhere.'

'With Humphrey? Can't wait!'

'We Survivalists love to learn more about love, oui! Anyzing from archery to Zen Buddhism, from beta waves to yarrow sticks, from cabbages to. . . .'

'Kings?' contributed Alice, as if coining a quote for further use. She was tapping her toes, impatient to move off again she knew not where.

'WAIT! Time for ze biggest adventure yet!'

'Time Travel. . . ?'

'PAIN, mon bonhomie!' cooed Viv. 'You fall in love!'

'I DO NOT!' snapped Alice, her jaw jutting. 'Love is only falling when it's failing. I want now to RISE . . . like teacakes!'

'Wiz many randy boys, mon pretty mongoose! Choose! But stay aware. You'll recognise. You'll feel. Ze magnetism, ze sexual bait, both hung drawn and s-t-r-e-t-c-h-e-d irresistibly. . . .'

'But all these boys here have dressed up as GIRLS!' protested Alice. 'With water-pistols, too! Karma, is it? Group consciouness?'

'Grope consciousness more like. Some re-cycled nunnery what fell 'ook line and sinker for nearby monastery. Such confusions 'appen. C'est lá vie! But love, mon darling, love know no separations. Before ze atom was split, so was 'uman consciousness even more. Man and womb as cracked looking-glass lessons. . . .'

'Now we've sunk so far down the ladder of learning . . . it hurts.'

'Only bodies. Or brains. Not Soul's older zan Angels, more flexi zan unisex, more fluid zan KY jelly! On earth, we like English weazer, change-able! Unpredictable. Philosophical. Zat 'ow in zese lower worlds, we balance out ourselves: girl/boy; black/white; empathy/alienation; past/present; young/old; good/bad; etc. Drama, she needs contrasts. Not ze ethics of ecstasy but ze tit for ze backstage tat. Drama, she never a neutral Muse. . . .'

'Tits?' asked Alice looking around as if she had used a swearword. 'Like rose buds. On all babies. Boys and girls. But why stuck on . . . BOTH?' Losing breath, a blush was suffusing her cheeks.

'Tits should be on everybody's side, mon darling . . . Like God. Like ze best playwright!'

'Now tell me, is Humphrey handsome? Where will I find him, sing with him, dance with him, holding hands. . . ?'

' 'Ere, I give you. A clip.'

'Not round the ear?'

' 'Umphrey's ear, maybe. And yours, maybe. Glue ears, togezer, zat how sexy snails mate! Watch your carousel of karma. Each role repeat, till we free ourselves from all joint tortures. . . .'

'TORTURES? Don't . . . again . . . don't hurt me, please. . . !'

'Watch mirror. NOW! We chop again . . . as in butcher shop. . . .'

'Human MEAT. . . ?' Alice, hands over both ears, hoped not to listen, not even to look.

'In thick mists of 'istory, TWICE in one dark lifetime, my beautiful body was your virgin victim. In Paris. Me ze experiment, you ze wizened, wicked Alchemist . . . with meat cleavers. . . .'

'I like games of Let's Pretend but not horrid ones.' Even as Alice spoke, Viv was undressing the reluctant girl and, again using theatrical grease-paints, preparing her for their next operation. Or was it for her last one? Alice was getting too flustered to think clearly.

'Drama is always a Mystery Play. Ze audiences, like initiates are led, so to speak, into echo chambers of zeir own collective conflicts. Zis ghost training we call IMAGINATION!'

'Me – an alchemist, Viv? No, NEVER! Please no torture, not hurting me this time . . . PLEASE. . . .'

'Time reminds us, again and again. So listen good. Tired of failing to turn lead into gold, mon darling, you decided to cure your own greed for fame and power. After circumcising, you chopped off penis fast. Zat was ME. Re-member, re-member, re-member ME, child. . . ?'

Was Alice going to cry, trying to avoid all responsibility? No, though trembling, she stood her ground, defying all she dreaded most, uninvited nightmarish ogres.

'Sliced up, me, bit by little bit into test tubes. Everyzink from tonsils to tibia. Jars and jars of meatballs, pickled bits; brains, double-chins, tongue, knee-caps, tripes. . . .'

'Awful!'

'Offal, too!' On that, Viv placed on Alice the wig of a gnarled old wizard. In the make-up mirror, a dwarfish Alchemist appeared. In the same way world leaders are drawn magnetically towards their own assassinations, deaf to all warnings, so Alice found herself magnetised to the grotesque image in the mirror. 'Ah, 'ere will loom anozer me, two in one of your ancient victims,' says Viv, salaciously. 'Remember my penis? Remember my clitoris? I looked like an Angel. Zat hermaphrodite, me, you snip, clip, snip, clip, SLICE! Zen red 'ot iron rod you insert so brutally . . . 'till screaming, I split apart . . . like zis OZER victim – HERE!'

Blinking unbelievably, Alice sees a plump cherubic teenager. Awkwardly, he is standing beside her. While Viv ogles the young man, Alice scrutinizes the spotty face with distaste. If Alice had wanted a boyfriend she certainly would not have picked such a plump, gawky specimen, his spotty face pock-marked as any golf ball, his knowing eyes steady as those of a vulture at suppertime.

' 'Ere is Humphrey!'

Like Pandarus introducing Troilus to Cressida, Viv pushed the gawky lad towards Alice. He is dressed up in some of her own discarded clothes, so at least her dress on him looked familiar, like a family friend. Disturbingly, what then emerged was an overblown version of one of Lewis Carroll's own original drawings before these were sanitised by Mr Tenniel's talent to please the middle-classes.

Alice averted her eyes. For a swift escape she looked in the mirror again. But snarling back at her was herself as the raddled old gargoyle of the Alchemist, a revolting dwarf with nose dripping slimy snot, like sea-green ectoplasm. . . .

'We're beautiful,' insisted Humphrey.

Ignoring that misguided compliment, Alice turned to Viv, asking, 'Pray, what else are we to learn from these ugly disguises? Before I meet my kind, lovely, handsome young author in Oxfordshire. . . ?'

'We're still beautiful,' suggests Humphrey unblinkingly, his eyes boring into her skull.

Alice, apart from being beside Humphrey – if that indeed was his true name – she was also beside herself. Not only in relation to the image of the old time Alchemist, apparently one of her past selves, but also because of her disappointment in Humphrey's plain spotty face, surely an imposter. He didn't even stammer.

'Theatricals? They act as alchemical magic,' continued Viv, powdering Alice's latest make-up.

'Transformative. . . .' added the gawky spotted youth.

Scowling, she snapped at him, 'Why do artists often feel ugly?'

'Oui, oui. Soul's gold curdles into lead. Earthly fame, adulation delays our self-awareness. You my girl, as Alchemist turned butcher; myself, and 'Umphrey 'ere, your victims . . . will re-live, and RELIEVE, all of your screams in painful role-play. . . .'

'Oh, NO!' Alice was anticipating revenge. 'Hurting is horrid. Please, NO!'

'To be precise, you sliced us up while still we breathed. Alive again, facing each ozer, we all now shall enjoy playing CONSEQUENCES. . . !'

Writhing with painful expectations, Alice tried to delay matters. 'In his lives, man plays many parts, I know; but how can I be IN the next re-play and WATCH it at the same time . . . let alone learn anything good . . . through pain. . . ?'

'Easy! Good actors, zey sit inside zeir roles,' explains Viv, 'but also on zeir own shoulder. From zere zey drive ze playwright's vehicle, steering transports in audiences. Also, zey sit wiz ze gods, above it all, watching from on 'igh every gesture and nuance. . . .'

'Like Upstairs Downstairs. . . ?'

'Ozerwise. . . .' On that, Viv taps her own temple, flippantly, 'Like Snow White above ground now, leading ze society she not believe in, into ze bleakest winters of discontent to end ze Cold War.'

'Poor dear, locked out of Warren Row. Perhaps we can help her some more.'

Pre-emptively, Viv barks out. 'OPERATION 616!' Alice's front teeth are painted out with black enamel, Viv yelling. 'You pulled us living patients apart. Now we pull YOU apart, till you respect all parts of life, the union of all in Spirit. Occultists would call zis an eye-for-an-eye. Dentists would call it a tooz-for-a-tooz. 'Umphrey and me, we call it LOVE. . . .'

'LOVE?' spluttered Alice.

'We're beautiful,' says Humphrey, his eyes scanning her but now set on action. Was he, after all, just a cold-blooded surgeon . . . into tunnel vision . . . only after her entrails to eat them alive. . . ?

Through the looking-glass, another ominous scene looms into view, absorbing all viewers.

Central is a white altar, like an operating-table, or a slab of marble as used in temple morgues. In the distance Alice, as the old Alchemist, thrashes about in hemp vest and loincloth. Cowed figures in black surround her skinny male body. Alice's own voice cries out for mercy. She has been here before. This Alice now knows, this Alice now dreads, dreads with every shred of her flesh. As in a re-enactment of a crime in a televised documentary, even a simulation makes her shrink in terror as Viv removes her vest. Alice screams. Revealed is her scabby flabby chest, a wrinkled slab of raw whiskered meat, the writhing hair alive with tics. 'Surgeons, NO!' she shrieks. Their face-masks seem to grin. 'Spare me! I won't do it again. Too kind now to . . . I CAN'T ever again . . . PROMISE!'

'No such word as CAN'T!' replies Viv, curtly. 'We never get more bones of contention to chew on zan we can grow and bury in our own garden. Can't? You CAN! What we cause we can cure! Courage, mon brave!'

'We're beautiful,' adds Humphrey, implacably. His smile though contagious like that of a dolphin, Alice saw him as a deeply dangerous shark lurking around her in the name of love.

'No, no, NO!' wails Alice and then hits Humphrey hard across his face. CLICK!

A freeze, like a still from a film. Even though, for the past four minutes she had felt it brewing, she had hoped to avoid striking him. Immediately released from hysteria, and as quick as a laser-beam, Alice projects herself into the body of that thrashing Alchemist. Though the same Soul apparently in two different bodies, operating in four rather than in just three dimensions, the two stay inter-connected. A strong but barely visible silver-chord links each body at the solar-plexus. Pull either out like plugs from electric sockets and Alice, as current body energy, would surely fuse. Not death but PAIN, that's what Alice as the old alchemist now fears most.

Music. Mix.

Cross-fade.

Zoom in from above high cliffs, racing clouds, raging seas, jagged rocks, flocks of raucous rooks, seagulls screeching and wheeling in bouts of black and white battles as scraps of flesh are viciously torn apart, mid-air.

A corpse on top of a knoll.

Below, a transept of trees, a sacrificial altar, a place to encourage open-heart surgery. And hooded vultures, being glared at by the slavering wolfhounds chained to the nearby wych elm.

Tied to the other side of that tree, the wizened dwarf Alchemist, frothing with terror, bulging eyes bloodshot and weeping. His mouth gibbers with the shrill, piping sounds of Alice's own voice. To the Masked Carvers, she cried out for help and mercy.

'OPERATION 616!'

'No, no, Viv, NO. . . !'

'OPEN!'

'Not torture! Kill me first. . . !'

But the shrivelled old dwarf is dropped on the altar and tied there by four hooded figures. Then, like fielders on a cricket-pitch, they spread out as if to anticipate the best catch of the season.

Like a psychic surgeon, the tallest man in a sable cowl, his face in a bird-mask, loose black sleeves like vulture's wings, rubs together his chapped hands. Now he raises only his left palm. The cutlass he grasps flashes, slices downwards as in his Teutonic rasping accent he screeches out the one word, 'CHIROPODIST!'

With that, the masked surgeon throws the old dwarf's left foot to one of the cowled figures in the field. From an unseen Pavilion, dark vulture angels clap this catch. And the face of that skilful fielder? Not Viv's face grinning there, but that of Alice.

'Stop squealing, pigshit!' Commands the Masked Surgeon. In upheld hands above the cringing dwarf Alchemist, a pair of glinting secateurs. These he clamps on the victim's podgy nose. With a flick of the wrist and a final twist and wrench, he calls out, 'E.N.T!'

He tosses the severed nose to another specialist in the field who, despite competition from diving herring gulls, catches it. Unseen applause. His, too, is the grinning face of Alice.

'Dark HEART!'

Giant curved gleaming serrated grapefruit knife swoops down. Blood spurting, it scoops out the pumping organ from her mangled dwarf carcass, Alice screaming. Now another slice. As through cheese with a wire, the scalp is removed. With naked hands the Surgeon, like a twin-set of pearls from its hard casing, lifts out the slimy brain like spongy white packing from a hat-box.

Each excised bodily item, from the man of many parts, is thrown to different medical experts in the field. Each in turn is seen to bear the grinning face of Alice herself.

The dwarf's baggy scrotum, sliced off, is slipped into the shark-like jaws of the tethered wolfhound nearest to the operating altar. It, also, has the grinning face of Alice.

'W-H-Y ME. . . ?' whines her ghostly voice through the slavering lips of the ravenous dog.

She wanted to tell it off for speaking with its mouth full. But all her excised and writhing remains refuse to die quietly at the hands of these so-called doctors, Soul defying all such deadly experts. 'Why kill a blow-fly,' aloud, her Higher Self asks the Alchemist in her, 'until we know how to create one with love?'

To no avail.

Surgeons continue to weigh the heart; psychiatrists probe the brain cells, dentists excavate the molars. All the specialists, advancing their latest theories, return towards the screaming stump of a patient on the slab, Alchemist's twitching reflexes on autopilot. Alice, appalled, still consciously watches and wonders. And even as her teeth-rattling screams continue to ricochet between the distant trees, her old decapitated body vanishes.

Wolfhounds' red tongues lick their chops, then skirt round their genitals, penises erect as glossy lipsticks at the ready.

CUT.

It was over. That patient was voted incurable, the experiment's findings ignored, the case remaining inconclusive. Left, that was, in a state of suspended animation, Soul working elsewhere towards its next set of earthly adventures.

Alice, her girlish body shaking, was convulsed with wild sobbing, her howling mind racked by having seen such visions. She even forgot about Humphrey, he no longer to be seen or heard, anywhere.

As if nothing extraordinary had happened, Viv lightly continued her instruction. 'Cure Soul and all else will follow, mon darling. Separation from wholeness and we're all ze walking wounded, even wizout wars.' As Alice spoke, the make-up of the old Alchemist, with lashings of vanishing cream, was fast disappearing in a searing downpour of Alice's latest tears.

'I don't want . . . I don't want . . . ever . . . to be cruel again, Viv,' she gasped between sobs.

'So say all of us!' sang Viv, flippantly.

'I MEAN it, though. Really, I do not wish to . . . to . . . go back through that mirror ever again . . . to earth again. Don't make me. I don't HAVE to, do I. . . ?' Pointing at where Humphrey had stood, Viv nodded, as if reintroducing Alice to a shadow of her former self.

Like a computer hacker onto a Top Secret, she swore she heard Humphrey wink. Unfinished business? With him? With that spotty putty-faced puppy trying to hide his acne with dark-glasses and now invisible. Alice burst out with, 'Show me your eyes, you!'

'*In healing, we see the whole person as a hologram, perfect in potential. But m-m-moribund, like today's technology compared with that under ground in the City of the Gods. . . .*'

Was that a stammer? Humphrey had sounded like a smug computer buff, one not easy to pin down and, Alice had to admit, one that sounded disconcertingly like herself when in a huff. Glaring at his invisible outline, Alice remembered playing touch-and-go with the imaged apple in the Hall of Holograms. As if reading her mental picture, Humphrey continued, '*An apple a day m-may keep the hacker at bay, but not if we don't eat it all raw, skin, pips and stalk, holistically.*'

'What about that last sorcerer?' challenged she, interviewing the air. 'And his Adam's apple. . . ?'

'*You mean the apple of Newton's eye, that young m-mathematical coxcomb he was infatuated with?*'

Izaac Newton gay? Whatever next?

'*M-m-maybe it was their taste for cox that suggested the fairy-story of the falling apple. Certainly, Newton fell out with m-most of his friends,'* announced Humphrey with an audible wince. Before Alice could challenge his story, uninvited, he continued. *'Break a hologram and each bit holds in itself a m-m-miniature of the whole picture. When every puzzle-piece fits, inter-dimensionally, the whole picture's one of complete health.'* On that he re-appeared in person, standing mute, like a plum pudding on a shelf before Christmas.

Weary of counting blackheads on the left side of Humphrey's nose, Alice asked, sharply, 'Then how many different bodies DO we have?'

'Bods for God? Guess!'

She soon counted SEVEN blackheads, so far, and all of those on the left side of his rather too podgy nose. Further, Alice was wondering if the good Lord could send young Humphrey a more handsome face since his own present-day one was a pock-marked and somewhat over-uphol-stered blotchy pasty phizog.

Humphrey smiled, winningly. So brightly indeed, Alice counted her invisible toes instead of his spots, eyes kept downcast.

'Touch 'im, mon darling. . . .' suggested Viv.

Alice turned away to study her tear-lined face in the mirror. Humphrey's smug sense of secret knowing did not engage her affections. Still beam-ing her his dazzling teeth, he placed a finger alongside the left of his nose, hiding all offending blackheads. Why do boys so often fiddle with their noses? Said Humphrey, 'Smash this looking-glass and each shard has only a bit, YEP!' With a fist he shattered the mirror. 'So it is with "experts". Specialists splinter off, work only with their bit, not the whole picture. Sickness comes from unnatural separations. From Spirit's purpose for each of us.'

'US?' asked Alice, edgily.

'Let's heal all of our past images, Alice, shall we?'

'S'pose a m-m-mirror shows me what I CAN become . . . (Gosh, why did I stammer?')

'Beautiful!' said Humphrey, unblinkingly. He turned his other cheek in case Alice wanted to land a swipe. After all he knew that adolescent fluff and blackheads were not the real man.

Then, smiling like a cheeky cherub, he waved his hand across the shattered shards of glass. As if obedient to his command, all the splinters leap back into the looking-glass frame. Through that replaced and perfect looking-glass, Humphrey dived and vanished. Gone? Again? Alice then noticed that her dress, the one worn by Humphrey, had re-appeared on the floor, lying there where he had just stood before in person. And gone so suddenly! Why? Because undressed? With a pang in her fast-beating heart, Alice dare not face that fact that she was already missing him, despite everything, plus his seven blackheads. Recovering, Alice turned to Viv for comfort. 'Could we have met before, that boy and I? In different bodies? And what's his real name, please. Is it – was it – really . . . you know?'

' 'Umphrey.'

'I see. Not much 'umph, has he? Almost as lumpy as. . . .' She whispered, wriggling with expectations in case he was eavesdropping. After all, it seemed that Humphrey was the less catty owner of her inner voice. 'Does that mean it's our re-play time, he and I! Will we meet again? Is Humphrey my inner guide, Viv? Oh, no, he can't be, can he? He didn't stutter. Well, only a bit. A couple of hiccoughs. Hardly . . . and yet . . . oh, please stop laughing at me. Confused . . . aren't I? Perhaps, m-maybe . . . only . . . shut me up!'

Desolate, all romantic aspirations left her as quickly as had Humphrey's presence in physical form. Viv, an arm round Alice's tense shoulders, pointed to another group of mixed children. Engrossed, they were dressing-up in everything from cloaks to clogs, representing all the different periods of mankind's playtimes on planet earth and elsewhere, maybe, as in extraterrestrial cultures also under ground.

' 'Istory, mon darling. Notice 'ow quickly ze kids, left to choose, select. Zey seem to recognise zier own best lesson, unaided, choosing zeir own learning groups. If we let zem, kiddies always get true glimpses of their karmas.'

'Glimpses, Viv?' gasped Alice. 'I was nearly driven mad, blind and . . . and . . . so stupid, STUPID. . . !'

Viv hugged Alice harder. 'As Soul, you kids are nearer to Source, 'aving just recently returned from IT. Such insights into earlier lives! Zese customs, archives, props, maps, artefacts which Survivalists preserve, zey all can 'elp us link with past lessons, free all inner blocks and blotches. Zen all shadows evaporate!'

'What, even blackheads?'

Before Viv could reply, zat is exactly what s/he did, EVAPORATE!

Undisturbed, even after witnessing mysterious acts of disappearance, a ten-year-old, aping a chalk-and-talk teacher, asked the assembled children, 'What was Henry the Eighth?'

'A dirty old man!' answered a podge of a girl called Jan.

'Who was Mrs Thatcher?'

'The Black Prince,' said Alice changing back into her own clothes. 'But who's **M** who leads us out of all ages of ugliness. . . ?'

As the children spontaneously hummed their **M**-sound Alice felt such an outsider. Not having yet learned how to evaporate herself, she tiptoed back into the corridor, leaving behind that Cavern of Customs.

'I knew who I was when I got up this morning,' said Alice to her other ubiquitous voice. 'Cat, I think I must have changed several times since then. But which way now?' The Mancunian Cat wasn't playing. But HE WAS, damn it! Stammered he, '*M-m-m-miaow!*' then Humphrey within the inner ear of Alice, purred m-meaningfully soft and sensuous m-male m-m-m-music.

Feline nails extended, Alice hissed. Suddenly, she also needed to escape. How? Oh yes, re-visit the plight of the important two top ladies. They MUST become her top concern. Much better than his romantic overtures, no matter how seductive. Anyway, his bum fluff might tickle.

Scene 6 – Warren Row. Exterior. Nuclear Winter Day or Night?

WHITE QUEEN	Do you suppose our butter mountains have melted? Like the Pyrenees? Like the chunnel?
SNOW BLACK	ChunnELLE! After SHE who made History.
WHITE QUEEN	What is the score now, I wonder.
SNOW BLACK	Britain 22 nuclear power plants, France 38.(*frowns*).

	Oh, you mean my nails. Seven down, three to go. But think Liz, what opportunities this waste gives one now. No essential services to cut back on. Such a clean sweep. Lots of space to build palaces.
WHITE QUEEN	I still worry about our generals. And judges. Were they too rich to get into heaven?
SNOW BLACK	White Judges so much easier to sway our way than juries. But see! What a new Empire we can build, Liz. All opposition floored. Free enterprise, no handicaps like handouts. I see it all now!
WHITE QUEEN	Not the ghost of Denis?
SNOW BLACK	A little Grocer's. A little corner shop. Over there (*points through the fall-out fumes*). A modest enough start, I know but. . . .
WHITE QUEEN	Margaret, now there are no corners left to cut. . . .
SNOW BLACK	(*With rising conviction*) Organically grown vegetables, of course. No tinned rubbish.
WHITE QUEEN	Could Oxfam donate to one a tin-opener? No, in your brave new world, will the customers, next time around, BUY it. . . ?
SNOW BLACK	They already have! (*Grins, teeth now blackened.*)
WHITE QUEEN	I have remembered that codeword. Charles promised that in deserts, it is much better than Feng Shui. Or even the Black Rod. Or any other open sesame known to corgies. Watch!
SNOW BLACK	Our one sure word, ma'am, is wealth.

BACK TO BACK, THEY SIT ON THE IRON DOOR OF THE UNDER-GROUND BUNKER. CROSS-LEGGED, FIRST FINGERS AND THUMBS JOINED, EYES CLOSED.

WHITE QUEEN	Let's pray for a miracle, Miss Maggie. . . .
BOTH	(*Together, chanting*) OM!

*

As Alice surged down the next corridor at the rear of a crowd, she saw a stout god ahead. The on-coming Pluto made her wobble. She quickly turned this into a shaky curtsy. His sigh sent shudders through her every fibre. While in transit, Pluto placed a baleful gaze on the distant horizon, on the next human challenge ahead. Pluto was supposed to be a good market indicator. Might Pluto say something helpful about Alice's investment in Humphrey?

Again safely below ground in both Spirit and in body, screwing up her pretty features, Alice bravely tried to picture Humphrey's face. Behind eyelids closed, she saw only blue spots, dancing like fireflies in moonlight. Well, better than blackheads. How odd it was that she was so longing to see someone she didn't apparently know, let alone know intimately, or yet trust. Who were Humphrey's parents, where his home? Did he have ambitions? Perhaps, like Newton, he seemed to prefer young men. Alice did, so why shouldn't he?

As Pluto proceeded away from her, in a small plaintive voice to his departing powerful back, Alice dared to ask him, 'Have you seen my friend Humphrey, please sire?'

While still wandering, he raised his leaden elliptical crown made from pulped newspaper. Like tatoos, it had left imprinted all over Pluto's shadowy features and small bald head, bold black menacing headlines, all slowly changing. That montage of future necessary disasters Alice saw while his heavy crown was raised. All pollution was being purified, and before the next Golden Age. Meanwhile, maybe leaked reports on current accidents had been blacked out above ground for none showed on Pluto.

Alice noticed all past headlines were printed back to front.

But where is 1984's up-to-the-moment news? Not to be seen. Because Big Sister was watching them, had her 'wets' maybe turned it into a damp squid? Are nuclear threats but a myth too serious be taken lightly, like Aids and other global warnings? NO!

So what other disasters were printed back to front. . . ?

A Wall Street crash in 1987. And that, only one year after something to be called CHERNOBYL. Without reading out more future headlines, Alice thought many would involve underground eruptions through the use, misuse and abuse of nuclear fuel-rods.

Pluto lowered his crown. A blackout on all future bad news.

Would stored nuclear spent fuels get upset, like Black Rod who had overtaken the powers of White Rod, he then long forgotten by most historians unaware of nuclear explosions before the next promised deluge?

'I'm going west,' said the god of plutonium, late as usual. 'Rare though I am, I'm about to be discovered again . . . and again and again . . . like recycled young Souls. . . .'

Alice watched him plod his weight down the slope, breathing heavily, his smoky-blue velvet cloak barely billowing behind in the wake of his stately gait, Alice watching with breathless awe. Spread out before the god, like huge glass toys upon a vast green eider-down, was a star-like city called Plutonium. Each scintillating crystal structure was tinted in delicate shades of the rainbow. The glacier-like buildings were gleaming brightly, many studded with multicoloured jewels. Terraces of radiant flowers were being sprinkled by a tall, sparkling fountain in the central square and, in the distance, a massive Blue Dome on a high, emerald hill. That, surely, would be where Humphrey was. She hoped that he, at least, would impart the secrets of **M** to her when she was ready. Given, that is, that she could find him in time. Maybe he would even lead her to the golden key seen in her recent daydreams.

Or would that distract her from her real mission?

Suddenly, Humphrey was a certainty. With new pluck, she followed in the measured pace of the god of the Underworld taking the chance, along the glittering high street, to do some sight-seeing in that crystalline city of breathtaking grandeur.

From the Blue Dome she could hear a treble hum. The letter **M** was being chanted inside it. Magnetised by the music of those angel-like voices, Alice entered.

CHAPTER SIX

THE BLUE DOME

'Will you, won't you, will you, won't you,
will you join the dance?'

After dismemberment through ugly role-reversals, relief. How beautiful to see the naked children in the Blue Dome. Alice, like Peter Pan, was suddenly certain of one thing. She never wanted to grow up, or to become all plump, smug, pockmarked and middle-aged, like young Humphrey.

Inside the Blue Dome, Alice felt herself shrinking. Yet its mighty magnificence rising above her filled her heart with wonder and strange comfort. What spaciousness! What uplift! The happy sky-blue of the ceiling's high central six-pointed star, light streaming through at all angles, all made everything within the Blue Dome tingle with an energy that radiated a vibrant brilliance.

Embossed words above the front portal had caught her eye. These Alice mouthed again, always her way with residual fears of embarrassing word blindness. 'UNLESS YOU BE LIKE A CHILD THOU SHALT NOT RE-ENTER.' Then she remembered the underlying riddle in small print. That read: *Do the Gods make OMelettes without breaking eggs?*

OM, the original Seed-Sound of all Creation? Not having used OM to get into the safer environment of the Survivalists, Alice could not, at that stage, be too certain of anything based on sound logic. Fun, trying to find out, though. . . !

Apart from uninvited voices, mostly Humphrey but sometimes Mancunian Cat, something else niggled and nagged. What? Ah, yes! Which key word HAD allowed her access to the safe Chambers of the Deep? As if an answering echo, the sound of the children chanting the '**M**' sound grew louder. That persuaded Alice to proceed. Floating in the wake of other circulating stragglers in awe of the charged atmosphere, she advanced deeper into the Blue Dome.

Seated on a purple podium, Pluto on his throne was smiling gravely, unseen except perhaps by Alice. His helmet-shaped headpiece looked odd. It must have been made by the Mad Hatter. Though robed in dark grey, his helmet kept Pluto unseen by earthly eyes. Above all visitors, Pluto solemnly nodded greetings, but not enough to dislodge the helmet. That was too heavy for even atomic physics to shift. Gods often stay invisible to human eyes, even when disguised in modern mufti.

In the expansive wide-open space were three circles of naked children, facing inwards. Holding hands they were preparing for some gentle ritual. Glancing around, Alice was appalled to find that she was the only young-ster there who was clothed. 'I do hope that Humphrey has not got black-heads all over him,' thought Alice to herself as she peeked about deter-mined to find his puppy fat moving in one of those slowly rotating circles of nude children.

'Whether for long or for short spells in their zodiac, some still call me a new boy. But I was always open,' announced Pluto, his voice as if on remote control. 'Not so much BRING OUT YOUR DEAD as GIVE THEM THE KISS OF NEW LIFE.' While his body remained invisible to most seek-ers there, his potent presence was sensed, especially as his sonorous voice intoned, 'Open now for business. Re-evaluate. What no longer serves us all is eliminated.'

As if responding to a psychic circle, the clothed adult spectators looked increasingly alert. Shaking their tensions away, they slowly opened them-selves to all fresh developments, both inner and outer. Neither adults nor children had yet seemed to notice Alice.

Pluto sounding like an ageless Old Moore, announced, 'As born-again Survivalists, as Keepers of the New Consciousness, as Stewards of

Earth's ethical future, using your innate wisdom, you are invited to devise a new system of waste and energy exchange. One which is based on the spiritual sciences. Beware of scare mongering. Globally, is not a plutonium economy, the root of all. . . ?'

'MADNESS!' That word screamed in Alice's head, yet did not obliterate 'FEAR', the word next chosen by Pluto.

'Ask yourselves,' persevered Pluto, 'will Noah's Next Children still favour full employment? And the nuclear arms' trade? It's a multinational business, but one based on economics and widespread alarmism. The Market Monster, like radiation, is neutral. Having no in-built morality, money as an energy form. It can strangle prince or pauper alike.'

Challenged one naked kid, 'Ain't it always the rich wot survives?'

(Simmering was Alice's concern for the Top Ladies. Would they survive without her help. . . ?)

'Whether gold or God, or both together, setting dream goals can lead to the pauper's prison or kids, to the grandest palace.'

Some were unafraid of Pluto's unseen influence. Others terrified. All knew of his reputation for sweeping things squeaky-clean, that his re-forming powers operate at the edge of a creative human chaos. 'Rather than offering to help God's overall plan,' challenged Pluto, 'who likes telling God his job? For example, to save the queen above is a goodly idea. . . ?'

Like an electric jolt his words hit Alice. Was he instructing her to stay true to her wish and to save the queen from radiation poisoning? And in time? Even her less appealing 'Prim' Minister also. . . ? Oh dear, deci-sions, decisions. . . !

'Ask this: would the presence of two ladies, your Queen and her Prime Minister, add to your collective gifts of human wisdom?' Pluto's question was posed as if his listeners had the same ability as the god himself; namely, to rise way above it all; even above all so-called nuclear accidents without stress or alarm-bells or even one blessed death. All that while knowing, like all gods, one day he'd get demoted to a dwarf.

Continuing his theme, Pluto added, 'Pride before a fall? Dubious. Of those two remaining Top Ladies demanding asylum in your midst, one has no sense of community, tolerance, or humour, especially about Oxford University; is against railways which serve society, rather than private cars that exhaust oxygen and people's purses and private patience! Yet, in charity, though the Survivalists could never be her natural home, may we still ask ourselves how she can best contribute to the Corporate Citizen? So let's suggest to her, some universal ecological yardstick other than money? But beware of her heavy handbag!'

'What about the other lady, the White Queen?' asked Alice, telepathically.

'The White Queen owns no money, only material possessions,' came Pluto's answer. 'Land, castles, jewels, paintings.' Perusing this point, he then asked them, 'If they should ever listen to you children, ask them: Why should such a Prime Minister and Queen reign over you?'

'Acid rain were enough!' quipped one adult spectator.

'You Rainbow Rebels, listen. Are they not begging to join you smiling Survivalists underground? You few, you healthy few. You all who deserve such godly congratulations!'

Hugs all round. Alice is still unnoticed or ignored.

'Pride before a fall?' asked Alice of herself. 'No, those two poor toffs upstairs aren't like me. Or these children here. Not enough supernatural daring. So, without help, they'll never find, even by accident, the Word which opens all doors. Surely, it's M-ME they need! A MIGHTY M-M-MIRACLE – and NOW!'

Another dark cloud dampened her ardour. Oh yes of course, that's why not one person present had yet hugged her. They could not see her, or her m-mission. How could they when she herself could not yet see it clearly enough to forge ahead with confidence? Till then, it often felt she did not properly exist. Then another doubt deepened the darkness across her brow. Would not Pluto try to persuade her to leave alone the two Top Ladies to their own searing fate, like bitter, biting punishment? Tears pricked her eyeballs. Where were Humphrey's arms?

'Wasn't it the wish to be better endowed than others that caused this devastation above ground?' asked the god. 'But the basest materials are also on the way up. Otherwise they would not be based again on earth as humans. Real poverty's not knowing one's own true worth. So let's love folks' deafness, their short sightedness and seek to love their own blind spots.'

Even acne and blackheads? But that question was left silent in the turbulent head of Alice. Indeed, lesser god or not, Alice wanted to hug him. Pluto, that is. And yes, whatever the price, she intended to enter Victorian life, not as a street-wise urchin picking pockets, but as a well-heeled church-going Christian, like the Reverend Dodgson in Daresbury. Pluto interrupted such thoughts by requesting, 'Before business commences, step forward all those who defected from the nuclear sciences, any who threatened the healthy wholesomeness of Mother Earth in any way.'

Not sheepishly but with excitement, three men and one Jewish granny, Miriam, stepped forward, their arms opening with expectation. Each physicist in turn was handed a rotting apple.

'With only one bad apple, each covered with ants,' announced Pluto, 'you four scientists will be locked up. In separate microwave ovens. With thousands of urban termites whose ancestors, unlike Neanderthal or Cro-Magnon man, lived in specialised tunnels and chambers. From such underground cities they launched wars, used chemical sprays and child labour, captured slaves. Human evil only delays supernatural evolution. So now, earthlings, it is not arrogant to know you are all godlike!'

Restlessness seethed in those in the crowd unwilling to elevate their horizons. Not true of the four scientists being addressed. They leaned forward as if to be bathed in Pluto's words. 'Only one apple for all to share in each oven. For 40 days and 40 nights. In that time, can you name each ant while crop farming takes place in their carefully constructed chambers? Only through love of all learners is release possible . . . release from poisons which pollute...carcinogenic waste . . . release for all peoples who hate . . . release for all dead thought forms . . . before they kill the future. . . .'

Eyes radiant, the four physicists stared towards the voice from the throne, still unable to see Pluto but offering him obedient worshipful salaams. They trusted they would not be roasted alive.

'And the apple?' asked Miriam. 'Vy only VON. . . ?' She sounded like a poor and small Arab nation complaining it could not afford one A-bomb, unlike its up-market Jewish neighbours. **M** for morals?

More like a frown, Pluto's smile slowly spread, his answer sounding somewhat lugubrious. 'Who eats up what first? You have forty days to find out. Esoteric entrepreneurs might open up new frontiers in free enterprise. Just know this. You all started equal, with the same physical resources.' Then came the last order, delivered as if for late night drinks to invisible bar-staff. 'Scientists, ants and apples,' declaimed Pluto, 'time to be locked up!'

Three of the four scientists produced not only gleeful smiles but also brandished a hefty iron key. Each waved it high like an emblem of victory. Not so Miriam. For the three men, though, it was as if they had just been released FROM jail and found at long last to be entirely innocent, joy in their jackass expressions suggesting freedom from all guilt.

Watching the four scientists leave the Dome unaccompanied, Alice was puzzled. Why should nuclear 'terrorists' be free to walk themselves unac-companied towards their own punishment-cells?'

'Astrologically, major shifts are being empowered,' stated Pluto. 'Uranus and Aquarius, like Death the Abyss, are associated in the Cabala with the secret dark tunnels between the Seen and Unseen. On earth, only hu-man sound can open such portals.' Suddenly, as if to subdue even thunder, the god's brass gong voice reverberated his final command: 'MEDITATION! Ask "What does it mean to be hu-man"?'

'**M**-M-M-M-ed-it-ation, is it?' called out Alice aloud. She was hoping to reach Humphrey wherever he was hiding. Might her stammered plea become some sort of secret Morse Code signalling to him the need for a closer understanding soon? Was he helping the Top Ladies? Closing her eyes, Alice ASKED to be transported again above ground to check on their progress.

Success!

From tree-top level, Alice was again able to watch the White Queen, always one of her favourites. Still with her was Snow White. Or was it Snow Black? By some miracle of nuclear science, her once ivory-beige complexion, and her swept-back Dallas-style ash-beige bouffant mane, had both turned jet black. As black in fact as the complexion of any rare miner finding himself still with a job; but without a healthy air-blowing helmet to prevent silicosis. In Nagasaki, the miners deep underground survived the nuclear blast, a blessed escape overlooked by Nostradamus. And a fact one Snow Black (née Snow White), had wished to keep secret. Like, indeed, those Top People's private underground lairs, laden like overloaded larders in banqueting-halls, lying in wait for the self-selected elect, for each galloping gourmet in expected times of crisis.

In Spirit-form, Alice surveyed the surviving two Top Ladies sitting upon the scorched earth. Both, apparently, still remained dedicated to death by deterrence. No crocodile was big enough to shed all the hot tears that Alice felt well up in the deep wellspring of her world-weary, heavy heart.

Scene 7 – Warren Row. Exterior. Nuclear night, or day

STILL SITTING BACK TO BACK ON THE IRON DOOR SET IN THE GROUND, BOTH HUMAN BOOKENDS ARE STARTING TO WILT, WHILE QUEEN AND SNOW BLACK STILL GAMELY CHANT ALOUD BY ROYAL DECREE. ONLY THE QUEEN'S FACE IS STILL BLEACHED WHITE, LIKE HER INCREASING BALDNESS.

BOTH   (*Chanting together*) OM!

AFTER GULPS OF SULPHUROUS, OILY RED SOOT, THEY STOP.

SNOW BLACK   Oh Jesus, no room at the Inn. . . ? (*A sob.*)
WHITE QUEEN   Smile, do. I can only cry in private. . . .
SNOW BLACK   Useless. What did the prince say OM meant?
WHITE QUEEN   Short for omnipotent.
SNOW BLACK   But one either IS or one isn't.
WHITE QUEEN   Then short for omnipresent.
SNOW BLACK   Now yes, that I DO recognise as my sort of truth. And
               even when they turned against me, again and again I

143

	made a present of myself to my constituency. My word I always kept.
WHITE QUEEN	'Cuts?'
SNOW BLACK	They thought me some old battle-axe. Yes, like Boadicea. But peace in our time was preserved.
WHITE QUEEN	For those with bombs in their handbag.
SNOW BLACK	Oh yes, thanks to our nuclear Buttons, I got to the Ball. All over the world I've shared royal toasts out of silver. . . .
WHITE QUEEN	(*Kindly*) I say, Cinders, do shut up. Here comes Doctor Charles. He can cure anything. Except unhappiness . . . one's duty. . . .
SNOW BLACK	Nonsense! Work at it, Liz. All hours, like me.

FROM BEHIND SNOW BLACK, DOCTOR CHARLES APPEARS, A THER-
MOMETER IN HIS HAND. SEEING SNOW WHITE NOW QUITE BLACK,
HE GASPS. SNOW BLACK GASPS. THE THERMOMETER IS POPPED
INTO HER. SHE FAINTS.

DR CHARLES	I'm taking her temperature.
WHITE QUEEN	(*Not looking*) Which end?
DR CHARLES	The noisy one.
WHITE QUEEN	Peace, at last.
DR CHARLES	Baked beans beyond reach, I see.
WHITE QUEEN	Not that she needs them for fuel. She only created vast unemployment so that she'd have more work to do. I mean, look at her NOW. . . .
DR CHARLES	(*Reading thermometer*) Over the top.
WHITE QUEEN	Yes. Every muscle still working. Teeth being ground down like the poor, but capped. Unlike the rates used to be.
DR CHARLES	Very tiring, not listening to Luddites.
WHITE QUEEN	Surely, power need not be quite so . . . so strident. Or might we mean 'Trident'?

DR CHARLES	What shall we say when she comes round?
WHITE QUEEN	Round? The lady's not for turning.
DR CHARLES	Haven't we terminal cases the right to KNOW. Look at her face. It's as black as the ace of. . . .
WHITE QUEEN	Clubs?
DR CHARLES	Spades. After the Brixton riots, we could always export her to South Africa. They'd love a Black Queen. Say, in a Cape Town Waxworks.
WHITE QUEEN	It was the black children I always loved best. Such laughter!
DR CHARLES	A jab of plutonium, ma'am. . . ?
WHITE QUEEN	Like those rejuvenation pills you gave me all those years back?
DR CHARLES	(*Singing, loyally*) Long to reign over us!
WHITE QUEEN	Inject one, you said, like Mother Earth.
DR CHARLES	Mercy killing now seems a more enticing option, ma'am. With one fatal knock-out rocket-shaped jab, perhaps. . . .
WHITE QUEEN	A radioactive overdose? As with homeopathy, would one say!
DR CHARLES	If only Mother Earth would give the word. . . .
WHITE QUEEN	The word stronger than the sword? Who wrote, 'Whatever weapons we take up to defend ourselves will surely kill us'?
DR CHARLES	The German physician Samuel Hahnemann.
WHITE QUEEN	A German Jew? Well, well. Not for me.
DR CHARLES	Relative of yours, ma'am? How tiresome.
WHITE QUEEN	Doctor, as I always said to my husband's bag of shot grouse, since life after death is inevitable, there's surely no need for any defence against it. (*Brightening*.) That's why birds of prey don't carry guns. I always feared the nuclear industry was over-rated and under-manned.
DR CHARLES	Like sex. How strange. At last, she stirs. . . .

145

SNOW BLACK RECOVERS CONSCIOUSNESS.

SNOW BLACK	(*Weakly*) Where am I. . . ?
WHITE QUEEN	There, there. . . .
SNOW BLACK	Where, where. . . ?
WHITE QUEEN	Here, here. . . .
SNOW BLACK	Ah, everyone agrees with me. Back in business. Now listen here, you lot. I always said it was unthinkable.
WHITE QUEEN	Retirement?
SNOW BLACK	Life after the bomb. That's why THEY stockpiled warheads. Remember the Battle of Plessey? Cheap, unreliable military partners, the French. No taste.
WHITE QUEEN	Oneself they always admired. Like the Impressionists.
SNOW BLACK	Not the Spitting Image brigade? – Not those PUPPETS?
DR CHARLES	They're not even in NATO, the French.
SNOW BLACK	Yes, I blame Nelson for defeating Napoleon. So, in revenge, how the French competed. All out to overtake our nuclear capacity. . . .
DR CHARLES	To increase the chance of them NOT using their nuke bombs, erroniously?
WHITE QUEEN	One's palace vaporised. In a millisecond.
DR CHARLES	CND was wrong. The firestorm was worse, the death toll higher than their most conservative guess. We're reaping our own doomsday whirlwind. This moonscape is NOT the fault of the French.
SNOW BLACK	Whatever your morbid diagnosis, sir, THIS is NOT THE MOON. So kindly let me finish.

WHITE QUEEN BURSTS OUT LAUGHING. SNOW BLACK FROWNS. HYSTERIA IS TAMED BY THE PRIME MINISTER'S VOICE.

> No laughing matter! Ask yourself. How CAN this be the moon? There are no lunatics present.

146

WHITE QUEEN LAUGHS LOUDER. SNOW BLACK MORE HAUGHTY THAN EVER, SCOWLS.

WHITE QUEEN　　　(*Laughing*) So sorry . . . it's my . . . my famous sense of hu . . . hu . . . humour. . . !

SUDDENLY, THE TRAP OPENS INWARDS AND THE QUEEN DROPS OUT OF SIGHT, DOWN THE SHAFT OF DARKNESS. THE DOOR SNAPS CLOSED WITH A LOUD RESOUNDING CLANG.

SNOW BLACK　　　Well, at the helm, that still leaves ME. (*Picks up hand-bag*.) Queen of all we survey.

DR CHARLES BOWING, SINGS 'BA BA **BLACK** SHEEP', BADLY.

As the White Queen tumbled further down into the inner earth, the Mancunian Cat appeared on the same branch of the astral willow-tree Alice had chosen to weep upon. A comforting paw round her shoulders, the Cat whispered, 'Long ago, the King of the Underworld prophesied that a cat may look at a king but that many monarchs would continue to fall. . . .'

'Does Humphrey's surname start with a **M**?' asked Alice all in one breath. 'I m-m-miss him, stupidly.'

'Want to be 'is Mrs, chuck. . . ?'

'Mrs Who? Please, DO tell. Is Humphrey in hiding with you?'

Instead of answering, Mancunian Cat pursued more immediate matters, 'White Queen must be placed in one of the Decontamination Chambers. There, like all others, royal or commoner, she will be debriefed. That, luv, is not quite so cheeky as it sounds. See, she'll be checked for radiation. And for rabies. In reverse order. Royalty has to pay up, just like all else. Since they usually travels everywhere with empty pockets, she might not be able to proper contribute owt.'

Alice was quick to protest. 'But the White Queen has given all her life to the service of. . . .'

'Whist! Wait for Judgement, chuck,' came the curt reply. 'If she fails to produce a gift, pet, she'll not get processed proper.'

'What sort of gift? A racehorse would never fit through that trap-door.'

'Fruit,' was the Cat's only silent answer as the cat's face faded from view.

Alice feared that the White Queen, despite her late peachy complexion, would never be granted a Clearance Certificate. And that would pose another puzzle. Why had not she, Alice, been sent to a Decontamination Chamber? Surely, she also might catch radiation sickness, even in an invisible weeping willow tree.

Mancunian Cat was heard to purr. It was a real comfort to Alice that her feline friend stayed with her faithfully even as Alice, also in her astral body, watched the lurid sights below them. The boiling Thames was still curdling into waves of gold, purple, violet and blue. Warren Row had by then been transformed into a non-glossy advert for the Apocalypse, a photo opportunity sadly missed by packs of reporters and by their readers, the late silent majority.

Scene 8 – Warren Row, Exterior. Nuclear Winter night, or day?

THROUGH THE FOGS OF FALL-OUT, TWO MALES HAIL WHAT THEY TAKE TO BE THEIR SURVIVING QUEEN. SNOW BLACK, RELUCTANT TO DISENCHANT THEM, RAISES HER VOICE AN OCTAVE AND HER WHITE-GLOVED HAND EVER HIGHER. SEEN IN THE MURKY DISTANCE, THE POLICE COMMISSIONER AND THE BISHOP, CHARLES CARROLL. THE LATTER IS NOW FRANTICALLY LOOKING FOR SOMEONE, ANYONE, TO GIVE THE LAST RITES TO BEFORE HE, TOO, BECOMES REDUNDANT. APPROACHING SNOW BLACK, HE STUMBLES OVER TWO CROSSED AND BURNISHED THIGH BONES. RECOVERING THEM, HE RAISES BOTH LIKE A BLEACHED CRUCIFIX, ALL PAST PRESENT HUMAN FLESH KINDLED INTO KINGDOM COME.

BISHOP   Jesus saves, Jesus saves!

SNOW BLACK   Now Bishop, one's Welfare State should never

become some dog-eared Building Society.

COMMISSIONER (*Coughing politely*) S'cuse, ma'am. No buildings left. (*Strokes his small black but singed moustache.*) Bloody right, eh? LOOK!

SNOW BLACK Wrong. We made the rules clear. No-one with more then £300 in the bank is entitled to any State Handout, no matter how homeless. Or hopeless. Give 'em gumption.

COMMISSIONER Like us bloody now. Homeless.

SNOW BLACK Well, we did warn you to take a firmer line with those inner city rebels. Global warming will protect us all from chilblains. The same with our own dear fair weather friends. Brother Sun and Sister Moon give equal chances to one and all, sun tan or sun burn.

BISHOP (*Piously*) Even in South Africa, ma'am.

SNOW BLACK Precisely!

BISHOP Yet the Great Leveller abides by no etiquette. In all climates, fells bandit and Bishop alike. . . . (*knocks on hatch door. No answer.*) No room at the Inn? Surely not. I was appointed by you ma'am, not by the queen.

THE POLICE COMMISSIONER PRODUCES A GUN, BRANDISHES IT, MENACINGLY.

COMMISSIONER It's THEM or BLOODY US!

SNOW BLACK Charles, that's not the way to package our policy. Presentation skills. Image. Now hide all guns, do . . . and SMILE!

THE COMMISSIONER SMILES, LEERINGLY, THEN TURNS THE GUN ON SNOW BLACK HERSELF.

SNOW BLACK Revolution? This isn't froggy France, chump. Besides, I'm a devotee of Saint Francis, so why try to victimize

149

	ME? Frankly, such absurd VANITY even trying to enslave one!
BISHOP	It's your black face, Sister Francis. Sort of reflex I'd suggest, that's all.
SNOW BLACK	Then it's high time we all reconditioned ourselves at once.
COMMISSIONER	She's taken away our bloody right to our bloody lodging allowances.
BISHOP	Sir Charles Wigton has denounced that ruling. AND, may one say, all swearing.
COMMISSIONER	Don't give a monkey's what any judge says. I'm no bloody criminal, I'm a Top Nob. A cop, not a yob on a Y.O.P. scheme.
BISHOP	Look at the miners.
SNOW BLACK	The enemy within. (Points at hatch door).
COMMISSIONER	They've commandeered our nuclear bunkers. And you, Madam Margaret, also propose to abolish the death grant. I've got to fire somebody before I bloody explode. . . !
BISHOP	Not hell fire? With Jesus, my son, save your Soul.
COMMISSIONER	I can't afford to go on the dole. If I goes on strike, I'd have £16 a week deducted while the likes of you get tax-free perks and expense account lunches. Tell you, it's THEM or US!
SNOW BLACK	(*Staring steadily at his raised gun.*) I see you have the law in your hands. Well then, quite obviously, to keep you sweet, to keep you, Charles, as one of our special Boys in Blue, we must AGAIN raise your salary.

INTEREST AROUSED, THE COMMISSIONER RELAXES HIS AIM AS SNOW BLACK FORAGES IN HER HANDBAG. FROM INSIDE SHE PRODUCES HER OWN PEARL-HANDIED REVOLVER, AIMS IT AT HIM, MENACINGLY.

	Time to raise the stakes. AND your hands. Charles, we suggest you drop your bloody complaints. ALL of them!
COMMISSIONER	Mine ain't loaded. Empty! (*Strokes singed moustache with gun barrel.*)
SNOW BLACK	Neither is mine, dear. Empty. (*Strokes chin with gun-barrel.*)
BISHOP	Ah, a blessed truce!

AT THIS, THE POLICE COMMISSIONER PLACES ANOTHER BULLET IN HIS GUN. NOT TO BE OUTDONE, SNOW BLACK IMMEDIATELY FOLLOWS SUIT, LOADING HER OWN GUN WITH A SECOND BULLET.

SNOW BLACK	(*Both*) Two each. Equal!
COMMISSIONER	
BISHOP	(*Sadly*) Now BOTH will lose. Might I inspect your weapons before they proliferate? Not to niggle but . . . 'Thou shalt not kill' . . . YES?

BOTH GUNS TURNED ON THE BISHOP, HE CROSSES HIMSELF, HIS FINGERS, LEGS AND EYES.

	Have faith! I believe you won't kill. I believe (*cowering*) you both. Let's all believe . . . (*He kneels before them*).
COMMISSIONER	(*To Snow Black*) I believe you. . . !
SNOW BLACK	(*To Commissioner*) I believe you. . . !
BISHOP	Alleluia! Fearless Christian Truth United!

SNOW BLACK PUTS YET ANOTHER BULLET IN HER GUN. NOT TO BE OUTDONE, THE COMMISSIONER FOLLOWS SUIT.

BISHOP	(*Agitated*) Real Russian roulette requires that you leave one empty chamber. It discourages overkill.
COMMISSIONER	But encourages bloody accidents.

BISHOP   Like this Cold War we're in the thick of just now, sad to say. . . .

AFTER A MOMENT'S CONSIDERATION, SNOW BLACK AND THE COMMISSIONER TOGETHER PLACE NOT ONE, BUT TWO MORE BULLETS INSIDE THEIR OWN GUNS. LIKE DUALISTS BACK TO BACK, WARILY THEY PACE AWAY FROM EACH OTHER, BOTH WADING THROUGH REDDISH-GREY DUNES OF POWDERY ASH.

BISHOP   (*Praying, sinking into sand*) Dear god, dust unto dust. No good can come of this, gentle Jesus, no good. (*To them both.*) Can't you just kiss and cop out of this arms' race rather than out of the human race before it's all done and dusted? A divided house must FALL. . . .

BOTH GUNS ARE AGAIN TURNED ON THE BISHOP. HE BLESSES BOTH WITH THE RESULT, THEY AIM AT EACH OTHER.

                (*Cringing*) Pax . . . vobiscum. I'll bless the winner. I'll bury the loser. (*Conducting a countdown.*) 5 . . . 4 . . . 3 . . . 2 . . . ready for blast-off . . . FIRE!

INSTEAD OF FIRING AT EACH OTHER, AS EXPECTED, THEY BOTH FIRE SHOTS AT THE IRON HATCH WHICH BARS THEM FROM BAKED-BEANS. BOTH BULLETS RICOCHET AND BOUNCE OFF. THUS EACH GUN-HOLDER IS SHOT IN THE CHEST, BOTH FALLING INTO DUNES OF CRUMBLY DUST AND RUBBLE.

SNOW BLACK/   (*Both collapsing*) Got me. . . !
COMMISSIONER

BISHOP   Snap! Thank God GOD'S NEUTRAL, saving me to save you BOTH!

THE BISHOP KNOCKS AT THE IRON DOOR, THREE TIMES.

BISHOP I feel re-born! Eternal Welfare for all and at such a good price! Now, dear God, hear my plea. I'll live, live for Thee alone! So, open up in the name of the Lord. . . . (*No answer. He KNOCKS again.*) God, you can't have heard me, ME, your faithful servant . . . now in my hour of need. These good Souls have locked us out of the bargain basement. We need your comforting hand. Knock and all shall be answered, eh. . . ? (*Again he knocks.*)

NO REPLY FROM GOD, THE COSMOS OR FROM THE DUSTY DOOR BELOW THEM. SNOW BLACK AND THE COMMISSIONER STILL APPEAR DEAD. CHANGING TACK, THE BISHOP SNEAKS THE GUNS FROM BOTH BODIES, HIDES THE WEAPONS ON HIS PERSON. THEN, FROM SNOW BLACK, HE TAKES THE DRIPPING PEARL NECKLACE. HOLDING THESE ABOVE THE IRON HATCH HE KNOCKS. HIS HAND HURTING, HE USES ONE OF THE GUNS.

BISHOP But I come in peace, hippies! (*To himself.*) Is that the word? (*To the hatch.*) I bring peace, yuppies! I bring beads, yobbos. Plus the book of our Saviour, the Lord Jesus. (*Suddenly bursting.*) CHRIST! Let me in you buggers. It's a nuclear winter out here and I'm bloody freezing. . . !

LOUD EXPLOSION IS HEARD SHAKING ALL AROUND. AGAIN AND AGAIN, THE BISHOP BASHES THE HATCH WITH HIS BIBLE AS, IN HIS HAND, THE BOOK DISINTEGRATES, PAGE BY PAGE CARRIED AWAY ON THE WINDS OF CHANGE. WIPING TEARS AWAY WITH A LOOSE PAGE, THE BISHOP LOUDLY WEEPS.

BISHOP (*Crying*) No room . . . no room at the Berni.

SUDDENLY, THE COMMISSIONER GRABS ONE OF THE GUNS. HOLD-
ING HIS WOUNDED CHEST WITH ONE HAND, WITH THE OTHER HE
AIMS HIS GUN AT THE BISHOP'S THIRD EYE.

BISHOP   (*Trembling*) You're both bleeding. I have a bandage.
                  Yes, I was on the way to bless a new hospice. Instead
                  of cutting a ribbon to declare it open, I suggested I'd,
                  (don't shoot please), I'd cut this bandage . . . and,
                  d'you see, save us from more red tape. I hate guns. I
                  only blessed bombs not . . . how else could we have
                  won two World Wars . . . defeated godless evil?

SNOW BLACK   That bandage. Before I bleed to death. If Liz with no
                  tin-opener can get into their baked beans, I most
                  certainly deserve special entry, urgently, before they
                  enthrone her instead. Even if I have to adorn hippy
                  beads and speak in bloody Cockney slang. . . .

COMMISSIONER   Know what Bish? Make me a bloody miracle now,
                  mate, or I shoot. . . .

BISHOP   Lo! – A MIRACLE CURE! Take this bandage. Behold –
                  I hereby cut it in half. . . .

SNOW BLACK   Bags I get the better half. . . .

COMMISSIONER   But I've biggest bloody wound. . . .

SNOW BLACK   Tough titty! I have the bigger heart. Dear Bishop
                  Charles, bless ME first. . . !

THE BISHOP LOOKS SUSPICIOUS.

SNOW BLACK   Otherwise, no promotion. . . .

THE BISHOP LOOKS AUSPICIOUS.

COMMISSIONER   (*Clutching BOTH guns*) And before I eat you both for
                  breakfast . . . like bloody bangers and mash . . . I'm
                  going down in the world. . . !

*

'Why are those above ground, the surviving men that is, all called Charles?'Alice heard such thoughts in dialogue with themselves, sharing a chat-show. 'Could it simply be that they're all Charlies, those Top People? And that Commissioner's a swine? A pig with pretentions to become a pearl from the top drawer. And Snow Black pretending to be a hippy, instead of a whited sepulchre, a hypocrite. What could possibly be their gifts to our underground Survivalists?

'Two guns.'

Alice was shocked. 'Cat, we must warn the Rainbow Ravers!'

'Why?' asked Mancunian Cat, conspiratorially. 'Just bite the bullet, luv. . . .'

'Bullets? Not just one Cat, but LOTS!'

'Then what about regicide? Did the White Queen manage to produce some healthy fruit as a gift to the future? No. The nearest she came to that luv, is she dislodged a grape pip from her dentures. Passed off as fruit was that, if you please, and paraded in't Blue Dome as a right royal gift of superior preciousness!'

Mancunian Cat described how everyone who had entered below had carried with them some gift for the future. Boys carried maggots in match-boxes in case fishing was ever possible in the promised subterranean rivers and kilometre-wide lakes. Girls carried silkworms, mindful of the time their clothes would fade. Young men carried phials of their own powered sperm; pre-bomb samples preventing later contamination. The bi-sexuals carried spare pints of their own pre-bomb blood; grandparents were more inclined to carry garlic or pumpkin seeds, wheat germ or apricot kernals to tackle any unexpected cancers.

All aspects of a fruitful future were to be buried with them rather than leave any legacy of their earlier natural life to the over-paid and over-sanguine Top People. Should any one of them, that is, survive their own homespun holocaust.

'Hurry lass. Lovely procession next. You'll learn loads' purred the Cat with her usual Mancuian persuasiveness.

*

Back inside the Blue Dome, Alice watched a procession of twelve person-ages gliding along a balcony, all with silver stars attached to an extravagant hat provided by the Mad Hatter. On each headpiece there was a symbol to represent different signs of the zodiac. Each statuesque personage stepped down a spiral glass staircase that started high up near the curved roof. They re-assembled on a lower gallery, behind the embossed fretwork in amber and aquamarine of an overhanging and elegant Minstrels' Gallery.

Excited, Alice was speculating again. Was life with the Survivalists more real, she wondered, than the stoical lifestyles she had endured on stolid earth before the nuclear confusions? Often she longed to be less aware, less sensitive to the silent sufferings of others.

With a squeal of anticipation, the naked children ran off to eat their raw food snacks.

Even though Alice had seen so many do-gooders doing themselves down in the name of good deeds to others, how could she balance out the needs of others with her own budding needs? That was her perennial fascination. Would warning them against any bullets below ground turn her into a pariah, eternal optimists dismissing her fears on invasion as groundless. . . ?

Another puzzle. Just how did people before the disaster find enough satisfaction in beer and bingo, juicy gossip, spicy scandals, shaky marriages trapped in mortgages; all dependent on the muffling material-ism of paltry state benefits, all sapping personal autonomy, initiatives and pro-active energies? How come those state-imposed straight-jackets had been accepted for so long as national health-giving? And all that crushes the human Spirit unquestioned by so many sleep-walking sheep looking for their next Judas ram?

By then, Alice was set upon living by eternal principles, whatever they might turn out to be; living in the moment even, anything rather than by short-term conveniences, even if Humphrey and she had to split before they again met. She smiled at the irony of that since Humphrey, of his own volition, still remained as elusive as an elf. Was he nervous of close human contact? If so, couldn't this, also, be challenged? And by herself . . . single-handed? But what had Pitta advised? Oh yes. Never trust a lad with a runny nose or one who's never heard of a clitoris. No mention of black-heads though. Clitoris, chakra; Alice made a note to ask Humphrey to explain those mysterious words to her.

In the Blue Dome with society's self-selected rejects and their families, Alice felt more vital, more religiously REAL. At best, like a seafarer of old, she was exhilarated enough to face all weathers, to sail unknown epic oceans, the wind of change singing in her middle ear. At worst, she felt as frail as some cobweb dream-boat, a free-floating radical, a single seed adrift of wispy thistle-down rocked by restless winds. The need for an anchor made her yearn for the elusive Humphrey. Why, WHY did he keep on avoiding her? A reassessment was necessary. Let go and let God or . . . invite into her lifestyle more of unknowns, like the mysterious clitoris or chakra? Something was about to happen, something disturbing. But what? Antennae probing, tummy trembling, Alice felt her fragile self more fully present. Yet somehow not sufficiently protected; from what, she could not yet be sure – but perhaps from psychic attacks, possession, and even from Satanism itself.

'When troubled, lass, work things out for yourself first, pet.'

That advice from Mancunian Cat comforted Alice. It helped her decide to watch the astrological ceremony, without reservation, poised and prepared for her next set of revelations. Risky, maybe, but at least, adven-turous enough to arouse more excitement.

In her programme, before the Blue Dome spectacle started, she read about the likenesses between the parading personages and characters in works channelled by one known as Lewis Carroll published in the fifties by the astute occultist and writer, Joan Reveille. Their dates with 'Fate'? Yet weren't all the best insights, because of Free Will, also somehow time-less? How could the Creator of All That IS ever restrict inspirations by copyright?

The programme notes stated that Saturn's influence brings down the value of stocks and shares, and that Uranus can split stock holdings. Had

Pluto also dictated what Alice read next?

'*Every major crash this century has occurred during the same 40% of the Mars-Uranus cycle.*'

For further insights, readers were asked to share in the MON-EE MANTRA, such experiments to follow in a later workshop with the naked children. Meantime, the spectators were persuaded to relate the following proceedings to further astrological vibrations effecting the use and abuse of money as the energising oil of temporal power.

Her chin cupped in hands hoping soon for some free popcorn, esoteric theatricals began to relax Alice. In the hushed Blue Dome, the next ritual procession started.

Would Humphrey be part of the parade – and would she recognise him if he was. . . ?

First, for ARIES, came the Queen of Hearts. In blind and aimless fury, she was shouting 'Off with his head!' Such orders, like all necessary cutbacks, have a way of aggravating opposition. Being painful, they do so seem to lack compassion. 'The same,' ruminated Alice with a shudder, 'could be said of the butcher's knife in a Welsh Chernobyl lamb.'

Dolled up as a TAURUS, came the Mad Hatter, looking like Bertrand Russell. Or was it Bert Rant Russell looking like the Mad Hatter? Either way, Alice had learnt not to enjoy his sloshy dentures. Even if he did passionately wish to ban the bomb, he shouldn't spit so indiscriminately.

Thirdly came the Siamese twins, Tweedledum and Tweedledee. Or was it Tweedledee and Tweedledum? Both, relishing metaphysical fisticuffs, were representing GEMINI. As if waking up in the same dream, they yawned together, walking side by side without putting a hand in front of each other's open mouth, when so required by a good upbringing. Mirror images, when they didn't frighten her, still also fascinated Alice.

Next to appear was the Mock Turtle, more used to being under the sea, like CANCER the crab, than under the land as such. In a voice thick with sobs, he was still singing the melancholic 'Beau-ootiful soo-oop.' Snow Black was in the soup all right. Sadly, no more turtle soup for her, not on Berkshire's new nuclear beach.

The Tarot card for the Sun shows Humpty Dumpty's wall in the background so, for LEO, who else other than that superior egghead, the boss of E.M.B.E.R.S. himself? Or his representative since his eggshell seemed to be without cracks. That of itself was unlikely following a fall, let alone after hitting the addled earth after a nuclear explosion, all the Queen's horses and all the Queen's corgies obliterated into ghosts. . . .

Meticulously clean and neat, his star sign well polished, without his partner Pitta but representing VIRGO, White Rabbit came next. Though jumpy with over-anxious wishes to be more kind and useful all round, this Caribbean helper was obviously NOT the power behind Humpty Dumpty's high dudgeon and throne. Too anxious. In fact, so anxious was this Virgoan to be seen by everyone as conscientious, he kept bumping into the portly egghead strutting ahead of him. It was as if that twitchy bunny was blind. 'Obviously needs to eat more organic CARROTS,' observed Alice.

Next, representing Monarchy, the King of Hearts, the opposite sign to that of his Queen born under Aries. As a calm LIBRAN, he preferred to pardon even the most explosive expletives of the Queen's manic croquet-players. As far as criminals were concerned, balance for him meant 'Sentence first, verdict afterwards'. In contrast with his wife, a sweet and reasonable personage.

Alice and crowd then watched Jabberwock waffle and wiffle down the crystal-silver staircase. A double-act since the beamish boy, with the flashing eyes of a killer, pursued the Jabberwock, hot on his victim's heels. That irresistible combination of villain and hero was typical, of course, of sexy SCORPIO. For some reason, Alice wanted to ask that lad if he also had a clitoris.

But where was Humphrey?

Next the Gryphon. A cheery, optimistic beast, he was never to be over-shadowed by the Queen of Hearts. Half man, half animal, that is SAGIT-TARIUS, a life struggle to gain freedom from the limitations of both aspects, philosophical eyes on distant horizons. Looking for Humphrey. . . ?

The Red Queen, eyes fierce as with a governess, manner formal but not unkind, inculcating business etiquette in the name of good manners, this was CAPRICORN. A stock of very dry biscuits was kept to hand, the Red Queen ever ready to catechise and castigate impoliteness in all impostors and pretenders to the throne. Alice couldn't help saying to herself, 'Watch out, Snow Black, should you ever make it among us Survivalists, watch out for the Red Queen. . . !'

The White Knight coming next, for a split second Alice hoped it was Humphrey. She did not even know his star sign but maybe his was AQUARIUS. With his prying eyes he LOOKED as if he was inventive, a stare that showed such nerve it verged on the neurotic. Look at the way Humphrey had let her slap him. Still, even a podgy genius can be masochistic. Disappointingly, the White Knight, though a living caricature of Dean Dodgson yet to re-appear, was only the White Knight, not Humphrey in disguise. How Alice wished for even a brotherly hug, to hear him again whisper in her ear, 'We're beautiful.'

PISCES being last, desperately Alice looked to see if it was Humphrey. But no, that was the White Queen herself. Even though Humphrey might be some teenage transvestite, having already donned Alice's own dress, Alice recognized the lady in question as the royal Top Person who had recently fallen below from above ground. Ideal casting for PISCES, maybe, had given her a gentle and dreamy look in her sad wrinkled face. The White Queen, not used to being the last in any procession, seemed in a faint muddle. As if she was a middle-aged filly afraid she was on the way to the knackers yard instead of The Royal Horse Show. One, what's more, tolerated only because of public duty done to others less well orf than her benighted self and her family, all so boarded-up with good breeding. Indeed, under capitalism or under socialism, are not most subjects happy slaves? And as if assembling for some underground gathering of a newly conceived Commonwealth, the colourful characters in The Minstrels' Gallery all bowed to Pluto's apparently empty throne, a fact that the White Queen found galling beyond belief. Yet, for two minutes, lights were lowered in memory of all loved ones lost in the recent nuclear incident. In silence, they grieved for all the unseen elementals in the Fairy Kingdom despairing of mankind. They also sent love to lost Mother Nature and to those thousands of Souls hoping to be re-born on earth in order to mop up their last karmic debts before the final Silent Spring and the next Long Sleep.

In memory of the warning no-one had received in time, the silence lasted longer than planned.

That is, for four and a half minutes.

Again, Alice had an out-of-body projection, this next one worthy of much personal angst and regret. Were not her worst fears about to become realised – underground?

Scene 9 – WARREN ROW. Exterior. Nuclear night, or day

CHURCH AND STATE ARE BOTH PULLING, TUG-OF-WAR STYLE, ON THE ONLY SURVIVING BANDAGE. GETTING WEAKER, AND LIKE THE COMMISSIONER ALSO LOSING BLOOD, SNOW BLACK IS TRYING TO DECIDE WHO WILL BE THE WINNER SO THAT SHE CAN GIVE FULL SUPPORT WITHOUT HER REPUTATION BECOMING FURTHER BLACKENED.

SNOW BLACK   Oh boys, you're both so strong, so . . . so . . . Tarsonesque!

THE BISHOP LOSES HIS MITRE AND TOUPEE IN THE STRUGGLE. HE IS ALSO IN DANGER OF BEING DEFROCKED IF HE LOSES THE CONTEST. EACH MAN THINKING HE IS BEING CHEERED ON, THEIR STRUGGLE TO THE DEATH, INTENSIFIES.

SNOW BLACK   Much better behaved than the poll tax riots. So educational. I say, this is our best Baker Day yet!
COMMISSIONER (*To Snow Black*) Tie a bloody knot in it!
BISHOP   (*Inspired*) Good as done, old boy. . . !

THE BISHOP RUNS ROUND THE COMMISSIONER, PINS HIS ARMS TO HIS BACK IN A HALF NELSON, TIGHTLY KNOTS THE BANDAGE THERE.

Wasn't a Boy Scout for nothing, ma'am

161

THE COMMISSIONER IS DUMPED ON THE BUNKER'S HATCH DOOR.

SNOW BLACK   Now grab the guns before. . . .

COMMISSIONER   Too late. In my pocket. Demote me, mate? Think again, brother. I'm as good as bloody Houdini. In fact, I'm Super Human! (*The hatch opens inwards.*)

WITH TWO LOADED GUNS PC, POLICE COMMISSIONER, FALLS DOWN THE OPEN SHAFT WITH A RESOUNDING CHEER.

SNOW BLACK   (*Calling*) Quick! Tell them I'm after him. . . .

BUT THE HATCH DOOR CLOSES WITH A THUD.

I was always for arming the police. Let's hope his guns get those hippy yobs to pull their socks up. Now then chaps, where's my ambulance got to. . . ?

As if suddenly invaded by an invisible fox, the skull-shaped Blue Dome became like a hen-coop seething with urgent anxieties about survival. At a high point of rising neurosis, the descent into the underworld of PC (the ex-Police Commissioner), was only known to a few below ground, namely those Survivalists dealing with him at GCHQ, in their Decontamination Chamber.

But Alice KNEW. Ammunition and the means to use it were now in the person of that swearing policeman now sheltering below the radiation belt on earth. Also below her own worry-belt. Just what was starting to rack her conscience? Of course, PC's bullets.

But like everyone else there, PC needed sanctuary.

In the Decontamination Chamber, that dangerous stranger convinced those in charge that his police uniform was a cast-off from Oxfam. Unlikely as was this lie, so loving were those below ground that they preferred to give the benefit of the doubt to everyone alike. PC therefore had no difficulty in persuading them that it had been issued to him when he joined the homeless before the day disaster struck.

Painfully aware of his presence underground, should Alice tell all the Survivalists that PC was well armed? No, the Sensitives among them would surely know that already. Or would they? Such contradictory tensions were battling in her brain, Alice nervous of would-be mind-readers which seemed to probe every psychic shadow within the group consciousness.

In the Whispering Gallery, the broody Mediums continued to flutter over their new laid occult eggs, wondering which had psychic salmonella, which were china eggs and which, if any, fertile. Which, indeed, might hatch out helpful reliable guidance about their new arrival, the one dressed as a Police Commissioner. The Blue Dome's internal energy-shift had fatally disturbed their fragile sense of safety. Had nukes exploded, or just power stations? Had World War Three started? Or, worse still, had all future wars on earth already been ended for good, killing the barren earth itself? Even the best Psychics were wobbling on the seesaws of uncertainty.

In the Lighting Gallery below the buzzing psychics, the 12 personages representing the signs of the zodiac were preparing like a backstage cast. Each took charge of a spotlight in that star-studded orrery, all beams pointing at the three naked circles of children below. Though aware that only 5% of earth's light spectrum can be seen by the non-clairvoyant eye, they were using infra-red and laser technologies.

Pluto had already instructed all present about financial debt, money being presented as the lowest common denominator. Inwardly, they had been asked to invite into use a far more rewarding currency through the will-to-goodness in all to prevent the need for future usuries. But Alice wondered why he had not mentioned loaded guns under ground, let alone specifically warned against the gun-toting intruder, the ex-policeman. No, each child with others born under the same star sign would chant the word MON-EE as a mantra. That process, suggested Pluto, would make the most profound of sound investments, whatever the rising stars in their birth charts. Each child was therefore invited to see how the energy known as MON-EE could be spent, changed even, under the 12 astral light-beams as the children paraded through each in turn, seven times. Such a grounded spiral of aspirations would last till sound Redemption of Mon-ee had earned enough to reduce unique, individual karmic accounts.

Even as Alice produced a notebook to record what would happen to the children's voices as they processed, inner tugs were pulling her in several different directions at once. Nothing new in that. Low threshold of boredom, pro-active curiosity, restless loneliness were ever-present with her. New, yet worst of all, was the knowledge of the explosive newcomer in their midst, PC. Though unknown to the majority, an uneasy feeling had already disturbed the seismic centre of their underground group consciousness. Threats implicit in the presence of the ex-policeman felt to Alice that any consequences of such a threat would be entirely due to her keeping such a dangerous secret to herself. For how long could she – or should she – keep quiet?

Bugging her mind yet again, the soothing yet stammered inner voice of Humphrey instructed her, '*M-minding the greatest good, m-m-more important than trying to save folks from their own personal karmic debts.*'

Not convinced, despite her longing for the boy, Alice examined her conscience again. At that crossroads, she seemed to have at least four options. These first two she saw as:

(1) Stay put in the Blue Dome while she watched and learnt from SOUND MONEY MEDITATIONS, mantras serving to balance each Soul's internal Bank Manager. After all, Humphrey might show up, reveal his all to her. Or get shot. Agonised once again Alice asked herself should she warn the naked children that PC was armed with a brace of pistols?

(2) Check on Snow Black above. Would she survive her chest wounds (or the fall-out?) before the Bishop gave her the Last Rites? IF he outlived her in time. Or, might both surviving Top People show shame for their shared crimes against humanity and Mother Nature? And, as a consequence, could their fear of destruction have led to a mutual suicide pact? Could – or should – Alice therefore save them from such a fate without infringing upon their will-to-live or to die?

Interrupting Alice's decision-making process, suddenly the Blue Dome lit up. A lattice-work of colourful lights made a living hologram. Ranged around the spacious floor, bathed in the twelve laser-like beams, waited the three circles of naked children. The youngsters were swaying on their feet, entranced. Each tuned into higher dimensions in order to serve the future more fruitfully, not as a servant but as a master-in-the-making. And not for self alone but for the Corporate Citizen, for Plutonium, a city built for and by those with a far-sightedness best suited to physical survival under the earth, guided, no doubt, by earlier inhabitants from extraterrestrial cultures.

Why had Humphrey apparently not joined the others to hear Pluto's words? Perhaps, like Alice's heart, his teenage voice was breaking and shyness and acne had taken him into hibernation.

In sepulchral tones god Pluto announced, 'After the recent destruction of fail-safe nuclear systems, a less expensive way is now necessary to suit a workable future. On the Astral plane meanwhile, there is no fear of unemployment, Souls working overtime on themselves, millions having blown it to get there, prematurely. But here, underground,' he continued with a chortle like thunder, 'you Survivalists, you few hundreds now saved, you are all invited to find more creative outlets, a more positive re-deployment of all destructive urges.'

But what about PC? Would they decommission him in time? No-one was telling.

'As Pluto, I rule after finality, the points of no return. That includes nuclear power. You, in ancient Atlantis, also failed to ban the bomb. Warfare always fuelled the need for more welfare since underfed soldiers don't kill efficiently. Being Spiritual Beings, they deeply need a spiritual cause to believe in and to kill for – themselves or others.'

TWO guns? Oh God, but how many BULLETS? Alice lost count. But at what cost her miserable maths?

'Whether it is Boom before Bust, or Bust before Boom, welfare and warfare keep Souls trapped in passive and active pain respectively. Before every State Benefit was blown to bits,' intoned Pluto, 'Britain had been spending £40 billion annually on Welfare, up to one-third of the nation's budget. How much of the other two-thirds was spent on Defence of the indefensible? £30 million per annum on Military Bands, while the entire budget based on threat assessment, equalled that spent on BOTH education and on housing!' From the no longer homeless, a big cheer.

Topping their cheer, Pluto's voice regaled them further. 'The whole Civil Service numbered over 80,000 drones, with over 60 different types of honey to dole out, directly effecting over 20 million other drones. Now the whole hive has rendered itself milk-free and honey-less.'

Alice wondered how the four physicists were coping with all those ants in their microwave oven. As if Pluto knew, he continued with, 'Ants were farmers about 50 million years ago. Ant architects inherit what's left of earth because they are co-operative BUILDERS. Like you all here, below. What insects, bees, wasps, ants, destroy their nests? Only humans have earned that privilege.' He paused, allowing his ironies to filter the more slow-minded. 'Divine Spirit,' he concluded more jubilantly, 'is always economical. You children have chosen to short-circuit your Soul's last lessons in physical bodies. This now is your hour. So, out of the mouths of babes, SPEAK.'

Alice was in two minds. Dare she ask that unseen god whether or not she and Humphrey were meant to get close together in the underworlds? And if the answer was NO, would she suddenly stop loving him, especially given her lover boy's obstinate invisibility?

Just formulating such a question, then and there, Alice's THIRD possible choice clicked into place as if the most natural thing. At her personal crossroads, why not choose the third way?

(3) Find Humphrey. A MUST! And perhaps, through his guidance, put their feet on their future path together. That is, IF she could find him. Was that wish selfish, putting her own desires before the safety of others given that PC's guns were still loaded?

In her Third Ear, a whisper. *'Not over yet, our dancing duet. Not till m-me and you are fully beautiful!'* Yes, it was Humphrey's voice! Again! Watching a timid little girl wink at the timid little boy next to him, a pang of pain shot through her whole being. Alice realised just how much she was missing Humphrey. So why not leave the Blue Dome before her girlish dream began not to flourish into a really rewarding romance . . . but to fester from neglect?

Pluto's next statement helped her decide. 'Mankind's long slow fuse, resisting all reforms, gives generous time for all books to get balanced. All buttons to be pushed. However,' continued his oracle voice, 'money, like buttons without clothes, is worthless, useless on shrouds. That's why you children are naked now. Some corpses, those who contemplated their own belly-buttons throughout centuries, could only ensure personal survival by committing communal suicide. Terrified of hell after death, that's EXACTLY what they CREATE – HELL, Hell on scorched Earth, themselves as suffering salamanders writhing with cries of ugly belated searing remorse.'

Snow Black – writhing with remorse? Wasn't she glad those guns had gone down below with PC? Oh dear God, weren't guns like passive smokers, a hidden danger to all those beautiful Souls underground?

Asked Pluto, rhetorically, 'Since the paymasters are the button-moulders of society, why be amazed when secret nuclear buttons get obediently pushed? Or secrets explode in the face of their own fail-safe protectors? So, instead of money – WHAT? Go, within, you children of the future earth. Check out your own personal accounts. Seek the inner city, Soul, the true Action Resource Centre?' Then like a reveille, Pluto bugled out the one word – '**S-O-U-N-D!**'

Outer silence, inner symphonies.

'**Sound** wealth? **Sound** health? What blessings! For humans in love with god-given free will, the pulsating heart of humanity is **sound**. For Planet Earth, you are its most precious gift. So, after MON-EE, what other **Sound** symbol of exchange is called for? Find it. To raise Consciousness, to raise the roof, find the right universal healing **SOUND!**'

Before even the baby Aries group could start chanting MON-EE, Alice using their proactive untaxed energy, tried to forge her FOURTH choice into focus. But, like a lot of rich and quick minds, she'd forgotten, forgotten already what might be her fourth option. **H-E-L-P!**

Mancunian Cat, purring through her watermelon grin, lifted a paw and cuffed Alice, patting her chin four times, saying, 'Check out today's inventory of choices, chuck:

1. Invisibility. In the Blue Dome. Achieved.

2. Out-of-body projections. Astro-shamanic trips. Achieved.

3. Spirit Travel. Try next TIME TRAVEL WORKSHOP.

4. Four? Seems yer sticking point, does this one, pet!'

'Aye, does an'all,' replied Alice. Even though their communications were telepathic, Alice found herself slipping into the cat's Coronation Street accent.

'Think on. Wot's quantum physics got wot you ain't got yet?'

'I've forgot. Wot newlyweds get up to in bed, int it?'

'Aye, an' cats on a hot tin roof!' grinned her feline friend, salaciously. 'You thought the fourth choice should come before you could sleep on it, eh. Nicer sleeping on it AFTERWARDS!'

'On what?' And in case that sounded too abrupt, Alice added, 'So what IS my fourth choice, please?'

'Well luv, let it sneak up on you again.'

'You mean Humphrey?' panted Alice, she getting hotter, and not just under the collar.

'We speak of Black Holes. . . .'

'Blackheads?' Even the thought of Humphrey's blotchy acne got Alice feeling all spaced out. Like staring adoringly at the milky-way at night with eyes closed in anticipation.

'Before you practise bi-location, it might help you luv, if we speak of the two-way W, up and down. That is, W-plus and W-minus, two-way, but interchangable bosons, m-marching in step. . . .'

'TWO-way BOSOMS?' chided Alice with disguised passion. 'Bottom, chakras, clitoris and now tits. Humphrey isn't here. So can we please leave sex out of this, pussy?' Then she snapped her fingers. 'Cats!' When they fall, they land the right way up. And W? That's **M**! That's an **M**, upside down!'

'VAT 69, aye, luv. Sorta heads to tails, Tweedledee and Dum!'

'I'm not too dumb to see past and present are like upside-down twins. W and M kissing each other's finger-tips. Like magnets, really. Or see that Humphrey's past love, back from the future, can still stay around – to reclaim me. Can't help hoping!'

'Even while coming again . . . right here in yer warm lap, pet, in yer warm moist crutch, luv, all strokes and purrs. . . !'

'Really, Cat dear, I think you've got the hots for Humphrey. Not ladylike. Besides, Humphrey I think, would not like me stroking him. Perhaps we'd rather hit each other. Again.'

'Might be why he stays close to you, eh! To see if you'll duck, chuck. So, my angel, why not test it? Meet up wi' 'im on an inner journey. Out of time, you might even learn 'im some tenderness.'

A shiver shimmied through Alice.

'Aye lass, turn yer virgin ears into Dumbo's wings. Listen like a lynx. That is, if you need to meet Humphrey that bad. So now, crunch time. Do you, or do you not, want 'im that bad you could explode?'

'Kind Cat, that badLY. Good grammar, please.'

'Even if you don't fancy wot Humphrey's up to with that PC?' That last question hit her solar plexus with a thud. 'Even if he don't fancy the pants off yer?' Another thud.

'Well, not that badly, I suppose,' hesitated Alice, aloud. 'But I m-m-mean, why can't I learn to love him better first, better than ever before?'

'Then chuck, t'is time to try bi-location – OK?'

'Is that like a banana-split?'

'Bi-location is what Humphrey does an'all, see.'

'So we'll both go bananas – together?'

'Well, ready to give it a spin, chuck, beyond time and space – and bite the bullet?'

'Aye-aye, Captain CAT!' agreed Alice getting more intrigued, and yet not at all certain what she'd just agreed to with such alarming alacrity. 'Bi-location? Biting bullets. Sounds dodgy.'

Still, no pain ventured, no capital gained. Apart from that, the nuns may not have taught her what a clitoris is but in Sports in her gym-slip they had admired her doing the splits.

Surely after that, bi-location should be a pushover. . . .

'SMILE – Say CHEESE!'

'Cheshire Pride?'

'Aye, lass. You can be in't Cheshire AND Manchster at same time.

Boundrey changes makes no difference to us, pet. . . .'

'As with bi-location. . . ?'

Mancunian Cat sounded business-like. 'Do two things at once and, like, in two placs at once, see. Want to 'ave a go, chuck?'

'Like two for the price of one! So long as I'm the Shepherd, not a lamb to the slaughter. But about that PC? And about Humphrey? Worries me, still. Don't trust him. PC, that is. But maybe bi-locating will help. Will it help us spy on them both, at once, and without. . . ?'

'See, you can run, walk, kiss, fly two bodies, concurrently. . . .'

'Humphrey? Can he, will he . . . kiss both my bodies, all over me, all of my four cheeks . . . bosoms . . . the lot . . . all at the same time and. . . ?'

'All 8 cheeks, at once!' Her unseen guide playfully cuffed Alice with a paw on her bum and then was heard to purr, operatically.

Alice couldn't wait. 'Split no more hairs. I'm up and away. . . !'

CHAPTER SEVEN

ENEMY OVERHEADS. . . ?

'It's very rude of him,' she said,
'to come and spoil the fun!'

'Nay, you stay 'ere in't Blue Dome as Alice GREEN . . . ok. . . .'

'Making notes on those kids chanting MON-EE, ok dear Cat!'

'As well as, at self-same time, luv, sending off Alice GREY to see, like, the Decontamination Chamber. She'll watch over the new arrival, PC, the butch bent copper, getting 'isself strip-searched. . . .'

'Be-briefed is nicer. Let's ask Humph. Maybe they cure schizophrenics there! Is what bi-location does for us – gives flashes?' Through Alice's brain, answers quicker than lightning. Twice before she had been a split personality, both times under the occupation of the Romans. Entranced, Alice received these fleeting glimpses of past times: *'JCs. Yes, Julius. Two. JCs I loved Jesus deeply . . . but . . . refused to play follow-me. Ripped flesh . . . whiplashes, bleeding back . . . split minds. Result? An aching Soul. Then guidance. From whom some still call their Saviour, Jesus himself. As their Holy Ghost he practiced bi-location . . . before . . . after his so-called death. After too, that Mad Hatter's tea-party. No, sorry, after the Last Supper. But how now will I fly two flight-paths? Oh, I see! Soul is ALL paths at once! I am the pilot under training, Pan Airways my inter-dimensional airport. When the pilot is ready the right plane appears. But before omnipresence, first try bi-location. WHAT I HAVE DONE OTHERS WILL DO BETTER. Buddha at last got his come-uppance under a living tree, not on dead wood. But after a staged crucifixion, how else could Jesus have appeared to doubting Thomas . . . except through bi-location. . . ?*

'Aye, like dyslexia, schizophrenia, possession. Two-edged psychic swords, free gifts, but not for woolly-minded sheep. . . .'

'For bald Shepherds, then – ones without crooks?'

'Like as not, luv, On their way to OM-ni-presence.'

'Like me, Cat, when I'm feeling all beside myself. . . ?'

'First, though, practice being able to appear in't ONLY two places at same time. So, READY? Ready to steer two vehicles, two bodies at once?' Alice nodded. 'STEADY?'

'And ever-ever ready!'

'Decide to learn gnosis in action, survive all under ground tests, become like Purrsephone, Queen of the Underworld' smiled the unseen Mancunian Cat, 'one of God's extra special Secret Agents! Right?' Alice nodded. Twice. 'So fly Alice GREY and Alice GREEN – THROUGH THE LOOKING-GLASS like two. . . .'

'Two – yes, yes . . . like . . . like. . . ??'

'Two kites with one silver chord- Ready, steady, go girls, **GO!**'

ALICE GREY
Outside Decontamination Unit

Police Commissioner released. No tash. Shaved off. Why? He's regaling besotted groups of teenagers. Among them HUMPHREY. Freeze. Can he see me? Will he be pleased? Shh! PC Charles speaks: 'Whether we follow the morality of thrift or the morality of care, each choice remains accountable, has to be paid for. Does a grocer's shop only survive if too much protection money's paid up front?'
Sounds like Pluto, not him.
'But if extortion wins, the rest of world's corrupt nuclear Mafia will reap the final whirlwind their selves. . . .' *Bad grammar. Maybe PC's own thoughts, after all.* 'Then the nuclear freeze they pretended not to prefer will become their chosen frozen asset; namely, permanent nuclear winter.' *Look! Him! Humphrey – all goggle-eyed. PC's golden-eyed boy? In sunshades! He's sitting at the copper's now sandaled feet. URGH!* 'We orphans of the earth, we late homeless helpless hippies, inherit the honeypot.' *Does Humphrey KNOW? PC, a CND cop-basher . . . allowed innocent pacifist marchers to get beaten senseless?* 'Friends, we've won. If not heaven ON earth since the bomb may have banned itself by now, at least we've won the rabbit droppings of the Welfare State, their warm safe burrows as well!' *Didn't say 'bloody' once. PC's cleaned up his act all right.*

ALICE GREEN
Inside The Blue Dome

Sound investments? Can I write notes quick enough? Snapshots! Soundscapes! Sensations! Short-hand! Kids swaying in and out of multicoloured beams, light bouncing off the crystal floor, lamps above held by the 12 Planet Personages. Sound-Webs, God-Energy, inter-linking all life-forms, so said Pluto, on all planes of existence. And all at once . . . Isn't God-Money neutral? Pluto says we need it more than it needs us. But cash, unlike God, can be changed by us from neutrality, and into partiality, I say. 'Yep, many ARE somewhat partial to it!' Kids laugh. They see me now. And my joke!
Think. If not barter, then find the right agencies for honest dealings not based on dead gold standards and cold consumerism. But first, centre myselves. Leave double vision. Re-zero my GREEN half. Kids tune-up. Blue Dome filled with **M**-sound. It starts staccato, in a cleansing stutter. Mucus moves. Throats open. Each kid holds in open hands a small gift for future common wealth; a dandelion seed-head, a grain of wheat germ, varied fruits, an acorn, a free-energy invention. Pluto guides us from Alpha to Zikar. Kids to circuit 7 times through 12 light-beams, chanting throughout, letting the currencies of green Spirit change their notes and expense of energy accounts.

Humphrey besotted. Leading applause. He's so naff! 'For Survivalists, WORKFARE makes a Utopian Society with all help welcomed!' *CHEERS? They're all trusting PC.! Guess they're just being conned by him. Even Humphrey. This hurts. Yet not so much as by the fact that I might be wrong about PC. Well, I hate suspicious people. OUCH! Has PC been converted? In the Decontamination Chamber. . . ? Ask that Sister who nursed me. Bet Pluto's voice was on tannoy there. Bet PC pinched Pluto's words to show those teenage twits he's really a goodie now. If Humphry falls into PC's arms instead of mine, what then. . . ? Warn him the cop can fire him, shoot . . . kill . . . murder him . . . me. . . !* 'And free education, friends? Looks generous on paper. At first. But it's based on state law; i.e. on coercion. This can kill initiative in all but the low criminal classes.' *GOT IT! Where PC's learnt his con tricks. From posh crooks.* 'While your dear parents fretted over mortgages, they're more upset over mags what teach better mating skills than by TV what teaches how to commit violent bloody GBH, murders, rapes and the like!'
BLOODY? So PC HAS written his speech not the pope! Out of the mouths of saints, sinners, crooks or cops, adult lies all taste YUK! They must see that PC's a two-faced conman. . . .

New images ready to master Money, Matter, Space and Time, change the world's cash-tills with love. Cogs of naked kids. 3 cosmic clocks circling, will sing the MON-EE mantra, all under each star-sign in turn. 12 lamps for the 12 signs of the zodiac suffuse the floor with different coloured beams. First light for ARIES hits the crystal floor in a blaze of sparky bouncing raindrops, drenching its slice of the Blue Dome. Now the central floor, a revolving stage, spins under the kids' nimble feet, as three cogs of bodies, step clockwise under each star-lamp through to **Pisces**. Are pennies from heaven too pure to keep as a concept, or too soiled for old Souls to buy into? LISTEN!

ARIES:

Keen kids croon MON-EE under the red beam of the Queen of Hearts. Curt wee rams make MON-EE sound like MAG-EE, on a wet Monday Market Day. Poor little ewes morph into Marie Antionettes, then bleed black economy to death with cruel cuts. Worthy privatized patisseries stockpiled with piles of dough, upwardly mobile, making a self-raising future for fancy cakes with double thick cream fillings, all teeth capped with gold, all loud bossy-boots fiddling their figures, pound for pound. Also their fat Corporation Tax!

PC stroking his top lip. Looks softer than while up on earth. No, still don't trust him. See what he DOES, not just what he rants using fancy words. . . . 'I say let us balance all our group energies, each as a reliable self-monitoring barometer. . . .' *He's vanished! Must of blinked. Or has he too split like a banana? Panic!* **Humphrey?** *Where you both gone to? What if he saw me? Cop and kid, if you're kosher karma, you win me over now!* 'Thanks for hearing me out, lads. Balance of power, men? It bred a dependable balance of loot in the bank, not bread in folks' bellies. So, see, this balance, it always favours them what have power, using force against the unforgiving Divine Will.' *Nods all round. This cop's a fake, trading on old one-party tricks. Decided. Not playing. Not while . . . Wow, can PC see me? So what. . . ?* **(PC's reference to mon-ee rings till-bells. Unseen eyes flick over to ALICE GREEN.)** *I and me watching all. Blue Dome kids noted. By my other half. Kid crooners on the way to CAPRI-CORN, like born-again capitalist Happy-Clappers. Can't see Humphrey.* **CLICK! (Channel switch! Back with ALICE GREY.)** *Why? What next?* 'We're still beautiful!' *My heart leaps. Good, on cue! Where are you now,* **Humph**?

TAURUS:

Spitting Mad Hatter dampens down inflation at the expense of sound MON-EE as if, despite market pressures, cattle cake must wait for bargain prices. By 4th time around under bovine management, **mon-ee** can't bulldoze deals into regular wage packets, taking stock of all lose change by bedding down with billions. Dairy farmers sell no air, yet come their last breath, rich cremating stock-holders will die for more **mon-ee** to burn. Some bank on fossil fuels' foul profits, and military arms, sold as smiling alms, keen to earth all practical comforts.

GEMINI:

MON-EE sounds doubly mean-minded and generous in turns with twins Tweeldedee and Dum both likely to borrow each other's socks and shares from a joint account; these are sold on at a profit to less deserving poor vicars. Some cheeky kids inflate, till all chant 'Double yer **mon-ee**.' Commerce and breath control, double dealing, two sides of every coin; over-spending on hot air as if folks are all free floaters with free capital reserves, no purse-strings attached. Mercurial **mon-ee** soars, making all sales talk for marketing, gilt-edged dreams. Twins won't die broke but more like restless airhead Bingo Callers – at the Ritz!

'**Here. Within.**' *HIM! Cross my legs. Can I keep Humphrey now, my silly secret self, all safe?* '**Nowhere to go but everywhere, Alice Grey.**' *Oh, he also knows my alias. I feel naked.* '**You've met my M-m-Mancunian Cat!**' *HIS PET! His familiar? So, can my Boy Witch and magic Cat, fly us all to Master M. . . ?*' **(CLICK off!)** *What earthly use is Humphry to me with no body present to play with? And especially a birthday-suit present! Won't give up though. Please God, let him soon lie in my lap like Kitty as I dream of a picnic rug on green earth. Near my next home, let me hear him purr like Kitty, even if I do rescue all her timid mice and let them go. Listen! All God's giddy planets purring on their own pitch. Humph, where are you –* **VENUS**? '**Astral**' *Blackheads there, too?* '**Past-future toys, gismos. Artists, inventors in pink specs. Ah,** FOUND IT**. . . !**' *Not dark glasses?* '**No, Lot's Hall and these vast healing Museums. My inspiration. Wait while I find what I'm looking for, Alice.**' *I'm HERE, Humphrey!* '**Not ALL of you, eh? On earth we're never complete. So be patient.**' *So be DOCTOR then. Let's play patient and . . .* **(CLICK!)** *Oh, phooey! Gone. Again. And before he could count on my panting pulse . . . SHAME!*

CANCER:

MON-EE sounds like MOON-EE, loyal gamblers lamenting the loss of lunatic loans. As their interest wanes, debts wax fat, expenses reaching the sort of crescendos heard in Requiem Masses for the Mafia. I see Noah's Ark top-heavy with hoarded barrels of nuclear waste sinking fast, despite Greenpeace, for whom MON-EE never grew on evergreen trees. Hear sinking oil-tankers crushing the last sentimental Mock Turtle, his faithful tears generous to a fault, locked up with liquid assets in a crab-shell strong-box, unwilling to splash out till shelling out on profitable dreamy moon water.

LEO:

Under the effects of portly Humpty Dumpty's beaming patronage, singers are losing their notes. Roaring through six rounds of costly expenses, MON-EE sounds like **many**; also flush, as in spending a penny in **many** mansions. The wages of sin – loadsamoney – take the lion's share, sums left to sunshine cubs. Not even sulky family pride curbs Big Spenders' over-loud gifts of generosity, giving many to all prodigal golden spendthrifts. King Leo, in the business of looking his best, in the main, fears he can't buy homage and after all his bluster, fears his fake crown's still sadly hollow.

Heart-shaped stethoscope falls at my feet! From HUMPHREY? A proposal? Knees knocking, eyes front, stay stern, keep steady. Yes, there's my scowl in his dark-glasses. WOW! He appears – what for? For me? **'Got it, Alice!'** *But not me. I deepen my frown. Me in charge. God, we're touching! He's warm as burnt toast.* **'A Blueprint! A m-m-modern Medieval head-piece!'** *It's a spitting image of a hat in the Cave of Costumes. So, keep it from the Mad Hatter. He spits enough as it is! Oops! Suddenly! Holding my left hand. Squeezing. Is he* REAL. . . *? Eardrums beating, eyelashes dancing, kneecaps melting, my scolding frown, it feels so fake. Oh, squinting at my budding tits, he is too! Tighten frown. No more fidgets. Oh, so close. His blackheads winking at me!* **'In the Middle Ages, lady's left hand was bound. With a ring coined by Alchemists.'** *Oh, no more horrid re-plays. . . ?* **'Gold blocks all good flows, Alice.'** *All this, yet he kisses the sods PC would march over.* **'So don't wed. Get energies balanced. Listen, hear. Let mon-ee get balanced like karma.'** *Escape? to Alice Green? No. he'll boast I want him to chase me, gawky lads watching, learning how to play it on their first date. PC's a card, stuck in M-monopoly not Happy Families. But I'm game, boy! Bet Humph won't play. . . .*

VIRGO:

Chanting, as if short of the readies. Sounding skinflint. After **Leos'** inflated gifts, cut-backs on deposits of breath, kids conscientious as little treasures; Civil Servants, at the Treasury. Honest, hating waste, they lend **minn-y** in neat piles, too small to boost reflation, risking no flutter. They bank on reserves, on currencies high on interest. Rich in finesse, far too posh to try football-pools. Swelling lungs like silk purses, they sound lonely but reasonable, handling no begging-bowls. If fasting and you need fast food, they will serve you up a feast.

LIBRA:

The dole not boosted under Tory King of Hearts, despite their picnic trade, BlueRinse Hampers', and labour-saving plans – i.e. unemployment. No handouts to tramps. Caution tightens idle tonsils. Highest voices rise up salary scales. Coughers, coffers too, get uncongested by using a well-balanced expenditure of breath, I hear **mon-ger**, as in fish merchants, angling for fair trade; free gifts as bait, donations being more restful. Sense shareholders say yes, then no to a sensible merger, having sought best advice in the bank, from the cleaners. Those born expecting the best also look a 100 dollars.

He bows, on my head places a blue dunce's cap. **'Good fit'** *boasts he. A blue fit? Just what I feel like having right now! So cuddly, yet distant even when close. My cone-shaped cap, I see it, in his dark-glasses. Me, a* DUNCE? *Take it off! Titters from gawping yobs.* 'Knock 'er off!' *they shout as Humphry whispers,* '**D** *for* **D***ivine!' A cherub's smile and his plump hands arrange the tall cap's tassel down my spine, he touching my . . . oops! Tingles. Nice, though. What next. . . ?* **'7 chakras. Barometer for both Alice's' 7 busy body's power cogs. Yep, all plug-holes need self-discipline. . . .'** *Chakras? Power cogs? PC speak? But PC's a cop not a church canon. Loaded. Not just with MON-EE. Bet PC's a Capricorn. And plug-holes? Who does he think he is – a plumber's mate? Best I don't blow a fuse. Or ask him what a clitoris is. If he's so shy, HE might blow a fuse without me . . .* WHERE. . . ? *Deflowered? Nuns said we'd lose our bloom if . . . Still, he doesn't smell like compost, more like soft moss.* **M** *for Merlin? His eyes now hoover my spine. Oh, I'm leaking. Will HE know why? Mustn't cry too, not while trembling. Can't see if his eyes ARE a golden honey hue. Phooey!*

SCORPIO:

Pluto says Scorpio effects nuclear power, fuels eagles to fly above the snow-line free from all mints and meltdowns. Or they pluck out their own guts. To put safety first (for US not THEM), **boom and bust** means big bucks. On EE of **mon-EE**, voices rise like gilt-edged wings seeking alliance with the sun, that huge nuke fusion furnace, our pulsating exchequer funding all life. In frequent depressions, prices pitched too high, enterprise stretched to giddy limits, not nice to hear in naked nuclear orphans. In 1930 cash-flows, the capital Hitler Youth Choir must have sounded like this, pricey. Hearts like Fort Knox, their booty stays locked up like deep-sea liquid assets. Over taxed, they sound out golden verses on abolishing all local exports, all polluting food miles. In business, driving hard bargains, they're experts at keeping up their interest, even in bed, spent energy sounding extravagant. Girl fans of Pluto not to over-power the shy boys, purr like kittens, saving on air till shrieking **mon-EE** with out-bursts of unexpectedly cool generosity. The boys, their reserves secretly intact, hold in, and bank on, an over-heated horror of all forms of outer extravagances.

'Cap's chord, here, shows us bio-feedback at each chakra. Thus each Survivalist can become his. . . .' *HER!* 'All can read their own vibe-meter.' *Me? Haven't got eyes at the back of my head. So there!* 'Have.' *Haven't!* 'All teachers have. Yep, we're all teachers. So use 'em, Al; read yourself from top to bottom.' *BOTTOM! His hand. Yep! Just brushed my . . . Wow! Stop quivering. . . .* 'Notice the cap's peak, like a pyramid. Its top crystal is a transformer of cosmic Light and Sound flowing through the crown charka. It opens up the Third Eye at the centre of your brow. . . .' *Face me so I can count all your blinking blackheads. How else to stop my horrid hot flushes from boiling over, his fingers probing my spine. . . ?* 'Intuition comes next, going down . . . going down. . . .' *Like a lift? Wonder what he'll ask to buy in my bargain basement. But can't protest. Frog stuck in my throat. Maybe a prince!* 'In throat, block shown here! So prevent all ills before sick Mind boxes you in.' *In bed?* 'Orange memories lasso the human heart.' *Piss off, boy, or sing me a soppy love song, so I can puke up in private! Don't mean it. Unfortunately.* '5 lower bodies fizzing! So be my D-Cap model, Al!' *Repay me in hot kisses?* 'Maybe, Al!'

SAGITTARIUS:

They pay for all challenges, well afforded but, in spouting new-minted truths, they risk optimistic overdrafts. Betting MON-EE flows into a chorus of curlicues and over-tones. . . . Speculations spin more than heads and tails, sounding like MONK-EE. Impatient, direct and honest door-to-door sales-men, quick foot in the door, the other in their mouths, often too late. As if bankrupt, MONKEE'S tight, on account of air being exhausted. So, high rises get curbed, then fall flat broke, curious big noses for bargains bruised. Next deal excites them most!

CAPRICORN:

Thrusting ambitions make MON-EE sound like music is worth $1,000 a minim, if a crotchet never quavers. Red Queen goes deeply into red, loses face like Snow White in the black, all 'borrowed' nine crowns and 23 Windsor tiaras as unsafe as a backstreet pawnbroker, the queen the scapegoat for the Maunday Thursday poor. 7th round, **money** harmonizes all currencies into the higher octaves of human dealings at top income levels. High value they aim to gain, trading on the word **mon-ee**, keen to be seen working on the most classy, high-powered poker-faced sales team ever heard.

'GIVE 'ER ONE, MATE!' *Yobs! Humph blushing Astral Pink. Fingers his nose, facing me. PC's lads drool.* **'7 chakras act as flute holes, serve all tunes. Like perfect pitch, perfect health's one clear endless note, music the first language of love.'** *Lads take notes as if he's a Prof, finger hiding his star cluster of blackheads. What's behind his shady specs? M-memo. Don't stare at him like a fish.* **'Every chakra gets balanced. 2-way flows see on D-cap's seven pigtail dials, SOUND the Master Key. Let Souls sing pure songs above the five lower psychic octaves. Natural laws always follow the Spiritual.'** *The clever sod glows, smiles at last. D-Cap? Does* **D** *stand for me, as in his My Old* **D**uck*? NEVER! He's too plump. So off-putting when he's too cocky. God now, NOW, beaming me his best sizzler! Seriously, Humph, how do we pay up for our* **D**-Caps*? Monopoly* **MON-EE***? LAUGHTER! BULLSEYE! Just heard Pluto chuckle! Tell ALICE GREEN! But what in the world did I say?* **'See, Alice, God's Greatest Good needs us all as equal partners. This D-cap's for self-monitoring, helping life on all its precious sacred levels.'** *And I thought I was smug. Maybe we're a good m-match, after all. . . !*

AQUARIUS:

With this Sun Sign's magic, kids devalue MON-EE as an ideal yet still sound rich. By all means of accounting, music and maths are good for breathless outpourings soon boosting universal goodwill, while rude boys shout, 'up, uranus!' On their 5th circuit intuition, the finest psychic gift rises. Over new interest rates few rebel. By 7th and last round, boys back in platonic embraces, even with girls. Feel my pen is writing, not me, automatically. Will I understand my scrawl later? White Knight's coinage is uranium. SOS! Its radioactive metallic chemical's found in large corporations, and in small combinations. Look at the White Knight holding the lamp of AQUARIUS! Makes me think he is wearing illegal uranium combinations under his conventional armour. His corporation's big enough. After a free market crash under CAPRICORN, with its huge pockets of poverty, competition gives way to joyful co-operation as song and singers become sound in wind and limb; these inventive universally curious brothers and sisters of our over means-tested Nu-Age suspicious of **mon-ee** madness. Friendly prompt payers, credit cards often seen as less ideal debt.

PC's certainly not full of wise words like Pluto. See, Humph on his knees beneath towering PC in full flow. Yobs and snobs lap up his words like nectar. Want to buzz off from his tricky-sticky Venus fly-trap. Who wants my challenging insights? M-maybe, just maybe that far off donnish Oxford cleric I dream of so often. If so, what else might the ox of logic need to marry the Sacred Cow of intuition? Of course, ME! First, collect more good and bad experiences! Hope Humph's one of 'em! A good baddie? Or better, a bad goodie! Clouds of unknowing! Worse! I'm in a pea-souper without a map! See through your shades and toy hero, PC's a shallow show-off. Must go! What did you call it, Humph? **'Our carousel of karma.'** *So jump off, you jerk! Kick-start our future before it flies past us!' Oops Al, too pushy. Yet he also told me about weather control. Yep, and 32 steps to Self-Realization. But not how. Wonder if **M** guides us.* **'Only if we ask.'** *Better try asking. Best of all, find mysterious **M** . . . We all need protection . . . from our fears of death. Show us how to avoid leaking poisons from nuclear power stations and the like. Is THAT what Alice Green and I are being trained for, like spying? Must catch her up and ask. . . .*

PISCES:

Into a Black Hole, the kids' pocket-money falls further into the enchanting black, burps coming from lungs and rumbling tummies. MON-EE'S swallowed wholesale, like junk food; enzymes killed. World poverty is the biggest backlog of debts in history. Like bloated tiddlers, our small fry sink to the bottom of the goldfish pond, too lazy to sing for their supper. Outpourings of compassion help, municipal swimming-pools drowning apathy. Now MON-EE boosts faint-hearts with uppers and downers as with stocks and shares, the whole unhealthy business based on drugs to aid inner city illness. Kids now sound drunk, doctors suicidal, their patients as poisoned salmon, unable to leap with a love of life. Deprived of earning, they become deprived of learning. All the aches of unhappy humanity seem inept. Only proactive contributions, not punishing taxation, awaken the doped and duped dodos. Too much Welfare? Few kids work milk-rounds, no longer suckled by shrinking udders of the Socialist cow chewing homeless cardboard-boxes, re-cycling spent consumers' inner riches for sharing in all ways. Divine charity now sounds the truest wealth!

Agreeing on a merger, Alice **Grey** and Alice **Green** got their heads together again. They compared, as it were, bank notes. Such sketchy scribbles were difficult to decode. So, pulling themselves together more closely, they debated the issues.

To expand one's own good fortune, both interior and exterior, they decided, first it's best to expand the imagination. Unemployed imagination, like a muscle under-exercised, gets flabby. Investing in sound imaging, like breathing more deeply, can revitalise the health and wealth-making agencies in human l/earners, in all who love all of life's necessary expences of energy.

Having completed seven circuits through the zodiac, the children embraced. All present improvised a spontaneous choral oration. Yes, as if it was already composed, all voices harmonised, children and adults all chanting in celebration:

CHILDREN   Karma can create. . . .

ADULTS   And karma can kill. . . .

CHILDREN   It can kill . . . but only until. . . .

ADULTS   It can again create. . . .

ALL   (*together*) Us all. . . .

MALES   (*together*) He. . . .

FEMALES   (*together*) She. . . .

ALL   (*together*) All apes and Angels before the Fall. . . .

ADULTS   Then as men and women, again, and then again. . . .

CHILDREN   Who when ready, need never visit earth again. . . .

ADULTS   Uncoupled we're each free to fly . . . Two birds from one egg aiming high. . . .

ALL   (*together*) No longer constrained, All Souls' love unchained . . . Like every wing can widen the sky. . . .

So what had Alice learned? That small investments of belief, for a mere song, can be rewarded with the most bountiful wisdom teachings. That memories, like films, can be turned into stills, pictures caught in freeze frames. A chilly reminder to stay active and in flow. . . .

Alice also remembered that LET'S PRETEND games are some of her best pastimes. So, in Monopoly for instance, she usually wins more office-blocks, hotels and make-believe money than other players. 'When I'm next grown-up,' she ruminated, 'I'll be on the make. Imagination MAKES. If LOVE is the main means, I'll make myself into a billionaire of love! Humph can be my toy-boy!'

'*We're beautiful!*'

'Humphrey, stop bugging me, cloth ears! I didn't . . . I don't . . . I do . . . oh shut up, and piss off!'

'*Keep love on a seesaw, chuck, an' you'll up-chuck. . . !*'

'Whose side are you on, Mancunian Cat – Humphrey's! So how can I trust you? Either of you. So says both Alice Grey and Alice Green, so now you two, double PISS OFF!'

Who was left to trust?

Feeling like an over-dressed untouchable, Alice identified with the deprived-looking 'wallflowers'. Like houseplants left behind on a family holiday, such clumps of kids were wilting there, unattended, not joining in any of the activities. Alice, using the royal 'we' to celebrate their first bout of bi-location, asked themselves this: 'How can we help those up against the wall...? Surely the right to EARN is more important than even the right to WORK: meaning, I suppose, that WORKFARE must be better than blan-ket Welfare? Welfare saves faces but the eyes are blank and listless. WORKFARE saves money but eyes shine with the pride of earning one's own keep, of contributing to the whole community at large. . . .'

Such ruminations obviously led to concern for the suffering Snow Black and the Bishop so near to death above ground. Save them for the Survivalists? Snow Black's earnings by then were useless, of course. As a life-support system money is, after all, more **M** for Mammon than **M** for Messiah. But it's also the breath of life for those, like Snow Black, on the pay-role of a global tobacco company. Money the root of all evil? Mother Nature's Tree of Life to stay healthy, the roots and the branches need to become perfectly balanced. So with Snow Black, the Prime Minister. So why shouldn't Alice persuade the Survivalists to let her into their inner sanctum, give her the chance to change . . . like that other queen of all she surveys. . . ?

Three smokers pointed out that smoking only 20 cigarettes per year can ruin the equivalent of 26 trees, annually. But what if there were no available leaves left to smoke? That counter argument, Alice was determined to defy. Hope, like a human ghost, must always hover around surely, hardly to be seen. Like Humphrey's bum fluff?

What was next mentioned had the hairs on the nape of her neck standing up on end. Suggested a white witch; 'Of itself, dear, human hair can be used to clean-up super-tanker spillages and save beaches and birds from black tides of crude oil-slicks.' No-one believed her.

Another daydreamer lounging against the wall in a caftan, suggested something even more epic. Hardly audible, pockmarked with tattoos, this girl suggested radio-active poisons need not harm those who protect themselves in advance against it. How? By using crystal-bright lazer-beams.

Two choices: Save Snow Black and her self-appointed Bishop . . . or . . . leave them to their inevitable fate, bar them from underground shelter. Yes or no? Such a decision should surely be reached, democratically.

While votes got counted, Alice wrote in her diary her concluding thoughts on her out-of-body flights that day. What by-line might suit? No, all that came to her was Humphrey's dazzling smile. Even the memory of it gave her jet-lag. She pictured herself stroking his dimples with breathless tenderness, until his smiling podgy face crumpled into a fierce frown. How could she feel less jaded and rejected? Surely not by meeting him again face to face, no matter how briefly . . . or how spotty.

Time to remove her own light from under the bushel. Alice decided to reveal herself like a bare sapling, like a delicate silver birch in the middle of a mixed deciduous wood of clothed adults refusing, it seemed, to acknowledge her presence. So Alice, at last, will shed her own leaves and reveal to all present, bit by bit, her whole naked body.

Undressed to the floor, hiding nothing of her true naked self, she announced, 'Whatever the eventual profit and loss of all lifetimes, money's only window-dressing. Like clothes, of passing interest, a matter more for Caesar than for God.' Thinking of Humphrey helped her to become more lucid and fluent. 'Friends, in this vast cosmic oratorio of God's own score . . . MON-EE, like tree leaves in a winter breeze, are but a handful of fluttering, airborne notes. Friends, I wish to find the First Word, the golden key, the missing link, the inter-connecting currency, the Lost Chord, the ghost in the machine, all that's eternal and imperishable, with or without the help of you all. Any takers? And givers? Who will join me in this most sacred search? WHO. . . ?'

In the dome ceiling, a hidden hatch door opened wide.

Hundreds of blue dunce's caps floated down towards the assorted and grateful hands reaching upwards to catch them. The excitement of it made Alice want to spend a penny. No, of course not. Old fashioned use of mon-ee might soon become outlawed.

Well pleased, Pluto still not seen by most folks, started to leave the Blue Dome. His departing message was delivered as dunces' hats were being placed on children and adults alike, a sparkling crystal on top of each pyramid-like cone catching the light.

Walking backwards, Pluto's sepulchral voice intoned: 'One day, each grubby caterpillar, with or without the help of a Hookah pipe of peace, or the Flute of God, will spread its wings. On such fine days dull caterpillars become bright psychedelic butterflies. Till then, for those who see change as pain, the pain itself will seem permanent. . . .'

The message delivered, Alice gasped as Pluto in a whoosh of an up-draught, his body like a barely visible string-vest, got catapulted upwards and vanished through the ceiling of the Blue Dome. On his departure, the roof's hatch door closed with a resounding thud.

As one, all assembled greeted each other in their new peaked D-caps, all blessing each other. 'We're beautiful!' They all agreed. Presumably, the headpieces had been sent down by Humphrey or PC. From wherever. Oh no, not PC as well. . . ?

Alice had to agree. They were BEAUTIFUL. And so was she. And so, surely, was Humphrey, whatever he chose to do for her or for others. Or might be choose not to face her nakednss?

Suddenly, all the astral chakras started ringing like discordant alarm-bells. The children's tassels started to bleep and blink, like single tendrils hanging from weeping willow saplings before an imminent earthquake or a freak tsunami.

The grand double-door, encrusted with diamonds, opened majestically. In paraded the ex-policeman with a gang of severe-looking acolytes. In dark glasses, these included HUMPHREY!

'In future,' announced PC grimly, 'no nudity. Each must wear a purple tunic. To be issued tomorrow. Everybody, GET DRESSED!'

To punctuate his rhetorical authority, PC and Humphrey let fly a couple of bullets.

Screams and panic as Alice fumed. Why hadn't she warned them all? Afraid of not being believed again? Had she, though daring to appear naked, turned into a moral coward? Starting with her nose, Alice burst out in a rash. Blotchy blemishes spread all over her bare flesh as if it was blotting-paper, Humphrey she was afraid, watching her turning out to look like a spotted dick, her favourite pudding.

Alice quickly got dressed before Humphrey raised his dark glasses to check on her spotted shame and peer at her more clearly. Or worse, more nearly. Her hot blushes of anger and disgust at his cowboy tactics in support of PC, were further helping her to come out in livid orange goose-bumps, the prickly rash spreading all over her body like acne. Having started down the left side of her nose, were the spots symbolising her resistance to Humphrey's own blackheads? Surely not.

Before more bullets could shatter the cool of the Blue Dome, the naked children checked the digital meters at the end of the silver chords hanging down from their peaked D-caps. Yes, emotionally out of balance, their Astral Chakras were showing a high intake of FEAR. They were in debt to themselves, to each other and to the universe. Only LOVE could conquer such fears so, to balance the books, so to speak, they had to refuse to invite more fear in and, instead GIVE OUT an equal amount of LOVE. As one, this they all did. Or tried to do so before drooping back into deadly dread.

Calling out, 'DADDY!', the kids rushed towards the armed ex-policeman with shrieks of joy, as if he was Chief Cook at a Nudist Camp, one who had just yelled COME AND GET IT!

Grabbing back the second gun from Humphrey, PC brandished a brace of pistols. 'HANDS UP!' the copper shouted at the little bare bodies as they hurtled themselves towards him, all arms and smiles wide open. And again, he commanded, 'HANDS UP!'

Hearing that instruction from the stern bristle-face in front of them, they did just that; they put their hands up. They put their hands right up his tunic and tickled him all over, as others started to remove his uniform. A born Leo, he might like to growl loudly, to swank and to swagger grandly, but they'd taken a risk with that King Lionheart of earth's asphalt underworld jungle. They'd turn him over, tickle his tummy and watch to see if he rolled over and became every body's, like a playful pussy-cat.

Such unashamed recklessness in all the naked kids frightened PC more than a battalion of riotous inner city football fans.

Humphrey watched Alice. She was still dressing furtively. Dreading his disapproval, she was also watching his every eye blink, suspiciously, a bitter taste flushing through her mouth.

As the bare boys slipped off the policeman's trousers from beneath him, PC struggled to save his skin and dignity, a tiger trying not to become a tame fireside rug, especially as the lads eased off his y-fronts. Those he tried to catch before they, too, followed his trousers into a shredder. A cherubic lad unhooked the guns from both his trigger-fingers. Being debagged by little boys was bad enough, but it was the naked little girls who really got on his tits. Tunic removed, shirt unbuttoned, they soon found the bullet-wound under his vest, below his right shoulder, while soothing him with creamy finger-tips.

With a whoop of delight the Sister appeared, her second patient in two days. PC was placed on an altar, operating-tables being redundant under ground. His bottom, on making contact with the cold marble, jerked upwards. With that sudden movement a bullet shot out from his flesh but caught by a slick kid cricketer. Meantime, little girls massaged him with quick flexible fingers. A big magnetic purple plate strapped over the wound, plus dozens of warm hands with herb-scented lotions, all contributed to the healing process. All the while, the twelve planetary light-beams still played over the body of the pampered ex-Commissioner as, slowly, his aches and his angers seemed to become more soothed. Every so often, though, fearing submission was softness, PC's need for aggressive authority rallied. His self-image feeling threatened, he ordered, 'My bloody uniform. Get it! I give the orders round here.' He hadn't seen the shredder. 'Everybody, get dressed!'

'Alleluia!' bellowed Humphrey with a salute like a karate chop. 'We obey!' He also had not noticed the shredder.

'Streaking,' insisted PC, 'flashing, it's a dirty exercise, also a disturbance of the peace. . . .'

'What, STRIPPING? After dirty nukes just BURST a GUT?' So questioned one of the little lads, disgusted.

'No panic. No nukes dropped in on us' insisted Humphrey.

'But upstairs. . . .' started Alice as she wrenched on her tougher undies. Upset by Humphrey's barefaced lie and her own barefaced spotty body, she became incoherent.

'What's just dropped,' said Humphrey implacably, 'not just tougher knickers but brilliant dunces' caps. . . .'

'And quartz CRYSTALS. . . !' corrected Alice.

'And these crystals,' continued Humphrey avoiding Alice's accusing stare, 'do not corrode, erode, decay or change with time. They can't even be carbon-dated. They'll protect our auras from any radio-active leaks, from all disorientation, when recharged.'

Alice wanted to ask about Snow Black and the Bishop. The voters' verdict was what? Were they allowed down into the safety of the Survivalists? On cue, the result came through. A resounding NO. NO MORE ADMITTANCE OF REFUGEES TO UNDERGROUND SHELTERS. Alice took such sad news personally. Numbers of surplus crystals lay about the floor unclaimed like sparkling tent-pegs. Definitely, pulling them off from the D-Caps, Alice quickly collected them up. Her impulse to help those less blessed above her was burning a hole in her heart.

Soothed by the girls, the stirrings of an erection in PC's pants was spotted by the cherubic-looking lad who was already playing with one of PC's guns. 'You a poofter?' he asked the supine copper, sweetly.

'That's loaded!' grimaced the ex-Commissioner, nodding at the gun.

'So's my question,' smiled the cherub sensuously as his hands slid up and down the phallic barrel, suggestively. 'My dad was bent. He's the biggest arsenal in Europe. Worked for Nato. Bent as a boomerang. Died, of course. On picket duty. At Greenham Common. Call me Dick, Mister Misty Eyes . . . how's your cosh. . . ?'

Hypnotised by the cherub's cheek, perhaps by all four of them, PC was, for the moment, rendered speechless.

Not so Humphrey. As Alice dropped a crystal, having collected too many to handle, Humphrey offered her something to hold them in.

'What's that?' asked Alice suspiciously. She was hoping that her long hair would hide most of her spotted face from him.

'PC's y-fronts.'

'Why?'

'Because Alice, they're tougher than your knickers. Want to prove me wrong? A kiss m-m-m-m-might help. . . .'

Thinking, 'I don't want to make money, I don't want to make love, I don't even want to make conversation with a two-faced fart,' she ignored him. But not before he shot her another unforgetable smile. 'Your physical body might be blotched and horrible,' said he, hardly the Prince of Tact, 'but Al, you've got FIVE lower psychic bodies to beautify. Play with tri-location on the Time Track. Better than silly dolls. See you there, Alice. . . ?'

WHOOSH! Where? He'd gone! Through the roof. . . ! Why? Had she made Humphrey that angry? Good!

Her orange hot spots, in her unhealthy state of fevered frenzy, got hotter and hotter at the thought of following Humphrey . . . skywards . . . like an obedient Dalmatian puppy . . . in a cartoon movie. . . .

'Don't point that gun at me, Richard, or else I'll. . . .'

'Dick!' said Dick, interrupting PC. 'Looked like you, dad. Was a spy, too. What shall us call you then, smartypants – Mr Plod?'

Finding a voice rather lower than normal, the PC boomed out, 'Charles!' But having caused giggles all round, he quickly raised his voice to a more conversational tone, adding in a fake posh accent, 'Victor R. Charles, actually.'

'R for Rupert?' asked a saucer-eyed girl. 'Oh, he's so butch. . . !'

'Just like a bear!' agreed others.

On that, the naked children climbed all over him for a hug, to give comfort, to tame and to to soothe that bear with a sore chest.

Alice smarting with orange blotches, consulted the ecstatic Sister again. Yes, in the Decontamination Chamber there was a tannoy so, yes, PC could have overheard all that Pluto had said in the Blue Dome and recycled his words to entrance his young followers. Proof, surely, that PC was a shallow sham determined to convince others he was a benign and decent-minded democrat and should therefore be blindly obliged. He was just the sort of bait Alice liked tackling, to challenge her resourcefulness. Everyone underground to be dressed in purple uniforms? – no way.

Before getting too delirious, PC rallied again and in a ratty voice, shouted, 'You won't get away with this. We're surrounded. My men are out there, all on Purple Alert. Any trouble, I'll call my men. . . !'

'Oooh,can't wait, ducky!' smirked Dick, licking the tip of the gun-barrel then bending over, rubbing it between his legs.

By then not amused by such camp cavorting, Alice gingerly made her escape from the Blue Dome. With her was a bundle of nine seven-sided clear crystals. The sound of running water was magnetically drawing her further out to . . . she knew not where. . . .

Or yet indeed, WHY. But never too early to know, being just in time you're not too late for a most important date, be it with destiny, or with Fate, a fate better than rebirth...and twice as exciting! Gurgling with girlish glee, she started to dance along the bright green bank of the underground stream. . . .

CHAPTER EIGHT

TIME TRAVELLING

'Now, HERE, you see, it takes all the running YOU can do,
to stay in the same place.
If you want to get somewhere else,
you must run at least twice as fast as that!'

Outside the Blue Dome Alice followed the chuckling stream. The orange-tinted water often flowed under crystal buildings. Who built a city so magnificent as Plutonium? As she reflected on the elegance of the structures, Alice wondered if the Survivalists had designed such fine dwellings. Or maybe the vast megalithic metropolis had been discovered by them already complete. Together with hydraulic underground waterways and chambers larger than cathedrals.

Perhaps it had been built by that Super Race of beings said to reside within the hollow earth. The family au pair from Guatemala had told Alice that the world is not spherical. At both poles, apparently, it is more dough-nut-shaped, especially so at the area beyond the north polar entrance. Why else are tropical seeds, plants and trees seen floating in the fresh-water of big icebergs with multi-coloured pollen spreading for thousands of miles. . . ?

Is a Super Race hiding within? Could there be roundish unisex blobs like Plato said the first happy humans were? Had they always been awaiting mankind's self-destruction, aeon after aeon? Or were they, in fact, the dreaded Saffs so feared by the militaristic PC and his fast-growing gang as he claimed to be teaching them about all the inner mysteries of existence?

M for **M**ystic? For Alice, another insightful flash. **M**etaphysics! An open paperback. Page 142. Quickly, she added the three page numbers together. Good heavens, yes 7. On the mystical TIME TRACK, the book showed Alice that since the past and future are only reflected images, they can be changed by an act in the present. 'No wonder I feel Christmas Day should be every day! Yep, to master the present moment is to master eternity! – Like this flying book of wisdom!'

'*Do we see ourselves dying with eyes open like shutters. . . !*'

Drawn to the early days of the camera, Humphry toyed with photographic imagery. '*Negatives nesting in the mind's darkroom,*' he reckoned, '*last longer than snaps hatched out with bromide. Though Divine Spirit, of course, is necessary to develop our inner pictures. How? By travelling, not by staying still. That's what makes our own personal movies materialise. So, keep on going. When in doubt, DO. No matter what destination, don't delay. Procrastination is the thief of time, Alice!*'

TIME!

Her mind rose to higher octaves. Humphrey. Yuk! Yet, how had he risen in the air like that, through the roof of the Blue Dome, like a jet-propelled podgy penguin? Should she join him if she could? Opinions split between the earthly Alice and the Astral Alice.

Re-adjusting her 'mad-cap', she let the silver chord dangle down in front of her so that she could monitor it closely. The orange level was bleeping around her heart, no doubt in sympathy with her rash of itchy orange spots.

As if hypnotised, Alice found herself drawn further along the gurgling stream, its water as pure as fresh orange juice. She wanted to play Pooh sticks.

But what with?

'All solutions were there before they were problems,' decided she, buoyantly.

Alice threw one of her nine seven-sided crystals into the stream. It sank. She retrieved it. Could the crystals become Pooh sticks if they were purified? Eyes closed, in her imagination, she rubbed all nine seven-sided crystals, watching them. As they got brighter and lighter they grew larger. Experimentally, she squeezed her eyes shut, asked for the crystals to grow smaller.

By the time she opened her eyes, all nine crystals, hard as rocks, were larger than ever before. In fact they were almost too heavy to carry. So, as if to defy Humphrey, Alice slipped off her itchy knickers. Her long range idea was to save Snow Black and the Bishop by transplanting the nine cleansed crystals above ground to diffuse there the local fall-out. But how could she if the healing crystals were too heavy to float or to fly. . . ?

M for **M**agic or for **M**iracles! What's the difference, anyway? Wonders are always wonderful, and natural, in all ways SUPERnatural! After all, Saint Peter walked on water. And Jesus called him a Rock! How did Peter not sink like a fake photograph drowning on its own developing-tray? So Alice again launched the large crystals. To her delight and amazement, they floated. Not only did they float away but continued down the sparkling orange stream, then disappeared under the nearby golden six-sided building, a Healing Temple. And Yes! her orange spots were fading fast. 'By the time all nine crystals reach the other side of that Temple Park,' thought Alice, 'I'll find my next set of directions written on water. . . .'

To reclaim the crystals, she ran down an avenue of tall elder trees. Alice felt she was in training. But for what? As she passed by, each pair of elders spoke in arboreal unison.

'Reality's in reverse,' advised the first two elders, rustling their leaves, 'like your reflection in a looking-glass. . . .' She fancied they bobbed a curtsy and then bowed towards the next pair of trees down the line as she kept on running.

'. . . Spirit's like sparkling orange juice, ever fluid. . .' said the second pair together, bowing as Alice ran on, panting past them. . . .

'. . . mankind's a shower in sunshine, rivers choking with flotsam and jetsam. . . .'

'. . . till each dewdrop wriggles back to the promised Sea of Love and Mercy. . . .'

'. . . evaporates . . . re-turns to the end-start of all Spiritual Freedoms. . . .'

As Alice flashed by them, tree barks peeled back to reveal secrets imprinted on their trunks.

'. . . meantime – not that time is mean – disasters, droughts, deserts . . . poison the awakening path . . . harmful petrochemicals keeping vibrations too low. . . .'

'. . . until reveilles before rebirth . . . reawaken the wilderness of Earth's heart. . . .'

'. . . with springtime's siren Seed Word . . . OM!'

As both lines of elders chanted 'Ah-Oom' instead of 'Amen', Alice stopped in her tracks. She yelled against the chorus of quietly chanting trees, 'What poisoned dams can't be freed into fresh and purified crystal waterfalls. . . ?'

'Exactly!' agreed the two trees at the end of the avenue nearest to her. 'Acid tears and windowpanes clash time and time again. But the qualities of $H2_0$ stay the same whether as morning dew, iceberg, or as vapour. Resurrection? Re-birth? Conscious re-condensation!'

Suddenly, Alice found herself running backwards. Each pair of trees encouraged her as she sped towards where she had started, at the top of the avenue.

'All's a stream of dreaming waters . . . our bodies thermal bathtubs . . . as brittle as splintering icebergs. . . .'

'. . . single Souls swim in fickle waters...which each can drink or drown in. . . .'

'. . . long-lasting water remembers dinosaurs and you too, Alice, when once a dancing dodo. . . .'

'. . . each dewdrop. . .' agreed the last few trees, nodding '. . . like Soul, spiralling, explores all of its properties. . . .'

'. . . to express its full potential . . . to rise and shine. . . .'

'. . . to its own multiple levels, to the highest water tables of evolution. . . .'

'. . . through all drinkers...till three cheers, water's sweating it out, in and out of striving cross-channel swimmers. . . .'

'. . . as they brave all turbulent storms. . . .'

'. . . and go for Olympic Gold . . . on the Other Side of life!'

Alice heard Snow Black calling for a drink. Or was it the ghost of Denis? 'Isn't it painful that drought, that curse of deserts, such quantities of sand are also man-made?' Alice asked the trees.

And the elders answered, 'Drought spreads where fatalistic man is most passive. While bribed loggers count beef burgers, whole societies month after month sit, like cattle-ticks on fallen sticks, waiting for a cow to pass. . . .'

'A sacred cow, of course!' added Alice.

The chorus of elders applauded her, their leaves sounding like sea waves on a shingled beach. 'Yet if the Spirit of water can move mountains, why not rivers also? Instead of inventing fiercer and fiercer desert-making bombs and burgers, why don't you humans simply fire missiles, ballistic icebergs, from Antarctica to Ethiopia? Instead of people fighting people, why not join and together fight the biggest enemy . . . starvation . . . bring clean air and clean water and clean food to all in need. . . ?'

The images of bloated, flyblown children sucking on stones brought tears to the girl's eyes. How to get those healing crystals to the dying Prime Minister before she also perished? In her inner eye, Alice saw a black oil iceberg. As big as a petrol-station, it was perched in the centre of the Sahara Desert. As the vision melted Alice, eyes pricking with tears, ran off to greet her crystals just in time she hoped to see them float into view.

'*In and out of different bodies, Al. The best bit, that!*'

CHEEK! That was Humphrey chipping in. '*Alice, let's m-m-make more jelly babies!*'

Double CHEEK! But before Alice would slap his invisible face, a flotilla of crystals appeared in the dazzling light. They even steered themselves on the stream towards her welcoming hands.

Alice checked her meter. FEAR and ANGER were both registering. Had Alice fuelled the shared failings of mankind by giving negativity too much attention? BABIES? With bulging populations, who wants to compete with nuclear fast-breeders, with flea-ridden rabbits? Who wants to breed babies?

'*WE DO, m-m-mate!*' – Humphrey again!

Checking her dials, his last comment had made her Astral Chakra move six points into the pink. A signal, maybe. Should she ride the tide and visit above ground again . . . and fast. . . ?

With the sound of AH-OOM still resonating, her dream diary blew open. Confronting Alice, written in a strange handwriting, were the words: TO CARE, LEARN NOT TO CRY.

Outraged by such callousness, her Astral reading shot up even higher. Yet Sweden and Switzerland, for all those nuclear bunkers under their mountains, might have done the cause of world peace far more good in their state of neutrality than all the angry Easter marchers from Aldermaston. But wasn't Snow Black against such demonstrations? So, let her sit and stew!

Without closing her eyes, other images formed. Bleak mountainsides. Caves. Were they housing elderly CND marchers? No. Open mines. Alice pictured narrow-eyed workers near a petrochemical factory. They were dismantling a treeless mountain so that local poisonous fumes would not stay trapped in their own polluted environment but would, instead, be wind-driven into somebody else's backyard far away from local nostrils. . . .

'This the Nu-Age. Chambers hidden under the Sphinx. The inner room of the Great Pyramid will be opened,' sighed the chorus of trees, 'to reveal a radioactive sarcophagus.'

In her head, the number 86 kept flashing like a belisha beacon. By then, Alice felt invaded, like an ever-open dovecote being raped at every orifice by flocks of hungry hawks.

Until, that is, the nine crystals decided to soothe Alice. Basking like gleaming fish near the bank of the stream, gently rocking there, they sang to her:

'OTHER ANGEL BEINGS YOU WILL MEET
THE VEILS BETWEEN ALL WORLDS MUCH THINNER.
FURTHER FUTURE MEMORIES YOU WILL GREET
REVEAL ALL POWER SPOTS WITHIN EACH SINNER.'

Power spots? All she could think of were Humphrey's blackheads. Oh, what about the Rollright Stones? Were her crystals more use there than above with the sickened Snow Black? And before the end of the avaricious eighties? And before the predicted Wall Street crash?

The picture changed. Her dream diary closed. A Big Mountain appeared on its front cover. It showed streams of weeping children being forced to leave their ancestral homelands. The US government wanted Big Mountain. Why? For its uranium. For atomic energy. For nuclear weapons. Who will reach heaven first: imperious American Senators, or indigenous North American Indians communing with Nature Spirits, those tribes our good Christian folk once called savages? What of orphaned Snow Black, née White? She hadn't been donated one ethnic blanket, not even by Oxfam. Compassion and curiosity fighting inside her, Alice was transported to above Warren Row, on a reconnaissance trip.

Scene 10 – No-Man's-Land. Exterior. Nuclear Winter Day/Night?

SNOW BLACK GAZES AT THE STEAMING FOGGY GREY BLEAKNESS ALONE EYES GLAZED, THE LOOK OF BARELY DISGUISED INSANITY. WOUNDED, WEAK AND NEARING HER LAST GASP, SHE IS SO BADLY BARBECUED, HER FACE IS DRIPPING LIKE FRIED LICORICE, A MOSAIC OF MASCARA-LIKE PUDDLE CONGEALING AROUND HER BLISTERED FEET. IN SAND. AS SHE WRITES, USING THE WHITE QUEEN'S ABANDONED SCEPTRE AS A PEN, SHE TRACES THE WORDS, READING ALOUD TO SCORCHED TREE STUMPS:

SNOW BLACK WRITES:

And Mark, don't forget to change your socks at least once a week no matter what your wife may tell you.

Lastly, a confession.

They said that I was inflexible, that I never listen. But isn't that just like God? Isn't He sorely lacking compassion also, allowing so many wars? According to my last Bishop to defect, gods cannot decide which side to be on, even after an obvious victory. And even when alive to tell the tale. The Bishop that is, not God. Oh yes, Runcie still rankles. God and the gold standard might have declined but I still battle on.

However, dear boy, I digress.

After the French detonated their bothersome bomb (on account of some deign failure, I suspect), I was plunged into a most frightful dilemma. Whether to yield to the prevailing wind, or to change its direction with one of our own NATO warheads. Frankly, I didn't wish to let down the party, myself or history. And in that fatal last moment of lonely decision, I remembered my chum Laurens. He once said, 'OM 'unlocks all life's lessons. Press on with the OM. How can only TWO terms in office be long enough to do all there is to do? The Buddhists, he said, claim that to contemplate one's navel, chanting OM, brings far greater peace and glory than the sinking of Rainbow Warrior. Or even, unbelievably, Belgrano. Whether or not to retaliate with one of our superior nukes, it was decision time.

Still feeling guilty about PC's guns in the underworld, Alice had blocked her ears to Snow Black's 'confession'. Too much like being told what sins to admit to before mandatory Mass. It was hearing 'TIME'. On that word Alice shot back down below.

There, she checked. Yes, the nine crystals were still at her feet. And her meter showed a six-point gain. Alice needed her emotional levels to become neutral, herself unaffected. Neutral? Glancing down at her dream diary, in stylish handwriting, a new message had appeared:

To fly, first learn to glide. But had not the crystals floated already? Well, she'd relax, and trust. Or try to. But first, a sign, please. If the nine crystals were to be Snow Black's rescue remedy how could she transport them as well as her astral body to where she could most help? Ask and ye shall . . . WHOOSH! Suddenly, Alice was with Saint Peter, surfing sea water, waves leaping high above the shipwrecked Ark, way above bubbling Mount Ararat seen far below her feet. So, had earth just been cooked like a Christmas Island pudding in boiling seas?

WHOOSH! Alice watched herself sucked upwards, then floating, gliding over the glittering jewel-topped roofs of Plutonium. Overtaking Time as if there was no tomorrow, she just knew that she'd find the very PLAYshop she needed next, TIME TRAVEL! Since Time is always coming, she reckoned she was bound to jump into it somewhere, some time.

Yes Time, the destroyer of worlds, had always fascinated Alice, despite the fear of being hi-jacked by Black Holes. Such revived dark doubts had an immediate effect. She sank, dropping right back down to below the earth's crust again asking, Is it not Time and gravity make the worlds go around? Surely when God made Time, wasn't plenty of it kindly provided. . . ?

But below again, how to sustain higher levels of activity by her own volition? How safely to transport her magic crystals and her physical body to the poisoned top-soil above, save Snow Black?

M? That letter again branded itself inside her brow. Surely not **M** for **M**egatons? For **M.A.D.**, **M**utually **A**ssured **D**estruction? Then what? **M** for **M**aster? But which one? Second-hand spirituality? In the New Age Supermarkets, there were so many more self-help books . . . all forbidden fruit as far as her rigid nuns were concerned. Not that that ever concerned Alice beyond her last 'bad' confession. How unsatisfactory to be forgiven by a steaming priest the other side of the police grill, especially when invited to discuss her private 'fantasies' over fairy cakes and lemonade, her Confessor tying her in knots. Was he hoping for a boy Scout?

'*A M-M-Mirrorcle! Reflect! Let's reverse time Alice, get together one more time?*'

Yes, it was Humphrey, again not putting in an appearance. Very sneaky.

He asked did Snow Black need the nine healing crystals more than Alice needed the Time Track? She'd consult Alice Grey and Green. Instead, Humphrey butted in again. '*If you want to learn Time Travelling, you'll have to develop your Causal Body first.*'

'Find another body to invade, Humphrey, not mine,' snorted Alice. 'I'm NOT getting possessed by YOU, young pup. So bugger off!' But would he go, really do a bunk? To cleanse her turbulent mind, Alice glanced in the stream. It had become a tributary. Seven multicoloured spring waters were weaving in and out of the central current. Such springs, she'd been told, hale from the North Pole. Emerging through the stream's rippling glitter, Humphrey's face appeared. Through the stream's surface, he gargled *'Looking--glass love, Alice, m-m-y love! Good girl! Clear as crystal when polished with our own spit! Enjoy your Causal Body. Wear SAFFRON!'*

Wear orange so that Humphrey could squash her? Never! Not while he was still in the grip of that PC and his power mania . . . and, maybe secretly on the side of those legendary OMinous Saff monks in, what was, Magic Mountain, many wearing saffron robes.

'Watch this m-m-mirror stream. Let's send love-beams straight back to their hidden source. Water carries memories. Reverse light, and Time also. How else can we float in and out of our looking-glass worlds? Before flying, learn how to float. Safely. Alone. In charge. Then let's kiss and cuddle in the Flying Flute.'

That sounded uncomfortable. Squirming at his word 'cuddle', her watery image superimposed on Humphrey's beaming features, began to curdle. Both faces reflected in the stream below her gaze slowly rippled away from her. By way of au revoir, he chuckled, *'We're beautiful!'* Then he burst with rapturous laughter, bubbles popping up everywhere. That outburst made both sets of liquid features expand into further spiralling rings as both fluid faces, together in flow, weaved away down a chuckling orange-juice sluice and were swallowed wholesale out of sight.

Is Humphrey some apprentice shaman, spy, lover-boy? Some evil adolescent guru on an ego-trip? A salesman for Time Travel Dream Services? Why should he be so smitten with PC, that street wise cop with the phoney posh accent? He who commands all young recruits to wear purple. Aren't uniforms for fighting wars, for killing others of a different belief? In a state of confusion and misery, trying to stay impervious to passers-by who offered cheery help, Alice delayed her next move. Humphrey wouldn't leave her. Or was it that she wouldn't leave him? Either way, Alice felt heavy with the desire to do the right thing by Snow Black and others in need. When depressed, Alice found that GIVING, rather than asking to GET, was the quickest relief for self-imposed sniffles. Don't our enemies need our love most? Trust! She'd again go above. Yes, she'd plant the nine sacred crystals around Snow Black hoping the PM and her followers could be healed in time.

Scene 11 – No-Man's-Land. Exterior. Nuclear Midnight/day

SADLY, ALICE TIPTOES. SHE'S SAFELY PROJECTED HERSELF BUT NOT THE HEALING CRYSTALS. THEY REMAIN UNDERGROUND, HIDDEN IN HER KNICKERS, LIKE BALLAST.
WHILE ALICE LISTENS TO SNOW BLACK RANT, UNSEEN, SHE SEARCHES FOR THE LAST TRUMP. SHE REMEMBERS WHAT SOME CLAIRVOYANT HAD SAID: MATERIAL OBJECTS KNOWN AS APPORTS CAN TRAVEL THROUGH THE ETHER. THEY ARRIVE BEST THROUGH A TRUMPET. FIND ONE IN THE NEARBY SCHOOL . . . AND FAST!
FROM ITS SKELETAL TANGLE OF SEARED ORCHESTRAL INSTRU-MENTS, COULD THE LAST COOKED MUSIC DEPARTMENT PROVIDE AN OLD TRUMPET? IF THEY HAD NOT ALL MELTED INTO A SILENT BRASSY SLUDGE.
PLUCKING A PASSING GOOSE-FEATHER SINGED BUT POINTED, SNOW BLACK CONTINUES HER LETTER TO HER SON, MARK. WITH INKLESS GOOSE-QUILL DIPPED IN THE TOFFEE-HOT SAND, WITH OVER-BRIGHT, NEAR-SANE OPTIMISM, SHE SCRIBBLES, RELENT-LESSLY, MOUTHING THE WORDS AS IF TO A DYING BABY.

SNOW BLACK SCRIBBLES:

The main UN support for us over the Falklands War came from Oman. And OM, dear boy, takes me back to today's pickle. Well, remembering Laurens and his advice, down the hot-line, I gave the word. 'Don't press the button,' I pleaded, 'CHANT OM!'

Despite elocution lessons from Saatchi and Saatchi in the bunkers of our own dear Conservative Office, unlikely as it seems, they misheard. Assuming me to be inflexible in crisis, they only heard what they wanted to hear. Instead of 'button' and 'OM', they heard 'BUTTON ON BOMB' and so pushed the button for blast-

off. Thanks to me boom is here to stay. I took the decision no sane English MAN would ever dare to take. This is not the first time that failure in phonetics has accidentally sunk a battle before it's launched. But you know Mark, progress matters more than personal grandeur. Perhaps that's why I've been spared.

No longer can they blame us for their own laziness. Here Mark, here we have history. In one fell swoop unemployment has been wiped out. And let not the French try to collect all the praise. This victory is ours alone. Oh Mark . . . MARK . . . though your mother bleeds for it, you may have besmirched the family business but, dear son, the kindest healer is still time.

TIME?

Jolted back into dark passageways below, Alice stopped at the sounds of ticking clocks, talking clocks, tocking-clocks, cuckoo-clocks, striking clocks, see-through clocks, grandfather-clocks and thousands of watches of all sorts and shapes, all ticking, tocking, clicking, chiming, stopping. 'Must beat Humphrey at his own game,' thought Alice, as she opened a barrel-shaped door with the face of a sundial.

TIME TRAVELLING PLAYSHOP

She stood amazed in a cranial cave. Dozens of men, no caps on their heads, were almost too ugly to watch. Scissors lashed into fob-watches, carvers into grandfather-clocks, axes into alarm-clocks, hammers into atomic clocks, bricks into gold watches, the different weapons struck again and again at the heart of the chosen timepiece. She averted her eyes, covered her ears.

Curious as ever, Alice immediately uncovered her eyes.

Murderous faces were mercilessly mutilating a range of time-pieces. All the men's features were grotesquely disfigured. One man in a butcher's uniform bespattered with oil was attacking a Mayan calendar-clock with a steel machete as if there was no tomorrow, or no safe year ahead for mankind after 2012.

Some were twisting the arms off clocks as if to make them scream. Others were wrenching the pendulums off antique mantelpiece timepieces, garrotting clocks until their springy innards were smashed into quiescence.

Glass clocks got gutted, cogs and wheels, spindles and other bits flying all over the workshop area as if the men were so many psychopathic poachers plucking chickens as they clucked, such fowl alarmingly late for the Christmas market in a callous cacophony of mechanical murder.

Mildly smiling throughout was an Indian gentleman in a white turban. 'Velcome, Miss Alice,' said he with a gracious double-handed bow as an extra heavy pendulum hit the floor an inch from his open sandal. 'These fellows,' explained the Sikh, 'they not so much killing time. . . .'

'Could of kidded me!' said Alice, adopting brave-sounding slang. To hide her discomfort she chewed imaginary gum, like a holy cow before clumsy slaughter at the hands of heartless infidels.

'No, no, no, no, no!'

'No, no, no, no, no?' responded Alice, catching his Indian intonations. And that despite the fact that he sounded clever enough to be from the late city of Oxford, successfully lecturing even bullish criminals on the blessings bestowed by Sat Nam.

'Permit me to tell you, child. These brisk fellows are doing time.'

'Sure, man,' agreed Alice as if gnawing indestructible gum. Such pretence she hoped would make her look tough enough to cow even a hungry herd of abattoir butchers. Indeed, she was being confronted by grunting ranks of brutal-looking bruisers, all smashing things, all gnashing their teeth, each one wishing her brave smile to shine just on him alone.

Under their collective and unprotected pug noses, a shiny glass clock suddenly shattered into a thousand splinters.

Bowing, Alice and the Indian withdrew behind a silk curtain as flimsy as any sparkling Karachi sari.

Though safe from prisoners' tormented eyes, clock-breaking bashing still failed to shatter the Indian's over-polished courtesy.

'To lock up violent men no good. Like Gary Gilmore, these fellows murdered in their previous lives. Now they vish to do time in own chosen vay. Some like to electrocute themselves on high voltage clocks. Time, they say, an illusion. Like murder. Like suicide, passing trade. Yet accountable. In this vay no permanent harm done to dharma. They now balance out karmas . . . meditating.'

Alice nodding, glad to show she could contribute, offered 'Something to do with OM, eh?'

The Sikh closed his eyes and placed both hands on his upright Dickensian desk. Poised like two hairy tarantulas, where might they jump to next? Or herself for that matter? Relaxing her mind, Alice asked to float astrally. Like a pink kite over the blighted English shires, she hoped to find the Last Trump. Her dearest wish was to practise teleportation. Psychically to send the nine large crystals to above ground and, surrounding Snow Black, plant them in the sterile earth to neutralise the effects of fall-out.

But first Alice needed to know which way to go for the two-way Time Track. She was still wondering if Time really started with the Big Bang.

And bang, she was out of body, back above the earth again!

Scene 12-Warren Row. Exterior. Nuclear Winter Midnight/Midday?

AS IN SOME SAHARA SWANSONG, THE LAST TOP LADY TIRELESSLY PLUCKS GOOSE FEATHERS AS THEY WAFT BY ON EDDIES OF ACRID FUMES. THE HEADSCARF INHERITED FROM THE RECENTLY DEPARTED WHITE QUEEN, SNOW BLACK WEARS LIKE A YASHMAC. IT COVERS THE LOWER HALF OF HER BLOATED,TARRED FEATURES. AS IN A BLACKENED GOLDFISH BOWL, SHE DROWNS IN TOXIC VAPOURS, TEARS BLOTCHING HER FLOPPY MAD HATTER BOW-TIE. SHE BRAVELY FINISHES HER LAST LETTER IN CONGEALING SAND.

SNOW BLACK TIRELESSLY SCRIBBLES:

Mark, dear boy, do send your mother another yashmak. The headscarf left by Liz has seen better days and radiation is awfully hard on one's wardrobe. I've looked, but I can find no abnormal cases of cancer in the young around Aldermaston. So much for local leaks. I put such scares of radioactivity down to Russian hams. And their pink Soviet sympathisers. Now, like the Black Prince after the Battle of Crecy, your mother's fame is evergreen. (I nearly wrote Goose Green.) And even though France voted against us in the UN over the Falklands, calling me La Dame de Fer, my achievements will soon be trumpeted by those high-fliers, the Christian angels, AS I NEVER TIRE OF SAYING, A great healer is time.

TIME!

Again!

As if her cranium was an echo chambers, after a giddy moment of read-justment, Alice was back in her under earth body, Mr Patel mentioning the Milky Way, his rusty forefinger pointing upwards. The curved ceiling was painted like a Planetarium, each white star spiked with five radiating spokes which primed the night sky with a scintillating brightness.

'To understand,' said Mr Patel hoping to keep the restless attention of Alice, 'look less directly, see more deeply. Some need Big Ben. Some gang bang. Some Big Bang.'

BANG?

Timepieces were being slaughtered noisily on the other side of the silken veil curtain. 'So I HEAR!' yelped Alice, truly back in her physical body. Clapping both hands to her ears she decided to lip-read for a while.

'Timelessness ve all long for,' said the Indian gently, 'try to find on country valks, on long sails on calm seas. This, actually, is Soul as it tries to recall time in invisible spaces. Before, that is, there vas time or space. Vhen all vas ghostly gasses, slowly forming into habitable matter, from one originating monoblock. In quantum physics 'The whole universe appears the creation of decisions ve make' – Fritjof Capra' added the Sikh, happy to declare his source.

Not wishing to swop quotes (Alice preferred inventing her own) she nonetheless contributed one. 'And Einstein said that time spent with a pretty girl seems to speed up, whereas boredom somehow seems to slow the clock.'

Agreeing fervently, Mr Patel continued, 'He showed that space-time continuum cannot only stretch, almost like a rubber sheet, but can also be bent and distorted. Just as light rays are bent by gravity. Gravity causes time to slow down, so mental attention can be deflected to above gravity, above light and space. Once mind is above the illusion of time, its earthly machinery, as in body clocks, can cease. Some time, all planets like cogs, they vill also, one day, STOP!'

'How can atomic clocks be accurate to a fraction of a millionth of a second, if time is an illusion? Especially, since time measured by the sun or the moon is always lop-sided, not in neat equations. Answers, please.' Alice was asking, not Mr Patel, not Humphrey, not the Mancunian Cat, nor the mythological **M**, but herself. WHICH self? Why experimentally, all of them at once, of course!

With a click, an answer sprang out of her mouth. Alice found herself saying, 'Time has no absolute meaning outside itself and those experiencing it.' Rejoicing in finding a voice that sounded truly hers, Alice continued more confidently. 'Consciousness? As with colour. It's really just personal perception. Like digestion. Like diets. Personal. Watch astronauts. The faster their means of transport, the more time slows down.'

Mr Patel simpered with admiration. 'Using Big Ben, ve might all agree about time. But vhat about if we measure it differently? How can time be eternal if, before Big Bang, there vas no space to measure him by?'

'Bye-bye Blackbird!' sang Alice out of tune. Mention of the Big Bang reminded her to flick back for a tick and check on Snow Black's sandy last Will and Testament.

Clapping his hands like a child, and in order to hold Alice's total attention, the Sikh then phrased his next sentences like a concert hall conductor. Musically, he said, 'And after trillions years, if there IS contraction of universe and sun, our middle-aged cinder, then original monoblock vill reform itself, cause heat-death and vhite vapour . . . POOF! All vill again become super-hot plasma, ghostly gasses and TIME-LESS-NESS.'

The cosmos, a ghostly gasbag? Leaving her physical husk like the basket of a hot-air balloon, Alice again drifted to above the workshop's battle-ground of battered silent timepieces.

Cruising over latter-day Atlantis, the Americas, Alice enjoyed the bird's-eye-view. All seemed intact there. So she then whizzed over the super hot slurry that was Surrey, Sussex, Royal Berks, Bucks and other English shires that had hidden nuclear vipers in their lovely green bosoms.

Nuclear-age computers can't interpret pre-programmed instructions, only obey them, blindly.

So far.

Nuclear warheads are unable to read any scientific handbook on the holocaust. So far. Also, that all bombs are dirty.

And that remains true – so far – despite the Home Office's helpful tips in their thin publication, PROTECT AND SURVIVE. Survive? For what? And for how long. . . ?

Released radioactivity will last three times as long as mankind's recorded history, whether from France or from UK. So far – so good?

Snow Black still did not feel as indestructible as any Christian saint writing sacred memoirs in the sands of time. Humphrey's voice, then contributing, said, *'Imagination manipulates m-m-matter. So why can't it also alter time?'*

TIME to . . . switch. . . ?

No. That time Alice, decided to keep her Astral Self above Time. Staying aloft, her reproof was quickly turned into a telepathised question. 'Humphrey, do you watch over me in the loo as well?' Then another: 'Humphrey, do you even sleep in your dark glasses?' If so, how could she ever read his eyes . . . or his real intentions? Worse, could he see she'd got no knickers on?

'No knickers or knockers, what m-makes you think, I think you're the bees' knees, Alice?'

HELP! Had their programme just crashed?

Humphrey, happy as an occult hacker flicking through a stack of file-names and passwords, quickly re-booted their quantum computer. *'Time? Cor, it's like your knicker elastic, Alice – plenty of s-t-r-e-t-c-h!'*

'Well, mine's more secure than your precious PC's y-fronts – so there! I'm trying to make this my last trip to earth as a slave. Without the aid of cops, thanks Humphrey, so back to your precious PC and stop poking your nose into my. . . .'

His boyish laughter, quick as some fast-breeder reactor, stopped Alice from hearing the rest of her demand. Probably because it was so half-hearted.

'Bonking in blitzes, eh?' chortled Humphrey with a wicked twinkle.

'Wars, disasters, plagues, famines ... they always produce lashings of sex, sex and more SEX!'

Oh, dear, for a girl whose dream was always to stay a teenage virgin – and pretty – what a daily dilemma to dally with! With a quiver and a quaver in her voice, Alice loudly insisted, 'Humphrey, go play war games with your putrid policeman but leave me in peace. No son-of-a-gun boyfriend for me. GO AWAY!'

Next? A quick creative distraction, please.

Back in Astral form, Alice finds what she had been seeking, a trumpet. Its silver surface is scarred with third degree burns. How could any psychic medium manage to get nine crystals to drop through radioactive ether? But with her rescued trumpet, could Alice yet save Snow Black from the ashes, like Cinders in the fairy story. But saved for – what next?

'HITLER'S ONE LAST BALLS-UP!' chuckled Humphrey.

She had tried, but Humphrey's triple use of the word SEX still proved irresistibly haunting. Powerfully, it was pulling the earthly Alice down-wards. As if after a catnap, she was sucked back down to the timely playshop below.

Alice, like some Yogic yo-yo, was enjoying her elastic trips up and down Jacob's ladder, like an Astral Astronaut.

Astral clouds clearing, Alice returned to complete physical vision. But the silence among all the clock corpses was eerie.

Whatever had happened to the bullish clock assassins?

The quietness soon un-nerved Alice. Peeking through the silk curtain, she saw the men frozen in a trance while still on their feet.

Watching over those time-killers was a very tall, gangling man in his early thirties with long neck and hair so blonde it all but dazzled Alice as he hovered over her like some big-brained stick-insect.

'Tim,' nodded Mr Patel, jerking his head towards the man.

'Instead of counting sheep,' announced Tim in thin, metallic tones, 'try counting seconds. Keep at it for an hour and then watch, check how far the clock hands have moved.'

Listening intently, the men tensed their shoulders, then relaxed. Alice could see some lips moving. Seconds had started to be counted. Towards Alice, tip-toed Tim as his knee-caps seemed to touch each of his nostrils. Alice was pleased to meet such a pliable and genial giraffe.

Jerking his head at his clients, Tim whispered, 'A multitude doesn't make a miracle more true than just you, doll, doing your own thing.'

'Yes, I'd like to learn the difference between miracles and magic...' whispered Alice, keen as mustard to amaze all of her multiple selves at once.

Tim took Alice further into his own den. 'One miracle is just as real as a hundred conjuring-tricks and quite sufficient to establish the existence of. . . .' He paused.

'Stick-insects!' blurted Alice, mesmerised by the glassy stillness of his blue eyes. If only Humphrey's eyes proved to be so bright.

Like a locust in love with a wilting lettuce leaf, Tim appraised his new student, the only female present. 'Might I check your dials?' Taking permission for granted, Tim consulted the tassel hanging down from her D-Cap. 'The TIME TRACK is set on orange. That's why those who chant OM awaken memories and often find, willy-nilly, that they're into re-birth.'

'Forwards, or backwards, aren't we repeating all ways ourselves . . . trapped in patterns . . . in different body-clocks. . . ?'

'Either way,' replied Tim 'that's exactly what TIME TRAVEL is. So, whatever you stare at long enough fades from vision . . . unlocking our ideas of reality. Even this clock here. . . .'

Before her on an oak table, Tim placed the face of a large station clock, saying, 'The aim is to stop it. Master Time. As you produce theta waves, trance will follow. Watch the second-hand in a will-less way, unfocused. When silenced by you, the clock will vanish from view. . . .'

'So my own body clock, and the cogs in that station clock, will all chime as one.'

'Mesh together with the inter-planetary clockwork, Alice,' added he, getting closer, 'and that shared consciousness is only real, so long as we each agree on what our joint reality is.'

'Or is not,' said she, edging away from his nudging elbow.

'Right, while we operate at these rather low levels of reality, we. . . .'

'LOW?' protested Alice, interrupting him. 'How can the TIME TRACK be low Tim, if it overrides all earthly events?'

'Right!' praised Tim, 'not till you can stop a clock. Choose. This station clock? Or this cuckoo clock? Mind, you as observer, MUST stay NEUTRAL. In the ETERNAL Here-and-Now. That's if you want to become Omniscient, Omnipotent and Omnipresent. Like HUMPHREY!'

'That creep?'

'Focus lightly, Alice.'

'I'm trying Tim, but memories are swarming like ants. In my baked apple brain, they ring some bell. Which? What? Where? When? Oh, HOW do I escape all of these confusions, please?'

'Patience,' soothed Tim, 'a good old-fashioned virtue to go with this Victorian clock. Its chimes too, ring a bell. LISTEN!'

In her head, bells rang louder than bees in a bucket.

'Help time-less-ness. Weave daydreams. Like Einstein, in a sunbeam receive the theory of relativity,' encouraged Tim. 'If science fiction's always in advance of so-called science fact, how can we time ourselves when travelling from one dimension to another? Yeah? DETERMINATION does NOT do the impossible. Not even for scientists. See Alice, instead use the law of reversed effort. Even individual subatomic particles can move, unseen, either way. Once understood Alice, this discovery will quash the notion of causality, it being the chief obstacle to Time Travel'. He moved in closer.

'So what must I do?' (Apart from moving away again.)

'MUST?' asked Tim quizzically. 'If you WISH to, CHOOSE non-attach-ment. You can only ask to travel to, say Mars, if it's already part of your own undiscovered consciousness.' His voice got younger as he explained *'The sharp Cartesian division between Mind and Matter can no longer be m-m-maintained.'*

What a bummer! That was Humphrey's voice coming out of Tim's mouth. How obscene!

'This opens up the possibility,' continued Tim quite naturally, 'of travel beyond the fourth dimension and even through other voices . . . other voids. . . .'

Hearing Humphrey's tones like sprinkles of caster sugar on glowing clinkers, her heat bumps became a bonfire. Was Humphrey to become her own fall guy, and for keeps. . . ?

'*Unlike my m-m-mate Alice*,' continued Tim in Humphrey's voice, '*falling down the rabbit-hole like death, from whose bourn no traveller fails to return in a reconstituted and cute new body*.'

'Body?'

'CUTE!' chimed both men in unison, flirtatiously.

What next would they get up to? 'For time-less-ness' they offered her as one, 'try M-M-MIND-less-ness. . . .'

Was this to be some sort of psychic gang-bang? As if engaged in a three-line telephone chat-line with two heavy-breathing stammerers Alice, wearing her top-of-the-class hat, heard what she hoped to keep to herself. Nonetheless aloud she said, '*To reach other dimensions we need to be "out of body-clock" first. A rotating Black Hole, in theory at least, is a physical time M-M-Machine. So TIME TRAVEL becomes inseparable from . . . yep . . . bi-location*.'

'Hi, Humphrey!' greeted Tim, giving Alice the thumbs up. Humphrey, getting the credit? That made even her curls start to curdle! So defying the boys, in tetchy tones Alice stated, 'For the Time Track, before I clock you both, what exactly do I require?'

'A threesome!' chortled Humphrey and Tim together, bonding blokishly.

'Is that TRI-location, please?'

Since they ignored this, she added, 'If I've karma with you, I'll collect it, OK – OK?' More suggestive noises. 'Got the tee-shirt, boys! Through role-play with Viv. Wasting time here.' But before departing, Alice begged to know how she could catch up with Humphrey's body, stroke him gently till he didn't want to shy away like a stallion afraid of a comfort blanket. Should she reject him before his visits inside her became too frequent and, what's worse, too addictive?

'Change your m-m-mind about m-m-me,' promised Humphrey, still using the handsome Tim like a Direct Voice Medium, 'and I'll leave you. Like I left m-m-my dad . . . bereft.'

'Threat, promise or enticement?' Alice was weakening. His stammer was getting to be somewhat endearing. And Tim was so good-looking it hurt. Would he – or *they* – both hit her if she stroked Tim's downy cheek, pretending it was Humphrey through and through?

Tim cupped her chin. 'Humphrey,' he confided, 'he's on. . . .'

'POT?' gulped Alice, fearing the worst, or the best, at once. No, what Tim next whispered she must check out for herself. Would Humphrey kindly confirm he was not on the CAUSAL Plane.

'Above it,' boasted Humphrey through Tim. 'M-m-mental!'

'Yes, I know we're both loopy in love but why keep on playing leap-frog with me, Humphrey?'

'Follow, Princess. But first, master your own m-m-memories.'

'Like you're m-m-mastering your own stammer?' asked Alice, tartly.

As tutor, Tim crowed, 'One of my best students, Humphrey. Has passion. Now rides the Flying Flute. Kept all promises, dates, deadlines, Humphrey. Always did do, spot on.'

'Spot ON what – his face?'

'Alice, he's a champ! Promise you. Got passion . . . like me!'

'Passion? Champ? He's a lumpy chump!' Champ – Humphrey – passion – promises, promises . . . ESCAPE!

Back to above, please.

NOW!

Scene 13 – Scorched earth. Exterior. Midday (or Midnight?)

SNOW BLACK (NÉE WHITE) BLINKS IN DISBELIEF. EYELASHES DROP IN FLUTTERS OF FLICKERING FALL-OUT. SHE PONGS LIKE OVER-FRIED RANCID SPAM. IN SPIRIT FORM, ALICE WATCHES SNOW BLACK FINISH HER FINAL LETTER;

SNOW BLACK WRITES:

You're surely under less of a dark cloud there in the Oman desert Mark, than if you'd stayed in UK. A good omen. Oman starts with OM. And think what their unemployment would be like without you.

At least the French did not outbid us in the sewage works there! Never mind what a stink good business causes, just so long as mother's behind you. And just so long as you can smoke as much as you want, (you remember which brand, of course).

Being rich has never been against any law that I'd allow. It's thanks to we with enterprise that the Third World is too poor to start the third World War. Debt keeps us in charge of their small loose change. Yet, if your grandfather had known that one day Harrods would be sold of to the Arabs, he'd never have gone into the grocery trade. Then where would I have been now?

Oh, if only your father had stayed put in the wine-cellars like I said, he'd have been able to bring me my usual gin-and-it.

Still, with Cementation Construction, you CAN build a chain of nuclear shelters, below the pyramids and along the Nile, like underground Safeways, well stocked with long life milk and honey. Uncontaminated, of course.

Charred cattle bones are good for absorbing toxins. Good pickings around here just now. Might they top up our export trade?

A GHOSTLY BUGLE IS HEARD

Must rush or I'll miss the last post.

THE BUGLE PLAYS THE 'LAST POST' DISCORDANTLY

Mark dear, if I'm too late, perhaps some archivist will rescue this from the dead letter department. Already I'm seeing things.

THROUGH THE MOUTH OF THE HOVERING SILVER TRUMPET, FIVE CRYSTALS DROP ON TO THE PUTREFIED SAND, FOLLOWED BY A PLAYING-CARD – THE ACE OF SPADES. UNSEEN BY SNOW BLACK, ALICE WHO WANTED TO PLACE THE CRYSTALS IN THE SHAPE OF A SIX-POINTED STAR, HAS NOW INSTEAD TO RECONCILE HERSELF TO A PENTAGRAM AS SHE CHANTS 'OM'.

SNOW BLACK STILL WRITING, CONSCIENTIOUSLY:

Mark I've just been sent jewellery by some grateful council house owners. Delivered to my door, as it were, through a musical instrument. Not to blow my own trumpet, but you know dear, third time lucky or not, being Prime Minister has prepared me to meet my Maker. I expect God, who is surely no Quaker, will enjoy my answers at Question Time. I have, after all, become quite an expert at the strident riposte. (I nearly wrote TRIDENT riposte.) And it'll be nice to thank Nelson personally for decimating the French like that.

FAINT ECHO OF GHOSTLY CHEERS FROM THE HUSTINGS

No, your mother never did go round the bend, or break her word. Far better to get others to do it for you. I alone made a virtue out of good old-fashioned rectitude under fire. The French can keep their St Joan. Who needs a witch when they can have their own Black Madonna?

SHE BLESSES THE FIRST FIVE CRYSTALS NOW PLANTED AS A PENTAGON

And now for the peace I've long deserved. I thank God that your father's optimism always kept me cheerful, even in my darkest hour. How? By keeping my Think Tanks always tanked up. How I shall miss him. You too, dear boy.

A loving kiss, Mother.

P.S. Mind you have many successful years in your own blooming desert. And Mark, it WAS right to battle with France in the arms race, especially since they haven't forgiven me for selling Tornado aircraft to Saudi Arabia before they could clinch a deal themselves. Such single-mindedness wins every war.

HAVING NOT FOUND A FIRST-CLASS STAMP WITH HER PICTURE ON IT, SNOW BLACK SLOWLY SCRAPES HER SAND LETTER INTO A BLACK ENVELOPE. THIS SHE PLACES ON A SILVER SALVER WHICH, LIKE THE ENVELOPE, HAS SOMEHOW SYMBOLICALLY SURVIVED IN THE NEW ALDERMASTON DESERT.

P.P.S. Mark THIS. Even if it kills me, I'll never again reflate.

SHE BURIES HER HEAD IN THE SAND.

EYES DRY, ALICE IS STILL WATCHING FROM A TRANSPARENT WILLOW TREE AS IT QUIETLY WEEPS.

ALICE   Poor charred mummy.

AS IF HAVING ESCAPED THE POISON GAS INSIDE A SHRODINGER'S SEALED BOX, THE CAT GRINS LIKE A DOLPHIN WITH OVER-SIZED DENTURES.

MANCUNIAN CAT   (*grinning*) Send white light, luv.
ALICE   Like from your teeth? They're dazzling!
MANCUNIAN CAT   (*with a nod at the slumped corpse below*) It's easier for salaries to be raised than dead Top People. Specially in a depression, chuck. And a desert.
ALICE   She's one of the Astral Jet-set now.
MANCUNIAN CAT   More like one of the debt-set. Think of her karma. No rest where she's going. Astral Holy Days ain't holidays up there, chuck. Seems you'll meet her there.
ALICE   Then she'll rise again, you think?
MANCUNIAN CAT   (*through grinning, gritted teeth*) Aye, luv. Like a tough rich doughnut. . . !

CLOSE-UP OF THE CORPSE'S GRITTED TEETH AND CROSS-FADE TO THE PENTAGON OF CRYSTALS AS THEIR PRISTINE BRIGHTNESS

GETS BLIGHTED BY DEEPENING DARK SHADOWS DISSOLVING INTO
NUCLEAR WINTER.

'TIME TRAVEL, SPACE TRAVEL, ASTRAL TRAVEL, all three are parallel
modes of transportation' This bald statement from Tim got Alice firmly
earthed again below ground as he continued to explain, 'The word 'transport,' also means a form of reverie. Cool for those addicted to dying . . .
like Humphrey'. Dying? Not Humphrey, surely. But why had five, not nine
crystals surrounding Snow Black, turned black? Were they slowly dying
for more time like Mr Patel's murderers? Bellowing at them, Tim told the
men to estimate how much more time they had thoughtlessly killed since
his last check on them. Most said about twelve minutes. But no. Not half-
an-hour, nor fifty minutes, but an hour and twelve seconds had passed.
So much for time-less-ness. 'Correct,' emphasised Tim 'astral journeys
take up no time. Why? Time is frozen for anything travelling at or beyond
the speed of earthly light. Now concentrate,' said he with a curt nod now
that he saw she didn't really fancy him.

Alice herself was nervous that she'd never be able to stop the station
clock in time, as instructed by Tim, just by staring at it. 'Watch a star!'
snapped he like a teacher too keen to help dimwits. 'Try the simplest form
of Time Travel first.'

Alice refused to frown in case she got confronted with an explanation
that she might have been able to work out for herself. Getting more irritated with the somewhat oppressive Tim, she let him impose yet further
explanations. 'A virtual particle Alice, is able to move sideways in time, like
a two-way stretch, say in a prison sentence, while the light of a star is
looking back in time, just like Humphrey likes to do, stare at faint spots on
the sky's face, eleven billion light years away.'

Before Tim could edge his body nearer his student, Humphrey inter-
rupted. To Alice he revealed that he was communicating with other
Gilmores. Not just with the multiple murderer Gary Gilmore, and with
Christopher Gilmore author of ALICE IN WELFARELAND but with the
American writer Robert Gilmore. Humphrey, meanwhile, felt he was being
prepared to become thrilled with yet another alluring little girl called Alice

and maybe in Oxford or maybe in Daresbury, wherever that is. In some timeless zone, Alice might disport her nubile form on a velvet couch as he photographs her naughty knowingness.

'*Bi-locating virtual particles can appear as an uncertainty in time, able to turn time around, antiparticles being particles travelling backward in time so that an anti-Alice in Quantumland could, for example, have been destroyed before she was created*'. Hardly pillow talk.

So Tim was right. Humphrey was more interested in death in the past than in life in the future. No wonder on earth they were saying that romance, like God, was dead. Yet sensing her partiality for the invisible Humphrey to his non-effective handsome self, Tim got more strident still. Trying to get Alice closer, he repeated his demand with an edge of menace that she found somewhat daunting. But at least Tim could hold her if she fainted. 'Stare at a star,' demanded Tim as he pointed to the painted galaxy on the ceiling, 'and, Alice, you report back if and when movement has occurred.'

'YEP!' announced she, brazenly refusing to avert her eyes from the station clock before her. 'The star has travelled to earth using its light body. I do Spirit Travel. It does Astral Travel!'

'Sure thing, doll! All atoms are created out of the same explosive super-nova,' said Tim coldly but wanting to embrace her. 'Souls, soils and stars, we're all of the same Cause-Essence. Every person's body borrows a dusting of every universal element. Even the seven families of crystals, Alice, are inside you now'.

'*Like m-m-ME*,' agreed Humphrey. That time his voice again came out of the mouth of Alice herself before she could throttle it. '*Alice, you and m-me, we're both private parts of the first night's cosmic orgasm – BEAUTIFUL!*'

Oh, boy! How Humphrey kept banging on about beauty as if he couldn't get enough of it for himself. Maybe, like a eunuch in a Sex Shop. Again, Alice was feeling ganged up on by those two guys. She was getting to feel too clammy. So, nothing for it, she had to lash out. 'Then the chosen enemy must also be within. And sorry boys if you're both mates, but Humphrey, I think you're one of those!' To aid direct contact, she glared into a looking-glass.

'*M-m-marvellous!*' said Humphrey.

'You're not hearing me, Humphrey. I mean,' insisted Alice, glaring at the station clock, 'I think you're SHITTING shadows! That's to say, you are my chosen life-defying, stinky, putrid Enemy Number One. GOT THAT BUSTER?' Silence. No response. Suddenly, after ten minutes, loud ticking brought her back into sharper focus as, with a tinny-sounding scream, the two hands on the station clock dropped off and fell to her feet. That left a timeless clock. Recovering from the shock, Alice used the blank face as a mandala and went into meditation. Quietly, she requested something to protect herself. Abruptly changing her mind, she instead insisted that Humphrey in person should materialise. And without his dark glasses. Time to check if he really was from Venus, not from Mars or somewhere worse. And appear he did. But would his eyes be a golden honey hue. . . ?

Then and there, the plump impish face of Humphrey popped out of a nearby cuckoo-clock. '*URGENT!*' he cried, '*I've got important duties. That cop intruder. He's trying to tunnel out, let in nuclear fall-out fumes. Gamma rays he'll use as a tactical first-strike deterrent against the Saffs.*'

'But that's not logical. And you're GRINNING like that unfeeling cat!'

'*Nice you noticed,*' clucked the face in the centre of the cuckoo-clock. '*So, what you going to DO about THAT bald threat, Alice? NOTHING? As usual!*'

'Seems it's only the inner earth left now,' said Tim showing signs of alarm.

'Ve've poisoned ozone with aerosols, earth vith fall-out rust,' agreed Mr Patel.

'And now that lunatic wants to puncture our sanctuary,' said Alice, 'and let in. . . .'

'Cuckoo!' agreed the clock, eleven times.

'Don't go!' pleaded Alice, unexpectedly. 'You're always flying off some-where. Why won't you take me with you, please?'

'*Five points first, like fingers and toes. Five passions, virtues, continents, and five psychic planes. Five for magic, black or white. When the sixth sacred crystal appears again, you will be ready to reach the Flute's Sixth Sacred Portal. Then we'll celebrate. A free ride, you and m-m-me both,*'

Alice!' With that, the cuckoo popped back inside the clock and the hatch snapped shut. Oh bother, she'd forgotten to check on his eyes.

'Vill you let him go? Actually, I should,' advised the kindly Mr Patel, backed up by a sexy look of encouragement from Tim.

'Who's cuckoo, him or I? All I want,' said Alice, 'is a friend I can rely on. Somewhere soon, please.'

Tim, like a choirmaster of troubadors, led the Time-Killers into an affable litany, the men dancing round Alice to comfort her. With Tim and Mr Patel, the lumpen oafs intoned in unison:

'Stars fall . . . LIGHT!

'Rain falls . . . LIFE!

'Lava falls . . . LOVE!

'Love FALLS. . . .'

The loving space they left for Alice she filled, like a well of tears. 'I know 'cos I've fallen. I love him, Tim. I love Humphrey. And all he does is rise above me, ever out of reach. I hate his Flying Flute. I've been using the OM but he still stays beyond me. There must be a better way, a better word than OM.'

Their litany and dance steps continued lightly:

'Dew rises . . . LIGHT!

Steam rises . . . LIFE!

'Lava RISES. . . .'

The loving space they left for Alice she filled like a well lit up with rippling laughter. Staring, the men froze in wonder.

'LOVE! Yes, LOVE RISES like skylarks! What IS love but joyful Soul recognising its next best teacher!'

Tim's brawny Time Tyrants, staring dumbly, all nodded.

'Come back, Humphrey!' called out Alice as if to a universe gone deaf. 'I'm willing to learn, learn all about LOVE!' Shamelessly, in front of all those murderers, Alice shared her upsurge of new misery with unmaidenly abandon. She even lost her cap and tassel, ready to forget Humphrey's behest for her to monitor all her feelings so that she could stay in charge of her own emotional tool-kit.'Help me, God! Where does Humphrey park his Flying Flute?' asked Alice, she desperately gasping by then for any morsel of mystery, sacred or profane.

No answer. The men stayed mute as Tim tried to slip his hand around her waist like a stealthy python.

Pulling away, shuddering with inner sobs Alice, all the same, led the next round of the litany:

'Sea-beds burst into flames. CHAOS!

'Fish FLY!

'Volcanoes burst into flames. CHAOS!

'Birds fly!

'Forests burst into flames. CHAOS!

'Seeds FLY!

'Thoughts fly. Dreams fly. Time flies – LOOK!'

She pointed to the floor.

The two clock hands which had fallen there started to rise up. Flying round the cave like a lopsided clockwork bird were the two-handed wings of the station clock. Was that potent magic, full of profane pendragon-like powers? Or was it a time for sacred miracles to manifest more abundantly?

'Dark angels still fall,' frowned Alice, doubts nagging. 'Not me, so who on earth let in that gunman to the Rainbow Survivalists?'

'PC? – Humphrey did.'

'Humphrey!' she repeated, appalled by Tim's revelation. 'He claimed PC said the magic word.'

'Told him by Humphrey?'

'Why not?'

'The OM? PC used the word OM! – I don't . . . I CAN'T believe it.'

Tim shrugged with a relish that made Alice even more wary of his intentions. To take her from Humphrey was he lying?

'HUMPHREY? He let in that Police Commissioner?' wailed Alice, still reeling, bewildered, and back on her seesaw of uncertainties. 'But why didn't I stop that? Is this why I can't get a life of pure love down here? Is THAT why? Is that really WHY?'

'Why Hitler?' asked Mr Patel. 'Why Satan?'

Alice had no answer.

Not yet.

But HAD Humphrey all the answers, damn it! Alice had to find out.

Soon.

Before, under ground, PC's lethal poisons could contaminate all the earth-loving Rainbow Survivalists. And in the sacred name of protecting the sanctity of life and liberty. Of course. And in good time for eternity itself to be kept safely intact.

CHAPTER NINE

ANTS AND APPLES

'Do cats eat bats? – Do bats eat cats?'
'But answer came there none -
And this was scarcely odd because
They'd eaten every one.'

As Christmas approached, Alice was not alone in her desperate search to make sense of her new life, underground. To get Humphey to remove his dark glasses, she'd even dreamed of giving him a white stick...across his backside.

Pitta, that chirpy soul, had just left her boyfriend White Rabbit. Unexpectedly, she was claiming she now desired celibacy. He didn't. Well, which rabbit ever did? 'Doc told him to cut down his sex life by half.'

'Which half?' asked Alice, still wondering about bi-location.

'The BETTER 'alf mate – ME!' laughed Pitta. 'And that's not the 'alf of it. For me, the best is our nights to remember. For 'im, guess the best is what he can boast to 'is mates about. Still, like you, I'm hunting for a more healing lifestyle.' While still skidding lip-gloss around Alice's mouth, she joked, 'Now don't snog any bloke what might mind looking like he's been mobbed by snails!'

Hardly giving them a glance, dozens of dozy youths clung onto outmoded beams of meaning, sometimes upside down in Yoga postures, not working of course, but passively waiting; for 'Something real BIG, man', to appear. Pitta felt that their macho erections to date didn't fit the bill. They hadn't hers so why should boys find them something worth holding onto? With all the salacious glee of a born-again celibate, Pitta riveted Alice by sharing facts about the clitoris and about Dr (Sex) Kinsey.

When he wished to film 2,000 voluntary masturbators, a line of male recruits stretched right round Kinsey's block. 'At only two dollars a toss, it was hardly a Christmas present,' quipped Pitta, 'even if they was all singing COME ALL YE FAITHFUL with gay abandon! Now one Senator wants wanking taught in schools as a stress buster. What a giggle, eh!'

Hardly listening, Alice sighed, 'I feel like a computer who's lost her hacker.'

'An apple a day keeps the Humphrey at bay!' She offered Alice a rosy one to match her newly rouged cheeks, determined to update her image. Passionately, Pitta was listing the 500 atomic tests carried out in the atmosphere from the 1950s onwards. 'So Rudolph's red Nose is now radioactive.' About to take her first bite of the rosy apple, Alice then let it drop.

'Yeah, Santa's reindeer, like the lichens they live on, contaminated. Strontium 90. And the Saami farmers, instead of noshing reindeer, now nosh junk food. Result? Nuclear-age cancers. Feeling better, mate?'

Alice, picking up the bruised apple, nibbled it experimentally.

Around them, PC's growing number of groupies gathered, lethargically. 'Look at this shower!' sneered Alice, dismissively. 'Reared on state handouts. Too idle to even try Workfare instead of Welfare. So what's left but WARfare and playing with guns?'

Behind her new rouge, Alice blushed. Was PC to be the **M**ao Tse-tung of the inner cave Survivalists? Somehow, she felt guilty.

'Now to become high-flyers, limp balloons need blow-jobs! See, 'eaven on earth, girl,' encouraged Pitta, 'it ain't just Welfare on Wings. You know somewhere out on a limb near Cloud Nine, Right? No, it's 'ERE! Starting with these.' She pointed at her bare feet. 'So go for it, girl. Flash 'em yer tits!'

'Pitta. Don't give me pity. I need praise, please.'

'Humphrey's a workaholic,' teased Pitta. 'Wish he'd work on YOU a bit harder, eh, gal?'

Looking for her shoes, Alice asked, 'Is HE amongst those yobs, Pitta?'

'PC? 'E's inspecting their purple uniforms.'

'HUMPHREY in. . . ?' she wailed, inconclusively.

'WELL! White Rabbit an' all! My randy EX. Shit! In uniform! Joined up! Still, more than 'is 'andwriting ever did! Fuck me. Must be PC's way with words. Know what PC's motto is?'

'For you sometimes, for ME always?'

'IF WE CAN'T STIR THE GODS THEN STIR THE UNDERWORLD!'

Alice peeked at the youngsters with PC, their newly adopted father figure. 'Gold teeth! PC and Humphrey, close!' hissed Alice, bewildered with bitterness. 'And Humphrey, he's still wearing dark glasses. Gold-tinted. To match PC's teeth?'

Softening, Pitta added, 'Told you. He come from Venus.'

'PC? From Mars, surely!'

'Humphrey – Venus?'

'I dreamed he got gorgeous honey golden eyes. But he keeps hiding behind shades. Why?'

Aware of her voice being too loud, Alice crouching, hid from view.

''Ave it all out with him, mate!' advised Pitta joining Alice.

'And then where would we be, Pitta? In LOVE?'

'With a fucking FANTASY? A figment of your unripe tight little fanny?'

'Fanny? WHERE IS SHE?' Rising abruptly, Alice's blazing eyes scanned the crowd. 'You're wrong. I love God, too. Love's not a fantasy. It's NOT!' Seeing Humphrey, she ducked down again beside Pitta.

On command, Humphrey organised the recruits. Amongst the spectators, Pitta heard rumours that all PC's recruits had accepted celibacy. She felt rejected by White Rabbit. And for what? Purple tunics, silver epaulettes, and tourniquet tight trousers. He looked so captivated. And handsome! 'What real man,' asked PC, 'can never resist a smart uniform?'

Pitta became conspiratorial. 'Takes real guts to learn from baddies. Get that crafty little 'Itler sussed,' pursued Pitta, 'and we won't need no Master

Race to rule us. So, mate, let's join up!'

Alice gasped. 'Pretend we're one of the boys?'

'All dolled up, good for a laugh, eh! Watch 'em stand errect!'

'No. Let's watch from a safe place.'

'Bet you'd jump at it if Humphrey asked you to join up!'

'Bet YOU only asked ME, Pitta, 'cos you want me to help spy on White Rabbit! As one of PC's yobs, no way. But as ME – maybe!' Agreeing with glee, they hugged each other. Left on Pitta's shoulder was one false eyelash and a smear of lip-gloss.

Swashbuckling his muscles, PC was imprinting his vision of uniformed oneness on the vacuous fan club of raw recruits. Those growing ranks of bodybuilders soon attracted nubile girls, shapely as scent bottles. Along the lines of martial males, unattached prowlers in red leather hot pants sniffed like smouldering panthers. It was those predatory chicks that Pitta again tried to encourage Alice to join.

'Knock 'im off – 'is glasses, I mean, ducks. Get a butchers of 'is eyes, mate. Call 'im HONEYballs! And GRAB. . . !'

If Humphrey's eyes truly were Venusian GOLD, a combustible kiss would surely spark off more than fireworks.

Alice felt her cheeks flush behind the rouge camouflage.

'First, get your arse back of the crowd, mate.' Still hidden Pitta, surreptitiously, started removing her own garish make-up.

'Before it was too much sex and do sod all,' explained PC through a megaphone, encouraging inter-gender Martial Arts. Combat training was part of PC's New Moral Map campaign. 'No more smoking pot in the cancer wards of worn-out Welfare. Vote for Personal Virtues,' commanded PC, persuasively. 'Vote for personal Victory, not victimhood. Vote for the vision of a cleaner, freer, more enterprising future, all mankind's failings conquered. Vote for ME and together let's forge a glorious future, all as one, TOGETHER, as one, we promise to magnify our magical mandate!'

M for **M**andate?

PC like Hitler was also a democrat. But training the youth for what? For death, slyly disguised as a better afterlife?

But in which dimension, high or low?

'Time to move in closer' whispered Pitta, taking two steps back.

Noticing that, Alice asked, 'Even if it means...losing both our boys?'

As the two stared deeply into each other's eyes, they were sensing that such pumped-up male libidos so tightly harnessed would shortly be aching for outlets. What sort of releases? Sex was discouraged and masturbation outlawed by peer pressure. Maybe bloodshed? War? So often wars, as in menstrual cycles, seem to release bio-psychic discharges, society's hidden poisons. To become randy enough for battle, even impotent young men must feel fully loaded, guns all cocked.

Humphrey, flash in gold-tinted glasses, announced that their saffron-robed enemy, the monkish Saffs, were said to be about to let in nuclear leaks from above ground.

Terror tactics, scare tactics . . . or both together. . . ?

Earlier, PC himself had posed the direst threats. WHY? Alice dare not yet tell Pitta that at the time Humphrey had announced that piece of news, he was appearing through a cuckoo-clock.

Widespread deaths, PC still claimed, could be prevented. How? By voting for him and his Rainbow Warriors. And in time. With urgency the air tingled as psychedelic smog-masks were issued. Persuaded to 'COME CLEAN, COME STRONG!', PC's recruits were to be trained in his newly formed Occult Academy.

It was decided.

Alice and Pitta would continue to monitor both Humphrey and White Rabbit. After all, where else was safe for them all, except under ground? Unless, that is, the dreaded Saffs DID puncture the earth's surface and let in toxic fall-out fumes.

Did the Saffs want extra supplies? Reserve rations had been squirreled away by the late Top People. One of those food stores was not far from Warren Row. Could it get looted without letting in the cocktail of toxic abominations blanketing southern England? Suffocation or starvation, either way, a sinister scenario for unprotected Survivalists.

Alice and Pitta watched PC steer his followers from Yoga, through Martial Arts, to macho robotics. Such a path, some hoped, might lead to the dark heart of Black Magic. Already PC, his new moustache bristling like charred stubble, was priming his young hopefuls with notions of superiority as they gave blood transfusions, swelling the local blood bank.

Alice, feeling trapped underground, had no idea which blood group she belonged to. As a true Aquarian, her inclination to keep free of all groups kept her lonely despite dreaming of a Golden Hearted Land of Loving Friends.That's why Humphrey's support of PC's dubious crusade distressed her so much. Surely, like her, he was destined for something better than mere politics and crowd control?

Catching her despair, Pitta declared, 'There's got to be a way, mate. Otherwise, right, we wouldn't be looking for it!' Truth to tell, she was missing White Rabbit, and his evergreen ribaldry.

Alice demurred. 'How can we do our own thing, when most of life's lessons are through other unhappy people. . . ?'

So many choices. So many signposts. But was over-dosing on self-growth playshops just a distraction from the real issues, stopping PC from getting elected?

Alice decided her personal development was her real mission. Even though she and Pitta did agree that no workshop, any more than any one religion of itself, seemed to advance them fast enough towards Total Consciousness without the fatal ferryman.

Where next? Death Row-Boat. Named in memory of Charon.

Inner Earth's Death Row-Boat was a chain of caves hewn out of granite rocks. Within each of these was set a man-sized microwave oven. Into these cells of self-adjustment, four nuclear physicists, defectors from their chosen career, had agreed to fast for forty days and forty nights. Taking guidance from Pluto, they had been locked up, with one rotting apple each and a thousand assorted wild ants. This arrangemnt was supervised by PC.

Billed as THE MAN OF THE MOMENT, curious Survivalists of all colours congregated to hear PC. Crowds made it easy for Alice and Pitta to stay hidden. With his magnetic certainties, PC persuaded his listeners that it was he, not Pluto, who in the goodness of his heart felt it was time to give those scientists freedom, and the square meal cooked by his young devotees. 'Supervise 'em, son.' That command was to Humphrey. Like a ringmaster, PC then introduced Old Adam.

The first physicist to emerge dazed from his micro-oven was shrivelled up and pixy-like. His usual quick movements had slowed down. Though weak and unshaven, eyes glazed from lack of food, he keenly shared his insights. Bemused and exhilarated both at once, he intoned, 'IMPERSONAL!' several times as if not believing in himself. 'Impersonal. Black and red. Two ant armies. Ate my apple. Then, all impersonal, they ate each other. Ready to be killed . . . ready to kill . . . till I stopped them. . . .'

'Like the Saffs!' agreed PC, his blazing eyes sweeping the crowd, his hypnotic gaze supported by a generous gesture that included every listener there. 'Fear THEM! But not fear itself.'

Continued Old Adam, somewhat confused, 'Enemies function best as artefacts. Impersonal. Friends, to protect myself, I killed. Those ants . . . hundreds . . . killed . . . hundreds. . . .'

PC led a cheer.

'Both armies. I killed them all.'

PC led a louder cheer.

'Both sides. All. Every ant. Dead as dung.'

'Dung' rung a sour note. Cowed, the crowd fell silent. 'Before the ants ate me alive.'

Giggles. Not Alice. Not Pitta. Notably, not Humphrey, either.

'Even if I'd known each ant by name, I'd have killed. To keep myself sane. To survive. I killed! Impersonally. A hobby, to keep boredom at bay. Well, you smug pacifists ask this; isn't war earth's purpose . . . like Mars before it?' Old Adam like a crazed hunger striker, blurted further thoughts. 'To teach killing? Well? Don't we all murder oxygen even as we breathe it? Yet if death doesn't exist neither can permanent murder. . . ?'

'Mankind's only cure . . . manure?' was Humphrey's offering, without one stammer.

Though PC was having the meeting filmed, Alice saw him note 'manure', Humphrey's latest word. Was he a Sunday rose grower like a lot of soldiers? Seeing her distress, Humphrey buzzed her inner ear with, '*M-*

M-MATTER CAN'T BE DESTROYED. DEATH DOESN'T EXIST!' Panic stations! He did not stutter with PC, only when relaying his so-called wisdom to her in private. Had Humphrey fed Old Adam and PC only life-threatening warmongering ideas, notions of poisonous personal powers?

Regaining crowd focus and acclaim, PC explained that consciousness is like a cage. Open it, and most songbirds choose to stay inside it.

'Sheep? Is that what you want?' asked one potential recruit to the cause of war as regaled by PC, 'SHEEP?'

'Shepherds, son. Like you!' parried PC with a winning smile.

The phrase 'JUDAS RAM' suddenly pierced her ear, Alice alerted again to alternatives.

As if to the cenotaph on Poppy Day (before Whitehall was vaporised, of course), that pixilated physicist returned to his microwave oven. Inside again, Old Adam quickly atomised himself, and the six remaining ants hiding inside it. Fascinated, the crowd watched through the oven door as if it was an episode of DR. WHO. On the microwave, who indeed, had pressed the button?

'Bloodless roast lamb,' muttered PC darkly.

With a gulp, Alice tried to trap her scalding tears.

PC was well launched into a speech linking Nietzsche with Winnie-the-Pooh. No longer a despised pariah, PC was fast becoming more of a pampered paragon. Under PC's patronage, he made his devotees believe they could become SUPERBEARS! But who would own the honey-pot? That question was only asked – so far – by Alice. She hoped the thought had come from Humphrey.

Ben the second scientist emerged from his oven. In the glare, his shrivelled wrinkles widened into bright smiles. Ben described how his ants had received every possible comfort in their homely new habitat. He had counted some 130 ants, of some 50 different species, within a single square yard of leaf litter. Among those, the leaf-cutting ant had actually started to cultivate its own crop of fungi. Ecstatic, even in a state of starvation, that willowy scientist waltzed as he talked, his large mottled hands screwing hanks of white hair to the nape of his neck, his head looking like a washing-up mop left out to dry.

Alice nudged Pitta. She'd noticed how PC was getting edgy. In what way was Ben, this second scientist, not politically helpful?

Well, Ben was greeting all around him as if long lost relatives. Even Alice herself got a hug, despite her defensive deportment. And that had happened as she was still trying to hide from Humphrey – should he be looking out for her. Alice often felt threatened by an open display of emotions. In the eyes of that old scientist though, she saw an inner light. It illuminated Ben's ageless face with untold tenderness. For a moment Alice enjoyed being flustered by his attentions. Why? Because secretly she hoped that Humphrey was watching her closely with his x-ray eyes, inwardly.

'My ants built me a mushroom to sit on! Yes, while I sucked my hookah-pipe. Their patrol leader tipped them off. After a huddle, the scout who had located the best place for it, returned to mobilise their building teams. Fascinating! Never nipped me, not one of them. And look here . . . what magnificence! What grandeur! They built their own elegant cathedral! – LOOK!'

'And the apple?'

'The pharaoh ants rolled it down their cathedral nave!'

Alice noticed PC record that last fact, the ex-policeman by then a bit more open to Ben's sunny nature despite the crowd being so enthralled by his near hysterical exuberance.

'I expect to mummify the apple, in their altar tabernacle. . . .' chuckled the scientist, rapturously. 'Such skills! Such architecture! What organisa-tion! And all, it seems, without one order from a tyrant . . . what a lesson to us all, eh!'

PC expanded his chest. He intended to stop Ben. Reclaiming his listen-ers, PC loudly rhapsodised. 'Modern desert storm troopers couldn't even build . . .' He left such a long pause, curiosity alone got reluctant ears pinned back. As a trained orator, he knew that to hold your breath for too long sharpens concentration in the spectators. Eventually, he added, '. . . a mud hut never mind a pyramid. We self-chosen Saved Ones, friends, we're FANTASTIC! For a good future, we Survivalists deserve the best possible leadership. That right, son?'

230

As Humphrey saluted him, Alice grit her teeth.

A question. Whispered by Alice it was repeated loudly by Pitta. 'ANTS DON'T NEED LEADERS SO WHY DO WE?' That chilled the crowd. Was PC's power-base being challenged? 'WHY should we need GENERALS?' demanded Pitta.

Not wishing to be associated with Pitta's heckling, White Rabbit, near PC, ducked as Alice, beside Pitta, also ducked down.

Even in the face of PC's silent scowl, Alice again prompted Pitta. Before it got aired, PC rose magnificently to the challenge saying, 'By the agricultural standards of Biblical times, the fungus-farming and aphid-herding of ants are eclipsed by our own dangerous land-management crafts, folks. Farmer ants secrete antibiotics to control alien fungi, like garden weeds, and spread this waste to fertilise their crop. Further, desert ants, the like of which will have survived fall-out despite instant nuclear ash, navigate by integrating compass bearings and distances as they consult in what looks like rugger-scrums. These signposts they continuously update. So what ants can learn even in desert sands, my Psychic Specials can and will learn, as well as improve such skills before insects rule the roost instead of us. YES?'

Not cowed by PC's biblical rant to beat Ben's appeal, Pitta shouted out her next provocative question. 'Where is the apple now mister, in your belly?'

'Apple energy is everywhere!' was Ben's delirious reply. 'Like Apollo! A symbol of immortality. Welcome all, welcome to my playshop. Just as soon as I've recovered.'

HEALTH AND LONGEVITY! That PLAYshop offered by Ben was a MUST! Alice had such a deep wish to fly with Humphrey unencumbered by all earthly aches, pains and unanswered riddles. While still in such romantic reveries, she received another hug from the waltzing scientist, Ben singing out, 'Apple tree, apple tree. Tree of Life. End all conflict, end all strife!'

The delighted crowd found themselves singing the Apple Tree ditty, PC getting agitated at the crowd's spontaneous raptures. Might that engaging ant-lover become a dangerous rival candidate in the forthcoming election, a beloved tribal Elder? Confirming PC's fears, the scientist uplifting their spirits, said, 'The Tree of Life grows through all earths, skies and heavens. Its balancing roots remain hidden in all Inner Kingdoms,' he explained, expansively. 'Oh dear Eve, how we men have maligned you! Your seduction of the first Adam speeded up our human progress most wonderfully . . . like all epidemics and all wars!'

Pitta nudged Alice, winking towards Humphrey. 'What you got to sow, chick, but your wild oats, eh? So, lose yer virginity gal and GAIN yer own centre of gravity!' As usual, shooting from the hip, Pitta added, 'Just make sure you choose a smoking gun, gal!'

On the word 'gun', Alice again squirmed with simmering guilt. Before she could decide to confide in Pitta, Ben spoke.

Ben was clarifying his last point, saying, 'Science has no morals. Destructive powers can be much more quickly curative than the creative...in fact speed up our joyous return to the Golden Gardens of Eden!' Resisting subsequent praise from PC, Ben's integrity was almost tangible as he entranced the crowd. 'Such unlimited, irrational HOPE! That's what those ants taught me! Building health and beauty out of waste litter!' Then his smiling wrinkles wilted. 'Yet, equality? Can that be the real answer? Not when few voters went to Eton while many others were sent to Borstal.'

'What if all ants started off as equal, but their own experiences makes . . . each of them, despite looking like cloned soldiers, UNIQUE?' contributed Humphrey.

Alice was worried. Humphrey's pearls offered in front of a pig like PC, his words were being tape-recorded. Why so? As evidence against him for later power plays endangering Humphrey. . . ?

'Take Anthony and Anthea here.' Ben was pointing at two ants recognising their faces. 'These two learnt not to commit mass suicide. But the majority still blundered into the glass door, multiple deaths splattered like moths on a windscreen, like kamikaze clowns trying to escape the oven. At least they were willing to die more ALIVE than those who stay back and just sulk.'

Insisted PC, 'Brave, glorious SACRIFICES for the sake of society's survival! Give ants democracy and what would happen? They'd allow total annihilation. DEATH is the lowest common denominator.'

'The HIGHEST!' countered Ben.

Battle-lines were becoming clearer.

'Only benign leadership saves us all from DEATH!' bugled PC, robustly. 'Discipline must pass from their chosen Shepherd to his disciples! Folks, ALL folks, must bloody choose – wisely!'

Even though PC had refrained from saying MY PEOPLE, Alice and Pitta wanted to puke.

Rightly or wrongly Alice was still feeling that the presence underground of PC and his Gun Law was all her own fault. While she was still writhing with guilt, PC produced the third physicist, Casper, a retired beekeeper. Though Casper was a podge on two dumpy legs, he praised fasting as a way to purge his body even though it had stayed obstinately plump. In short pants Casper announced, 'Bees make nuclear nectar. Till every worker dies. In a litter of husks. Till then, each season, bees stay ready to stab. To die in one fatal, defensive sting. Honey bees are not cute!' He took a moment for the full picture to etch itself in its mental acid.

Before PC could intervene, Casper whose eyes were fired with irony continued. 'Yes, bees respect monarchy. But that won't save them. Nor will God. Bees believe in their deterrent. God may be dead but not bees' own in-built time-bomb. Nuclear power lives. It works. For or against us, it works'. Then after another panting pause, he added, 'I'd rather trust ants!' With a wry grin, Casper pulled down his bee-net, veiling his entire head. A weary shrug of his shoulders and he sank into lassitude refusing all food.

There followed a break for refreshments, Humphrey presiding.

Beaming Ben, the second scientist, took centre stage again. While spoon-feeding the reluctant Casper, he said, 'Yes, better respect the bomb. It's quick, obedient, and efficient. A fast-breeder of cancer cells, cute enough to fell Olympian gold medallists. Let's relish profits before people, hamburgers before hardwoods, paper before policy, or vast wastelands of radioactive ruins. And, if the rest of the circus does survive on toxic sawdust. . . .'

'Not long to go!' clarified PC, a clarion-call to reclaim the limelight. 'The Saffs are going to swamp us with leaks of fall-out fumes. Will we let these killers blackmail us all, man, woman and child, or. . . ?' Like a lethal vapour cloud, the unspoken threat hung over their heads. What, PC and Ben, both on the same side?

Stressed Pitta, 'Nosh more food before . . . We ain't safe, see. From underground nuke tests sites never mind new earthquakes. . . .'

Not Humphrey, not White Rabbit, nor any one of the scientists responded, all looking down at their shoes as if wearing magnetised soles. Only until PC hyped up the hysteria with tabloid terror-tactics. Then PC's 'disciples' gazed up at their leader like refurbished glove-puppets. Without him, they had no life. WITH him, their survival through all dangers seemed secure, flirting with dangers a sort of masturbatory foreplay. Silently, they begged him to intervene with resolute phrases to thrill them into actions they could be persuaded would soon benefit all Survivalists.

Except those called enemies, the savage Saffs. Invisible enemies, even the threat of them, are always the most potent.

Keeping a wary eye on Humphrey, Alice prompted Pitta to voice her next urgent question. 'How would we all, like, spend our last four-minute warning?'

An uncomfortable silence.

After two minutes Humphrey farted. Laughter, Then Ben sadly proclaimed, 'Two hundred more acres of tropical rain forest now destroyed.'

Casper yawned out, 'While Cyclops sleeps, we all turn a blind eye.'

Arm around Casper, Ben almost carolled out this next lament, 'Flying ants taught me to preserve power. Now I'll help to save nuclear fuels for posterity.'

Alice became disturbed as Ben continued, 'Even if we have to claw our way through with broken nails. Who will join me . . . before our food supplies run short . . . who will rescue enough rations . . . from the selfish claws of those infidels, the Saffs hidden in Rainbow Mountain? Show me who's willing. . . .'

Pitta and many others put up their hands.

Alice did not. She was disgusted by Ben's apparent conversion to the cause espoused by PC and Humphrey, their ideals, steered by PC, as flexible as anthrax on varied airwaves.

Feeling threatened, PC grabbed back the focus. Loudly he declared, 'We should be sealing ourselves in friends, against noxious fogs. Imperative we block the Saff monks who would control us lot, stock and barrel. Before hereabouts . . . becomes airless . . . like the earth is . . . above us now.'

Led by Ben, a band of like-minded folks together with Casper decided to take off. They would risk collecting food from within the network of secret tunnels under Abingdon town.

Abingdon was rumoured to be hiding one of 330 stores situated around Britain. Such emergency supplies in the Excessive Eighties were for what the late officials, despite public concerns about the Cold War, had been instructed to call 'NATURAL disasters.' And of course, officials denied the existence of such underground provisions even around London's Westminster, let alone the 30 unused tube stations or their extensions. These were protected by the official Secrets Acts, presumably because they're to be converted into nuclear bunkers for the Ministry of Defence with a convenient tunnel linked to the Palaces Westminster and Buckingham.

PC's henchmen blocked their path. Before Ben and others could desert that vast troglodyte city and perhaps turn into defectors, PC insisted, 'WAIT! Not tins of food. It's nuclear waste disguised as baked beans. Bait! Bait placed there by the Saffs! A Pandora's Box of poisons to kill us all.' Whatever fears PC could not exploit, he might be inventing in order to keep them trapped in a vice of anxieties from which only he could release them. 'Any one nuclear power plant cracks and – SPLAT! Like bursting a pod of poisoned sweet peas. Now! Threat's bloody present – omnipotent'.

'But we've five hair trigger fail-safe mechanisms,' protested Ben. Armageddon is now us! Will laws prevent substances like alpha-emitter Plutonium-239 with a half-life 24,000 years, or Tritium which forms radioactive water. . . ?'

Supporting his colleague, Casper said, 'Corn, as it happens, cracks open less easily. Each seed's now more resistant to ultraviolet radiation. Adjusting, you see . . . evolving. . . .'

'Ants and beetles are not so easy to crack open either,' added Ben.'Is that why cockroaches get stamped on? So, with my hungry beekeeper here, who's for reclaiming self-raising flour . . . not organically grown . . . but awaiting the no longer privileged consumers. . . ?'

Topping all possible arguments, while arranging for iodine pills to be given out like sweeties, PC made his final plea, declaring, 'Armageddon now belongs to the late dead ones above. What we are threatened with down here is the aftermath of Doomray. Death by small doses . . . death by silent stealth . . . threats worse than the fire in Windscale . . . worse than Three Mile Island . . . and worse than what happened to all of those who prayed for peace whilst seeking protection with their implicit prayer, Let's help an Accident! All it took upstairs was the failure of a 5-cent chip. Fear of war don't lead to peace. Bad eggs will always explode.'

Pitta returned to Alice. Change her mind, would she? 'Join PC's lot, eh, after all? 'You knows why, yeah! Let's go for it, gal!'

Alice stared at Humphrey, her loyalties painfully torn. Corn from the underground store in Abingdon or perhaps, choose the more dangerous option; stay with Humphrey and therefore the pushy and overbearing warmonger disguised as a peacenik, PC.

Alice shrank. Pitta pleaded. No? Then off she'd go, herself and Casper. As to food-miles, Abingdon was about six miles from Oxford. Oxford? Alice would remember to honour another date with another Charles, one Dodgson, in some circular time warp resonant with déjà vu. Alternatively, should Alice risk losing her beloved by discovering, maybe, what secrets lay behind Humphrey's tinted glasses that so needed a good clean?

With a gulp, Alice said a firmer NO. She'd not go with Pitta.

The parting of the ways.

With a final wink to the recoiling Alice, Pitta left with the others, defenders of the faith or defectors, whichever. As if on eggshells, the small band of explorers tiptoed along the passage that led away from Death Row-Boat, 800 miles under the mantle of the airless earth above them.

Still hiding at the back of the crowd, Alice was persuading herself that fears of annihilation could never compete with the joys of Total Consciousness. Unless they were the same thing!

'Right on, pet!' praised her inner feline, comfortingly. 'Pigmies with blowpipes envy Giants with bazookas. Till polarity is gained with weapons like boomerangs. Or one big cosmic threat. Never since Atlantis has Goliath so needed the next King David; filthy seas the next Noah; human Souls the next Living Master; Jerusalem run by inter-denominational Priest Monarchs. Our crucial crossroads always return . . . even on the most moral of ordinance survey maps. Aye, rightly so. So, think on, chuck!'

Think on, she did. Risking all, she would dare to declare her public opposition to PC, Humphrey and all who traded in fear.

Later the same day, PC rallied the crowd as usual. Proudly, he announced he was about to unveil the secrets gleaned by the fourth 'microwaved' scientist, Miriam.

M for Miriam? Alice hoped she who would reveal secrets from beyond and before Christ Consciousness. Even if the sad scientist thought God has deserted her tribe even before Golgatha.

PC riveted those present with this thought: 'In breaking into that cache of emergency rations, how long till they bombard us with radioactive smog? Those deserters who just left us, friends, how long before they trigger terrorist activities? Our underground streets, Plutodenium City reeking with nauseating odours from our own wasting away dear ones with blue-black blistered necks is that what we want. . . ?'

Protective yasmaks were tightened around nose and mouth, the crowd gasping in a more shallow way.

Bursting with defiance and distrust of the man, Alice cheered up. Instead of a yashmak, she put on a bonnet covered with fruit and flowers. Boldly, marching straight up to PC and his sick 'son' (meaning Humphrey), she told them to explain themselves. 'How can a beehive be saved when 2.4 billion pounds is used on making nuclear honey,' she asked, sharpening her tongue, 'all so that bees may buzz in Easter bonnets more safely if, in using their ultimate deterrent, each bee dies by losing its own sting? And the beehive. And all flowers. And their fruit trees.' On that she produced what she had carved earlier. 'Isn't the atom bomb the ultimate boomerang?' In conclusion, she snapped it in half. 'Gentlemen, donnish logic has no answers worth dying FOR or living WITH, have they?' Pause. 'HAVE THEY?' she bellowed like a bulldog bitch on heat. BullDOG because the words felt given her.

'Machines chew up one entire tree in 60 seconds!' Surprising them, the voice came from Ben. He and two other stragglers had returned. 'Takes centuries to grow one sapling'. The crowd sighed as he added, 'But five minutes to murder a tree.'

Like a quiet beligerent bishop with God on his side, PC cooly answered Alice's outburst with, 'Young lady, live every day as if about to die, and live every night as if you'll live for ever!'

Round of applause for PC!

Surprisingly, his adherents were joined by some of the returned Abingdon group. Though believing the end is nigh like Jehovah's Witnesses knocking on locked doors of nuclear bunkers, they had quickly split up over tactics. Ben had done what no politician ever dares to do – a U-turn. But not Pitta. She was not with the returnees. Alice still missed her jolly support.

As spokesperson, Ben told PC they had become afraid that in breaking into food stores, they might accidentally unleash some leaking nuclear waste products supposedly safely buried beyond harm to human life. Music to the ears of PC and his supporters, this seemed to vindicate their leader's earlier warning. The threat of earth changes was bad enough. Contamination of their groundwater springs was indeed another hazard. Even without the Saffs preparing their epic attack from within Rainbow Mountain.

Pip added another suggestion. Like a male version of Pitta with the crystal ear-studs, Pip said they were all better off tunnelling, through to the Rollright Stones north of Oxford. At the mention of Oxford, Alice found her eyes flicking over to Humphrey. Suddenly he looked older and thinner, as if his new found hero PC was shaping up his plump sheep-dog pup into a manhood that applauds the ethics of dog eats dog. Was that what her nightmare Black Dog had warned her to avoid?

'Like, on this dawn raid, right,' said Pip picking his nose, 'we sensed microwave activity. All round the Rollrights. Like light and sound are one, psychedelic. Standing Stones the first rock opera! Primitive, man! And like, we wasn't stoned at the time! But at sunrise on the solstice, right, the electrons in the stones got sorta excited. I heard sommat. Even-toned. High-pitched. One note. Like the press at home call 'THE BRISTOL HUM'. Yeah, blew me away, man. Sufferers of tinnitus get uptight, right. But what if these sounds are, like spooky mystical messages. . . ?'

M for Mystic?

Pip grimaced. 'Listen, this ain't 'arf groovy. Radioactive. Them Rollrights. That henge what would of, like, kept at bay all man-made radiations . . . shockwaves, yeah. Know wot I mean? From them recent nuke explosions, man. A safe haven, right, in amongst them wizard's tall stones!'

Possibly. Alice was remembering how the first five of her nine crystals had become tarnished when placed around the dying Snow Black. Was that not like Pip claiming that a magic stone circle might protect all life within it? If so, yippee!

'Nein, nein, NEIN! An operatic howl came from within the fourth oven. 'No better than the blue Star of David'. These howls came from Miriam, her hooked nose squashed against the microwave door, splayed hands battering the glass.

Miriam's cries PC ignored. So, of course, did many of his fans. Instead, Pip introduced a second psychic researcher. One who had been present that day at the Rollright Stones. Into the limelight stepped Humphrey, the plumpish psychic ventriloquist.

Alice gasped. Humphrey with second sight also? To check out his eyes, when would she get to see behind his gold-tinted glasses, shades seeming so suspicious. . . ?

Humphrey reported what infra-red photography had revealed, glowing just above the ground near the King Stone. 'As well as around the rest of the megalithic site, a mysterious cloud appeared! Now m-maybe, we should turn all underground nuclear waste dumps, yep, into Sacred Sites, not into mushroom clouds.'

The crowd became hushed.

Alice was furious. So inconsiderate! How could Humphrey confuse her about where he was really coming from, all over again? Still, the inside of the Rollright Stone Circle, she felt, would stay safe against nuclear fall-out. Being a sacred site, it would be the best place to wait for rescue from any passing UFO or Flying Flute with or without her two-faced lover boy, Humphrey.

But truth to tell, suddenly Alice was hoping that the pilot might indeed be Humphrey. And in a different uniform. Not purple but a Venusian gold. Yes, in her private heart, Alice nursed the vision of Humphrey waving her aboard his own escape craft to higher regions of love on planet Venus with all mod cons.

To a saucier angle, purring like a bumblebee, she up-tilted the brim of her fruity bonnet. Surely she'd soon get close enough to check on the colour of Humphrey's hidden eyes. If he truly was mystic, they'd be all golden, like the eyes of a messenger sent down from Venus. Had she not also remembered that Venus was once known as a loving MALE entity with an earth-like atmosphere curiously modified but with strange dynamics? An enticing prospect, or what?

Humphrey appeared to stay besotted. Proverbially, he was licking PC's jackboots every step of the way . . . every day of the election campaign . . . to WHERE . . . and WHY. . . ?

'Open up, son!'

Following that curt order with its slight Cockney tones, Humphrey broke the outer cobwebs draped over the fourth oven. Like a self-elected celebrity opening a cake-stall at some village fête, PC then presented Miriam.

Ingrained with grief, the granny appeared. The only woman amongst the subterranean scientists, Miriam confessed. She had failed to name all the ants that had amassed on the apple under her protection. Dark lines streaked her tense face, her stringy neck wobbling like a turkey dreading Christmas Day. Not that her religion would have permitted such a thought. Miriam had always found ovens deeply disturbing ever since reading Jack and the Beanstalk. Enjoying quantum physics by dodging electrons or

falling into an atom hadn't helped either. Such studies seemed to be leading to nowhere better than to a nuclear no-where. Indeed, she thought
splitting the atom humanity's most odious sin since the destruction of
Atlantis, with or without warped cystal powers.

PC posed the question printed out on a crib-card just handed him by
Humphrey. Who else but Alice in the crowd was noticing such tell-tale
details between that martial mentor and his adopted 'son', her would-be
lover, Humphrey? Resolutely, PC asked his awe-struck acolytes, 'Can
anyone get comfort from a quark that doesn't bloody well seem to exist?'

'Only ... zose ... beyond all ... Milky Vay agonies,' surrendered
Miriam, the Viennese mystic, her face writhing. 'Forgive, David's Star.
Stars only but evolution's ovens, cosmic furnaces in ze high firmament,
zem zat bake kosher bagels for space-angels past and present ... and
future ... to consume.' She looked deranged.

'Like them late crazy ants on only one apple, eh?' asked Pip.

During her atonement Miriam claimed with a wince her warring
thoughts had gnawed. 'Two ant armies zey attack my apple on two fronts,
ja. My sparring empire, Mind, a battlefield. Inner umpire, Intuition, it sing
to me vespers. Zese I studiously ignore. Sorry to say, civil-var, she still so
raw, blazes inside of me now, like pins and needles ... like some say,
ARMAGEDON, ja!'

Trading on visions of terrestrial terror, PC intervened. Dramatically
waving an old copy of TIBET NEWS like Chamberlain declaring peace in
our time, he read out, *'Less than half a decade to its birthing will see the
waters breaking on a world event that will polarise our attention!'* PC
further painted a graphic picture of earth's crust, the ceiling of their underground cities, being punctured and paralysed by the Saffs.'Pierced like an
upside down colander, deluged with toxic oceans, all underground get
trapped like ants in a cosmic toxic washing-machine, no mercy.' That
threat, claimed PC, was enough to justify pre-emptive attacks on the sinister Saffs in order to prevent further cataclysms.

'Mother Earth ... we veep for you!' wailed Miriam. With pity, they
watched her fists beating her sagging breasts. 'How we hold onto
sufferink. So now, riddled I am! YES! Half a THOUSAND Pharaoh ants,

241

vampire ants, all inside me. They can live in von keyhole only, so . . . omnivorous.' Wild eyes flashing but too weak to stand, her stocky body fell to the floor like a rag-doll.

Through the fazed crowd, the full implications of Miriam's condition spread like a virus. Soon vampire ants appeared from out of her ears. After the bad apple, too little was left to eat for the tiny thousand carnivorous jaws. Through every orifice pierced by ant patrols, marching columns had mined all of Miriam's entrails while chewing out a whole body network of ant tunnels, yet against all offered comforts, her baleful eyes stared, blankly. Sympathetically, the crowd moved in closer so that the old lady need not shout. 'It vas like four ages . . . stages' explained Miriam in her German accent. 'Being a biologist, I got to break zese all down you understand, even if both voracious rival ant armies intend, how you say, to break ME down . . . first. I must zink zis out nicely. . . .'

Humphrey offered Miriam a drink of water. As if a High Priest to a desert leper, she accepted it. Alice was starting to hate him. He'd followed a nod from PC, not volunteered that act of kindness himself.

'Living with ants' continued Miriam after four sips only, 'vas I Mamma, Papa, or . . . vot else. . . ?'

'Machine?' asked Humphrey, his tone growing colder.

'First, as Mother Earth,' said Miriam, gaining strength, 'I feel I should let my ants have zeir own vay. So swarms rape me, I may say so. My body just cheesecake, red pincer-sharp ants fighting black ants like schwarzers. Veaker ants, I intend to feed zese naturally, whilst the Papa in me, he favour only ze strongest. I spoilt them all, foolishly. Of course so. I'm a woman. How can von call Gott good and kind and Nature bad and cruel . . . someone tell me HOW zis can dare be so. . . ?'

Her pausing to sip more water gave a chance for those there to ponder her last point.

'Sex var. Ze Mamma in me, she had to, truly, interfere. To curtail all ants' apparent free choices. Zen kindly I am remembering LOVE. Be careful to little lives. So, I give zem vot I thought zey need most, my guts. I childless now, you must see zis.'

Breathlessly, Alice watched as Miriam's left eyeball ballooned. Her pupil bulging from inside its socket split open as if a seed-sac of a juicy bedside grape. Two twitching antennae appeared probing between her eyelashes as her words gushed forth. 'But vorst of all I could not, in love, kill my tiny attackers. So yes, now ants, even as I starve, eat me inside out . . . how to say? Ja, out of ze house and ze home . . . but sure, I vill love you all . . . each von . . . each small ant . . . as ze cruel Gott, he loves us all. . . .'

Those with ultra-sonic sensitivity, strained to hear worker ants as they bored through Miriam's brain, chewing their way towards both succulent eye-holes as more ant scouts sought a purchase on her lower eyelids. Behind, ranks of restless ants followed. Their nano-nipping jaws were likely to chew up all the rest of her insides to a husk, to let light into their dark innermost cave, Miriam's screaming skull.

'LOVE!' screeched Miriam, 'Love, in ze name of victorious villpower, this is NO PURE LOVE . . . but stupid fear-propelled victimhood, as if Gott vill not provide survival . . . zis I now learn!'

Alice saw that PC was itching to censor such insights. Unaware of his disquiet, Miriam continued like a demented New Age Mother Shipton. 'Individuals . . . of any race or breed...who vorship personal ego-power, zat dears, must be so purged, scoured out, purified . . . from vithin us all . . . even by beloved enemies like our darlink warring greedy ants . . . zis I learn now. . . .'

To please the crowd and silence the Jewess, PC ordered medics to attend to Miriam. Like Madame Curie discovering about radium by using her own experience as fatal evidence, Miriam rejected all help. Too soon. Howling with near madness, the agonised granny collapsed on to her knees. Once there, she sobbed over the corps of auxiliary ants she had just crushed under her own kneecaps, their death unlamented except by Miriam herself. Those ants, after all, had kindly refused her flesh and would have died anyway of starvation, or as martyred vegetarians.

Unaided, Miriam staggered to her feet, defiantly spitting out, 'As Papa, I try to use rationales; ze righteous Holy Var, like Holy Orders, is the supposed Divine Right to defend ourselves against all invaders, howso-ever small . . . however helpless. . . .'

Nods of squeamish sympathy all round. Keeping a sustainable peace had long inspired all those there. 'Borrowing from E.W. Beth, the Dutch logician,' Miriam continued, both eyeballs oozing, 'I kept quoting: *IF A MAN SAYS **I AM TELLING A LIE**, AND SPEAKS TRULY, HE **IS** TELLING A LIE AND THEREFORE SPEAKS **TRULY**.*'

Uneasy minds struggled with such a painful paradox.

But Alice had been deeply stirred. Empathising, she hoped to help the compassionate grandmother. If only she could hug her pain away.

'Nein, nein, NEIN!' screamed Miriam as if trying to call an ambulance before an emergency burst open like a boil or bomb. 'Edinburgh's first Professor of Parapsychology stated zis; ve can fake having a cold, but fake doesn't make ze cold any less real. To escape cold, Decartes went also into an oven. There he say to himself, I THINK THEREFORE I AM and perished, pissing against ze vind of changes . . . he now for ever . . . GONE . . . POOF!'

Ben requested sharply, 'Prevent a green holocaust.Consider the laws of nature and recycling. Like the METHOD OF TREES.'

'Vienna Voods!' Miriam sang a glissando of gratitude for the lungs of Austria, the lovely forests of her Fatherland.

Ben pursued her point. 'First, test the validity of forests through reduction ad absurdum.'

'You mean . . . like, blow 'em up?' asked Pip, appalled.

Determined to stay academically alert till the end, Miriam retorted with, 'The first vord of this vorld vas not EARTH. It was FOREST. And East Germany's favourite word is WALDSTERBEN. Means forest death. Privatise Vienna Voods? How might ve feel about this, tell me, HOW. . . ?'

'Vorried,' muttered Alice, quick to pick up any accent.

'90% of German trees vill die, thanks to fall-out from the Ruhr. Krupps still lives, OK? Vhat Hitler's war did not exterminate, recent accidents kill, acid rain VILL. Bevare, VILLPOWER KILLS!'

'I challenge that!' bellowed PC, his moustache as arched as his eyebrows. He was also rattled by Ben's part time support, Ben being a potential rival. 'The Fuehrer, he had all new forests planted. Hitler, as a vegetarian, loved trees,' added PC with forced bravado.

'So – bah!' sniped Miriam like a wounded rattlesnake pierced by spiked jackboots. 'Quick growing spruce, sir! To feed a quick victory! Hitler, believing in a pure race, did not permit MIXED planting. Or Gemeinshaft. Mistake! That is vhy he lost ze var, us Jews also, and our brainpowers. Hitler's forests still die, already! Just quick convenience conifers. No leaf mould to neutralise acid pine needles. No ants either. Greed alvays cause disbalances.'

Directed at PC, Ben shouted, 'Each year now, one family's garbage in wastepaper, disposes of SIX whole trees.' PC frowned.

Alice frowned. She was grieving over the leafy woodlands around Warren Row, all branches atomised in the first nuclear flash. One litmus test for a real leader is the way that probing questions are handled – or not. She decided to heckle PC direct. Since foxhunting tones upset PC's assumed Home Counties' arrogance, Alice disguised her voice. Sounding right royal posh and hiding in the crowd, unseen she asked, 'Confirm, if you will, sir, are we poised on the rim of infinity, on the edge of deadly doom?'

Defiantly, PC rallied with, 'The Force is with US!' three times.

'Not more FORCE ve need,' jeered Miriam, 'it's more freedom!'

'What country would dare fly a white flag as its national emblem?' demanded PC. He sounded reasonable yet, to the ear of Alice, still indulging in subtle one-upmanship while forcing his estuary vowels into well-bred utterances. 'Rabbits have white scuts not for themselves but to save the warren for future rabbits. But for Survivalists there's my Master Plan! This I'm ready to reveal if you wants all white blood corpuscle counts kept at a healthy high.'

Humphrey sank to his knees with a loud born again 'Yep – Alleluia!' Amazing themselves, many others followed his lead.

'But FIGHT for FREEDOM, we lose it!' yelled Alice like a tally-ho against fox-hunting out of season, she confronted PC head-on.

'Son!' PC gave another quick nod. Rising to order, Humphrey with a swipe of his hand hitting Alice in the face knocked off her Easter Bonnet, Alice faling to her knees. The crowd cheered.

Victoriously, PC, Humphrey and other recruits withdrew into Miriam's empty oven.

Alice was looking distraught. She'd not been quick enough to knock off Humphrey's golden specs in front of PC before they left.

Left, the crowd in Death Row-Boat resembled orphans. So insecure. Had PC planted metaphorical spores of myxomatosis in the rabbit warren? Before force against the Saffs could be democratically effective, highly spiced dangers were needed. For Operation Hope to work helped by Humphrey, PC was recognising the need for his young bucks to have dangerous Rites of Passage to prove themselves, to be given challenges in which to experiment with their own adrenaline. PC agreed that the time was not yet right for him to declare himself their General-in-Chief. For the RAINBOW WARRIORS to follow him into the bowels of King Kal's Rainbow Mountain, it was first essential that their ranks increase in numbers and in self-confidence. Should they be trained to serve the SYSTEM rather than their own personal mission to serve earth conscious-ness in their own chosen way? Or could not that become the same thing, anyway? These were the policies and tactics discussed in the fourth oven, a war bunker away from the crowd.

What could Alice do? PC's intentions were surely bristling with veiled but evil ambitions to become King of the Underworld. How could she, single-handedly, overthrow PC? And lose Humphrey? Nervously, Alice approached the forbidding Miriam even though she had refused all medical help and pity. If only Alice could express her big heart as easily as she could express her big head, by then, bruised by Humphrey. 'Peace exists,' ventured Alice, 'when we allow it to by believing in it as good and proper. Sadly yep, I'd say that's true of nuclear power also.'

'Nuclear fission! Nuclear fusion! Nuclear confusion! Nuclear eunuchs – PIGSHITE!' cried Miriam. 'Low level radiation is treated as being ze same as natural background radiation. But isotopes like Strontium 90 though artificial, concentrate in our very bones inducing mutations. Deadliest substances lie in vait underground, radioisotopes causing man-made diseases, fast breeders, caesium, and death in larger and larger doses. Intellectual defences of zis are trash. Nice non-sequiters abound like...like,' her shrug left an unfinished sentence.

'Like holes in a puzzle-jug, chuck!' suggested Alice. From within her inner ear, she'd borrowed Mancunian Cat's suggestion.

'A joke, ja! For Bavarian tourists!' she exclaimed. 'A jug riddled vith holes, making the storage of liquids impossible. A practical joke ja, for alcoholic uncles trying to dry out after years on ze booze bottles.'

'God's too holy to be logical!' offered Alice, consolingly.

'Like ME NOW!' scowled Miriam defying all help for her body but still wishing to use up her grey cells before the ant jaws ground her brains down into slimy white powdery droppings.

'Germanic lore,' suggested Ben, 'is infused with the SUPER-NATURAL.' Like PC, he used that SUPER word to uplift reactions.

'As are their best super allegories. Listen to Wagner!'

'Fascist!' spat out Miriam.

'Hitler was a red herring, deflecting Communism from world domination,' countered Ben. 'But the force is with US. Here. Underground. The race is on . . . here . . . now . . . today. We must grab back the evil Saff's Radioactive Rod of Power!'

Ben speaking? He was sounding like PC. That propelled Alice into stating aloud, 'Any acts not love-centred . . . they will FAIL!'

In PC's absence, Ben's attempt to win acclaim was short-changed by Miriam's cantorial-like hymn,'Ja, gentle gentiles, force-fed geese. Too fat to fly. The Force? Force self-destructs. . . ! Ze writing is on ze Vailing Vall. Ja, it belong to all goys, to schmocks too, not just to ve Chosen Vons who von't forgo egos . . . our pushy, self-opinionated villfullness, ja, ultimately, is our killer.'

'Action's essential if. . . .' Ben paused. He'd lost the crowd. From Miriam's oven PC had reappeared. In his wake his martial-looking squad of grim bald young bucks grinning in purple tunics.

As Humphrey, his head now shaven clean as an egg, joined the glowering PC, Alice dodged back to the rear of the crowd. Most misguided folks there were grateful to see PC re-establish his eminence in their eyes. 'It is not willpower which will kill all,' he proclaimed with renewed conviction. 'It is VRIL POWER which will THRILL EACH STUDENT OF GOD'S LOVE AND THE TRUE LIFE!'

A scream. Miriam, by then nearly blind in her right eye, had just suffered an extra sharp ant bite around her left nipple.

Many of the young got a more alert look in their eye. The new word VRIL has its own electrical charge. Like an ad-man not missing a trick, PC added the rider, 'The Real Secret of our Survival is unique. Simply, it's our own personal VRIL POWER!'

Another scream from Miriam. Bravely rallying, 'No, WRONG, sir!' she railed. 'As a Jew I say zis: zere be scarcely any event in Europe zat cannot be traced back to our superior tribal cleverness. Yet racism, it come vorst from its own kind. Check out Dr Oscar Levy of Vorcester College, Oxford. Read his vords, *"If you are anti-Semite, I the Semite am anti-Semite too, and a much more fervent one zan ever you are. Ve, the Jews, have erred my friends, ve have grievously erred"* – Unquote.'

Embarrassed shufflings. No immediate guidance offered by PC so Miriam persevered. 'And again, in his letter to George Pitt Rivers, Dr Levy wrote, *"VE WHO HAVE POSED AS THE SAVIOURS OF ZIS VORLD, VE WHO HAVE EVEN BOASTED OF HAVING GIVEN IT ZE SAVIOUR, VE ARE TODAY ... NOZING ELSE ... BUT ZE VORLD'S SEDUCERS, ITS DESTROYERS, ITS INCENDIARIES AND ITS EXECUTIONERS"*.'

More crowd unease.

'I, as professor . . .' admitted Miriam, 'have helped non-Jews study our Holy Book, The Talmud. Accordingly, I should die. It's forbidden to reveal our oaths against the Goyim. Reveal its secrets to Gentiles, the penalty is death. My Christian ants must know it ja. Now I opt out of every race. Even our human race. May my Yiddish sickness leave, never to return. Jehovah, promote me soon, I beg. To angel vings, I pray. Mankind is too messy for me to struggle any longer . . . I must fly avay . . . back home. . . .'

Erect with potency, PC massaged imaginations. 'Unify all races,' he serenaded, 'into one almighty Force and all will be wedded to cosmic obedience, each with Secret Powers, a Master Magician!' In young groins, the promise of personal power stiffened. Their resolve to serve PC was hardening into an urgent lust. Even Ben looked completely won over by PC's magnetic certainties, no matter who scripted them.

To Alice, Ben had seemed so liberal and kind. Was she to be left totally alone in her belief that PC and Humphrey were a threat worth exposing?

While Alice ruminated on that, Ben reminded them that in Parsifal, Wagner's opera, the secret of a long clean life was revealed as Pure Blood.

'Exactly!' exclaimed PC. 'That's why Vril Power is only for us, the Pure in Heart!'

Pubescent youths savoured a regime that would rate them as pure, important and permanently potent with VRIL POWER. That alone promised them a full life. And a long one too. Longevity in Utopia, for both sexes, was becoming the ultimate testosterone.

Miriam, meanwhile, was jubilantly improvising her own Dance of Death, driblets of mucus spattering her nifty raw feet. As bleeding fists punched the sky, overjoyed as any star footballer after scoring the best goal of the season, she whooped and wailed out:

'PUZZLE-JUGS, PUZZLE-JUGS,
LIFE'S MORE THAN FROTH AND FOAM,
SOUL IS GOOT, GOTT IS GOOT,
AS ALL ROADS LEAD TO HOME.
HUMAN HUGS, HUMAN HUGS, DON'T LEAVE OUT VON FOE,
GOTT LOVES US ALL, THOUGH WE MAY FALL,
JEHOVAH TIME TO GO.'

As they applauded, Miriam defied praise, screaming, 'GOTT, I ask zis. Where is Jehovah's answering-machine? SWITCHED OFF or vot?'

Sideways glances. In their purple uniforms PC's recruits did not like looking pig ignorant as well as bald. So Miriam topped her Dance Macabre with a spine-chilling cry, a skeletal finger jabbed towards PC. 'VE ALL are! Each is Gott's own answering-machine – NOT HIM!' A gasp! 'To survive ve seek more defiance, far less compliance. PEOPLE POWER, ja! I say again, not HIM!'

A tight posse quickly protected PC, isolating Miriam, many hissing at her. They wanted to become special in the eyes of PC, not in the fierce punishing eye of the unknowable Jehovah or by any one of His lower nom-de-plumes such as Moses.

Like a freak show at the funfair, Miriam's threadbare body again became the centre of attention. Rolling on the ground like a skinned gorilla demented with parasites, Miriam implored Abraham for release. 'Please! I must now of passed my nuclear tests. HELP ME!' she screeched, 'Inside ja, in zat big oven vith flying ants I felt so generous. Like Gott! Till ja, I . . . I bribe the Jesus ants already . . . vith my body . . . because I . . . I . . . DISOBEYED Pluto. Ja, ja, ja, to you, I LIED . . . sorry . . . sorry to say so badly . . . ja, I LIED to you all good folks. Me, here, you see me not as I am, ze bad apple. . . .'

Some listeners bit their lips.

PC felt crowd power deflected to the stark ant-bitten victim writhing on the ground.

Before blindness could blank out her brain, Miriam stretched every fibre of her old lady's ragged flesh to stay in focus. 'It's fusion ve need, not nuclear fission. Friends, friends, I am a shameful, shameful THIEF!'

Disbelief. The crowd frozen.

Rocking, she beat her chest several times, ritualistically. 'To myself I lied. To my ants lied. Zen to you all. LIES! Instead of von rotting apple, I sneaked inside zat oven SEVEN STOLEN ripe golden delicious. . . .'

The crowd dare not gasp. Or even giggle. Alice though, felt a kind of relief. Was that ALL the professor needed to confess! Was that small sin not as venial as her silence over two guns sneaked into their underground paradise?

Grateful for their silence, Miriam continued, 'Like my tribe, I was afraid, ja. For my own survival . . . always AFRAID. . . .'

'Why SEVEN apples,' they asked as she beat the ground.

'To prove myself through lies. To survive in your eyes as special. God's mysteries are best revealed slowly, over centuries. But zis I now know.' Whispering reverentially, Miriam grimaced at the bee-keeping physicist. 'Zere are 7 veils, 7 earths, seventy-seven heavens to fly to . . . so. . . .' Her raw hands clawed at her dress.

A clump of callow youths started to shake. Could PC's orders on purity of purpose and intent be now compromised by nudity?

Stripping. Miriam ranted, 'So I say zis; ve must spend seven – at least seven – lifetimes in each astrological sign. Seven, too, is ze number of ze charkas, zis number of celestial symmetry. Spirit must flow through our puzzle-jugs, not be trapped. I, folks, serving ze greatest goot, ze Gott of Science? Ja ja, I fool myself.' Her laughter was rasping. 'Like any communist capitalist! By ze rationale of hollow materialism. SEVEN apples. Seven STOLEN apples! Not just von like colleagues. Ashamed I am. Like Queen Midas, like Queen Midas I need to die . . . please . . . let me die now. . . .'

M for Midas? Surely not.

Alice, aching because of not being allowed to help the old lady out of her pain, asked, 'Mother Miriam, do tell us, what you have learnt to help all underground Rainbow Warriors?'

Miriam obliged, grinning gamely. 'God's ants, I say zey all are Jesus agents, bless 'em. Unclogging my plumbing. Making me holy, into flow again. Better zan Yom Kippur.' Then a shriek of agony as ants bit voraciously at the centre of her brow. 'HOLY, HOLY, HOLY!' screamed Miriam. Then gritting her dentures, her voice grating, she obstinately insisted, 'Pain, I can take, ja. Ants I can take. Holy puzzle-jug I can swallow, even acute neuropathy, BUT . . . LOSE MY FIRST CLASS BRAINS . . . **NO!**'

Empathising, Alice clutched her own temples. Lightening searing pains zigzagged through her head. A maniacal cackle ricocheted around Alice's skull. Though sounding like PC, was that really Kal, King of Rainbow Mountain, the dark side of their underground Paradise? Through the evil-sounding hilarity, the words she thought she heard were:

FROM SPERM TO WORM, BECOME MY SECRET SPY!
HUMPHREY'S BIG BALLS IN HIS PUTRID SPUNK FRY!

Whose voice? Some Astral joker? Dump Humphrey? Believe Humphrey? And trust PC? Decisions too dangerous not to nag and gnaw at her conscience. Knowingly, the evil voice continued to cackle out,

TELL ALL! OR BAGATELLE WITH EYEBALLS – YOURS!
TILL BLIND AND DUMB YOU TOO BE RIDDLED WITH SORES!

More searing in her head. Alice couldn't even remember what bagatelle

251

was, horrid though that anonymous threat made it sound. And LOOK! Like a visual threat to her, from every orifice Miriam was exuding living lava of twitching red and black ants through a vertical line of gaping wounds. In all, that plumb-line of ant holes extended from her crown to her anus, ants seething, teeming, crawling everywhere, in and out of seven livid and frayed fleshy holes. Anxious to sport all war-wounds, from her thighs battle-scarred Mother Miriam was pealing off strips of flesh like wallpaper as if all her seven layers of skin were on fire.

Hiding her modesty, two Jewish girls gently sponged Miriam all over with milk and honey. 'Tears and she have been together too long,' they crooned, 'For her now, the Promised Land.'

A shriek from Miriam. 'NEIN! More pains! I need! Orgasms! Out-of-body trips, I need! Agonies! Exorcism, explosions, enemas, purge all termites, scour dirty bowels, boil, like skinned beetroot, in salt seas . . . but best, darling heartless Gott, at last You tell me zis; vy oh vy You say my earth race are Gott's own Chosen People?'

'Why? Why? WHY?' The crowd, repulsed yet fascinated by the struggle for dominance as both armies of ants, smelling honey, renewed attack, needling in and out of Miriam's raw pincushion body. 'For so many years I vould like to ask Mordecai Vanunu. But he going crazy in Israeli jail for disclosing his country's nuclear menu of toxic tonics.' A stoical sternness gripped her face as she stated, 'My race, my dear race pioneered nuclear nightmares. I, with researcher Jemma Cohen, ve vere Mensa's Top Brains. But poor Jemma, so clumsy. At Doomray Power Station. Two accidents. No face left. No press coverage. Plastic surgery. Cover-up. No compensation. No compassion . . . nozink. . . .'

Some disruptive yawns from non-uniformed yobs.

'Then cancer, I say, like self-inflicted mercy killing. Dead at only 56. All protected by Official Secrets Act. No brave vhistleblowers as the alarmbells kept ringing in D12. As Rumi, the Persian poet he wrote, SELL CLEVERNESS AND BUY BEVILDERMENT!'

Miriam's public self-persecution was unstoppable. 'Vhy ve the Chosen Ones you darlings ask me zis? Vhy?'

'Why, why, WHY?', they all echo around her in sympathy.

'Before, first I say zis. Turn your back on me and do vot I say, ja.'

PC gave this the nod, so the crowd obediently turned away from Miriam, all sitting cross-legged on the granite ground as Miriam painted a grim picture in their collective mind. 'See yourself near naked, friends. Three degrees off ze equator. See blowfly maggots on rancid pork chops, only fermenting veg to eat. Now push knuckles of thumbs into corner of both eyes. Keep elbows akimbo, ja, pointing outvards, pink fingers crooked, like me. Willing to be near blinded? Zis dears, vas von of earth's hot spots. Called Cook's Christmas Island . . . cooked, cooked alive!'

In the silence of the frozen tableau, Miriam's audience behind their screwed up eyes felt a sense of ominous anticipation, awaiting the testing sun-blinding flash of a nuclear blast.

'POOF!'

Jolted by the whiplash of her primeval scream, Miriam's crowd jerked upwards. Their quiescent heart had taken an electric shock. That kick-started them back into corporate life as Miriam continued her narrative. 'Though miles avay, back spines shattered. Some crooked pink fingers still stay frozen after more than thirty years. Var pensions ignoring the rights of so few survivors to a decent compensation. Ja, ve scientists of the civilised Vest rendered other's green lands infertile, zat cooked island now an un-peopled desert cemetery. So now, friends, I now believe Moses vas not a Jew after all. I also believe in kosha karma, friends. So vy Jews called Chosen People, you ask. Vy? 'Cos ve have most to learn! Too often ve doubted survival feared poverty. Crazed cuckoos, ve nested in palaces of clay, gorged on silks and gems. What conceits! Persecuted! Centuries of self-sought sufferance! Ve thirteenth tribe of Israel searched everyvhere for physical stability on drifting sands. Like nomad Arabs, our blood broth-ers in all but language. Like zose displaced by us. Only a couple of years back, Israel's Phalangist militia allies, started three-day orgy of rape, knif-ing and murder in Palestian refugee camps of Dabta and Shatila, taking nearly two thousand lives. What accumulating karma! What backlogs of blood money to balance out. Alvays fear before faith. Everyvhere initiating, pitting our skills and vits against the free vill of others, ignoring the incon-venient teachings of Jehovah, Moses, Mohammed, Buddha, Jesus and, no doubt, every Living Master throughout our shared and dismal human history. . . .'

M for Master? Suddenly Alice's headache was gone.

'I sank Gott, as only a temporary Jew, zis past life suffering is making me holy. So now, I sink, I can pass on in peace now as I pray for a Jewish Gandhi and an Arab Martin Luther King to sort out zis mess!' insisted Miriam. 'Hercules cleansed Agean stables. Hitler's holocaust more holistic, pointing to ze next terrestrial terror maniac. . . !' Jabbing an index fingers directly at PC, Miriam unexpectedly blew him a kiss, adding, 'Adolph's favourite vord vas VILLPOWER. Ve all deserved him! The vashing-up, it alvays come BEFORE the Last Supper!' Then too weary to even shrug, she simply sighed out, 'To the Laws of Life, I submit! At last I give back my vill to Gott – unconditionally – all my vishes, money, territory, terrors.' On that blessing all warring ants inside became stilled.

Agitated, PC shouted, 'Attention! I have a map. In case the Saffs swamp us with Anthrax. Or worse. Buried plutonium, used fuel rods, too hot to handle and lethal. Danger is everywhere. This map shows where we can stay hidden, protected, safe on the other side of forever! Believe me . . . LISTEN. . . !'

But attention would not be shifted from Miriam. Wrinkled with wry smiles, she was refusing to be worried by any whiff of mere physical fears for the future. Except one. Sharply pointing a seraphic smile at PC for emphasis, she crooned out, 'GIVE NO TRUST TO THIS TWO-FACED FASCIST!'

Afraid, Alice hugged her throbbing brow, her headache having returned. Was that due to empathy with Miriam? No, it hurt where Humphrey had hit her head.

Naked as a napalmed nudist nun, Miriam then offered herself to the microwave oven, a sacrificial beacon beaming love. Thus, before all the people, Miriam knelt inside it. Empty of emotion, all body wrinkles drooping towards bare feet like a discarded shroud, with an unearthly sigh she declared herself ready to be eaten to death by both armies of ants. 'Eat eat my evil avay, dear ants. Ja so, kindly now let me renounce zis life and die a stateless but loving human being. . . .'

Instead a miracle.

As if under a spiritual spell, the crown of Miriam's hair parted like the biblical Red Sea. Through her waving hair, hundreds of flying Pharaoh ants zoomed from her opened head like UFOs out of the hole at the North Pole. Swarms of wriggling ants lifted off like squadrons of tiny locusts. Below, they were leaving a bald patch on the old lady's pate, that tonsure a greasy gaping wound then bombarded by buzzing blowflies.

Inside, unheard except by Alice, the warning words returned,

'TELL ALL! OR BAGATELLE WITH EYEBALLS – YOURS!
TILL BLIND AND DUMB YOU TOO BE RIDDLED WITH SORES!'

Alice tried not to hear their renewed fierceness, wondering if she too was about to be rendered into rawness by way of a punishment like the reviving Miriam now refusing to die.

An interruption. The Sikh from the TIME TRAVELLING workshop offered an alternative view. 'Actually, nuclear bomb be old Indian tradition.' Many did not wish to hear this one out. But a gesture from PC silenced the would-be protesters. 'See the Vedas, chapter and verse I have to hand. Many fatal bombs before, many times. Every Gobi desert will revive, actually, with sunflowers and roses again. To fulfil all past projections, every bud and bomb must explode. . . !'

Alarm PC encouraged. It kept the plebes well cowed, easier to control. Also exhilarated by Miriam's operatic bravery, that ex-cop commissioner was satisfied his whole army of recruits would look smarter with bald heads, like an army of martial monks. The chaste kill keenest. Parades of Purity, no sex of any bent, would prepare them for surgical killing sprees before confronting the legion of celibate llamas, the Saffs. For the Rainbow Warriors, PC trumpeted the slogan, 'VRIL POWER TO ALL OUR PEOPLE!'

From the seven portholes of her husk of a body as from in a puzzle - jug, hundreds of glittering ants continued to leave Mother Miriam. Individual ants she seemed to recognise by name, sending love to them on the wing, blessing them for the lessons they had together survived long enough to learn at last.

*

That night, mixed nightmares – recalled in Alice's Dream Diary.

A big red toffee-apple, bouncing away out of my reach. Trying to catch it, my grasping hands grow in size, bigger than my shrinking body as I follow like a guided missile, streamlined. Now it is a scarlet potato. Blazing red eyes glinting all round it, a lit-up ball trying to blind me.

Like a Martian meteorite on a spidery yo-yo, it aims for my Sphinx-like face. Time and time again it nips my nose off piece by piece 'til now I'm pounding down through the new tunnel of my left nostril the only one left. There, it secretes hot seeds deep inside my yawning gullet burning my tonsils even though they got removed when I was six.

Alice, in trying to unearth the meaning of her bad dreams, was then reminded of reading about the Hollow Earth and its secret empires underground, long before running away to find herself. But not long after she had dreamed of foreseen titanic tidal waves hurling themselves over low-lying and sinking lands. After all, that's why the Rainbow Warriors as squatters had settled into nuclear bunkers in anticipation of a nuclear accident. Was Noah, like Christ, due for a Second Coming, they asked themselves? Uncomfortable questions were the only ones Alice found worth asking. Trying to keep her dream antennae in all dimensions at once, she asked for an interplanetary dream of peace. The Angels ever alert, obliged. But in their own mysterious way.

Next dawn she wrote out her disturbing impressions by hand.

<u>Mars. Trillions of years ago</u>
(*In Alice's own automatic handwriting.*)

Rival armies of Ants gnaw carbonate rocks down to the marrow. All nourishment exhausted. Primeval disaster. Swirling dust smothers pockmarked mountains. Water-ice clouds drift over hoar-frosted rocks under skies of shocking pink. UV radiation, acetylene-like, powders tableaux of riverbeds and oceans. Armies amass under the ossified crust.

On both sides of the war, saintly-looking Pharaoh Ants see through the myriad eyes of their shared but desiccated baked potato, then rendered as hollow as a husk. Predicting epic disasters, deep inside Mars they hide, awaiting repeated nuclear winters.

Opposing belief systems, in action. Civil War. Both sides driven by the same lust for conflict, comfort, control, survival at any cost. Both sides using ecological planetary engineering in order to prepare Planet Earth as a refuge for their imminent arrival. Meanwhile, a sub-species is being genetically engineered, also urgently needing to emigrate.

(NEWSFLASH: HITLER LIVES, OK? STILL BELIEVES IN RE-BIRTH!)

The Adepts of Mars emigrate. For centuries these Seers hibernate in Wonder World Emporiums inside a new paradise called Earth. With Cosmic Consciousness they enjoy longevity. (These secrets I have promised myself to uncover very soon.) In the Hollow Earth they preserve their physical prototype, ready to populate future galaxies with warring ants, peace not being the purpose of Mars or of Earth but to complete equations of all aggressive energies.

Aeons before the Ice Age, Pharaoh Elder Ants over-lit the construction of extensive networks of giant sub-celestial cites of sparkling gold and silicon, of pearl and polished ambers. From such noble unpolluted cities in the Hollow Earth, the Master Race eventually emerged into the verdant Nile Valley. Therein all recalled their chief Martian monument. They reproduced it as the face of the Great Sphinx of Giza. But even this did not unify the races of ants as they continued to fight for their different coloured gods, assuming victory as their right over all other holy lands.

Repeat, ad nauseam.

(NEWSFLASH: HITLER LIVES, OK? BELIEVES IN RE-BIRTH! LIKE SADDAM HUSSEIN.)

HELP! LET ME OUT!

Sweat-covered and screaming, Alice woke. Was she safe? She checked out her surrounds: the ceiling and sky the same reds and browns as the ground, no sign of the Black Sun that some Survivalists said kept alive those entombed underground. Apparently, like a poultice, the Black Sun draws heat into itself from the molten core raging at the centre of the earth, thus saving them all from becoming baked has-beens. Psychic Mediums foresaw America planning to colonise Mars despite it seemingly to be a parched inhospitable planet. In order to refurbish it as a human sanctuary once nuclear humans had obliterated earth, tit for tat! Summarising insights collected that far, Alice wrote in her dream diary, *Only puppies continue to chase their own tails and blame cat fleas.*

The ant-like Saffs needed to be exterminated. After PC's sweeping success at the polls, the more mindless youth, dazzled by the self-elected war leader, began to dig for victory mining under ground month after month. Alice, never fearing to call a spade a symbol of death, watched the Survivalists trust Humphrey more and more as, shrewdly, she herself trusted him less and less.

Ceremoniously, the ex-Police Commissioner placed a small red apple on a circular blue stone. That evening, in the Granite Cavern well lit by jewels, their OCCULT ACADEMY was declared open. 'No war was won with an elected general,' he said.

With all the gravity of a physicist splitting the first atom, above his purple-robed leonine head, PC raised a silver sword emblazoned with jewels. Intoning an incantation known to some police officers in the Freemasons, he sliced the apple in half. A karate chop might have sufficed but to be a convincing shaman you have to be a showman first.

'Orpheus was crucified, unmourned,' recited PC darkly, 'yet his Vril energies still snare us all in sticky webs.'

Humphrey then read from PC's Manual for Human Survival, 'Chapter Nine, verse three: Universal Redemption requires that each Rainbow Warrior cultivates Self-worth, trains hard, learns Occult Self-defence against all blood baths. As in an autumnal bonfire, survival necessitates that all impurities are sacrificially burnt. For the sake of the Highest Good and the Universal One, this Holy Cause we swear to serve!'

Students learnt that, AFTER matter, atomic energy is only SECONDARY. Further, that gravity gets stronger when approaching a massive object like Rainbow Mountain. VRIL ENERGY, however, is primordial mass-free energy BEFORE matter; and before humankind. Thus this SUPERIOR energy, Vril, can overcome the pollutants of plutonium and all its sterile spin-offs searing the windswept savannahs of the post-nuclear wilderness – wherever. Nervous, PC's numerous recruits requested Humphrey to train them in psychic protection against the sophisticated Saff psycho-technocrats.

The excavating youths had become exhausted, even though they had been provided with individual tepees. Shaped like hats worn by Welsh witches, and designed by the Mad Hatter, they acted as accumulators of Vril Power. Inside them, after secret rituals, not only did their faces glow, but the tent-like walls also.

Inside larger tepees, students studied the innate powers of the inner ashram, their own consciousness. These seminars were policed by PC's own Psychic Specials, regularly on their invisible beat, purging darker corners of doubt. To encourage self-controlled clarity, no pot was smoked or indeed, any Pipe of Peace. PC had warned that even a domestic smoke-alarm is radioactive. Like the lily, their radioactive flower emblem, representing Psychic Survival.

For starters, they all studied martial foreplay, the flirtations that had pleasured Ronald Raygun on his cowboy couch with the late Snow Black while they forged their shotgun marriage. Her subsequent dowry, it was later rumoured, had been accepted as a down payment on Trident, UK's Toasting-Fork symbol of power. They were reminded that the late Boudicca, the former Queen of Britannia, had also cherished the Trident. She it was who had burnt London and Colchester to a crisp. And then poisoned herself, some said, in the fumes of her own firestorms.

PC's mission was to control the whole known Underworld, to save it from Kal, King of Negativity, Master of the Saff monks and their occult empire. Thus, final preservation of Planet Earth could be in safe hands. His.

With Humphrey, they would break the Saff psychic codes, harness all invisible energies before the next Apocalypse. The four invisible reins of the Fourth Dimension PC would again hold. And by Divine Right as any born-again Atlantean monarch.

Fearless raw recruits were asked to consider why the good die young. But a tight knot of rebel peaceniks, those who had wearied of yawning, ignored that implicit threat. They complained that too many Rainbow Warriors had already gone missing.

Trouble-shooter Humphrey challenged PC's ambition to train Psychic Specials. 'How can anyone with the eye of all worlds within them, ever get lost? A sacred thread webs together all of creation,' argued Humphrey, his own gold-glinting glasses almost scorching his listeners. 'To each heaven, the gate is straight and narrow. But to Hades, the wide-open gates must be everywhere. That's why Cerberus has THREE heads. Two eyes are inadequate.' For good measure, Humphrey added, 'So remember to throw Cerberus, not one but THREE meaty bones!'

Calling naked Mother Nature a fascist, Humphrey bullied raw recruits with questions like, 'Do lambs vote on which should be slaughtered first?'

Confronting his youthful confidence, not yet one bleat. 'Which benign butcher in Animal Farm would survive as a democrat?'

Sheepish silence, heads bowed in supplication.

Such probing showed up those with heady idealism as against those hardened with a cynical pragmatism.

Even though PC, as top dog, often let Humphrey steer the Academy's curriculum, to reluctant recruits Humphrey looked too much like PC's puppy lapdog to be taken seriously. Encouraging outrage in rabid individualists, the Saffs were painted as hollow plaster saints; as empty wizards of welfare, insultingly over-kind to everyone alike. And in undermining all moral fibre they were spineless, too effete to live effectively. Prompted by Humphrey, PC was able to surf-ride most objections, restoring a surface calm, stealing his adopted son's aphorism, 'Lion Warlords make better Shepherds than lambs.' 'And then, you blessed chosen ones, in for a triple kill!' His hidden twinkle was magnetically menacing, and to his men, PC's oiled and rippling muscles strangely mesmerising.

Humphrey as PC's Standard Bearer was selling standardisation, the Martial Arts as Second Sight, blind obedience as Divine Guidance. And Apollo's Apple a symbol of personalised immortality. All this ensured for PC a tenacious, fanatical fan club.

Alice had to ask further painful questions. What if PC's apple-pie optimism was fatally poisoned? Were secret plans not fermenting like bad dreams? And they had a lot to do with Humphrey; she knew that for certain. Even though she was daydreaming of divorce far more often than indulging in night dreams with Humphrey on honeymoon. With her. In bed. In love.

In short, Alice ached to prove the deadly PC, and his sidekick Humphrey, fatally flawed.

But how?

CHAPTER TEN

HARROWING HADES

'And thick and fast they came at last
And more, and more, and more.'

Increasingly, the Rainbow Warriors saw PC as their Shepherd Saviour. While Humphrey, increasingly in private was seeing PC's followers as passive sheep.

Watching them whenever she could, Alice wondered for how much longer Humphrey would see himself as the Shepherd's favourite sheep-dog. Or tolerate PC's overbearing charisma, mostly indulged in private sessions of Consciousness Training?

Licking white-hot pokers; raising the Kundalini; Kirlian photography; auras; mirror-body massages, could PC's Psychic Specials be trusted not to abuse such secret two-edged energies?

In public, Humphrey was still PC's 'son'. Without a stammer in his presence, young though Humphrey was, he was captivating new recruits with PC's off-beat ideas. A favourite notion with the young cadets concerned Hitler. In his last bunker, the no-hoper Hitler being an occultist had, PC claimed, spontaneously burst into flames. A similar act of self-destruct had killed Humphrey's abusive father. One night, after thrashing his son with a horsewhip, his dad's genitals had burnt to a crisp. But not his dad's silken underclothes. On this news, PC's eyes narrowed to a steely glint.

Next day PC ordered all recruits to wear silky y-fronts. In seminar style, he regaled them with an alternative version of Hitler's fate in Wolfsschanze. That Wolf's Lair though wired up to self-destruct in the jaws of defeat, PC insisted that some doppelganger disguised as the führer was burnt like roast lamb so that Hitler, escaping, could be guided along underground passages by the Saff monks and safely delivered into permanent hiding in Rainbow Mountain disguised, of course, as a reincarnation of King Kal.

In recreational sessions after a hard day's dig, the burnt-out miners marched barefoot on hot lava. That was only one of the endurance tests provided by the Occult Academy. By then, the only strikes the Rainbow Warriors contemplated were military strikes, striking to destroy the King of the Negativity and all of his subterranean Mongolians. Humphrey knew that those advanced in the various Yoga techniques, like some Saffron monks, need no petrol to ignite themselves. PC's young recruits – all of them older than Humphrey – were being taught by him about so-called spontaneous combustion as a means of escaping torture at the hands of the enemy. The thought of subjecting Alice to such psychic secrets, given his plan of recruiting her as a spy, was a worry that Humphrey might, or might not, address.

Stacked near to the Apple Altar, the miners' working headgear looked like rows of abandoned space-helmets. Humphrey's latest invention provided, in the region of the Third Eye, a laser-like blowlamp. Dressed up in full gear, recruits felt proud, like spaced-out miners on a miracle cure for silicosis. Imitating their late lamented brother miners of the NUM, they also worked a four-day-week to boost their productivity, unbelievably.

Such a training programme suggested by Humphrey, PC stopped. He also blocked the boy's suggestion that if the miners excavated along known Ley-lines with, rather than against, the grain of the various rock formations, they would become less stressed.

Instead, PC let all know that, as the bible states, faith could teach them how to move mountains. Maybe not just his helmet invention would soon become redundant, but also Humphrey himself. This dodgy thought he tried not to leak, telepathically.

Moving mountains? Some Survivalists still dreaded meteors, as big as Everest, falling from the sky and puncturing their safe havens. Other folks feared mountains rearing up out of boiling sea-beds while they were sleeping. Indeed, would the destructive force of nature ever be controlled by mankind's use of Vril power? All Warriors were warned. Real dangers lay ahead as they forged towards the Rod of Vril Power in the 'immovable' Rainbow Mountain, even though it was still growing taller.

Caution was called for. The Saff forces can be dark, deceptive and, to defeat physically hazardous. So the quicker all Rainbow Warriors learnt to control their own Astral gifts the safer their future would become. Humphrey, it seemed, still supported that policy. Until, that is, PC started arousing the psychic fire, the kundalini dragon. Then Humphrey needed to act fast, one way or another. The risks in such activities Humphrey knew only too well, aided by his regular travels to laboratories on the Lower Astral Planes. Who could help him change PC's abusive tendencies? Alice? But after hitting her, would Humphrey dare risk asking her to help him?

Spiritual Adepts and accidents are, of course, a contradiction in terms. The initiate of sacred mysteries is after all, the co-worker in the evolution- ary process, never its slave. But PC's hard-working miners remained fiercely intent on linking up with the tunnels, the extraterrestrial culture of the Hollow Earth already established in antiquity, probably by a tiny black hole puncturing the ozone layer. Like columns of ants on the inner surface of a massive pumpkin rind, PC's forces, under oceans, under mountains, would crack the kernel of Planet Earth no matter how many burnt-out cases vanished in his crusade for New Inner World Domination.

Humphrey correctly guessed that PC, no longer guaranteed his adopted son's guidance all the way till victory, would himself set devotees worse dangers, said to heighten their inner powers of protection. For that, classes of telekinesis, working in cabins of weightlessness and, to match the Saff soldiers' prowess, in icy caves to lengthen the normal two-hour exposure time allowed to survive hypothermia. None were too congenial to Humphrey but at least his pursuit of eosteric studies was useful. PC, their sinister self-chosen Shepherd who gave them 'holy' orders, watched his young lads suffer gladly for him. Smugly, he whispered to Humphrey, 'The real sinners are not goats, but sheep. Nondescript as shitty nappies, disposable as diapers.'

Shocked, Humphrey knew a showdown was getting to be urgent. Who better than PC's long-trusted adviser to orchestrate rebellion, and before being fired? But dare he recruit Alice to the cutting-edge of risk-taking? Alice as a pre-teen Mata Hari on behalf of the Hari Krishnas? Alice as a bi-locating secret weapon of war? While considering these dangers on all four dimensions, Humphrey was still colouring in his map of the Astral Planes. Throughout, with the all-seeing eye of a spy satellite, he watched Alice's every movement …wondering just when to hatch out his new plan using Alice disguised as a raw cadet in male attire. Inwardly, he would continue to woo her.

HUMPHREY	Ding-dong! Eden Calling! (*PAUSE*) Knock-knock! Anybody there? (*PAUSE*)
ALICE	No. (*PAUSE*).
HUMPHREY	Hello, any bodies there?
ALICE	Two. And neither of them for you. Piss off!
HUMPHREY	Good. Telepathy in perfect working order, yep. (*PAUSE*) Ding-dong! (*PAUSE*) DING--DONG, DARLING!
ALICE	Yes, Humphrey, let's have an astral ding-dong. I say you've NOT got golden eyes. I say you're from Mars not Venus. And afraid of girls. I say that's why you hit me!
HUMPHREY	I say, I say, what did the Venus Fly-Trap say to the blowfly?
ALICE	Dirty jokes? Shows I'm right. How can a fascist warmonger bribe me with love?
HUMPHREY	Tests. Before Flying Flute with m-me over Rainbow M-m-mountain.
ALICE	(*bursting*) WHY? Why do you work with PC, that evil eel?
HUMPHREY	Electricity doesn't care if it shocks, kills, or illuminates us.
ALICE	So why work with shadows, not sunbeams?

HUMPHREY	To help with distant hands-on healing.
ALICE	Trust your hands on M-ME? Oh, if only **M** stood for Mahatma. Like Gandhi. You only fly the dark doves of war. What's so special about your secrets? Well?
HUMPHREY	Watch the ENEMY WITHIN. And the nine apports you. . . .
ALICE	Only 5 crystals. They appeared to protect Snow Black. But not for long enough.
HUMPHREY	WHY? Ask the hawks at the Pentagon? Ask the witches and wizards of war. We're all here to learn from conflicts. In eagles, the keenest, quickest killer's the highest flyer, yep. Better to eat with eagles than be eaten BY them. Bite their poisoned bait, yep. Doesn't m-mean you have to swallow it wholesale, eh!
ALICE	Sorry. Your truth disgusts me. So do you!
HUMPHREY	Nature's laws can't be defeated Alice, only obeyed.
ALICE	PC calls you 'son'. Is he your Dark Master, as bad as King Kal? Answer!
HUMPHREY	Thought he was better than my dad was. No beatings.
ALICE	YET! His god was Snow Black, but only when in power. But her pentagon of pure crystals turned as black as her handbag. Explain that, M-master M-mentor!
HUMPHREY	The crystals sort of lanced her m-milky poisons.
ALICE	You see lancing boils better than a poultice. Don't trust women either, do you?
HUMPHREY	Healing needs balance. Let's make a Peace Pact, Alice. PLEASE!
ALICE	With lances or with poisoned poultices?
HUMPHREY	There's one poultice big enough to heal all of our hurts. It's US! Working with love. For the sake of all of God's children – together. Yep?
ALICE	Funny. When you left me in peace I felt more aggro towards you than now when we're, well, arguing. Like now.

HUMPHREY	DISCUSSING! Yep, peace times are often the poultice that warm wars up to boiling point. Alice, I'm asking: Will you risk, like m-m-me, working with the purest power in the universe – unconditional love!
ALICE	PURE? LOVE? Do you APPROVE of his poisoned policies? PC, that is? – Well?
HUMPHREY	Does electricity care what colour its flexes so long as it doesn't fuse? Vril needs covert beacons, to balance out the blowlamps. Test my sincerity, do.
ALICE	Ok, ok. So, ANSWER this, m-mate! Are your m-motives pure, Humphrey? I don't think so.
HUMPHREY	First, your test. SPY! Peer through my dark-glasses! Go on – NOW!

RELENTING, ALICE CLOSES HER EYES AND INWARDLY PEERS.

ALICE	They're gold. Your EYES are gold, like two haloes – I see them! Hallucinogenic. . . !
HUMPHREY	So TRUST M-M-ME, Alice Green and Grey. You and m-me, we're about to become a brace of private Astral Spies!! Agreed?
ALICE	I'll . . . I'll decide after watching the next session. Bet your gold eyes aren't real. A con.

Alice, not yet disguised as a boy cadet, nonetheless attended the Occult Academy before it closed its ranks. All assumed the inevitable war was already won by PC and recruits. Attention was split. In their Astral Bodies, to date unseen by the supposedly clairvoyant Psychic Specials, Alice and Humphrey were then hovering like human humming-birds on two sides of the Cavern. Splitting their attention, they tuned into different halves of the apple on display. Alice was drawn by the left side, Humphrey by the right and both from their bird's-eye-viewpoint, while keeping their heads facing the East.

'I have split the apple, as man the atom, as God the human brain. Got a problem with this? Electrical, chemical, or BOTH? Or is the mind but a box of modelling-wax?'

Those were the scripted riddles set by PC, the martial arts guru, his trainees not yet committed. There was to be only one meeting more. Would Alice decide to attend that in disguise parading her physical body as a boy recruit?

'In the solitude of self-examination,' intoned PC, 'see if you can find eternal answers. Gaze deeply into the opened up apple on the blue stone before you.'

Alice winced. Smooth as syrup was PC. Where had he received training in Public Speaking? Not from Humphrey, surely. PC was starting to pontificate like a parson instead of a pirate. While not physically present, Alice and Humphrey nonetheless heard PC's words. 'The human pineal occupies only about 1% of the brain while in a successful homing-pigeon, it occupies 10%. Lose that one per cent and humans become totally lost.'

Like LOST SHEEP? Alice resisted both of those words. They suggested that only with belief in PC could those 'lost sheep' ever be 'saved.' Surely, the good heavens were not graded Welfare States where only the well-off got to play with harps. Surely, if she joined the cadets, she could bring to them a better way than military servitude.

PC continued. 'Lop-sided modern man is far too reliant on reason. Result? What we find today: diseases, disintegration and degeneration. In disgrace, sheepish victims have lost their One Eye of Goodness. Man, with our help, can now reinstate this personal blessing to those what believe!'

In him? Never! By way of a mutual plenary, Alice and Humphrey, telepathising, decided to book another astral chat.

HUMPHREY	If you can't beat him, become ALF!
ALICE	Short for Alpha?
HUMPHREY	On the way to Zeta will you go through Hades first – as a male?
ALICE	For you – anything. For ME – EVERYTHING!
HUMPHREY	The Freemasons pledge to put themselves first. Whether as ego or as Soul, I dunno.

ALICE	How consoling, not being sure of something so important, Golden Boy!
HUMPHREY	Reminder. You and I spy for the sake of Pure Love, Venus and Vril.
ALICE	Purity everlasting? A bit dull. Can't we enjoy just a bit of excitement too?
HUMPHREY	Watch out for Dick. Yep – and go for GOLD!
ALICE	Bet your earth eyes aren't real gold as well.
HUMPHREY	Won't you love m-m-me if they're only as blue as a six-pointed star?
ALICE	(*after pausing*) OK Honeyboy? (*capitulating*) What must I do?
HUMPHREY	Not school, no MUST. To save Survivalists from further nightmares, before the next golden dawn we can m-make m-miracles from m-mud through m-magic spells. Yep?
ALICE	You will lose your stammer for me! Oh, m-matey, pretty please, YEP!
HUMPHREY	Through **M**, Alice, everything is possible.
ALICE	**M**? for **M**an-date? Pretty please, Humph!
HUMPHREY	Golden-tongued God-M-Man, better than any wizard.

Alice had heard of Man-God, but not of God-Man. Perhaps that was like Eve, some sort of divine palindrome, Angels but two-way traffic wardens on the way to the heavens, no free harps, honey, milk or even non-alcoholic lagers. Yes, maybe all will work out well in the end, as in classic fairy-tales. And maybe as in pantomimes, with Alice swapping gender, becoming a honeyboy herself as Humphrey had requested. Yet hesitation still gripped her with the sort of fears that can ferment civil-wars or worse.

In their shared silence, Alice couldn't see Humphrey's earthly eyes for the luminescent golden glow around his cherubic cheeks. In such moments of astral intimacy, Alice longed for them to hug each other's earthly body, and together engender a warm and lasting emotional trust.

Then the crunch.

Humphrey had once stated that God wanted single spies not married couch potatoes or romantic soppy dates. Alice didn't give a fig for his relish for naked girls in summer meadows having simulated sex with a writhing shadow in the shape of a rampant man. Yet a seduction ploy or not, Gaki the erotic shape-shifting ghost, haunted her adolescent astral imagination. In training to become a psychic boy spy on the ground should she, Alice, learn about such intrusive earthbound spirits, ones that can change their sex at will in order to possess even frustrated mortals? When could she check if Humphey's earthly eyes, unlike his astral eyes, were truly golden? And so what if Gaki can make their bodies as small or as large as they please? Oh! Just as had happened to her in those different tunnels causing the bends! All part of her next set of testing timetables or what?

Humphrey's inner command used just one word – DISGUISE!

A FLASH FORWARD! Alice got an instant glimpse of herself as a young Adolph, almost as if she'd already agreed to the risky plan proposed by Dick. If Alice couldn't be Humphrey's child bride yet, at least she could agree to turn herself into another boy. The simplest way for the astral body not to miss a potential physical partner is to become more like him or her. Even braving, that is, the Monster Maze in order to qualify as one of PC's so-called Psychic Specials. With these thoughts and with hair cropped like Humphrey's, Alice flattened her budding breasts. She was about to volunteer and let herself get recruited as a cadet by the Rainbow Warriors.

Warm welcome to the Rainbow's JRR, the Junior Reserve Regiment.

When in doubt about boys' behaviour or attitudes Alf – for that's what s/he was to be called from then on – let Humphrey whisper instructions in her Third Ear. He was always within her in a much more intimate way than mere physical love can imitate. With practice, her voice soon acquired the right boyish cracks and sudden plunges in pitch and mood as puberty continued to pulse through 'their' veins, jointly. The role of Alf she was playing might be a bloody one, even without PMT and its private consequences. All this Alice knew. All this Alice relished.

Alf/Alice had more tests to overcome before s/he could qualify as a Rainbow Warrior Cadet. Would she survive them all? First, the DTs, the Disorientation Tests.

In twin caves, Alf was ordered to endure strong alternating magnetic fields and, while the dials on his bio-feedback meters whizzed out of control, s/he had to keep the four points of the compass clearly in 'their' mind's eye.

The first basalt cavern had been formed comparatively recently, while the second cave was around 20 million years old, formed in a fever of volcanic ferment. The cooling process had, as usual, been dictated by the prevailing magnetic field at its formation as well as by the interior Black Sun which absorbs heat unto itself rendering such spaces fit for habitation. The second cavern had its North Pole, so to speak, the wrong way round. Its solid magnetised lava was drawn towards the present South Pole.

PC explained to each raw recruit the fact that lava contains particles of magnetic oxides of iron, which, over a certain temperature, align themselves to the magnetic field of the time. This interpretation of invisible Ley-lines PC had always been happy to discuss with any scientific cynic, even among his own hardest working miners.

Side by side, what did the two caves together indicate? That the earth's Poles had already reversed, at least once, probably when Atlantis's fifth island sank out of sight.

Despite struggling with alternative magnetic pulls, the Third Eye buzzing like some overcharged voltmeter Alf, like Alice within, was able to withstand most outer distractions. So far, so safe.

In the second cave Alf, concentrating, watched an image appear to emerge through the ceiling of the basalt dome. Shimmering there was a swastika in red. But one vital difference, apart from its colour. It was in fact turning on its own axis. Yes, that ancient symbol of the sun-wheel was turning, not from left to right as depicted on Third Reich emblems, but from right to left. Accurate maybe, since 20 millions years ago the earth's sun, according to the evidence of the second cave, would have been travelling from West to East.

The left-handed motion of the swastika made Alice/Alf feel distinctly queasy, almost as if their shared body could be mutated through the use of magnetic pulls. Might Alf/Alice shrink and expand up and down like some adjustable one-eyed telescope caught in the crosscurrents of AC/DC Vril power? What would happen to her love for Humphrey if she was turned into a boy?

For good? For bad? Forbidden? Certainly, like many trained as coppers, PC was a homophobe. It was this stoic maleness that so attracted the wiles of Dick. Hard men were his hobby. It was the inter-dimensional Humphrey that attracted Alice to her calm and kind psychic playmate with a longing that others might show for heaven on earth.

Feeling bold as any boy on the block, in the centre of the front row, Alf sat directly in front of PC as he presided over the meeting. With the others, shiny in new purple leather tunic and leggings, ready to learn potholing or how to combat claustrophobia, s/he eased in between Dick and a gypsy-looking international caver from Ilkley, a graduate of Lancaster University known as Ferret. Alf felt the two recruits resisting his intrusion despite his engaging shrug. Smiling limply, his head sunk further into his shoulders, Alf's freckled nose wrinkled up as if asking them for acceptance from the territorial lads.

Alf and the lads then slid into the Apple Meditation as instructed by the presiding PC.

Outwardly, Alf looked devout. Inwardly Alice was in turmoil. 'They' had recognised Dick. He was the cherubic-looking boy who had checked the wounded PC when he had first arrived in the Blue Dome. Dick, that narrow appraiser of maleness, she had been warned against by Humphrey. And there he was next to her and already staring suspiciously at Alf and his pretty ways. Dick was obviously far from keen to share his brazen limelight with any rival, especially one as attractive as Alf. Unless, he had seen through the 'boy's' disguise, all ready now to blurt out such a revelation to his beloved boss, that well-muscled hunk, PC.

Watching the authoritative movements of the handsome policeman (whom Dick even to his face called Charlie), the recruits on trial all become engrossed in that all-male meditation. Dick suddenly felt cosy inside as PC placed both halves of the apple on cushions of moss. After all, wasn't he as Dick the better half, and wasn't he, as Dick, the apple of PC's eye? Re-living the memory of his first naked assault on the wounded Commissioner, braving even the guns, Dick still felt a warm tingle in his groin. Come hell or high water (or both), Dick vowed he would sleep with his ambivalent baddie, Charlie. The fact that PC was relentlessly straight added spice to the lad's erotic fantasies. In Dick's experience, it's the over masculine types who yield most easily, especially when erect in uniform.

'Uncircumcised!' Dick's sibilant whisper curdled with mock shock. He was staring at Alf's crutch like a President taking the measure of a new world leader's missile capacity. 'Well, doll,' he observed, tart as an acid drop, 'you're cute enough to become one of his precious specials, dearie!' A gulp clucked in what Alice hoped was 'his' own anatomically invisible Adam's apple.

Meditation proceeded, peacefully.

Watching the split apple some felt victimised by thought control. Especially when PC invited them to become freethinkers! After all, it only takes a lump of plutonium the size of a grapefruit (that hybrid breakfast fruit engineered in Israel) to destroy the whole planet – snap, crackle and pop. Who dare think otherwise? To follow was an open forum. Alf-Alice dreaded being exposed by Dick's loud-mouthed questions or by his camp quips pitched in such a high squeaky dirty voice.

Before becoming a Survivalist, Ferret had got trapped in cave water in only his underpants and wellies. That was for eight hours in South China, his burrowing techniques borrowed from the mitten crabs now mining the banks of the River Thames. In self-defence, Ferret discovered innovative ways of protecting himself from pain. Having already conquered cancer by playing a computer game in his mind, the red corpuscles against the white, he was too resilient to accept atomic radiation as a sure-fire killer. Though having just watched the grey-brown stain creeping across PC's red apple, Ferret claimed that not even decay was inevitable. As man can break through the bonds of gravity, decay too, can be defied. Hadn't his girlfriend Susie conquered her vertigo by climbing the Himalayas financed by her Sickness Benefit?

Jake Hooper, the leading American in the group, admitted that if the Saffs tortured him he sure would use Auto-Oxidation.

'SHC, son?' asked PC, acknowledging that Spontaneous Human Combustion was being openly aired. SHC and its sly indoctrination was the hypnotic PC's way for raw virile recruits to feel invincible as their orienteering expert, Ferret. Unlike laboratory rats, if cornered, PC's youths could become programmed to choose to self-destruct – once they had served his ambition enticingly camouflaged as their own personal mission.

Helping the growing gulf between PC and Humphrey to widen, Jake offered support. 'SHC? More neat than swallowing a capsule of cyanide.' Jake's voice was loud and American confident. Privately calling his students 'a bunch of victims, judge-and-jury junkies', Jake saw the convenient self-slaughter of PC's 'sheep' entirely acceptable, a form of DIY mercy killing. Jake Hooper had grown up thinking the electric-chair in Death Row was just fine and dandy. Thus Jake was being groomed for PC's War Cabinet. Humphrey was starting to sense that his removal as PC's top favoured 'son' was inevitable. How long could he keep dangerous suspicions at bay before both he and Alice were discovered to be in league?

'Nuclear decay in radioactive material can be effected, favourably,' explained Jake, 'even by passers-by. Thought-waves. Guys, tune in here, right. If Ferret's cancer can be cured by using visualisations, why not radioactive decay likewise? I guess councils of despair can always be reversed. Trouble is, you guys' cosy goodwill. Too often, uncritically, you let dodgy 'experts' ignite your own physical powder kegs. Why sure, your nylon tunics build up. . . .'

Before static electricity at 30,000 volts got spelt out, PC's charm held sway as he warned against all inflammable language.

Jake stayed stoney-faced, if not two-faced. Maybe he's OK after all, thought Humphrey, even though PC had just called him 'son' in public for the first time. All the same, knowing of the dangers of SHC, Humphrey would continue to watch his back.

Many Aquarian Warriors were not deeply devoted to conquering Kal, King of Negativity. They were more interested in conquering their own consciousness, raising their own lotus blossoms. As the shrewd Jake pointed out, enzymes in South American sludge had been found to behave in a way similar to that of cells in the human brain. 'Sure dos guys, God shot the Word into mud,' jested Jake, 'humans but a bunch of passing clay bubbles needing to pop off so often to fight for personal freedoms. And guys, best place you to stay safe from the bomb? Don't be there when it goes off! I ain't kidding you, either!' On that, PC allowed himself to laugh. For Humphrey it was painful to watch.

Being theatrical to his pink-painted fingernails, Dick had written **HITLER'S ONE BIG BALLS-UP**. He, Alf and others would perform that sketch for PC. Glancing again at Alice beside him, Alf knew what was coming. Alf should play the part of Adolf, that moustachioed, tyrannical Aries house painter. Alf-Alice was right. A crisp nod of the head indicated that Alf was game for any drama that offered acceptance amongst so many established male cadets with their mandatory backslapping and secret beer swilling.

PC, as their Damocles sword of Ceremonies, programmed his youthful excavators and their even younger reserves with a clean cut and imposing authority. With the eloquent arrogance of a self-anointed Lion King, PC continued to swell his pride, his lion's den buoyant with willing cubs. Alf, mimicking those older around him, assumed the required earnestness of the anxious-to-please male recruit on probation.

'Only the Chosen Ones may enter this Academy of the Occult,' insisted PC. 'Soon our own tunnels link up with those others networked by our Palaeocene forebears. But he prepared for attacks from those black forces, which protect King Kal. Watch out for Mogul Monks and those martial minions, their robot Pupes. Anyone a problem with that?' His question was rhetorical.

'Pupes?' asked the ever-curious Alf, risking recognition.

'Bagatelle. With calcified eyeballs,' stated PC, baldly. That voice! So like the metallic rasp that threatened her eyeballs earlier. Coincidence? Astral ventriloquism? Alice, on behalf of Alf, tried to stop trembling as PC explained, 'Pupes steamroller all what intrudes along their corridors of power. On the velvet throne of King Kal, lies the glowing sceptre of Vril Power. That potent golden Wand conducts all the energies of this world and all others in this galaxy. If we are not to be obliterated by further abominations, and/or by hell-fires ignited by King Kal and his tribes, we must wrest that Rod of Power from his evil grasp. Any problems?'

Led by Jake, concerted cheers. As if caught in sea breezes, purple arms like fern fronds waved in clusters, tight white fists swaying above them like lotus-buds yet to flower in mud-swamps.

'Those who conquer the King of Vril Power must become masters, of themselves, of their environment, of their own worldly fears first, before trying to escape to other planets.'

Like choreographed knee jerks, nods bobbed through the obedient ranks of PC's sprogs. Dick hoped some Masonic trouser-legs would get rolled up but, no, like Muslims on prayer-mats, all faced towards PC like squads of upturned feeding ducks, all performing a moonie to Handel's Water Music. No doubt the Alleluia Chorus would soon follow. Watched adoringly by Dick and with veiled wariness by Alf, PC continued in darker tones. 'As for nuclear energy' he stated entertainingly, 'a mere ant's fart compared with a volcanic eruption.' Imperiously, PC pointed at the split apple. The half that Ferret had chosen to send love-waves to was still looking crisp and fresh. The other half was stained grey-brown with slow creeping decay. 'Vril Energy can be used either constructively or destructively. Like God, fire, air, water and sunshine, all nurse no favourites. Friends, cast your eye again on this split apple!'

As one, the assembled cadets dilated their pupils like student painters about to see all the colours of the rainbow in a chunk of coal, unfocused eyesight opening many a psychedelic vista. PC further teased the wool away from their communal eye. His hypnotic words acting like some psychic windscreen-wiper over a large TV screen, enticed all into intoxicating insights, HIS OWN VISION OF UNBEARABLE BLISS! 'He who can use his total Vril capacity to its full potential,' crooned PC, 'can do with that apple what he will: make it whole again; erase all discolouring; stare at a pip and hatch it with the warmth of his gaze; grow an apple tree as tall as Jack's giant beanstalk. No personal limits. . . .'

Concentrating, giddy Dick was not the only male there who panted sweat through his pores (and his pants) to grow the fattest and the fruitiest apple tree in the whole underground orchard. But Dick noticed that Alf beside him was biting his lip.

'Circumcised, ducky?' hissed Dick in a prissy whisper. Again paralysed by such a question, Alf as Alice felt naked. 'Yeah, to me doll, you're as nude as a newt! And almost as fishy!' Before Alf could protest, Dick lisped, 'I read auras, dearie, like detectives read spy dust. In fact, cuddles, I can see your aura NOW!' Dick was staring straight into Alf's unpadded crutch. 'OOOOh, what a lovely big pink one you've got! Astral as anything!' Silently, PC was consulting Humphrey, not Jake. Seeing this, Alice bit 'his' lip again. 'Cut! Like Cowboy Jake. Prick, cut to the quick. No pre-med like all Yankee baby boys – OUCH!' pouted Dick, while still staring at Alf's absent member with apparent x-ray eyes. Reverentially, he gasped, 'OOOOh, turned BLUE for a boy all round its edges! Poor little thing, must have been sitting in a draught! That's the trouble with trousers. Two wind pipes. Mind, skirts encourage gales up the jacksie. Think of Marilyn Monroe over her hot grill. Gross!' Dick, as he wriggled and giggled, kept flashing his eyes over towards 'his' Charlie, ever alert to any flicker of recognition from the zipped-up rectitude of PC, favourable or not.

Instead, heavy SHH noises from behind. Dismissing Humphrey, PC's next pronouncement came as if from a Jesuit priest. 'Our infernal world spawns many mutants,' intoned PC, painting a Grande Guignol picture of Hades. 'The Saffs, for example, breed three-eyed Giants to defend the Garden of Grossocks surrounding King Kal's Mountain Palace. Trespassers get a steel-hot poker driven through their forehead even before entering their verdant pastures. Capture his Rod of Vril Power and their evil empire is finished. Anyone a problem with that?'

To the nervous Alf, Ferret explained that pot-holers and those lost on Dartmoor in a fog are only lost if they have a calcified pineal gland, like the savage Grossocks their ferric crystal.

'So men, toughen up. Get a grip. Challenge your worst nightmares. Accept more tests. Polish up all combat skills. Anyone got a problem with that?' No hand dares rise against PC's glare. 'So friends, hands up those who'd get promoted, become my Psychic Specials'.

Out of the sea of waving fists PC picked candidates in groups, each identified by name. Being in the front row, Alf, Dick, Ferret were told they were in the first group to be known as GOOSE. 'Bona, darling!' hissed Dick as if already sizzling on PC's spit and panting for more basting. He had heard a rumour that, after the MONSTER MAZE TEST, chief among the prizes was a private candle-lit dinner with PC. Knowing the quickest way to a man's groin is through his stomach, Dick just knew whose goose was about to be cooked.

Ferret did not show such cocky confidence despite his past exploits in the wilds of China. 'You're best of the bunch. Go for it, buster!' purred Susie, his glamorous girlfriend twirling one of her tinted ringlets. The 'it' referred to was a prize ferric crystal. After the next survival trial in the Monster Maze, a chief scout was to be chosen. Such a winning survivor would be sent on a perilous mission. In the Gardens of Grossocks, the brave victor's task was to prize out of the massive master Giant there his crystalline Third Eye, thus stop not just the mammoths, but also their enemy the Saffs, from getting too big for their boots. 'My engagement ring!' chirruped Susie, winking at her wiry as a whippet boyfriend, Ferret. 'Make me your Diamond Lil!'

'I will, Susie, I'll go for it, I WILL!' trumpeted Ferret, uncertainly.

Overhearing this was Jake. In the GOOSE group he was to judge the cadet candidates' individual talents and bonding skills. For PC, the two scientists, Miriam and Ben, both new converts to his crusade were monitoring other groups. Apart from the chief Grossock's ferric crystal, they were told that the second prize was a session with the voluptuous Susie. What naked? The third prize was also one that any young buck would give his eye-teeth for. Alf was not sure either he (or Alice) had any eye-teeth, whatever they were. So he turned to Dick.

Instead, Dick was keeping his randy eye on the ball. Not just his determination to stage his sketch, HITLER'S ONE BIG BALLS-UP, but on HE who could sponsor the sketch, chief muscle man, PC himself. 'Duckie, you can keep sexy Susie, and her ferret down her panties, doll.' Cooed Dick. 'Second hand massage not on, no way. Me, I'm after Mr Big's best prize undercover bulges!'

BLACKOUT.

In the new darkness PC intoned, 'Even radioactive homing pigeons safely navigate most hazards. That due to iron compounds in their beaks. So, you Goose group need to test and trust your bold 'beak' enough to go for gold!'

In the darkness Alf felt a hand groping him as Dick panted, 'YES, per-lease!'

Appalled, Alice pulled away from Dick's sweaty palm. Too late to escape? She didn't want ANY prize, let alone a massage with sexy Susie. Yet how could she excuse Alf without losing face? Further, how could she get nearer to Humphrey, a fake and a fraud though he might be. . . .

'That Humphrey, doll, what a nerd. Too plump. Be like being hugged by a plum pudding.'

Oh dear. Before battle commenced, what if PC ordered Alf and Dick to be billetted together with Humphrey staying in charge of the Psychic Specials? Psychic? Dick's clumsy grope must mean that he was only *pretending* to have second sight. Then, on second thoughts, maybe Dick was only wishing to prove Alf was no poof like himself but the real thing, a GIRL! Another hot flush!

'The Third Eye reveals its own light,' announced PC, sermonising again. 'In a moment, blindfold, candidates will enter the Monster Maze. You will successfully navigate the hazards – or not – and graduate. Or not. Not just through a nest of pythons, wade through a tank full of tarantulas and swim a pool of crocodile tears. No, for spy work, all Psychic Specials must first learn to survive the maze of abdominal mutant monsters captured from the Saffs' diabolical laboratories.'

Noises of excitement pierced the darkness.

Impossible to back out now, Alf felt locked in a vice of male pride, trapped in uniform, as if PC had already seen through the disguise, even in the blackout, yet was still keeping it a dark secret from her. And for his own suspicious ends.

'Further revelations before we start,' said PC, ominously. By then, Alf on behalf of Alice was really quaking. Laughing, PC added, 'Findings on the pineal gland were first revealed by a German radiologist. Guess when, men. 1894!' His unseen laughter invited others to join in. 'But our British Medical Association had a problem with that. So delayed publication of these amazing findings.' Led by PC, more hollow hilarity, obediently echoed by his raw recruits. 'Seriously, as you will see, the eyes of King Kal's silicon robots spit venom. Their eyes have ferrous crystal nerve endings, so piercingly accurate in their aims, they puncture even darkness more dense than you now sit in. Woe betide any of you who think the Saffs can see less well than any Psychic Special I appoint. Robots disguised as Tibetan monks guard the King's palace. Before each can become a Man-God, the eventual destiny of all, there are many layers of dangers in darkness. Will you . . . break through . . . all psychic barriers. . . ?'

From the crowd one forced cheer.

'Will you seek everlasting peace, the Rod of Vril Power blazing in your own hand. . . ?'

A second cheer, a little more confident than the first.

To raise their spirits further, PC declaimed, 'Through every anti-Christ, like Hitler, messy evil energies flourished. That's what fallen angels are for; to get the rest of us flying upwards, escaping their clutches – grubs into butterflies, not into the beaks of vultures! Corpses are but compost for little corporals to fertilise foreign soils. Like sheep droppings. Unless we defeat them in time, these same forces will rule and, effectively, destroy most of our own inner cities. My Psychic Specials will be severely trained to crush all threats to our stability. Any problems, men?'

A click of his fingers and, unnervingly, illuminated metal flowers sprang out of the darkness, opening like buds through both side walls. Through garlands of blooms an icon appeared, a glowing portrait of PC's own face, his mane of dark hair well groomed, a powerful image ready to imprint itself indelibly on the sturdy heart of each one there. In that solemn moment, PC lowered his voice to a churchy whisper, intoning, 'Friends, the road we must follow to Rainbow Mountain must be shortened. Though the Nazis failed to staunch the fires of subterranean evil, together friends, we WILL!'

With Miriam as recovered cheerleader they cried, 'We WILL!'

With scientist Ben as cheerleader they cried, 'We all VRIL!'

Alf nearly cried too. Not with adulation but at the thought of the pool of crocodile tears that lay in wait in the Monster Maze of mutants, ready to drown the Goose group contenders. Yelled PC, voicing his next octave of crowd arousal, 'The only need for fear is if we bloody agrees with our own assumed dumb impotence!'

Impotence? What a word for a girl disguised in drag to hear!

Then, with the skill of an actor seeking to win an Oscar for each of his followers, PC painted a picture of a neat and clean world of universal love, peace and organic wealth. 'Grow your own apple tree,' he encouraged with quiet urgent soothing. 'Watch it sprout winged leaves and lift itself up towards heaven. Lapped in inner light and wrapped in radiant love, let it open itself to the flows of its own apple sap within, to its own eternal springtime urge to flower . . . to fruit . . . to nourish us all, joyously, generously. Your goodness is the real wealth. It deserves to survive all our cruel tests and to strengthen your own God-given Vril-power.'

All there closed eyes, some to hide unmanly tears. Alice/Alf were jointly busy asking themselves whether or not Humphrey was PC's speech writer. It had to be someone much more posh than that ex-cop, despite PC's occasional lapses into bloody bad grammar.

Frisking his moustache, PC continued. 'With the anti-radiation Wand of Vril Power safely in our hands, future cataclysms we will ourselves prevent. Not leave them, friends, to the grotesque contortions of King Kal and to all of his millions of willing bloodless minions as we all sink, relentlessly, into the pitiless sewers of his spellbinding sorcery. This friends, is why each Psychic Special must be tested to the limits. Them with no problem with that yell out, Ready, Steady, GO!'

From the floor, a resounding response. Blinding light.

Startled, they opened their eyes in disbelief. Revealed behind a wall that had rolled up out of sight was the Monster Maze. But that was only a psychic mirage, one wrought through corporate suggestiveness. Worse, the real gothic horrors were to follow only too soon.

*

Holding court with Ben, Jake and Humphrey as his trusted sidekicks, PC confided in them how to control their 'Dragon-fire' as it flows along the body's Ley-lines by using Yogic breathing. At the seven charkas energies oscillate with an extra charge. 'We're able to control this like fire-fighters, right?' Or not so. Relying on charm, PC would drill all teenage slobs in smart purple gear, wearing regulation trainers with wodgy insoles made from the skins of pythons.

Ben explained, 'As in the holy Tree of Life. At the nodes, buds burst into flame like flowering chakras at regular intervals.' Others weren't listening, too worried about their future fate in the Monster Maze when tested in turn to survive all dangers.

'Let your Third Eye light the way like your miners' lamps deeper into the womb of Mother Nature. Controlled by you, Vril's sacred fire,' said PC, 'will illuminate all your sacred inner bodies!'

'Or burn you up to a crisp like a Hitler Guy Fawkes on bonfire night!' whispered Humphrey to Alice/Alf.

Meeting over. No mention of blood. Orgasms. Clitoris. And not one mention of women.

During the following sessions of heavy yogic breathing, one recruit was unable to meditate, to get out of his physical body. That was Dick. The whole apple exercise had not only given Dick the pip but had made him excessively randy. Nothing new in that. He had had so many erections in his nappy that his poor penis had daily got spiked with the so-called safety-pin. No wonder he grew up obsessed with pricks. Dick could even recall having a hard-on in the womb (a tailpiece of evidence not yet accepted by researchers into the Oedipus complex?). Even during the earlier WT (Weightlessness Test), Dick's only expansion of awareness had been between his legs. Never mind cocking a snook at Astral Travel; never mind his swelling insights, or his two unfallen cox apples. Almost unborn in Dick was his longing to show his own first pubic hair to Charlie; to produce his own spring sap and lounge about on silky cushions like a ripe and downy peach at picking-time. Would PC give Dick his first kiss, like his First Communion? Either way, his longing for the hard man of destiny inside him was growing more acute than constipation.

In the second cave during OT (Orientation Test), Alf had felt 'himself' grow taller, his skull expand, even membranes start to form under his armpits as though for flight. Dick promised Alf that levitation was possible. Wasn't his young penis often pointing heavenwards? Yet gravity and magnetic forces can sometimes seem in opposition, asking to be balanced out, as in the AC/DC currents of sexuality. Under his breath, lisping sideways, eyes on PC, Dick asked if Alice also had one.

'One WHAT?'

'An erection.'

'I've got a house,' replied Alf, huskily. 'Ran off. Parent problems.'

'I'm going to seduce him ducky! I AM!' bragged Dick, sibilantly as he jerked his head towards Charlie whose eyes were then as closed as those of St Francis when praying for birds. 'Who said pederasts never need a helping hand? Watch anyone call me innocent and I'll slosh 'em one with my Harrods handbag, darlin'!' Then, direct to PC himself, Dick chirruped aloud the challenging question, 'How about sex, Charlie?'

Silent gasps.

The meditating males brought down to below earth with a bump looked distinctly discomforted. Dick, scrutinising Alf again for any telltale bulge, decided that Alf was a 'bitch', like himself. Comforting for Dick, but not for Alf. Indeed, for him, it was fast becoming a drag.

The outsize cheek of Dick's last question was not ducked. Replying, PC snapped out, 'Sex gets. Love GIVES!' He then ordered the next exercise: How to control the kundalini fires; how to sublimate the sex-drive. Dick wanted to spit. Humphrey knew from personal experience that no amount of spittle could dowse SHC, Spontaneous Human Combustion, known as Elijah's Fire from Heaven. Were PC's acolytes being bribed with the rare possibility of generating the 'Lucifer's light', an auric-shaped circle of electro-magnetic luminescence dazzling to behold? 'Ekenergetic phenomena!' intoned PC gravely but with a sly wink that asked for Ben's support, as if they had pre-arranged such a link. 'So no pissing on the foe, even if the Saffs' teeth are on fire!'

Illuminating PC's jest, Ben said calmly, 'As in the holy Tree of Life. At the nodes, buds can burst through into flaming flowers. Our potential – all life's potential in Light – is dazzling!'

PC concluded with, 'So men, let your Third Eye enlighten your own Heaven Under Earth. Here. Now. And for EVER!' Session over.

Again, no mention of women. Periods. Sacrifice. Bloodshed.

Aroused by PC's intimidating masculinity, Dick felt certain that he, Dick, had more then a 50/50 chance to make it with PC. After quickly arranging for a rehearsal between himself and Alf for his sketch, Dick ambled out of the assembly. Hips undulating, buttocks pouting, eyelashes batting, Dick waved a saucy 'Au revoir!', publicly aimed at PC Charles' bulging crutch.

Stopped by Miriam before he could depart, he was instead ordered to join Alf and the others at the Monster Maze. It was their turn to be tested. A goose went over his grave.

The architecture of the Monster Maze was breathtaking. Epic in size it could have trounced the Coliseum of Augustus in ancient Rome. The rein-forced space age structure with a domed and colonnaded Brobdignag designed to last a thousand years was cathedral-like; in every dimension, splendid to behold. A glass lift gave an overview. In that magnificent matrix of zoo enclosures, grotesque was the scene even before the lift lowered spectators to the gate leading to the pit below. Competitors were confronted with a notice marked START HERE.

One gulp expressed it all.

Appalled, the group of contestants called GOOSE saw gargoyles spit-ting sparks, roving robots called Anthrax spreading white powder like confetti, prancing ratcrabs with pincers large enough to crush the heads of hippos, pythons hissing at both ends, upright snapping crocodiles marching over what looked like Mancunian Cat's flattened corpse. Further horrors were hidden as blindfolds, ritualistically, were fitted by Jake, Ben and Miriam. Alf found blind Miriam, by then in the clutches of PC's war ethics, as weird as when being eaten alive by ants. Alf, Dick and Ferret were now on the menu, left to survive horrors as best they knew how. Surely Humphrey would in some way help Alice no matter what her latest opinion of him, given that by then he feared for her life.

Too scared to get out of 'their' body, even the combined skills of Alice and Alf seemed inadequate. Praying that Humphrey would protect them from the maze of monsters, beastly and worse, Alf was dreading to have to compete with athletic Ferret.

As the wall descended behind the Goose Group, locking in potential victims in the Monster Maze, Alf and Dick both got a glimpse of PC and Humphrey. Apparently with no concern, they were enjoying a deeper bonding session. Not even a good-bye, never mind a two-faced 'au revoir'.

Though starved to sharpen their appetite for human flesh, all misshapen monsters there were lethal pro-active ammunition. Compounds contained elephantine tarantulas, flying piranhas and a herd of wolferines the size of bison. Unlike most circus creatures, the morbid cross-breeds before them trained in the killer's arts were capable of many lethal tricks, teasing their hapless victims.

The lift descended. The door slid open. The Goose Group was facing the first reinforced gate. Ferret opened it for the rest. On the inside of it as it closed were marked the words END DESPAIR.

Inside the first cage, Alf was howling, '**HUMPHREY!**' Dick was howling, '**CHARLIE!**' The two rottweiler monkeys were howling, '**DINNER!**', their fangs the size of carving knives. Both monsters then brandished guns. Alice felt this due punishment. Gun-law was over-due. Returning to kill her. With rapacious apes.

Believing psychic help is always at hand, Ferret in front again, donned a mask characterising the two hybrid monkey-mastiffs in the first cage, then nipped up onto the wooden stilts leaning near-by. Was that the sort of observation skills and initiative that was being tested throughout the Monster Maze. . . ?

Recovering from the shock of Ferret's antics on stilts, the monkey-mastiffs turned their guns on Alf and Dick, both of whom were clinging to each other like two cloistered virgins on the verge of being ravished by Cromwell's raving religious homicides.

*

Three days later, agitation, rumours and excitement grew apace. The Rainbow Warriors had broken through. Their enemy the Saffs were on Cardinal Alert.

Somewhere as yet unspecified, they had linked up with a magnificent myriad of avenues, corridors, a secret system of inter-connecting passages running in every direction.

They had reached near to the eerie Garden of Grossocks.

How had a good living been assured by the tribe of secret Giants? Certainly, in their garden beds were growing, some say, the giant white-gold apple with which King Kal blesses his besotted followers. And in their lily lagoons, some say, grows an algae which can cleanse water of all chemical impurities. And in the sandstone grows everlasting cacti which, some say, only flowers every few thousand years when the conditions are right; that is, after a season of nuclear tests and a strong whiff of fall-out.

True, no barbed-wire roadblock can stop radiation from spreading like unscented perfume but, maybe, cacti could do so. Ben and Miriam as scientists, without a belief in shape-shifting supernatural wizards or in fairies that turn wizened winter buds into beautiful springtime blooms, both physicists expressed optimism in their long search for an antidote for every man-made so-called tragedy. Those were just a few of the survival secrets protected by the Saffs, long sought after by even the more peace-loving Survivalists. That was why there were plans for them to become exterminated. And as anxiety grew intolerable to Miriam, Ben tried to calm her renewed nerves with philosophy, a fact she found more comforting than the arms of any kind-hearted man.

'Is not an innocent abroad, even in Israel or Palestine, an impostor?' asked Ben.

'Vy you ask zis of me? Because I say just Jews not deserve suffering, such progroms? Belson. Auschwitz. Belson, blindness.'

'An eye for an eye, what goes round comes around, even if it takes millennia. You see?'

'No escape from self-responsibility. Please, look at me. Really do so. Is it not plain zat I accept now. Zat though I choose to be a Jew, though many Orthodox believe in rebirth, many are atheist. If I was a PC, I vould tell all ze atheists to fight in ze front line. Zat vay, vatch zem all suddenly believe in a Merciful Loving Gott. No Ben, a name ve so like in Israel, I am now happy to ask myself, 'Miriam, vy you choose to become zis life time only a TEMPORARY Jew? For vhat long term blind Yiddish karmas, exactly . . . to recover?'

Dare Ben tell Miriam that planned for that Saturday night was a concert? The star attraction was to be Dick's satirical sketch, HITLER'S ONE BIG BALLS-UP. Alf, he knew, was to play Adolf, the name part. But no one seemed certain that, if surviving the Monster Maze ordeal, Alf would stay sane enough to partake. As it was, he was under-rehearsed. That seemed enough reason for the sketch to be delayed in case an understudy for Alf was . . . but no. Thanks to unexpected help from heaven, Alice/Alf was saved.

Like Alf, Dick was recuperating in the sanatorium. Dick was determined to proceed with the concert while PC was feeling so buoyant at the prospect of leading his tightly trained troops into the lower lands of conquest. Meanwhile, Alf, though still lying unconscious in the bed next to Dick, in a girlish voice, kept him awake at night as 'he' kept screaming out, 'Snow White, I'm not not Carol. Don't undress me . . . I'm NOT, not your little GIRL!' Not all nightmares go when past their sell-by date, death. Or before being revitalised by a brand new life, wherever. . . .

Welcome to Heaven, Carol. No need to scream. But of course you're my daughter. And you see Carol, ground-to-ceiling royal blue net-curtains, a spinning globe on one's desk. But of course I'm not dead, dear. Just famous. So Relax.

When one works hard day and night, nothing is wasted. Later, you must meet the Dodo family. Breeding fat pigs. In the Forest of Flowers. We only have a limited time here, so maybe the pig farm can wait. NOT to be confused with ANIMAL FARM. No. Or worse, with 1984. The late impostor Ferret is not one of ours, Carol. He admired Mao, so they're both now in some communist hell-hole. Serves him right for not smoking our international brand. You see dear, we make our own heaven. Or hell. But this lady's not for burning. Tell that to Christopher Fry. Those who work hard progress to the highest spheres.

Daydreams? Aberrations, dear. Mere day-trips for the idle and unemployed. Even we ghosts kept busy. Hence helping YOU!

Why did I return to earth to save you? Sent back. More work needed, they said, in the Inner Cities. I prefer helping those who stand on their own feet. Unlike that cheat, Ferret. He used stilts to get above the beasts, so, was easy meat to knock off his high-horse.

One's real props are self-reliance. Heaven is no Holiday Camp. Most people on benefit don't benefit. Don't need it, in fact. Let me finish, child. Oh indeed, we could agree that the queen is a prize sponger. Fed for free, like those zoo creatures in the Monster Maze. 1984, Liz had the effrontery to represent UK at the D-Day commemorations. Should have been me, the reigning PM, just as Mitterand represented France. So what did I do? Landing at airports abroad we had bands play God Save the Queen. Dick's favourite tune, you say. What a mercy we saved you two from the Monsters. Remember dear, we all get our Waterloo. For the Flood, Noah got his Ark. For Fortress Falklands we had HMS Cellafield. And dear Denis. He still hankers after Scotch on those South Atlantic rocks, one's Crown jewels. Told him, keep to a tight routine. You know where you are then. Heaven.

How those beasts attacked you. Like Poll Tax barbarians. No ghost of a chance. Except you believed in mother's protection. Took me back to you and Mark as toddlers. Francis suggested I guide you out of that tooth-and-claw pit. Such a saint. Like me, knows how to tame the wild ones. Agrees with one. We got things really RIGHT. Unlike that dreadful man, Humphreys.

If you'll let me finish Carol. I said Humphreys and I mean Humphreys so stop frowning, child, The only way to outdo such a rude interviewer is to terrify him. It was my blessed handbag, after all, that cowed all those raving socialist beasts within the Monster Maze. To guide you and your friend Richard to safety, a matter of compassion. The like of which you had shown to me in that nuclear wasteland. As I visited there, writing to

Mark with all polluting industries out of sight I felt satisfied I had given my all. Here one can safely draw net-curtains, open windows. One's not in the business of expecting gratitude, even though I never took my full pay. So now I return your crystals. Thank you for relying on mother. As with ghostly Big Sister Moon I'm always here for anything anyone may want. But the real thanks belongs to Big Brother Sun, always watching over one like Francis. As I say, like me, he's such a Saint.

The causes for worry were mounting up. 'Alf' woke up to find 'herself' not Carol, not dead, but a patient again in the men's ward.

Gulping, the inner Alice started to count up her reasons for alarm. First the ghost of Snow White (née Black) had seen through her cadet uniform while erroneously calling her Carol. Secondly – and worse – the delighted Sister in the underused sanatorium had undressed 'Alf' in the men's ward while Alice was apparently unconscious. Thirdly, sexy Susie, Ferret's new widow, was scheduled to give the winning Alf a naked massage by way of one top prize for wielding occult skills so surviving the Monster Maze and its bloodthirsty Frankenstein freaks. Though, in her nightmare 'Alf' had heard Snow White call himself and Dick 'our boys', Alice disguised as a cadet was increasingly nervous about further exposure before she as herself could conclude her mission by exposing PC as an impostor. And that mission to be completed for – and hopefully with – HUMPHREY. He, though, was her worst pain, her constant headache, mostly absent when needed most.

True, the nursing Sister had promised to keep Alice's secrets safe but Dick with his blabbermouth might prove to be a bigger problem. After the Saturday concert, Dick was aiming to achieve his prize, a candle-lit dinner with PC himself. Surely, they might pump each other dry, even though both would have different agendas and, in the case of Dick, two genders in one.

'You're not relaxed, sugar!' crooned sexy Susie 'It's warm enough to strip right off, honey. Like me, both girls, in the all together'. True to her word, her skimpy frilly black negligee fluttered to the floor by the bed, Susie wriggling it free as she poured more aromatic oils into her gleaming palms.

'Susie,' protested Alice, 'if I was you and knew that Humphrey, I mean Ferret, had been devoured by monsters, I'd want to howl, alone, till I had cried my eyes out.'

'I'm snookered, sure. But Ferret and me, dead or alive, we always had this understanding, see. Stay cool'. On that, she stripped off the bedsheet revealing Alice cowering in dungarees that went up to her neck. Surprised by this, Susie licked her lips and with a cluck in the throat, half way between a sob and a chuckle, said, 'A right turn-on, hun. Ferret's favourite outfit!'

Alice, allowing her anxiety over the missing Humphrey to overcome her, turned over to hide her eyes as they welled up with tears, crying out, 'Jake must have got him fired. Don't know if he's . . . he's in hiding . . . or liqui-dated . . . or left me for better girl, I mean boy. Oh God, I miss him so.' In her distraught state, she did not notice Susie peal down her dungarees to below her waist line. Not until, taking two of the crystals from the bedside locker and placing them on Alice's naked back that, as Alf, she yelped her protest. Tensing up, she tried to protect her tell-tale breasts from discov-ery, from Susie's warm exploring hands.

'I'm bursting my guts here trying not to cry for Ferret. But know what, hun?' announced Susie, 'He often said Jake would get Humphrey kicked off the team. Know why? 'Cos he's a Yank, see. They always join in wars late, then take all the credit!' Despite herself, she suddenly started to cry over the death of Ferret. The deeper the sounds of her late lament, the deeper furrowed Susan's massaging hands into Alf, tears dropping on 'his' well-oiled back.

Fearing Humphrey had also been killed, Alice/Alf also sobbed as deeper and deeper, Susie's probing fingers ploughed into the naked flesh beneath her accompanied by their duet of sobs. Gradually, sliding through the scented oils and tears, Susie's hands sneaked round the sides as if she was seeking consolation by way of grieving more fully. With the giddy sensation, both the girls' breasts were swelling. Revelation! On releasing Alice's breasts into mutual excitement, a sense of relief flooded them both. A yelp of pent up passion and Susie turned Alice over onto her back and a tongue as quick as a lizard's inserted itself.

Both startled by this momentary connection wrought out of despair, they pulled apart. At that second Dick entered the ward. Eyes down, he was holding two crystals like candles for some mystic ritual as he lisped, 'Think these will turn him on, doll? After what Charlie said about ferric crystals, they should be just the job. Candle-lit PC in moonlight with sizzling moths, can't wait, doll.'

Before Dick looked up or could grimace at her naked creamy curves, Susie retrieved her negligée. Having spotted blood on the bedsheet Susie, cautious as a skater on thin ice, smoothly switched tack. 'Oh poor shitty Alf' she sighed. 'Tough being a guy. Not allowed to cry, even in the Monster Maze. See blood there? Alf, you must of wounded one of them beasts real bad to get out alive.' Suavely, Susie re-covered Alice with bedclothes and, in emphatic transatlantic tones, added, 'Anyways, both you guys well on the highway now. Not long, I guess, and you'll sure be the best two Psychic Specials for PC on the whole goddam block. COOL!'

Susie? A second woman now knew the true gender of Alf. Another person for Alice to trust with her deception. Yet one aspect might help the disguise to continue in secret. Dick – of all people – had revealed that PC outlawed all sexual practices, except for regulated breeding purposes. In such a regime, Susie would not like her confidential bisexual impulses made public. At least one good reason for Susie not revealing Alf as really Alice. But what about that mother figure, the nursing Sister. Would she stay mum . . . or report such irregularities to PC. . . ?

Alf, relieved Dick had no x-ray vision, dismissing the dubious delights of being 'tongued downstairs', changed clothes again.

Dressed up as the Fun Fuehrer with charcoal moustache, he licked down a swath of black hair. Like Charlie Chaplin in knickerbockers, (not preferring the non-sexist word jodhpurs), Alf/ Alice/HITLER strutted the stage in dazzling black leather jackboots.

The real star of the celebration concert was, of course, the author himself, Dick in drag. Ballooning boobs filled with bubbly, he was playing the part of Lulu, the sumptuous German tart dragged up from the gutter by her garter, ruby lips as voluptuous as a vampire fruit-bat on heat.

All eyes were on PC as Dick minced on stage into the limelight. On high-heels he flaunted fishnet stockings, blonde wig and bouncing tits. Rapturous – almost rupturous! – applause.

Against a papier-mâché boulder, Lulu rubbed herself, seductively stroking the stone as if to hatch it. Suddenly, the boulder burst open. Inside it was what appeared to be a stuffed GORILLA. To this, Lulu drawled out, 'Dr DARVIN, I presume,' as, embracing the ape, the boulder closed them both away from sight of the audience to the sound of girlish shrieks of sexy delight.

Watching from the wings, Alice/Alf/HITLER were all, in their different ways, nervous enough without Dick springing unrehearsed surprises like that. Nonetheless, the audience loved it; Lulu's guttural German accent, her insinuating hand gestures, all had tickled their fancy, if not that of PC as Dick's celebrity guest sat and stared with firm, stern and poker-faced features.

Though the boulder stayed put, the scene was changed to that of an autobahn on a frosty night near to Christmas time.

Arching a shapely leg, Lulu tried to thumb a lift. Arousing male members in the front row, Dick persuaded them to role-play flashy drivers of fast cars with hot laps to cover, Dick in high gear, wriggling seductively into their clutches.

Though uneasy, at these suggestive cavortings PC seemed to be sniggering. In him, no sign yet that a conspiracy sexual or otherwise, might be about to direct itself straight at his own handsome short and curlies.

Seemingly, without the risk of any serious hitches despite too few rehearsals, the subversive sketch proceeded. 'ACHTUNG!' called out the Stage Manager. Sounding like 'Ah tongue!', Alice was reminded of her sloppy 'kiss' with Sexy Susie. Not yet sure how she felt about that, she tried to settle into her role, Nazi Germany's democratic dictator.

HITLER'S ONE BIG BALLS-UP

FROM DEEP DOWN IN HER AMPLE BOSOMS, LULU PULLS INTO VIEW A PHOTOGRAPH WHICH, ITS BACK TO THE AUDIENCE, SHE KISSES,

SIGHS OVER AND KISSES AGAIN MORE PASSIONATELY, LIKE MARLENE DIETRICH – IN DRAG!

LULU   (*to audience*) He not a vimp. He not even a Vimpy. He's a wegetarian. My hero. My veakness!

SHE GOES TO SHOW THE AUDIENCE THE PHOTO, COYLY CHANGES HER MIND.

LULU   He not a painting. He not a-painting houses, he's a painting picture postcards, my hero. My veakness!

AGAIN SHE GOES TO SHOW THE MAN'S FACE BUT, AT THE LAST SECOND, DECLINES TO DO SO, COYLY.

He don't drink beer or schnapps, only distilled vater, my hero. He nurse his mozzer till she die, supported by big hairy arms (*SNIFF-SNIFF*) and five thousand U-boats, the Luftwaffe and ze luff of one ageing canary. My, how he cry vhen she die (*SNIFF-SNIFF*) his beloved canary, my hero! My veakness! (*SHE SHOWS THE PHOTO, IT IS OF HITLER.*) He vote for homeopathy. Zat mean more of ze same. My hero, he cure a little death vith a lot of little deaths. Dear hero, dear veakness, dear Adolf, I luff you (*KISSING PHOTO*) I luff ze vay you kick ze goose in ze arse vhen you march. I luff ze vay you salute like Jack-ze-knife. Your eyes spit sparks, your voice fries ze cockles in my cockpit. But voe is me! (*PAUSE*) And voe is YOU! Ve can never meet, my veakness. How vill a lonely streetvalker on Horrstrasse, how vill she ever possibly meet her hero, her Adolph? AHHH!

IN ROMANTIC DESPAIR, SHE RUNS OFF THROUGH THE AUDIENCE

(*Dick, as Lulu, makes a beeline for PC at the back of the stalls. Many expect him/her to plant his/her butt on the policeman's lap to get yet bigger laughs. Dick refrains from doing so.*)

AFTER A QUICK SCENE CHANGE, THE BOULDER STILL IN PLACE, A MOODY HITLER ENTERS. HE HOLDS AN ALBUM OF PHOTOGRAPHS.

As a convincing HITLER, Alf/Alice's German accent sounds suitably messianic. But during rehearsals there had been no boulder or GORILLA. What was their purpose now? Feeling insecure even as she acted with apparent conviction, the Alice inside Alf calls on Humphrey, alive or dead, hopefully her Inner Master asking him to bless her. 'Wish us good luck?' she pleads. No reply. Again the request. Again silence, Alice getting panicky. Yet maybe the silence is because Humphrey never did believe in luck. Suddenly Alice wants his human arms to warm her into more confidence, to hold her tight. Anyway, where WAS Humphrey, the rat?

Aware the audience is waiting for him to speak, Alf as HITLER, continues as rehearsed until improvisation takes over. That is when the boulder behind Hitler's back and unseen by him, opens up and is again closed by the GORILLA. Standing bow-legged behind Hitler, the ape starts making suggestive gestures as Alice/Alf, HITLER stays on script, the ape getting Dick's sketch even bigger and better laughs from the audience.

HITLER   (*TO AUDIENCE, RESENTFULLY*) Adam HAD Eve, ja. Caesar HAD Calpurnia. AND Cleopatra. (*PAUSE, FOR MONKEY BUSINESS*) Antony HAD Cleopatra. AND his wife. AND all her friends, ja. (*MORE MONKEY BUSINESS*) Cleopatra had all zeir husbands. ME, behind my throne I have no-von, no vhipping-girl! (Alice/Alf had refused to use the word 'boy'.) I only haff skinny old Eva Brown.

To gales of laughter, HITLER steps nearer the audience. Behind him DARWIN, the gorilla, is showing off his range of rude gestures delighting the audience.

HITLER   (*INSPECTING LADIES IN THE FRONT ROW*) Who vill
                be zer perfect voman for ze greatest lover of zem all!
                Who says Hitler's only got vun Ballroom? Dancing's
                my speciality, especially ze Military two-step, ze
                goosestep, ja. Who vill join me vhile ve goose each
                ozzer?

DARWIN, the gorilla, offers himself, suggestively. This completely
throws Alice/Alf's fragile confidence off balance. Despite laughter,
DARWIN is pushed back inside the hinged boulder opening, out of sight,
so that 'HITLER' could get back on to the rehearsed script.

HITLER   All over ze vorld ve vill valtz vhen vell flattened. (I
                mean, flattered!) Vomen, who vill be my schnog-dog?
                NO? Ja. SO, mothers of all nations, come buy my
                dirty postcard. (*CRACKS RIDING-CROP ON JACK-
                BOOTS*) You like my knickerbockers, ja? My steel
                cool eyes, ja? Come, I vill vhip up your knickers, ja.
                Not just Eva Brown. In my Volf's Lair I vant big voman
                like Blondi my alsation, but much more . . . so to say
                . . . more . . . more roBUST!

By then in drag with a huge bosom, DARWIN the gorilla re-enters.
'HITLER', panicked, gestures for the ape to clear off stage. To no avail.
Audience even more delighted.

HITLER   (*twitching tash*) Much more roBUST here, ja?

(MIMES BIG BOOBS. THEN HITLER JERKS UP A NAZI SALUTE)

Imitating HITLER, DARWIN the gorilla simpers, then gives a Nazi salute,
Italian style. That is, with sexual overtones. Irritated at being up-staged,
Alice/Alf/HITLER again bundles the GORILLA upstage and closes it out of
sight in the boulder-like cave.

HITLER   (*REFLECTIVELY*) Picture my perfect voman. Big ash blonde she vill be. A bombshell, ja? Enough to ignite every lady killer. Dynamite! Miss Vorld for ze Third Reich's own Mr UNIVERSE – ME! (*TO AUDIENCE*) Ladies? Last chance. Anyvon villing to volunteer for zis? Don't be shy, you chosen vones. Valtz avay ze Blue Danute wiz Mein Herr . . . NEIN?

(OPENS PHOTOGRAPHIC ALBUM, SHOWS IT TO MERRY MIRIAM, ENJOYING THE SHOW, IMMENSELY.)

Look here! Ah, in zis album of street-Valkers, zere in Horrstrasse, outside ze leather shop. Lulu! Ja, mein Gott, a vintage modell! Vhat bumpers! Zoot! Von eyeball bigger zan ze ozzer. Still, ze lack of a little ball-bearing von't stop ME. Cue my religion, Vagner!

(TO RIDE OF THE VALKYRIES HE SHOWS THE AUDIENCE THE PICTURE OF LULU, DROOLING OVER IT AS THE MUSIC SOARS.)

Legs as long as Italy; thighs THICK AND pink as Poland; boobs big as Bavarian cheeses; smile vide as English Channel; eyes sexy as Vinnie's cigar smoke in Vhitehall's Var Bunker. Zis woman is my Miss Vorld United. MINE! I vill conquer; her every corner, crook, cranny AND crater. No crevice left untouched. I vill annihilate her vith hot scorching kisses. Vorldwide, The Perfect Race is now on. FIND HER! An ORDER. Achtung! For me now – FIND LULU!

Wearing a straw hat with fruit and flowers, DARWIN the gorilla, bursts out of the papier-mâché boulder and lollops down to Hitler's eye-level pointing to the back of audience. From behind it, Dick as LULU re-appears, steaming towards the stage with dainty little steps.

LULU   (*GOING THROUGH AUDIENCE*) I come, Charles! My luff, I'm here! Your Lulu, she come all ze vay. . . !

Many there had expected Dick/LULU to dive straight onto the lap of PC but, a theatrical improviser to the hilt, Dick steers LULU to a less expected target, DARWIN, the gorilla.

LULU   (*HUGGING GORILLA*) Oh, Darvin darlink, I luff you! Oh, Charles, I zink you divine, ze only hope for ze survival of me, ze fittest! Ja, me, I'm fit, I'm ready, villing and able, baby. Ravish me!

ALF   (*As actor, to Dick.*) That's not in the script. (*Resentfully, pointing at Darwin.*) Neither is that gorilla!

DICK   (*As himself.*) Get stuffed, darlin'!

At that, the gorilla goes wild with desire, DARWIN thinking Lulu's latest invitation means him. Hairy chest gets thumped like tom-toms, rubber lips pouting into kinky kissing mode.

LULU   Yes, let's get undressed, Charles, you hairy beast, you! Oh, Dawvin, may I call you Tarzan? Oh, OH, I can read you like a goot book – Genesis! Quick, rip off my fig-leaf! Damn zis top button! Undo me, darlink, from ze top to my bottom. Pop all press-studs, no flies on me, no fleas on you. Let us in under each ozzer's skin, for naughty naked monkey business vis me, pleaze. . . .

As the gorilla's skin falls to the floor, all witness the next revelation. Inside the beast's skin is a young monk dressed in saffron robes. Inside that outfit is HUMPHREY.

ALICE   (*As her unguarded self, amazed.*) Humphrey! Humphrey, you HAVE got honey golden. . . !

But before she can articulate the world 'eyes', Alice/Alf/ HITLER, together, all faint. Seeing Alf/HITLER on the floor unconscious at his/her feet, Dick/LULU slaps his face, starts to loosen the collar, and then Hitler's coat too. In removing this, with a gasp, DICK discovers ALICE and her tell-tale pubescent breasts.

DICK   (*aghast, as himself*) Ugh, Hitler's a VOMAN!

With a groan, Alice/Alf-HITLER all recover consciousness.

ALF   Who am I? Alice Hargreaves? I dreamed that . . . that
                        . . . Humphrey . . . (*on seeing him, she points*) that HE
                        . . . he is my BOYFRIEND!
DICK   (*to Alice*) Dirty dyke! Get up. Get yer finger out.
PC   (*rising*) Agents of King Kal – TRAITORS!
HUMPHREY   Too late. (*Waving papers.*) Got all your war plans –
                        HERE. . . !
PC   One of Kal's monks. G-R-A-B him – grab that SPY!
HUMPHREY   M-m-m-must FLY! BYE. . . !

Quick as a plump elf, HUMPHREY whizzes over to ALICE and whispers a word. It sounds like 'Venice'. Then, he pops a purse into one of Hitler's pockets and, swifly, sprints off, outpacing his pursuers, PC's Psychic Specials ordered to reclaim the stolen war-plans from the spy . . . AFTER HIS IMMINENT DEATH!

ALICE   (*as herself*) Humphrey, wait for me. . . !

Following the Psychic Specials who are chasing HUMPHREY, ALICE also sprints off, shedding her Hitler garb as she hurtles down the many winding corridors. Along both sides, they all fly past mosaic-studded walls, clouds painted on the ceilings, acrylic skeletons painted on mock doors. More baying of human hounds after Alice as her pace speeds up like a whippet on track. But might she be down the wrong hole chasing a false rabbit. . . ?

*

Spiralling along corkscrew tunnels Alice lost the Psychic Specials. Calling hoarsely after Humphrey she continued, panting hard, wending her way through a complex as dense as any medieval wall maze. In Palaeolithic times such labyrinths were made to test and stretch pilgrims' determination to find the true path home. But Alice kept going in circles, unable to find the entrance, never mind the exit. Somehow, she knew she'd recognise the centre should she find it. She was convinced that a sign of the centre would be a stone centaur.

Hardly had Alice received such a thought when an unexpected bombardment came helter-skelter, assorted Pupes descending as in a hectic game of bagatelle. Pupes were like colossal blind eyeballs, the network of tunnels being used as some giant pinball machine in a vast cavernous bowling-alley, Alice their latest enemy target. Hurtling towards her, repeatedly, came the massive Pupes. They got bigger and bigger the closer they got. From inside them she could hear a weird whining, like banshees trapped in billiard balls. Worse, their rancid smell was odious as every grain and speck of dust stuck itself magnetically to every rolling Pupe. That made them all heavier, thicker, harder, and more deadly as if Satan's eyeballs were everywhere at once closing in on Alice.

In alcoves ready to roll, other Pupes lay in wait, making evasion impossible.

Alice skidded in and out of their way, like an ant being eyeballed by barrel-loads of white winking apples. Urgently, she thought 'thin' every time yet another bloated eyeball thundered towards her and, like a cartoon character, she flattened herself against a wall as it hurtled past her. Then, as she quickly turned a corner, another giant ball knocked her flat. She heard a buzzer, saw a green light fizz, it spitting beams around the departing Pupe.

Alice also caught a glimpse of an ogre sitting at a console conducting the whole game as if it was just mechanised snooker. That was Cyclops. A gaping hole oozed where his own Pupe had been removed, rendering him useless; except to play that mindless computer game.

As Alice was about to discover, that blundering Giant was just one of many on the rampage after her virgin blood. Fortunately, the ground started to rise and Alice, as if running the wrong way round, up instead of down a bowling-alley, found that she was indeed freeing herself from the whining eyeballs behind, all closing in on her nifty heels. . . .

Brief was her next reprieve.

The ground became more vertical. As Alice started to climb a slippery rock-face, a massive perspex-type cover snapped over her. She was trapped. Yes, that game was worse than Bagatelle.

The cliff itself was a warren punctured with a pattern of rabbit-like holes. Each hole was large enough to swallow Alice's entire body in one gulp. Shot from below, bouncing around between the plastic casing and the slippery cliff in front of her, gigantic pellets appeared. They were huge leprous droppings disembowelled from giant rabbits that had died from myxamatosis. Like discarded 'eyes', each startled iris glared as if gouged out of a giant Spanish bull newly slaughtered.

Turning tightly in the cramped confines, Alice saw that it was Pitta's ex, White Rabbit, who kept firing off the five eyeballs at the base of that Bagatelle cabinet. Remembering his vital life force, seeing him so passive and zombified, made a sad moment for Alice.

Might Humphrey be the next to be so zombified?

Slithering about like a frog trying to climb a cliff, Alice found herself clinging to tufts of aconite and heather fringing the rabbit-holes. Weaving out of the way of the hard black balls as they repeatedly cannoned down the cliff towards her, she still forgot the talisman hiding in the purse given her by Humphrey. Instead, she hoped the new magic mantra would protect her. No, too fearful of sinking into stinking sludge on the far side of the nine black holes, Alice refused to use a stupid word like '*VENICE*', not even to save herself from drowning.

One by one, dropped the bombs of defecation, Alice hit five times. Eyeballs and the number five as a number seemed to be haunting her. Why could she never make nine as with her crystals?

After countless misses, the fifth ball sent Alice, feet first, down the near-est Black Hole. As she was catapulted, an eerie, empty laugh extended its earlier threat, screeching, 'HUMPHREY'S BIG BALLS IN HIS PUTRID SPUNK FRY!'

Another bleak passage. After four attempts to break through false doors painted on the long walls Alice, on the fifth attempt, found herself circling anti-clockwise and propelled back into the passage she had just left. But there was one difference. Despite being baffled by the intricacy of those alleyways and their deceptive shadows, she spotted the shape of a Centaur. Eureka?

Not so. A legion of Cenaurs.

The flying Centaurs, their jagged wings menacing and grotesque, were programmed to attack. Zooming down all the passages, heading towards her, a pack of winged horse-humans much bigger than pigs approached. Getting nearer, their posture became more threatening, as Alice started to shrink, her body crouched and cowering.

The first Centaur flicked out a single horn like a knife from the centre of its mock human head. Again and again, circling and lunging from above, circling Centaurs aimed their horn rapiers at her Third Eye, trying to gouge it out as if winkle-picking.

Ducking and dodging, Alice kept zigzagging as best she might in the narrow confines of the tortuous passageways. Pinned against false doors, her brow under direct threat from the one sharp-pointed horn of every low-flying Centaur, the door behind her suddenly opened. Spinning into another corridor, hovering at eye-level, more Centaurs hovered, all keen for a kill. Then, at the last second, the wall opened where no door was painted. In all, that happened five times Alice's yelps for help fast becoming yells.

Every time her body was skimmed by a metallic Centaur, she instantly aged twenty years, her hair turning progressively white, her mottled hands becoming warped with arthritis. Was she being turned into a wizened old witch like some discarded granny. . . ?

Eventually, at the hub of a wheel of passages, each corridor being as it were a spoke, the Centaurs had re-grouped. Frothing and neighing with frustration at her nimbleness, the spiky horse-humans attacked again, and again more successfully as Alice aged.

Sweat blurring her sight, Alice started to blubber. Afraid of looking hopeless to her robotic and relentless attackers, she had nothing with which to defend herself. She's even lost trust in her Humphrey's magic tricks. At last in desperation yet feeling foolish, 'VENICE!' she called out valiantly. The gleam in their eye stayed just as fierce, oily froth still plopping from their horse-like jaws.

'VENIS-ON!' cried Alice, hoping the extra urgent syllable gave her code word value-added magic. Instead, a sharper glint in the eyes of those beasts on flying picket duty. For their piercing jousting practice they still aimed to gouge open the centre of her ageing brow.

Finally, after five more attacks, Alice was able to nudge onto her open palm the object that had lain deep inside the velvet purse. Holding it out on an extended hand, Alice saw it for the first time. Honey golden in hue, it was an eye in a socket of silicon. On her outstretched hand, reminding her of Humphrey, the eye winked. As it did so, lightning flashes leapt out from the golden eye in twelve directions at once startling the flying horses. Neighing, rearing in the air, all the Centaurs turned round and retreated.

Feeling bent with aching age but safe from danger, she kissed the Magic Eye and replaced it in the purple purse. Hardly had she done so, when the next shock burst upon her. Shiny hooves and two front horns came hurtling towards Alice. The Centaur Cavalry had been called. All the reinforcements had two horns each, a double chance of blinding her Soul's homing gland.

An intrepid red Centaur led the fierce squadron. With the words GROSSOCKS branded into both of its sides, it dived down towards the quivering Alice. Before she could blink, it had scooped up the purple purse containing the Magic Eye. Off flew all the Centaurs leaving Alice without her talisman. Alone.

How could she then admit to Humphrey if he was still watching, that she was still very lost? And almost feeling too old to care any more.

Recovering some courage, Alice heaved her frail body on to the bank of the warren for human-sized rabbits. There she was relieved to find the Garden of the Grossocks. She has been warned, though. Grossocks was a tribe of cannibal Giants, ones she'd been told to AVOID at all costs. What, even at the cost of losing for ever her gift from Humphrey, her magic talisman. . . ?

Though blinded like Cyclops in the Third Eye, the Grossocks still possessed two ordinary eyes. Yet those Giants still lumbered grumblingly around their garden, bewildered and round-shouldered, their oversized hands trawling through the sea of grasses like mine-sweepers, each trying to locate his stolen Third Eye, all bemoaning their loss of ultra-violet vision in a garden once so beautiful.

Discreetly, as the Giants slept, Alice rested her throbbing body by a glittering pond. To reclaim her Magic Eye she needed a plan. Or guidance. Again, maybe, from Snow White. If she was not too busy filling her handbag with heavenly wisdom.

Entranced, Alice watched an assortment of birds, all bobbing and bouncing on the fresh clear sparkling pond. Gliding above her, dark blubber wings spread wide enough to cause a passing blackout. A pterosaur was cruising towards the castle ruins for night-time roosting. As it landed on a rampart, the paw of a brontosaur ripped up a birch tree and started to munch through it like it was chewing a stick of celery. Obviously, tooth and claw still prevailed in that wild garden, a danger, especially to all geriatrics.

Nearer to her, among those fabulous creatures, Alice gazed admiringly at a dozing unicorn. It brought back recent memories of fast flying Centaurs and of past flying centuries. All the same, there was something cuddly about that unicorn. Peering more closely Alice saw that it was, in its facial expression, not unlike Humphrey; the same earnest far-away look in an heraldic head; honey golden eyes; a deep-seeing yet flexible telescope curled up inside its Third Eye.

'And what's your name?' asked Alice. Not that she expected a coherent answer from the sweetly dozing unicorn.

On seeing such an eccentric old lady, it answered in a dreamy fashion. 'Venus. That's the word,' it offered in gentle tones.

'VENUS!' With a gush of juvenile warmth in her decrepit body, Alice thanked the sleepy unicorn for reminding her. Yes! Humphrey had not come from Venice but from Venus, the planet of love!

Then Alice caught a glimpse of herself in the pond. Indeed, she looked at least ninety. A mere youngster compared with Old Testament days, the days of the Giants. 'Surely, then, all life was much simpler,' thought Alice, pondering as usual. 'In four dimensions, not three, Peter Pan's primitive ancestors as high-flyers long before textbook learning silted up their pineal glands.'

Were not such ruminations more suitable to a Mother Methuselah than to a virgin teenager masked by the illusion – as she hoped it to be – of a reversible old age? Fancy still seeking the love of a plump boy on the run, her lover lad leaving her old bones without protection, like Mother Earth left vulnerable to giant eyeballs as large as asteroids.

Ever since being quite small, Alice had wondered if, earlier, some giant thud from outer space sent the earth spinning 180 degrees. Had its axis totally reversed, the North becoming South and vice versa? If so, was that why birds, like those preening by the pond, in freezing WINTER months migrated to the NORTH for more warmth? Perhaps the explanation was so simple it could only create ripples of derision in the scientifically trained mind. Might it be that birds seek shelter INSIDE the earth? Perhaps they joined other nervous creatures that hope to survive by staying hidden away from on-ground males with short-sighted and selfish lusts.

Philosophy never peeled a potato. What she needed was a plan.

Before she could form a strategy, three distinct howls rang through her head. Cerberus at the Forest Gate was ravenous.

Aroused, the Grossock Giants laboriously but with lumpen dogged-ness, lumbered over towards where old Alice was ruminating. Making disgusting chewing noises, hobbling, they shooed her towards where Cerberus was chained up between petrified trees, giants heavy and hairy their megalithic trunks deep in sulphuric mud spiked with long sharp pine needles.

A freak hybrid with three forked tongues slobbering, was not Cerberus some throw-out from the Saff's prize Kennel Club, three mouths being too expensive to feed?

'Where is my Magic Eye?' asked Alice while being hustled along by a gang of Giants towards that snapping, howling hungry three-headed dog. Old Alice, in a state of eternal hope, quickly intoned the one word – 'V-E-N-U-S!'

Opening her eyes, what she saw quelled and cowed even Cerberus. The red Centaur squadron leader was zooming with a sonic boom over the nearby forest. Shaking its horn, down fell the purple purse into a posse of the three most massive Giants.

Recovering, the Grossocks started to throw the purse to one another, as if practising for a primitive rugby match with a ping-pong ball. How could old Alice grab the purse before they saw it held her Magic Eye? Surrounded by what appeared to be massive tree trunks Alice, creaking into an upright position, saw that she had been hemmed in. Through her tired old lady's eyes she saw, leaning over her, looming large and hideous, the faces of three Grossock ogres, red ragged craters still bleeding in the centre of their brows, their other two eyes blank and drained of vigour. That clump of lobotomised Giants in the aqueous atmosphere of the mire under their feet, even without opening the purse, begged to keep the Magic Eye. As one, the Bible quote they begged old Alice to reject was, 'IF THY EYE OFFEND THEE, PLUCK IT OUT.'

'Maybe gentlemen, that's just what you each did thousands of years before. Thus you have stayed stuck-in-the-muds ever since, getting colder by the century.'

On impulse, the tallest Grossock ripped open the purse, started to fit the Magic Eye into the oozing ragged socket in the middle of his brow.

'Gentlemen, that is MINE!' protested Alice plaintively under the sweaty grunts of that rugger scrum of Giants as each in turn claimed the gem was his. The next game of 'catch' soon turned into a fight, the Magic Eye being tossed from one colossal clasping palm to another. Seemed the three largest Giants, though ugly and grotesque, were all aching to see marvels again. As the gem dropped into the mephitic bog, they turned nasty. In fact, they turned on Alice. Those ungainly Giants bewailing their lot reached down to pick up Alice like some shrivelled up old shrimp. Were they about to turn her into a snack? To her relief, they preferred to stay on a self-punishing fast.

The least kind Grossock of the three announced that Alice was too ugly to love, or eat. On that, a tear dripped from its nose. The kindest-looking Grossock told Alice that old age had put her beyond all the temptations of the flesh. That she was, in truth, too tough to eat. In a huff to be dismissed in such a tasteless fashion, 'Only till next springtime,' countered Alice, her withering gums drooling like an April shower.

Springtime holding no promise for the three Giants, to cheer themselves up, the anxious Grossocks above Alice all groaned out as one: '*Til-til-tisra-til, The Eye of Soul's our window-sill.*'

Choking, they sighed and sobbed. A braying of discordant laments enclosed her even tighter in their weeping midst. 'Old gentleman,' said Alice gently reminding herself, 'I need to become beautiful again. Let me go, please. Before we all slip into the mire like the lost Magic Eye below our feet. . . .'

'And for your next giant step?' they asked her.

'Humphrey!' was her quick, unconsidered reply.

The Giants shrugged.

'But how will I find him without my Magic Eye?'

With grotesque abruptness, they pushed the old lady down into the mire and ordered her to fish out of the sticky blackness the oily Magic Eye. Screaming and struggling, Alice felt her face getting nearer to slimy suffocation as the biggest of the Giants pushed her further into the slime, her neck nipped either side by a forked hazel staff, her face pushed further downwards.

Suddenly, they were surrounded.

Having sneaked up on them, a band of dwarfs attacked able to bite the ankles of the three Giants. As they hopped about dizzy and disorientated, old Alice was sprung from the sticky Giant trap of the lumbering and clumsy Grossocks. Even as they bellowed curses and threatened grisly revenge on her, Alice escaped.

Denied the help of her talisman the Golden Eye, and supported by the hazel walking-stick, old Alice hobbled on through that forest of petrified tree trunks. Leading her were the dwarfs. With the same tune just voiced by the Giants, but in a tone more treble, they sang, '*Vril, Vril, wicked Vril, One God our Goal, the rest is NIL.*'

*

Having plodded through acres of tangled undergrowth, old Alice rested her small throbbing body. Sitting in the circle of squatting troglodytes in multicoloured sunglasses, she tried to appraise them more closely. All seven dwarfs waved their stubby arms in a renewed welcome as if Snow White's grandmother had come to give each of them a fishing-rod. Did the brighter prospect of a suburban Garden Centre beckon, say in Oxford? Or only so long as they played possum amongst the potted plants, like plastic gnomes imitating statues.

Ignoring them a moment, Alice cogitated, 'How will I ever learn to inspire an evergreen classic,' she asked her private self, 'unless I myself become ageless first?'

'Yes. We all believe in happy endings' added their chief spokesperson, telepathically.

As one, the little men bobbed their heads. Despite some having beards they were longing to grow up, UPwards, above their adopted Granny Alice by at least two feet, while keeping two feet below them in size nine clogs.

Taking out the Golden Eye from inside his sleeve, their chief spokesperson breathed over it three times, gave it a spit and polish, and then pronounced the magic word – 'VENUS!'

Laughing like larks, the seven dwarfs rose up and ran to hug their new-found Fairy Godmother, they all growing a whole inch higher as they pranced around her. Then in a ring holding hands and dancing with Alice in the middle, she and they jubilantly sang out: '*Vril, Vril, Tisra-til, One God our Goal, Up each high hill!*'

Scarlet City.

A picture of that richly blessed city loomed through the Magic Eye. Enemy territory or not, before more misadventures, that was where they were called to face the next set of tests, maybe in Paradise Palace.

Inwardly, old Alice was experiencing a hell far worse than if she had been well and truly deserted by a scornful Humphrey. Instead, somewhere in the universe, might he be secretly praising her for learning to survive without him? If so, if her youthful bloom returned too late, would their under-cooked romance then become redundant? Especially if Humphrey really was a monk spy who had rejected female flesh. Could her love survive such hurtful tests? To find out more, that frail old lady resolutely continued to look everywhere she went for ways to regain her faded youth. And to refresh the ever-brightening memory of her beloved ghost made flesh, sweet boy Humphrey.

Yet irritating anxieties still clung, like the threads of a sticky spider's web making her face look more wrinkled than ever.

Dare she continue to believe in Humphrey's intentions; in his promise of the Flying Flute somewhere in the heart of the enemy's territory, Rainbow Mountain itself? Only, maybe, if he really was a trusted spy for the Saffs, Psychically, was he not already an astral Double Agent?

Tapping her way forward and holding the Magic Eye like a compass, Alice decided to lead the way to Scarlet City. That decision came to her because she dreaded being in a city overshadowed by prophecies of old that told of ultimate doom for itself and its flamboyant inhabitants. Yes, many fascinating conflicts still challenged the aching head of old Alice as she shepherded her seven dwarfs like a new-found family forwards towards a port of safety, one which on earth, might never exist.

Following her uncertain and hobbling lead were the seven skipping little men. Though heading towards terrain now preparing for war, there was a sprightly new spring in her step.

CHAPTER ELEVEN

SCARS –V– SAFFS

'The Carpenter said nothing but,
"The butter's spread too thick!"
'It was the BEST butter.'

Vril Power Hits Scarlet City

Scarlet City had the greatest grip on the inner life of the underworld. As a religious culture it did not lack imagination, so of course it was very astral. And very wealthy. The poor were always there though, laughing in back alleys under their graffiti and washing-lines of ragged washing.

Of course, pictures of Pope Peter consoled the poor who often cried in church. Firmly, they stuck to his belief that true welfare waited to welcome them. More in the heavenly hereafter, (as taught in Sunday school), than in – or on – Planet Earth, itself hardly a repository of grace. And their dear sweet pacifist Pontiff, a pastor they believed to be of exemplary morals, blessed that promise.

The latest Survivalists to arrive below, spearheaded by PC, had a different brief. Not Peace but War. Thus the need for PC's charisma to convince the infallible and popular pacifist Pontiff that a Holy War against the iniquitous and pagan Saffs was not only inevitable but JUST. And not just a con at that.

As rumours of war circled Scarlet city, the Palace of Pontiffs was packed to the doors. On stage were the recently promoted Jake and PC's finest young Rainbow Warriors. No sign of the would-be catamite Dick or of voluptuous Susie. Gossip suggested that they had been relegated to be PC's latest playthings, and therefore kept strictly for private parties beyond the eyes of snoopers. But, as events would prove, not beyond becoming PC's bedroom pawns for his own political advancement. His self-disciplined SCARS were supressing their battle jitters to express daily jubilation on parade, obeying PC's orders for their own good.

In the front row the Pontiff sat in his plush golden throne, like an over-stuffed Bird of Paradise; more a Mother Hen than a rooster with a wake-up call. On the right flank of His Eminence were his scarlet-robed Prelates; on his left flank the black cloaked Rooks. Prominent with the latter, sitting next to the Pope, was Cardinal Romano. With the beak of an eagle he seemed always to be scanning the Holy Sea for flying fish trying to get above themselves. The uprising of PC's army, the popular SCARS, had made the Pontiff wary. But not Romano. He was the Pope's chief adviser as well as the Rook's choice of successor. Best of all, Romano kept the boss of the Press Association, Rooters, fed on the choicest of the sacred city's underground scoops.

Presenting his drilled young bloods to the Pontiff, PC confessed, 'For me Vril Power, like radioactivity, like digitalis and God, is not easy to iden-tify. Yet having no taste, no touch, no smell, God is indeed a generous free gift to those who would exploit their own misguided version of the Deity's wishes. Like them evil Saffs,' PC further insisted, 'Those like their King Kal would convert us all to their foul ways in order NOT to understand their-selves more fully.'

Romano, noting PC's grammatical errors, nonetheless praised the man's words to the Pontiff. Privately, he made a note to find out why the upstart had used a word like *digitalis*, and in front of Holy Father?

Pretending not to notice the whispering Cardinal with the look of a bird of prey, PC declared, 'In the twinkling of an eye MIRACLES can reverse even the poisoned physical laws of the universe!' PC spat the word poisoned like a veiled threat direct to the closed circuit camera so that the whole arena could see him in close up. His piercing eyes set in such a handsome face were, indeed, so mesmerising that Romano knew there was a powerful threat to himself, therefore one worth cultivating.

On a nod from PC, Jake stepped forward. Like a magician's sidekick he snapped onto PC's wrists a pair of regulation police handcuffs. That somewhat homo-erotic act aroused from PC's troops behind the distracted Pontiff, loud applause.

Seemingly as calm as Sitting Bull before the Battle of Little Bighorn, the pacifist Pope dropped a tear. His mother was dying. Macho exhibitionism not to his taste, he should have stayed at her bedside. Normally, the popular Pontiff had the smile of a joyful cherub. He was equally at ease with the elderly as with infants. Romano, aiming to imitate such pastoral warmth, turned round and smiled. The Rooks' applause obediently increased in volume and intensity. Other clerics followed their lead.

One thing Romano and PC had in common. They both were determined to stay on the winning side. The threat of war made that more urgent. Romano was already slowly poisoning the Pontiff's pacifist policies, even the Pontiff himself. It was uncertain who would die first, Pope Peter's ailing mother or the Holy Father.

With a rousing gesture Romano led louder applause. Plus cheering. Approval of PC rang around the seven hills that, hopefully, would soon help to protect Scarlet City. But with Civil War brewing, even in the Curia between the tender hearted Pontiff and the would-be War Lord Romano, PC's skills of diplomacy were being challenged to the hilt.

Biting the Giants' ankles, the dwarfs fought back. In the Valley of Everlasting Flowers, they fiercely defended frail elderly Alice from attack. Seven lumbering Grossocks were gasping, groping, trying to snatch back the Magic Eye the granny still held on to in order bring hope into her ever shrinking heart.

The older Alice felt, the less complete. Even if Humphrey DID NOT want her love, more hazards can help her live life more fully. If death came before she found the waters of Eternal Youth, her current mission, like a love song without a lightning conductor, her mission would remain unfinished. Surely all human love needs more light. Depressingly, she had heard that certain agents of spiritual dis-ease thrive deep underground, even without sunshine. **M** for microbes?

Roaring Grossocks, hot on revenge, were ravenous. Though limping, their lolloping lurches outpaced the quick-witted dwarfs until each leapt onto his roller-skates, zigzagging through a dizzy maze of thick hairy legs. The Giants, pained by so many colourful meals-on-wheels flashing by, drooled. Her walking-staff grabbed by a dwarf, a chase as all raced off towards Kronos Corner. Scooting into the golden honeycomb of caves, they recovered. Until, clawing through the many cave portholes, hot Giant hands appeared, hot Giant noses snorted, gnashing molars helping the dwarfs into thinking that they were soon to make hot tasty take-away snacks. As well as being guardian and gaoler, builder and destroyer, the Kingdom of Kronos can also influence the inner-earthly realms of mining. Not a good omen for Alice and her dwarfs.

'Mars is unfavourably aspected?' panted Pinky in a paddy as usual. 'If so, God help us – major war and pestilence must be due any day now. We'll all die. . . !'

Inside the cave dwarfs' nerves twitched. Outside it, slobbering, the Grossocks licking their fat fleshy lips, Giant fingernails scraping at the cave's small openings, their hands getting ever nearer the cowering sweetmeats sweating inside. . . .

Pope Wooed Into War

Astonishing even the distracted Pontiff, across PC's throat Jake placed a seven-foot wooden pole. Not short on showmanship, PC had laid down, his bare back on the floorboards. Romano of the Rooks leant forwards to assess PC's self-promotional antics – and their value to his wily private schemes, these lorded as 'policies'.

Across PC's naked throat lay the thick ash pole. Two heavy weight-lifters knelt on either side of it, pressing downwards with enough weight to throttle an elephant. The heaviest of the wrestlers, a bruiser in hobnailed boots, jumped on PC's abdomen and, pressing his ham-fisted hands down on the men's shoulders nearest to him, added his own mighty weight to the pole across PC's larynx. How long could PC withstand such pressure?

The aching Pope, needing to feel his mother well again, was also under pressure. If destruction of Scarlet City was imminent, then why was Romano, when dispensing his nightcap cup of peppermint tea, advising against a Peace Treaty with the Saffs? Wanting a balance not of terror but of tenderness, the popular Pope decided to summon PC to a private audience before producing his encyclical to re-enforce the sacred commandment, THOU SHALT NOT KILL.

Aching for food, the dwarfs were planning escape, Alice helping. Had not past dwarfs been able to fly? Nods. Then, before the war, could they not rise above the reach of the Grossocks? Nods. Then each could climb his own hill for a superb take-off into higher adventures. Nods. But as the Grossocks howled outside the iron door, to distract themselves from their own hunger pangs, the dwarfs indulged in a fashion parade. That gave Alice a good chance to study her new-found friends. Stumpy legs and pug noses to a man, they each wore a different coloured smock.

'Not a cap. Home grown, organic!' boasted Greenie, nodding.

'Like a cock's prize red comb!' gloated the emotional Pinkie.

'Our decorative crests the Grossocks prize as delicacies,' confided Orangey with a gesture linking all the dwarfs.

'Our coloured crest sports a different number of "feathers," ' explained Bluey wagging a finger like a professor.

'Thus our colourful names,' beamed Goldie with a big grin warm enough to melt best butter.

'Do the Grossocks give you each a star rating?' Seeing puzzled faces, Alice expanded. 'By how many fleshy petals you each have in your cap. As for a Fast Food Guidebook for Giants. . . ?'

Watched the Giants' combined slobbering dripping into a pool of drool oozing under the door, the dwarfs were in no mood to be amused. Alice now felt guilty. She had not said good-bye to the Giants before running away from them with the terrified dwarfs. Not polite. Lack of food would

313

soon drive Alice and dwarfs from their Holes. Drooling Giants in wait, But HOW to escape – safely. . . ?

PC a loose 'canon'?

Though almost purple, PC was breathing with total self-mastery. Divine Vril in him firmly focused, PC escaped the mighty weight of the pole being pressed against his bare throat. In a trice, he upset the hefty wrestlers crouched on his stomach and, in a spectacular somersault, twisted himself free of the pole, the bodybuilders falling like puppets to the floor. He then shot off two bullets, hitting the first one mid-air like a cowboy. Impressive!

Backstage, Romano paid off the Rook wrestlers with scented ladies of the night as PC was admitted into the private apartments of the Pontiff.

Too gentle to call him a war-monger to his face, yet the Pope cross-examined PC about canon law, future weapons and his personal morals as if, instead of being a prospective General-In-Chief, he was a prospective son-sin-law. The Pontiff, meanwhile, might seem to be a Lamb of the Lord, but His Eminence was about to show he hid the claws of a lion.

Picks on shoulders, the dwarfs loved playing soldiers even in peacetime. Having lined them up, Alice walked along their multi-coloured rank feeling like a Queenly Grandmother inspecting some pigmy Guard of Honour. From left to right old Alice scrutinised them through her lorgnette.

First in line was Greeny with only four 'feathers' in his cap. Next came Pinky with six. Number three dwarf was Orangey. He disliked being called Orangey aloud in case the Grossocks thought he'd make good squash. Bluey the bookworm was like a miniature Doctor Faustus. Mauvey, with sixteen feathered flaps and humming like a giddy honey-bee, was suffering from tonsillitis. Goldy, next in line, had the face of a newborn babe, he being buzzed by a high-pitched note in his middle ear. Hobbling to the end of the line Alice faced Whitey. Marvellously upright, he was alert to any wind of fear that might disturb his whiskers. Much taken with Whitey, Alice found herself shaking his hand. As she did so, highlights sparkled on his rippling waterfall of a beard. Retracing her steps and imitating Snow White, Alice shook the hand of each dwarf in turn down the line. All but Greeny gave a curt bow. Instead, Greeny stuck out his stubby tongue and, devotedly, licked her hand. 'Must all my dwarfs turn into wets?' wondered Alice.

A dark rumble shook all. Even the iron door of their cave hideout shook, their bones tighening up in terror.

War? Earthquake? Underground explosion? Too near to Scarlet City, it reminded Alice that urgency was in the air. Their safe escape, to be successful, needed speed and surprise.

Pope's Mother Near Death

Having knelt to kiss the Pontiff's ring, PC was handed a flask. 'Peppermint tea. Survival needs the gentlest Jesus,' sighed the Pope. 'The first Socialist, he was a Buddhist, no eye-for-an-eye butcher. I believe you are trained in herbals, Shamanism and in forensics. They say that I am dying. Like my mother. Come.'

Abruptly, the Pope led the way to his mother's bedroom. On the ceilings of the corridors of papal power were painted chubby cherubs on pink clouds. Though suspicious of Pope Peter, his apparent warm-hearted trust, PC declared that repeated Papal Peace Treaties were but puny attempts to turn the age of gold into the Golden Age, prematurely. His prepared script was well learnt.

'King Kal's Rod of Vril Power means domination of the Survivalists through psychic mind control' proclaimed PC. 'War is a dialogue through violence. Your Eminence, I train our cadets how to avoid war and avoid unnecessary DEATH.'

'By killing others? By risking Hell?'

Unruffled, in carefully sculpted tones PC continued, 'Saint Peter's swing gate I've seen. It is like God's own servants' entrance. Universal evil, as in the savage Saffs, is just the ego of power freaks what won't kill off their little self to serve a bigger and better Cause.' A pause. 'What do you wish me to do with this peppermint tea?' At a bedroom door, PC waited for the distracted Pope to reply.

'The regular refreshment they administer to me? Drink it!'

On entering the opulent bedroom, the stink of vomit. The Pope's mother was dead in her bed, her mouth agape in a silent cry of agony.

Alice's plan was simple. Seven gemstones pealed off the cave walls, like marbles they were to be thrown under the locked iron doorway. But would that trick fool the Grossock Giants?

'Come and get it!' cried the hungry dwarfs.

Seven Giants lumbered after what they took to be gobstoppers or even their stolen Third Eyes. Using that distraction, even arthritic old Alice was able to bolt out of their hidey-hole. Quickly, they looked about them. Though all seven hills were said to be doomed, one was known to hide the Fount of Eternal Youth.

'I could do with a pick-me-up, chaps!' said Alice. 'So which hill is it hides the miracle water. . . ?'

'MINE, MINE, MINE, MINE, MINE, MINE, MINE!'

The towering Grossocks chorused that word as their immense size blotted out the surrounding hills from the dwarfs. After having skidded on coloured marbles, the Grossocks were in no mood for further tricks. 'Got all your marbles, then?' joked the little men. Then, perky coloured crests flapping in the breeze like pennents, each roller-skated away, racing up the hill that best matched his coloured smock, the stumbling Grossocks in clumsy pursuit.

Deserted, Alice felt like an Eskimo granny left on raw ice. As she watched each dwarf dodging, ducking and diving from the Giant on his heels, Alice couldn't help feeling some anger. How could they have left her on the outskirts of Scarlet city, unprotected in her aged frailty? Wrinkled as a prune, she might look past it but each dwarf in his own way was a little in love with Grandma Alice. This they soon proved. Despite alerting the Grossocks to their whereabouts, in chorus together, they each pleaded with her to climb up to hide in his own safe hillside cave.

Try each dwarf in turn? Now which dwarf needed her most?

*

Seven Hills Quake

The hills were alive with unseen forces shaking their very foundations.

The Rooks, the Curia's jackboots and Mafia, were relieved that PC, maybe more skilled in politics than the Pope (but not Romano), was recruiting young Scars from the back streets of Scarlet City. Saff superiority must be reversed before the true religion of the Scars was replaced. But was PC their best chance of corporate survival?

In the climate reeking with urgent rumours of invisible killing agents already causing panic, it seemed both PC and Romano of the Rooks needed to play on the same side. And quickly. 'Saffs zapping civilian Scars like insects,' reported the Pope's advisor, 'with weapons unknown in nature, like the deployment of depleted uranium.'

'And digitalis?' asked PC fixing Romano with a steely stare and offering him the papal flask. 'Peppermint tea. In the name of the Holy Father – DRINK!'

Scrutinising PC's eyes with vulture-like intensity, the Cardinal slowly unscrewed the top of the papal flask. Exploiting the latest rumbles and rumours of war to dramatic effect, Romano exclaimed, 'He who holds the Rod of Vril Power now in Rainbow Mountain rules the entire universal truth! This threat must be discontinued. And in our favour.'

PC knew that Romano, backed by the Rooks, despised Pope Peter's reforms, like red grape *juice* instead of altar wine. Like using yeast so that the hosts for the Holy Eucharist would rise. And his insistence that God was *female*, the Mother of All Life.

M for Metaphysics?

In short, the Curia secretly held that his blanket pacifism was a sure dead end. They themselves were certainly not averse to *violent* means to the end, not of the world, but to the end of every enemy evil. And that despite – perhaps BECAUSE of – ancient prophecies that the end of their line of spiritual teaching was imminent together with the seven sturdy hills of Scarlet City.

Like a bald eagle seeking giblets, Romano sniffed the contents of the flask, a pained smile glinting. 'The Holy Father believes in abstinence, as in the marital bed. Encouraged, terror is the best defence. Troops fighting for Heaven on Earth, the fires of FEAR in their bellies. I'm sure you will agree, the very best of personal poisons – FEAR OF HELL!'

'DRINK!'

With street-wise slyness, Romano parried. 'Peppermint tea, eh. And, shall we say, STOLEN? Taken from His Holy Eminence to boot. His private chambers, too. Tut-tut!'

'You're after his papal throne. So drink, father, DRINK!'

With a lop-sided grin, Romano poured out about three mouthfuls into the goblet on his desk, saying, 'I do realise that with your psychic skills, the last days of King Kal of Rainbow Mountain are numbered on one hand. On the other hand, before war is prohibited by papal proclamation, endangering civilisation itself, the Holy Father also needs a safe grave. By decree. No fuss. No autopsy. No suspicions – CHEERS!'

On that, Romano gulped down the contents of the goblet. 'Now if you'll excuse me, his mother awaits. We have a Requiem Mass to arrange.'

Said old Alice to the wrinkled Giant outside Greeny's cave 'Looking for your salad days, sir, like me?' She pointed to the cos lettuce by his massive feet. Then, to the sound of the Giant's stereophonic munching, Alice slipped into the Greeny's hideout.

Shocked, Alice saw Greeny groaning with constipation. Squatting on stumpy buckling legs, he was shoving handfuls of earth into his mouth, his anus like a church-organ producing contrapuntal farts worthy of Bach's Toccata and Fume in D minor.

The Giant sniffed. Food? Finding foul-smelling Greeny too offal to eat, laughing Greeny hacked away at the hillside with his pickaxe.

Dislodged earth produced not gems but Brussels sprouts, shoals of peas and a cannonade of soggy cabbages, dislodged, all toppling downhill as if chasing more food miles. Surely, no place for Alice to find the Fount of Eternal Youth. 'The answer lies in the soil!' sang Greeny, his anus pulsating like a sea urchin. 'Selenium! That's my cure-all!' With only vegetable mush with no trace elements, Greeny risked heavy metal poisoning with the Cadmium Bandits while singing into to a newly plucked head of broccoli.

Walkman glued to his left ear he writhed with constipation rock, seeking relief by the fetid wine lake. Police were already erecting electric fences there to keep out, not just Giants, but poor grubby nomadic kids from the piles of putrid waste on Meat Mountain. Handouts like off-cuts, said the guards, hurt personal pride. Yet risking arrest, nippers dodged in and out, scrounging valuable spare parts for War Hospitals. From pigs they extracted empty blood vessels, flaccid as string vests. From cow guts they pealed off the membranes that shroud their stomachs, all to help wounded human carnivores preparing to kill in the forthcoming battle against the Saffs.

From the stagnant lake itself, grubby boys fished for shopping-trolleys to sell on to arms-dealers. With war imminent, minerals in or out of vegetables were vital. Saddened, Alice watched urchin girls. To avoid call-up, they were throwing bananas with razor blades in them. Like boomerangs, they soon blinded their sender. Wars are best avoided, they boasted, at any cost.

Ailing Pope Rallies

A fearsome military junta, offered even by a peasant upstart like PC, was being cautiously considered by the grieving Pontiff. He was prompted into a quick decision by his pushy chief adviser Romano who had received security clearance, a relief all round.

Yes, the healthy Pope was relieved to be relying on his Chief Cardinal again, as in the good old days when his late mother was at the height of her powers. She had always stressed that the Prince of Peace was her son's real role in life. Surely, peace is the only way for the embryonic good-ness in all enemies to become honoured and, eventually, trusted. Even by Romano, the hypocrite.

At the time, the Pope was sipping peppermint tea, his favourite. He disliked all change, especially the deaths of enemies.

So loud were Pinky's sobs, bemoaning the waste matter tipped on his hill, so choking his cigarette smoke, that Alice yearned to ease his pains, even as the very earth beneath them became dislodged. Ice caps on Mutton Mount above them were melting. In the ensuing rainstorm, like leaking varicose veins, a filigree of haemorrhaging red rivulets stained the snow line. Frozen meats, dislodged, became a deluge. Like mother's bellies, caves aborted afterbirth, slimy sludge sliding downhill as Pinky's menacing Giant slipped and slithered out of sight. Like corpses in a morgue sit up and belch, so cattle down in the city valley were heard repeating their ghastly death rattles like ghostly bellows.

Another flash flood ejected old Alice and Pinky from their cave. Through uncooked goulash, they slurped downhill, ever faster towards the floundering Grossock below. As blistering raindrops dowsed his cigarette, Pinky bemoaned the cruelty of all abattoirs, clinging to what he took to be the rump of a hillside boulder.

Exhumed by the rainstorm, prime cuts, tripe and bits of giblets were swilling past the marooned humans, swilling helter-skelter, ever downwards. Bloodstained effluent churned around the feet of Alice and Pinky. Sheep heads, glaring with death-shock, were vomiting up their cud. Corpse calves, stomachs removed, were bleating like vacant phantoms. And as farmyard cadavers cascaded by, Alice lifted her lorgnette. She read out a note written in a script favoured by Saff monks: 'All that kill cows rot in hell for as many years as there are hairs on the body of a cow.' To their horror, they were clinging not to a boulder covered with lichen but a cow rump. Let go of the hide hair and they would drown in that stinking ulcerated khaki stew just like that cow had done.

General-in-Chief Appointed Soon

PC explained that the King of the Underworld had ruined the five lands known as Atlantis. They had misused Vril's crystal powers, forces that, till then, were unrivalled by all modern weapons. Thus the ageless King Kal needed to be obliterated before the same fate befell present-day rival cities, Scarlet and Saffron and the entire underworld.

As above, so below?

Passionate about peace, the Pope's sweet pacifism was again being threatened, like his popularity. Romano insisted that a way needed to be found for Pope Peter – or his successor – to sanction a Declaration of War, urgently.

The more PC was needed by Romano, the more PC watched his back. And Romano's hooded eyes. He had already noticed that the daily head- lines in the Rooks' own paper, THE CURIA, always seemed to LEAD on the next day's news, not just follow events.

Pope Peter was insisting that the embalmed body of his beloved mother stay in her own bedchamber, till no poisons are discovered in her bloodstream. There her santified remains would rest in peace; the cele- brant at the Requiem Mass, her son.

The trusted Romano, agreeing to be the only server at the bedroom altar, went a long way to help assuage the Pontiff's heavy grief. Laid out, did not the late mother resemble the Blessed Virgin Mary herself? But mid Requiem Mass, the Pope would collapse.

After partaking of the red grape juice in the name of the sacred blood of the Saviour, the poisoned chalice dropped to his dead feet before his head hit the marble floor.

Floating through the fleshly wreckage of Mutton Mount, a semi- submerged week old suicide arrived. Since she'd been addicted to junk food, preservatives had kept the body from rotting. Alice primly examined the starved corpse through raised eyebrows and lorgnette. After all, they'd not been introduced. Not believing in death, she asked, 'Not seen him on the Other Side, I suppose? Young Humphrey? He's lost me.'

'PARDON?' spat out the naked suicide gargling cow shit mixed with cattle blood.

Gasped Pinky, 'Didn't know the dead could talk!'

'Didn't know dead cows still shat,' spluttered the corpse.

'Have a fag, mate!' offered Pinky.

'Oh thank goodness, Pinky's found a friend at last,' thought Alice, hoping for reprieve from his emotional possessiveness.

Welcome War With Open Arms

Welcome PC with open arms – military arms – the Rook's long range investment was coming home to roost!

Addressing the cardinals in Scarlet College, Romano assured them that the late and deeply loved Pontiff had received the Last Rites before being embalmed. 'Overwhelmed by grief for his devoted mother, his sweet heart had broken as he drank the blood of our Saviour. Rest assured. In the Maternal Eye of God, he is at peace.' Such were the syrupy words intoned by Romano.

Given their state of multiple emergencies, Romano was soon voted in as wartime's General-in-Chief and as interim Pope. A matter of priorities in a time of tribal crisis.

'War, OK? Why the u-turn?' asked PC between gritted teeth.

'Short term, dear cop. City's not just reeking with incense and sin. It's reeling with grief. Peter was their beloved Mother Hen. He cared for every chick and cock. I am the long established and well-trusted second to Pope Peter. They know me. Love me.'

'Not what I 'eard.' His Cockney accent always returned when he was stressed. 'War's always a good distraction from. . . .' Pause.

PC was still struggling with doubts, niggles that can undermine those deprived in their earliest years. Offer eternal welfare? Through death? PC's occult training regime must be better than superficial psychic stage tricks. War, like all binary battles, must lead to much more competition than to co-operation. If civil war in the Curia was inevitable, to get on the winning side, quick action's essential. For political power Romano was ruthless.

'And your sly battle plan, Your Holiness-in-Waiting?'

'Copper, you use our psychic powers,' hissed Romano, 'to convince our grieving citizenry that against relentless Saff incursions we – you and I – can provide their best defences.'

'But brother, I AM – the BEST. ME! Make no mistake, mate!'

'Me! They will soon see my decisions are now infaliable. To prove to my people you can keep Scarlet City safer from the pagan Saffs than me, you will produce the stigmata. Bleeding you, on TV. We need to be assured PC is a rousing miracle maker. Like, we could say, our own psychic Jew who renounced his native Armenian tongue to become a suicidal terrorist against the occupying Romans. No passive wimp. You up to the challenge, or not? A fair Cop, or not? Top of the pops, or not? My time is short.'

'Ordered another assassination, then, have you – ME?'

Poisoned laughter, light as moths, flitted away into their dark frowns. First to recover is Romano, insisting, 'Together, we must fight them.' Bursting into a hymn, rousingly he sings, FIGHT THE GOOD FIGHT, his voice fit enough to fill an opera house.

'Look you. Told rebel Rooks you're General-in-Chief, mate? NO! Troops I train. Tell you straight, they won't never accept YOU, Romano! Even as Pope, never mind as bloody Field Martial. . . .'

'And I will never EVER promote you without the stigmata.'

'Both for warrior sainthood in their eyes! You first, father. . . .'

Came Romano's quicksilver command, 'Pray for me!'

Alice, coughing, was sharing a smoke to help tranquillise Pinky and keep the failed suicide company. To make conversation, she asked the corpse-like waif in sewerage, 'If we're all off-cuts from the selfsame star-stuff, does a White Dwarf eat a Black Hole, or the other way round. . . ?'

Answered the corpse, 'Only human herbivores agonise over such indulgent shit!'

'A worse sin was selling "indulgences" to rebuild St Peter's dome! After the expected ruin of Scarlet City, of course,' retorted Alice somewhat sniffily. 'Even constipated Luther expected the imminent END OF THE WORLD. But he didn't commit suicide. Or climb hills to seek safety. . . .'

Slowly floating by on her back in the slurping slurry, her cigarette puffing like a tugboat's chimney, their passing visitor's next remark was aimed straight at Pinky's 'JESUS SAVES' T-shirt. 'Pity you born-agains don't believe in rebirth. Fancy having to do all this shit, get rid of it all, and in only one lifetime. Some hope!'

The preserved corpse majestically floated off downstream on the bilious silage and slithered into the nearest sluice-like gully.

'You crucified cattle,' blubbered Pinky, screaming after her. 'Bet it was beefburger food poisoning what done you in. Serves you right, see! Jesus sacrificed his good blood for US LOT!' Blubbering Pinky doused his latest dog-end in the dead ear of a passing pig.

His tearful outburst disturbed Alice. Showing cosmic compassion, and sobbing with him operatically, Alice lit his next cigarette. 'National Health nurses are too expensive. War IS m-m-much cheaper' she cried. Her unexpected stammers reminded her how m-much she was really m-m-missing he who had disappeared.

'Doctor Jesus,' announced Pinky, 'can make all patients better.'

'Better what?' asked Alice surveying the bloody meat bath all around them. 'Better hips, better hearts, better limbs, ligaments, spleen.' Not mincing her words, she declared, 'Butchers' breakfast bangers even contain cows' slobber lips, snot and nostrils! Better?'

'Cowslips!' echoed Pinky, inaccurately. Then in a minor key, he sang, 'WHERE HAVE ALL THE FLOWERS GONE? – Christ's Second Coming will save 'em. And all the dodos!'

If Pinky really believes that, why did he still sob, splutter and smoke, his pink pug nose singed with nicotine?

'Only till next golden springtime! Then let young loves leap like lambkins!' chirruped old Alice.

But that born-again dwarf resisting the idea of reincarnation, instead preferred to smoke himself into an early coffin, thenceforward into the fires of one final but smokeless crematorium full of sobbing mourners.

Alice felt challenged. How could she help him out? With more emotional empathy, perhaps, not get tempted to reject him.

Carpenter From Nazareth Seeks Joiners

Romano, whatever lopsided game he was playing, was starting to limp. He needed a hip replacement. This limp was not on show when processing in long robes or when singing liturgy, mounting the steps of high altars, limps edited out from CCTV footage. Otherwise the Pope-in-waiting seemed well, not one apparent enemy in sight, his public acclaim of PC now an electoral asset. Romano, calling a spade a spade, launched PC into the Scarlet City recruitment drive. His crusading catch phrase was supported by THE CURIA's banner headline of the day and favoured by their secret astrologers.

To focus more public empathy with the Christ figure, Romano had devised a DIY Krucifixion Kit, PC fitted up with plastic nails, greasepaint scars and gaudy stage blood, all suitably kitsch, agreed rebel priests. Henceforth, the Rooks' joined in schemes best suited to their political ambitions. But PC failed to produce the desired stigmata, even SUPERnaturally. Having humiliated PC, Romano nonetheless then ordered pictures of PC as Saviour on the Cross, surrounded by Saffs all like gargoyles with zipguns. Such an image would spearhead a further massive recruitment drive. Lay brothers, their young blood emboldened, in deed, in prayer and in the need to feel safe from the pagan Saffs, would willingly lay down their lives, General Charles in charge. Though such cheap promotions startled him, in Scarlet city PC saw the need to appear compliant and grateful.

'If you'd not got to the top of your trade, Your Holiness,' asked PC with an apparent lack of irony as they relaxed over a carafe of red wine, 'what might you have become? Surely not a General, like me. Or is getting to be Pope top of the pops?'

'An opera singer, a world famous heavy base- without a dicky hip. My childhood dream, centre stage. YOU?'

'You bloody know. General Charles, Commander-in-Chief!'

Both men laughed, swigged back more wine.

For those reluctant to kill in battle, Romano produced the Rorschach Test. Starting at bilateral symmetrical red inkblots, recruits were asked to meditate on their sins. When the face of their Saviour appeared, (by way of a chemical conjuring trick) that meant the Lord had chosen them. Most reported seeing the new Pope-to-be, Romano. Further, when all the recruiting posters were distributed, the face on the cross was that of Romano's. PC had been airbrushed out of the picture. Romano was the new Pope.

Time for the fraudulent Pontiff to become unfrocked. Time for PC to deploy his hidden weapons. Bitchy Dick and sexy Susie.

'Could Jesus, a mere man,' asked Alice unhelpfully, 'have possibly died on the cross (if such was in fact true) for everybody's sins, without getting their permission in advance? At least the Saffs' eastern promise is that, for those who play their Akashic Cards right, paying back our own debts is

325

best. Is social compassion slowly killing off Christianity, caring do-gooders too liberal to impose discipline even on their kids? Was not Jesus more of a social worker than a Divine Liberator?'

Aggrieved, angry Pinky, with a deep desire to become a famous victim like Jesus, started to bleed with all the passionate masochism of a stigmatist. Identifying so obsessively with crucifixion (and cattle), even Pinky's feet started to bleed like pigs' trotters. In all directions, his plumbing burst, his body in small but magnanimous human meltdown.

'Don't . . . Pinky, don't!' pleaded Alice. 'You feel too much. It's not worth it.'

'WORTH?' sniped the dwarf, defiantly. 'WORTH!' Then he really cracked, his laughter more heartbreaking than any Mock Turtle's sobs drowning in oceans of sour soup. 'Why?' wailed Pinky, 'why should love HURT so much?' he asked, almost throttling Alice. 'WHY?'

'If only I could ask Humphrey!' wailed Alice, 'before I die of precocious old age, unloved by him. I need to cry too often now.'

Both struggling, their shoes squelching with red slime, instead of firm answers they found a stable rock ledge. From there they watched three pigs' defrosting necks set in frilly doilies bobbing by. Their spiky eyelashes were fringed with flecks of tinsel ice, nostrils grotesquely distended. In fear of postumous ham sandwiches? One such severed pig's head sloshed against Pinky's feet. Though retching, Pinky felt like a butcher's apprentice in a bloodied white linen trilby. In the pig's gaping mouth, Alice placed not posies of plastic parsley, but Pinky's next packet of cigarettes.

'Jesus! Without ASKING!' hollered he, his tiny mouth spurting spit like a punctured hosepipe.

Aiming to tickle his T-bone, Alice quipped, 'Faith, my little mannequin, according to Martin Luther, is beneath the third rib on the left, the side of your heart. There, where you now bleed. But don't die. Don't drown. I'm trying to care, to treat your wounds only . . . because I care enough to help you, even as it hurts me too!'

It worked, Pinky's bleeding, as with a crying baby, dried up mid-note. Less stigmatised, though still bemused, he risked the smallest of knowing smiles.

'Pinky dear, it WAS YOUR FAITH that got these meat products back into full flow? REJOICE! Even dwarfs can move meat mountains. LOOK. . . !'

From Mutton Mount's deep freeze above, a flock of unfrocked sacrificial lambs, like those favoured by devout Muslims, descended. Unable to bear the sight, Pinky the little lunatic, plunged into the scarlet slurry. With rotting rats, he swam after his packet of cigarettes swirling downhill in a frozen pig's mouth. . . .

As a last ditch attempt to save him, Alice shouted, 'See Pinky, we all live and die by our own free mistakes!' To her own surprise, they were swimming abreast, both swallowing sewerage, and in danger of drowning.

'Forget the other six, kiss ME, Alice,' demanded the dwarf.

A granny-fancier? Frail though she was, Alice wedged Pinky between two bulk-buy buttocks of best beef. Panting together there, wet through and yet steaming with sweat, whatever next. . . ?

New Pope Sings Warrior Songs

Invisible rays to fry all alive? On both sides? One thing seemed certain to PC. Only he, not Romano, could in time train a Warrior Task Force in psychic protection techniques to match the highly skilled disciplined forces under the influence of King Kal, in Rainbow Mountain. Psychic saboteurs and spies were known to be operating on both sides. Was that why Humphrey, as an alleged Saff spy, was on the run? PC's suggested plan: seize King Kal and his potent Rod of Power in Rainbow Mountain. Obliterate all Saffs.

'And FIGHT THE GOOD FIGHT!' sang out Romano. 'Let the clarion call be KING KAL – R.I.P!' Long live Pope Romano!'

PC questioned such a brazen call. Romano had demanded total control, total command and total praise. With his papal duties – and his weak and painful hip – how could he run military planning as well? 'I'm not blocking your skills, Your Eminence. But good soldiers don't limp. Not *before* battles. You need massage. Does wonders, soothing away pains. Like singing. In tune, of course. At High Mass. Some voice training would help you sing like a divine base, like a transcendent mudlark. Imagine. Can't wait to hear you reach top "C", mate, for Caruso, like a skylark, whatever!'

'Too high!' Nonetheless, the singing Pope agreed to ask Susan and Richard (not Dick, of course) into his private apartment.

Giggling like giddy long-lost sisters, Dick and sexy Susie went over their briefs, metaphorically speaking. Privately, PC had already trained them both in acts of sexual sabotage. To safeguard PCs war plans, time the base puritanical Pope got publicly exposed.

'Before I was seventeen,' his molten emotions in flow with tender tears, Pinkie cried, 'I wept over 1,600 murders on Smellyvision. Not ever once did they show disabled people making real love. Help me feel less small, Alice. You ARE so lovely to me!'

She considered his sincerity. Should she give Pinky the kiss of life? Or a cigarette? No. By then, they looked more like a damp packet of used dwarf tampons. Alice doubted Pinky was familiar with such sticky intimacies yet. He so loved his church organ each Sunday as he wept under the sway of its oceanic thunder.

From the crimson slurry, Alice managed to prop him up on a safe shoulder to cry on, another beefy rump to thump whenever his emotions needed to explode. Feeling limp but seductive, like a learner lover aged about nine, Pinky protruded his stiffening lips. As if he was a beached shrimp, Alice considered him, regretting her feelings of pity, her heart aching to help the pathetic little chap.

'LOVE ME, ALICE!'

Knee-jerk compassion plucked her heartstrings like a local urchin pulling her sleeve and begging for food. The Survivalists rescued 90,000 kids in Social Care in time before the Top People had blown it with war games. Though it's been promised the poor would inherit the earth, wisely, it was not stated which bits, if they survived starvation, might host such a sad situation.

'Kiss ME, Granny Alice!' As if expecting ravishment in the raw, Pinky closed his eyes. 'Jesus will love you for it, kissy-kiss. . . !'

Alice decided it wasn't a vegan's compassion for dead meat but the posings of sex-centred self-pity. Love is more than a meat market, Pinky. Even one on the decline, like here.' Extricating herself from Pinky's sticky emotions, Alice excused her confused self. She left him, playing with his imaginary church organ.

As quickly as her aching bones allowed, blocking her ears to Pinky's pleas, Alice slipped and slid down Pinky's hill back into the dark heat of that ancient old whore, Scarlet City.

Uncovered – Sound Secrets

Romano, by then Christ-like in looks, the marks of the stigma visible to all, was a convincing contender to hold responsibly the Rod of Power. As a born again Warlord he would lead the troops into battle against King Kal. With the Pope's blessing, (his own), all would become invincible. But practising his Battle Cry, he lost his voice. His hip also giving him gyp, relief massage was again advised before he could be convicing, himself sending others into battle. 'In case hip-replacements in heaven not on?' joked PC. 'Quicker than relying on doctor's waiting list is death! As for voice coaching, Your Holiness, what better than an ex-choirboy. A very experienced one. He'd just love it, kissing your ring. So would Susan into healing massages. A blessing them, OK?'

Halfway up Corn Hill, Orangey was caught by a Grossock. In a long scream the dwarf yelled, forehead being opened with a giant corkscrew, because he'd lost his memory. Trying to reach him after another steep climb, Alice found dwarf and Giant had vanished. So where was Orangey? Try the Survivalists' Tourist Centre for Lost Souls.

Present were orphans of the idle rich. To show cost-cutting kindness to their own kids, the dads had organised Food Mountains above as below. In rejecting such selfish tactics, children had either been disinherited, (the passive complainers), or run away from home, (the proactive rebels like Alice). Either way, the privileged kids, despite toys by the tonne, had escaped into underground bunkers.

'Hi, Hargreaves!' Under his breath smelling of marigolds, Orangey told

Alice that the Tourist Centre was really a cover-up. 'Records inside their safe hide decisions taken in advance by unborn Souls,' he confided, 'as to what sort of bodywork, cross-roads, breakdowns and rust they ordered well before their next series of driving tests on earth.' Displayed was a French road map.

'In 5554 AD, Scarlet City fathers, or maybe the Dark Monsters, censored us true born-agains,' recalled Orangey, sadly. 'To avoid papal pogroms, many hid in hillside caves, now haunted. In which country? 'Look, Hargreaves,' admitted Orangey as they climbed through tangerine-tinted corn, 'every time I forget who or what I'm here for again, my hair goes a bit ... See. Getting as white as yours, poor old lady. Such a shock!'

'I'm looking for the Fountain of Youth. Before war breaks out. It's on one of these hills. YOURS? I need to know this, fast!'

'Soon young again! Like you, Hargreaves.' The repeated name Hargreaves spooked Alice as they met the local Haruspicist. He knows by studying a radioactive lamb's heart, which gods are auspicious. Was the position of Mars, its atmosphere getting thicker with every war, about to prevent the final cosmic battle of psychic super powers? Would Orangey remember? Alice, screwing up her eyes as requested, untwisted the corkscrew in his brow. His screams shrank her sweet heart.

Highway To Victory

The inner city sex shops were doing a roaring trade. Romano on the Cross of Calvery was one thing, but more prominently displayed was the picture of his own upright naked member (of the church) being kissed by a choir-boy devotee on his knees. Spluttering spinsters and uptight priests were suitably disgusted while PC's storm troopers, up in arms, voted for it to go onto page three of THE CURIA.

For once, THE CURIA had failed to control the day's news. And as Romano struggled to reveal, not all, but the picture on hordings to be a fake, PC took his chance. To the Curia before they could arrange a cover up, decisively he announced that it was he, the best-qualified martial tactician in the field, who would lead the Scars into their next beatific and final battle.

'See, Hargreaves, ATOMOS means indivisible. Like all dimensions of omnipresent thought waves.'

'Orangey, why hold up your aerial like that?' asked Alice.

As he scratched his crest of eight orange petals, another shower of dandruff (or was it pollen?) fell. Remembering that good memories get good grades, Orangey blurted. 'Like an acorn remembers it's an oak tree. But not by growing backwards, like memory, into the ground . . . but up into more delight. . . .'

'If you can't prove things, Orangey,' warned Alice, 'know what Oxbridge dons do?'

'As a knowing brat, I always got slapped down,' agreed Orangey, wincing. 'Maybe that's why I grew up a dwarf! Memory? It's a magnet! Needs de-sensitising. Beware of memory.'

'Orangey, is that a clever excuse for having a bad one?'

'Well, only negative people want to look into the future, Hargreaves, in case it's not there.'

'Orangey, how do you KNOW all this?'

'Can't remember!' Orangey suddenly looked much younger.

And Alice much older.

Pope Blesses Troops

To reinstate his holiness, Pope Romano predicted raygun gas-attacks, Saff's Thought Police, earthquakes, all aimed to reclaim his authority in public affairs after losing more than his face in juicy private affairs. His private war he had to win.

Yet violent earth tremors in the seven hills of Scarlet City, the prelates at the Army Surplice Stores continued to ignore.

But not PC sporting his new-found role, by then publicly authenticated. 'The Saffs' man-made god-king Kal may be Big Boss at present but tomorrow belongs to those who conquer the constraints of the Fourth

331

Dimension, with occult weapons.' For promotion, PC's Psychic Specials paraded such propaganda.

Levitation and invisibility were the weapons that surely no military hardware could defeat. Certainly not under the gallant leadership of General Charles, and The Rainbow Warriors each having received a private audience with Romano, their blessed but maligned Pontiff who'd fight to override any evil attempts to discredit PC in public. By then, both men needed each other.

Alice in a back street sex-shop came across a flier showing the current Pope with his skirts up. Defrocked, he was displayed in a window poster decrying the 'naked perversions' of 'celibacy', the prelate's lop-sided hips in full view. Alice saw how raddled and wrinkled she had become. Yet a time-less desire to prize open all locked-up secrets kept her hobbling ever forwards and upwards. From the seven hills various cries for help called her. Five more poor dwarfs left she had to visit. For her, meanwhile, what hope of a mountain stream offering spiritual upliftment (and a face-lift)? Old Alice, like young Alexander the Great, aimed to drink pure waters to conquer the corruption of her own shrivelled body. Unlike him, she decided not to die young. Far better to love life alive by embracing the true Humphrey in or out of the promised long flight in the Flying Flute. Who of the five dwarfs left might yield a haven of everlasting health, a Healing Hive, so she with Humphrey can live forever? But find which first? Spring water!

Undercover Advances

Not long before Romano uncovered PC's plot. Something too furtive, too explosive, had to be handled with total caution. Namely, the dangers of SHC, Spontaneous Human Combustion.

PC's basic belief had hardened. It was that human futures, to thrive, need only a small flock of elitist 'Shepherds'. By their own self-assessments in action, herds of obedient yobs render themselves expendable. In contrast, Romano saw hordes of survivors on their knees all paying allegiance to him, submissively. Hell-fire flames like human fears, because they breed only Furies, can still be the ultimate deterrent. In one other way PC and Pope Romano were alike: Only those with cold hearts poke the fires of fear in others.

Blue Mountain looked headstrong. Having conquered such a cold long climb, Alice collapsed outside Bluey's cave. She heard rushing waters! The Fountain of Eternal Youth – at last? Hope springs eternal longings. . . !

Three ex-Rook clerics were drilling the blue-coated dwarf with facts, like dentists. Those catechising ex-priests, having rejected the Curia's hell-fire teachings, blamed the Scarlet Fathers for having blinded their all-seeing Middle Eyes. They were the equivalent of the Grossocks. Like Cyclops, the three clerics before excommunication had rescued damning documents, long warped shelves of looted archive materials, all confiscated by successive Popes from cathedral cellars and belfries. Their fattest tomb was being studied by Bluey. Every time he misquoted, one of the ex-Rooks nipped off another nibble of his sensitive head-flaps. Watching Alice flinch added spice to their peccadilloes as details of past Papal dissenters were being recited aloud by Bluey. More and more he looked like a bonsai version of Dr. Faustus in a painful brown study.

The Curia like the KGB had knowledge not just of Reds under beds but who was IN them. Historical figures, after face-lifts, needed unmasking. Image was all. Under covers, especially hard covers, celibates needed The Karma Sutra, The Tao of Sex, Tantric Orgasms, and Capers for Catamites. Yet they were tame compared with the wilder contortions illustrated in the sexiest of pop-up homosexual handbooks. Even nuns into S and M, wimples and whips, were catered for. All those archives the heretic Rooks had kept hidden in Blue Mountain caves preserved for each new millennium's further 'edutainment', as the planet of Venus grew ever brighter, and Mars darker.

Final Days of Deliverance?

Rumours calcified into occult certainties; Aliens' Mind-bending chemicals! Poisoned catacombs! Within Rainbow Mountain itself, seismic shifts on an epic scale! All feared!

On a countdown to the epicentre of doomsday, terror ticked away on the wrists of Romano and his Rooks as PC gave his troops the nod. Another order went out to the Curia's Marshall Guards. Attack Saffron City. Carry the bronze statue of PC as the Christ, ahead of the Scar troops; General Charles sacred VIP (Vril in Power). His battle tactics would undoubtedly decimate Rainbow Mountain's pagan monks. Time to sound the Scarlet City's seven sirens. From the evil King in his Mountain fortress they would wrest the Rod of Cosmic Power.

'But for whom?' asked Alice? 'And for how long. . . ?'

Klaxons blasting, hands over her ears, Alice felt unprotected by the tiers of tomes, parchments, pamphlets and tablets that entombed Bluey. Barricades of hardback books on apocrypha, black magic, liturgical scandals, paranormal practices, fallen saints and fraudulent stigmatists, smelt musty despite mountain breezes. Unconcerned by warnings of war, the ex-Rooks boasted about damning evidence of pogroms ordered by past so-called omniscient Pontiffs. And of Dead Sea Scrolls damaging to accepted beliefs. Included was Rerum Novarum, a divinely inspired document too uncomfortable to cosy up with. It condemned not just capitalism but also socialism. Could Bluey the dwarf recite it verbatim before all his blue cap flaps the giant Grossocks nipped off with pincers, bit by delicious bit?

'*A rare Scarlet Father, Lionheart the Eighth*,' droned Bluey, '*wrote that natural man has a right to property. His doctrine of Distributism his successors hastily discredited. They used. . . .*'

Hesitation. NIP, NIP, NIBBLE! OW! OW! OWWW! Three more bites from his flesh-flaps until to the ex-priests, Bluey quickly parroted out, '*The poor will inherit the Bread of Heaven.*'

'Papal Bullshit!' chortled the tallest torturer wielding his toothpick like a teacher's cane.

'*But that same Pontiff saw a society so mature, so prosperous, that a Nanny State would become. . . .*' His headache blocked the next word. The same pain sliced through Alice's brain as the smallest catechizer produced his last aspirin and split it in half.

NIP, NIP and NIBBLE! OW! OW! **OWWW!** Three more bits of Bluey's head-flesh met with amused licked lips as Bluey, handed only half an aspirin, blurted out, 'NO!' Quickly, he handed Alice his half of the tablet, concluding with, '*Such teachings lay dormant, until re-discovered by early Survivalists.*'

'Nothing new under the crust!' groaned Alice holding in her headache and sucking her half of the shared aspirin. Bluey, sucking his half, said, 'I think faster when I urinate. Might I, please, go for a leak. . . ?'

'All of these books,' protested Alice getting more heretical, 'they'll never cure his migraine. Or mine. Read rocks Bluey, not books; study insects and birds, nature's own university. God's lighter than all world bibles, all apocrypha.' Alice lit a match, saying, 'WATCH ME BURN THE LOT!'

'Oh shucks – my zip's stuck!'

Three lips gleamed with spittle. Was Bluey's trapped penis to be their next succulent tip-bit? A chase. Each time they all circled Alice, Bluey aimed his urine at the burning match in her shaking hand. Catching him mid flow, the biggest ex-cleric grabbed Bluey's left wrist. Alice pulled the dwarf's other wrist. Would he be split apart like that aspirin. . . ?

Suddenly, an explosion. Silence.

The dwarf cowered behind a barricade of blue books.

Only Alice seemed to hear, far in the distance, a healing mountain stream, as 'Thirst for Knowledge,' said she, 'leads to thermonuclear weapons and WORSE! The Fountain of Eternal Youth, dwarfs, fathers, heretics, all, WHERE IS IT?' Silence. 'Where can I find again my Eternal Youth . . . my Humphrey. . . ?' Getting deafer, Alice felt the eternal waters of youth had left her forlorn, smitten with a download of everlasting human tears. But hark, the sound of distant healing waters? No, Bluey's pee.

Back in Scarlet City Alice tried to block out further cries for help from her little men before they became war orphans, and she a wicked stepmother. Humphrey and Mancunian Cat, dead or alive, were still incommunicado. Being dead was no excuse for such unfriendly silence. Or had Humphrey left because, in her need to help others, she had become too haggard?

True, she was lacking cures for her hurting dwarfs . . . as well as one for her own love-sick heart. Alice knew she was suffering all the dwarf's ailments from constipation to migraine. Was it not possible to help others without harming one's own true inner growth?

'Welcome, Moonchild.' A tall dark-skinned man had spoken. With raven plaits he stood imposingly nearby. He was staring in the all-seeing, no-nonsense way of a Master Nanny. Raising his right hand, he greeted her again. 'Greentree. Inner City Guide. Pow-wow on peace?'

'With Humphrey?'

'With Great White Spirit.'

Astonished, she saw a ring of seven coloured mushrooms magically push their way through the marble floor. 'For eating?' asked Alice, hungry after all that climbing. 'I just KNEW I'd have a happy ending, Mr Greenpeace. Like a fairy!'

'Before healing waters above, three tests, old madam. . . .'

Excited, her breast wrinkles jiggled up and down like a loosely knitted old jumper, her eyes bright with expectation.

'Prepare for mountain flights. By Thunder Travel.' Sonorously, he chanted, 'Hin-mah-lat-kekht!' With a stately gait, Greentree then steered Alice towards Mauvey, the dwarf's hillside hideout a-buzz with bees. Secretly, Alice was hoping that at the end of the rainbow would be a surprise pot of honey called Humphrey. Secretly? Unlikely. Greentree was surely not alone in her protective aura, watching every heartbeat with holy care. Physical or astral, Alice longed to be embraced again by Humphrey's gentle affirmation, 'We're beautiful!'

Without warning, Greentree pointed towards Saffron Road as it sped away through green foothills below their gaze. 'When student ready, master he DISappear!' Greentree had vanished.

Alice, desperate for some sustaining contact, made a beeline for Mauvey's hidden cave. He surely needed her, badly.

Too Big For His Boots?

Leaving Scarlet City, PC ordered the Curia Guard to remove their face of

Christ. It showed that of Romano. Instead, he ordered his own rejuvinated image. Mesmerised by their Charles the Brave, all eagerly agreed. Their new battle emblem inspired them as they prepared to confront hostile hill-side heretics, all sides ordered to chant OM. Short for OMinous?

As Alice was panting up towards Mauvey's hideout Greentree, re-appearing, offered her a walking-staff. 'Flute to phallus, hazel-twigs to totem-poles,' warned he, gravely. 'Power Rods point us skywards. Land-locked battles solve little too late!'

Hoping he was not being rude about her dwarfs, she allowed him to lead her further through the purple heathers and bilberries. When they heard Mauvey wracked with whooping-cough, Alice hobbled forward faster, still keen to administer help. Would her do-gooding times end on the day she and Humphrey. . . ? 'M-my deaths never were extinction, I know but . . . well . . . I'll not ask if he's still . . . but . . . well . . . IS HE. . . ?'

Greentree's big tanned shoulders rose up like twin wing-tips. Calm as a graveside angel carved in burnished granite, he heard Alice admit, 'I knew you wouldn't say. That's why I tried not to ask. And,' she added with her usual honesty, 'why I HAD to. Oh, do stop grinning, Mr Greenpeace. If he's dead, it hurts. If he's alive, it's maybe OK. But if he still loves me, I'll . . . I'll. . . .'

'Say!'

'FAINT!' As if bursting out of a Victorian corset, Alice finally owned up. 'Oh, it's too horrible! I'm frantic! I can't pretend to stay detached, all spiritual! How on earth do YOU manage to stay so cool, Mr Greentree?'

With supreme serenity, the Hopi Indian explained. 'Faustians grow backwards towards re-birth, like you Alice, travelling from a future viewpoint. . . .'

'So,' asked Alice like a teacher trying to believe in eyes at the back of her head, 'am I in a state of decay, decade BEFORE decade, before . . . or after . . . or BOTH at the same . . . well . . . TIME. . . ?'

His noble head nodded. 'All matters – reversible.'

'That must mean that IF I go forwards to meet Humphrey's Astral Body I get older, but if, on the other hand, I continue to walk backwards for

Christmas, I'll get younger and prettier. Riper for romance, yes, but . . . but . . . m-might . . . I?' She could not bring herself to utter the obvious consequence, become all ripe and ready – if not randy – for the sex war.

On cue, another distant explosion.

'LOSE Humphrey?' Not daring to peek at Greentree after that bleak question, Alice trapped two pricking tears. 'God, what a choice. Win or LOSE. Just like in a war. Horrid!'

'Stay neutral. Like God.'

'But look, Mr Greenpeace. Straight AT instead of THROUGH me, please. Admit it. I'm like Methuselah's grandmother. A tatty old haggis.'

Chortled Greentree, 'Bernard Shaw, he tell of Ancients. Live centuries in young bodies.'

'Yes, I want my youth back. My straight spine. And Humphrey to love should I falter in self-esteem. In fact,' she concluded in a climax of generosity, 'I want ALL AT ONCE – NOW!'

'You – SOUL – speak. BRAVO!'

They rested on a plateau. Greentree slipped from his back an angler's basket and rocked it back and forth like a seesaw. 'Food for Soul. Food for body. Like acid, like alkaline, both at war inside this picnic basket.'

Pagan Practices

PC spiced further directives with crude references to the drinking habits of their enemy. Saffron City was notorious for Rose Cocktails, an ungodly habit found risible by the Rooks despite scientific defence of the high content of vitamin C in rose petals. All were warned. The Saffs had the deepest tunnels for experimenting in laboratories lit by advanced magnetics. Therein abducted Scars were mutilated like cattle, their sperm, and DNA stolen, ovaries ripped out, all for recycling in robots.

From the other side of the gully Alice heard Mauvey's hoarse throat rasping. Also a loud buzzing noise. Had he been poisoned? Stung by a bombardment of bees? No, it sounded more like whooping-cough. What was the cure for such a hacking cough?

Concern drew Alice so close to the lip of the rubbish-tip between herself and Mauvey that she nearly tipped herself over the brink. Dumped inside the deep crater were a million dispirited instruments of Soul Music. Alice shouted across the tangled tip, 'I want to help you . . . badly . . . but don't know how. The gully is too deep, Mauvey. But don't give up. Don't give in. I'll get there – somehow!' Then, feeling giddy, Alice glowered at the gulf that kept her from attending to Mauvey's cough.

The crater was choked, as if all the bankrupt orchestras of the under-world had cast their broken instruments down the cliff-face into a big mangled mess. Discarded harps, twisted cellos and tubas, mouth-less flutes, de-gutted pianos, skinless drums and filleted synthesisers, all showed a soundless sculptured montage at rest, and all signifying little or no peace.

Alice listened. But no bird sang there. Instead, they chose to sing for their supper away from such an unblessed symphonic cemetery. How long before such musical metals were to be shaped into lethal shells capable of silently piercing heavy armoured vehicles? Peering through her lorgnette Alice saw that on each rusty old instrument was scrawled one name: MAUVEY.

Feeling fleetingly helpless suddenly heartened her. As she relaxed, seemingly from nowhere, Greentree appeared again. As before, he cast no shadow on the ground. Humming to himself, he arranged assorted foods either side of Alice as he sat on the ground in front of her; Yin food on her left; Yang food her right. Which side should Alice eat? Reluctant to sit by him in case she couldn't get up again after food, Alice could not keep her aged eyes from straying towards the braying Mauvey too inaccessible, it seemed, to be given the help he urgently needed.

COUGH!

'Everything is as it should be.'

'Listen ! He wants help, not lectures!' protested Alice.

COUGH!

'And what might YOU need?'

'Me, sir? Want? Why, HUMPHREY!'

'That was not my question.'

339

'That was my answer.'

COUGH!

In Scarlet city, an explosion.

'Is Humphrey DEAD? Or with the Saffs, in the Flying Flute? No, no, no. Mauvey needs my help. He's got whooping-cough. No more questions. I'm tired of thinking. My head hurts.'

'Because you split that aspirin with Bluey? Now before Civil War gets too hot, EAT!'

'No, I've got no appetite. For conflicts . . . for choices . . . for food.'

'Same thing.'

NO COUGH.

'MAUVEY!' Alice's blotched old hand clapped against her right cheek. 'Needs me! Might be dead. Listen to him – LISTEN!'

NO COUGH.

'More than you need Soul Food? Choose!'

'I know a folk remedy. For his cough.' An explosion below. 'Must find a dead dormouse. . . .'

War Hots Up

Despite Romano's decline in energy, daily he fed more alarmist tales to THE CURIA. He feared PC's potential victory. Especially since PC had impressed the Rooks by suggesting that, as the Saff harvests had failed so disastrously, the Scar's Food Mountains might become a target. So feed the savage Saffs! What, to kill another day? That suited the Rooks' bankers! Rival religions maybe, but each side remained in debt to the same Arms Dealers. Each army needed its latest lethal technology to be tested. How else would secret weapons be kept effective without ordering further wars? A stronger poison than digitalis was killing Romano. The prophecy in which it is written: *No matter how holy, the last Pope must die out of office.*

Greentree sat as still as a Buddha. Delayed desires taste best. Despite yearning for youth and Humphrey hungry Alice settled herself between

Greentree's two picnic spreads.

Not a romantic pick-me-up, though famished, Alice found her chosen raw oyster to be unchewable. So Greentree imitated a steam train going, 'CHEW-CHEW, CHEW-CHEW, CHEW-CHEW, HOO-HOO!' On that the dead orchestra's musical instruments in the gully started to jig about playing unaided as all the vocal birds chirped up and starting singing. Until another bomb blast. Then silence. 'Saff's Holy Cows meditate as they masticate. Scars' clergy eat the Eucharist with no Es. YOU?'

'Now what do I want to eat? Humphrey!' Alice said airily, eyeing up the eggplants, red peppers, pork, potatoes, tomatoes, aubergines, clotted cream, coffee beans. But no refined flour to deepen her wrinkles. Instead, still tackling the rubbery oyster, obstinate Alice tried to look as cool as any vegan virgin chewing a sheep's eyeball as Mauvey's worsening cough grated on her nerves.

'Might he dream-catch own ANSWERS, young lady?'

YOUNG! The word stung her. But following his gaze, Alice eased herself over on to her right-hand side to examine the second spread of food. 'That oyster, Yin. Negative foods make acid. You slim, passive. Like Saffron City. Must turn meditation into contemplation. Like Scarlet City, must learn to be more detached. Contemplate. Visualise. Dowse.'

'And this?' With a forked twig she dowsed carrots, apples, cherries, grouse, buckwheat, watercress, goats' cheese, ginseng and mu teas. 'Positive?' asked Alice. The hazel-twig in her hands nodded up and down in time to the jigging instruments.

'Yang!' A grimace flicked across his face. 'Make you bitter. Like Scarlet City. Male. Mind. No humble. No submit,' smiled he. 'Both sides, male, female, fight for rights, for balance.'

'Don't like the taste of any of it.' With that, Alice spat out the oyster into the rubbish-tip. It silenced a stringless violin!

'A diet fit for seven dwarfs. No such thing. Yet food can cure constipation, emotionalism, memory loss, left brain indigestion, doubtful intuitions, etc., etc. Two dwarfs to go. What they teach you, Alice?' Listening, she heard only coughs.

'First, a mouse for whooping-cough. Shall I get Mancunian Cat to catch one for Mauvey?' She struggled to her aching feet.

Cool as a beach Jesus in jeans, Greentree plucked two herrings from the air, held them head to tail. 'Symbol of Pisces, passing Age of Christ. Believe life unfair. Stay dwarfs' victim.'

'ALICE – HELP!' called Mauvey between hacking coughs wracking his sore throat, and again 'H-E-L-P!'

'I do Yogic miracles standing on my head. Only like my dwarfs, forgotten how.' Almost silently she added, 'Sorry, Mauvey,' then doggedly sat. As still as Greentree, eyes shut, now the orchestra was on strike in sympathy with the violin that had hit with a flying oyster, she prayed for world peace.

The Heavens At War

Haley's comet had been referred to by an earlier Pope, Calixtus the Third, as 'An agent of the devil'. That self-same celestial agent was again snooping around the globe. Coincidence? NORMAD, the nuclear warning system had sent Seers of all persuasions to their crystal balls. Might a sudden change of the earth's axis disorientate all warring warriors as with nuclear explosions? After all, the split atom presaged an immense expansion of human consciousness. Categorically, PC announced that imminent catastrophes could always be averted. 'How so?' asked anxious Psychic Specials. 'HOW?'

'By us. By capturing the Rod of Vril Power. We can save the whole Curia, their seven hills from being flattened.' But could PC ensure survival of Scarlet City's universal creed, keep Romano as sickening Pope safe from harm; most of the believing sheep on both sides reconciled, assimilated, rounded-up, like singed leftovers after another cosmic culinary fry-up?

To Jake and other trusted Psychic Specials, PC dared use not the word assimilated but 'eliminated'. Ironically, he so despised 'the glorious dead' praised as self-styled heroes. Until sheep in boots refuse to be blindly herded into corporate slaughter, none will become his rival Shepherds. Good riddance!

*

'Fish?' gulped Alice, the tang of tough oyster still tingling.

'From atoms. Create form! See fish, Alice. Eyes shut.'

'Mine or the fish's?'

'See five white dots. Picture. In developing tank. Like blank TV. First, see fish atoms form. Now slow them down, down. Outline getting denser. Bless what you wish. Taste success, at one with fish-seed. Blink Inner Eye. Let go. Open! Receive full fish.' Alice came out of trance. In her lap she found five hot-cross buns. 'But I HATE fish!' growled Alice. Yet reluctantly amazed, her mouth was still gaping like an open oven door. She LOVED hot-cross buns!

Greentree frowned. 'French bread, wine, took years off the Gaspesian Tribe. Me – Hopi.'

Alice twinkled, 'Me Hopi, too! I hopi I have Humphrey in my next Christmas stocking!'

'Know Malarchy's predictions? Will Scarlet city survive droughts, fires, floods, wars . . . the next fat Pope. . . ?'

Squeals from five dwarfs as an earth tremor juddered through the seven hills. Below them, the dome of the golden basilica was split in twain, disaster causing raucous panic.

Said Greentree, 'Great Alexander left seven levels of Babel Tower in ruins. He just moved on . . . Move on, Alice . . . MOVE!'

Hundreds of worshippers, rising from rubble, fleeing from the mighty falling masonry, quickly sought safety. Adults grabbed children as boys and girls grabbed toys, all in noisy panic, racing, chasing, shouting, praying, looting, all on the run.

Asked Alice, 'Scars or Saffs, which will the Giants choose?'

'Food?'

'Oh NO, I've lost my Magic Eye, the one Humphrey gave me before.' Alice glanced at Greentree. No hint of sympathy.

'God-eaters rise, eat atoms only. Rise above worry-belts, astroid belts, black belts. Hear Mother Earth's heartbeat, RISE!'

They continued to climb towards Mauvey's cave. 'A folklore cure!

343

Ancient Rome! Should I cure his whooping-cough if it means killing a dormouse?' Mancuian Cat stayed mute.

Space Colonies

Was PC expendable? Like planet earth? Is it not written that he who shall control the Moon and Mars shall also control the earth? The more certain of marching to total victory, the colder grew PC's eyes, and darker grew the eyes of Romano and his Rooks, all pragmatically awaiting unknown outcomes. . . .

Whose number was up? Would any future Pope honour PC, posthumously, once his usefulness was over? Weren't their most valued servants, like Mother Teresa once canonised, soon forgotten? Romano was determined to keep the Rod of Power to himself, to be shared with God's own Righteous Believers he, not PC, at last in charge of all such humble Chosen Ones.

Mauvey was not at all shaken to see a tall Hopi Indian. Despite his fever and sore throat he welcomed them with, 'Tea 4 3?' Three not four? Odd that he should be so intuitive.

His next bout of coughing didn't quite drown out some rather tinny-sounding yawns. They were coming from inside Mauvey's teapot. Removing the lid, Alice was delighted to find a dormouse inside it rubbing its eyes at the sudden inrush of light. Along tiny eyelashes, sleepy-stuff was dotted like flecks of nectar. Before its yawning mouth he poised a polite paw and then, surprisingly, winked at them, sleepily saying, 'Quite exciting, dying. Better than sleep!' The mouse also intuitive?

'Hate killing, eh lass?' asked Mancunian Cat, on cue. Alice was comforted to hear again the phrase 'Mice have nine lives, too, pet, despite cruelty in medical research.'

M for **M**ice and **M**onkeys also?

Or for MEN only?

'Maybe next time,' admitted Dormouse, 'I'll stay awake for more mad tea-parties!' Then to Mauvey, it whispered, 'Eat, in memory of me.'

Greentree, with Mancunian Cat, used the old North American Indian form of grace: 'We thank our friend Dormouse for the goodly food set before us,' they prayed, 'and wish him well in his new Hunting Ground.'

The leather skin, toughened by having been boiled in tannin, was handed to Alice. Reluctantly munching the tender flesh, Mauvey protested, 'I'm not sure W.H.O. would approve.'

Distracting herself from thoughts of the Word Health Organisation (W.H.O.), Alice wondered what talisman she could keep in her new pouch of mouse hide now that Humphrey's gift of the Magic Eye had slipped from her onto any one of the five out of seven multi-coloured hills so far visited.

His cough and sore throat cured, Mauvey hugged Alice around the waist and Greentree around his right kneecap. Opening up their hearts and hands to the good heavens the three ended their happy jig with a mighty, 'Hip-Hip-HOO-RAY!'

From a distance it looked like rape. Seen nearer, the hillside was not covered with cattle-fodder or gold bars, but with frozen best butter. 'Crevice!' warned Greentree, 'Knee!'

'KNEE?' Fingertips freezing, old Alice was trying not to slip off the ice-dripping cliff, to accidentally abseil away from Goldy and his noisy tinnitus. For safer rock-climbing, Greentree was guiding the rope that bound them together, as they climbed heights too hazardous for a spinster beyond her sell-by date to enjoy with dignity and in the cleanest of under-clothes.

Somewhere high on the escarpment above, Goldy was screaming. Like a haunting jam session from Mauvey's hill tip, an inner cacophony of instruments rattled his brains with shrill whistles and blaring sirens, demanding attention. Had the stress of rumbling war and earth tremors unhinged his brain?

No thermal-jacket to stop her wrinkles trembling, but near to a water font in the flaking rock-face, Alice secured a foothold. Bending over to refresh herself the rope became slacker, her shallow panting less painful. While perched there so precariously, Alice met her next test head-on.

A voice imitating Humphrey commanded, 'Drink in m-memory of m—m-me.'

Hovering over a deep craggy crevasse, her brittle chicken-bones were losing their toehold as the rough voice rasped out, 'Water for eternal youthful beauty, DRINK!' Surely a false offer.

So which would win, vertigo or vanity? Or the intuition she'd just found with Mauvey? Alice decided to take the invitation, as inner guidance, and test her own temptations to disbelieve in miracles that aren't fully deserved.

Swinging on her fraying guide-rope, old Alice saw a goatskin gourd appear. As if by itself, the gourd dipped into the rock font's sparkling water. Accepting the gift, she gingerly lifted the gourd, her rope lifeline fraying fast above her. Dreading she'd lose her balance, slip and fall down the cliff-face, Alice thought, 'What if this holy water is POISONED?'

As out of icy hill mist, an old tramp loomed into view. Ragged and toothless, smelly as a billy-goat, he gobbed into the spring water. 'Old hag, help nectar harden into gold?'

'Butter Mountain?' Like her Black Dog was he tempting her into fear? 'You want me to fall, don't you? Fall . . . fall into. . . ?'

'Butter or bullion, let go of all that's heavy and hurts. Let go of all ropes. Let go,' he spat out, 'let go, LET GO!'

Glancing up to the summit, Alice saw Goldie was in deep distress. Snatching a glance down the deep ravine, fearing a fall, she nearly fainted. Was her life to finish like the crash that befell Humpty Dumpty? Like a spiked needle in acupuncture, a grim phrase kept jabbing her brain. ALL FALL DOWN needled her, the words digging ever deeper and deeper into her aching skull.

Inter-planetary Implants

PC's Psychic Specials tuned in daily to the Saffs. Warning visions. The ravings of monkish bulletheads manic enough to kill the Scars or themselves in states of drug-induced bliss. No need for priests. Their power, they claimed, came straight from the Rod of Vril. They were to project implants like pinpricks through the necks of PC's troops. Long known to the scientists of the Curia, the occult skills of such mind control techniques originally came from Mars. Historically, their army was known as Scars. Hopefully, a suitably sinister name for the Saffs to fear.

Horrified, Alice saw the flash of a penknife. The hobo was cutting through her frayed lifeline, his toothless gums grinning. But where was Greentree? Like the last autumn leaf afraid to leave its parent tree, the frail old Alice hung on, her heart pounding in her chest. Then, to prevent the rope being frayed even further – she was relieved that the penknife was less sharp than it looked – Alice holding out the gourd offered the tramp the first sip of holy water from the rock face font.

Instead of being grateful, he recoiled, saying, 'When Alexander were a lad, I had a drink o'that. Now look at me. Too ill to love, too ill to eat. Forever withered, ugly, like you old hag.'

Alice dared herself to lift the water, holy or harmful, to her own mouth. Snatching the gourd before she could drink, the toothless old vagabond, his body odour pungently male, demanded, 'Smack on me grizzled lips, old hag. Snog me quick, one last deep wet KISS!'

No hesitation. Visualising the Fountain of Youth, mineral waters trickling down her like liquid silver, letting her heart not her head take charge, Alice kissed him on his lips, generously.

Opening her withered old eyes, in her arms she found her lover boy. 'HUMPHREY!' she sang out to all seven hills. 'You're alive . . . and young and . . . and in. . . .'

'M-m-mighty hurry!' gasped he stuttering, delaying his departure as golden eyes scanned the skies. 'I'll call a taxi!' said he like Biggles on his Big Day. 'Fear old age less and live longer!'

Suddenly, caterwauling, 6 dwarfs again feeling ill, were begging their own magic Fairygodmother for rescue; to send an instant Air Ambulance before the war started in earnest.

'All dwarfs called to the colours!' shouted Humphrey. 'Except the one named WHO-itey.'

'Whitey, I think. Oh all right. But why WHO-itey? Irish is he? Sure sounds it. A bit like Orangey.'

'Yep, but neutral,' snapped Humphrey. 'QUICK NOW!'

Barely had his inadequate answer got accepted when a UFO hovered above them. A jokey, cackling voice from inside it accused Humphrey of kidnapping a granny for organ transplants; worse; of being a double-agent for King Kal. Sucking his body up into the belly of the UFO, the hatch closed. Humphrey was kidnapped. Broadcasting a promise his two balls in a bag would be stewed like two hairy dormice, the UFO skimmed the top of Butter Mountain and zipped away only to return seconds later.

Above Alice on her narrow ledge, its bowels opened and a torrent of entrails jettisoned from the craft splattered the hillside, a bleeding nose hitting Alice in the face and dropping at her feet. Examining the nose, Alice went white as ice. It was the same shape and size as Humphrey's. Yes, it was stippled with blackheads, a perfect fit for the pouch she kept in memory of her martyred Dormouse. In place of the Magic Eye, Humphrey's nose? She wanted to help him. Couldn't. What she had eaten at Greentree's hillside picnic, less the oyster, she spewed up.

A magpie lanced the nose with its beak and flew off with it. Was every-thing that reminded her of Humphrey and comfort to be taken from her? Why were only her worst experiences repeating themselves, again and again?

As gulls battled over the discharged cargo of giblets, six dwarfs wailed in a chorus of anguish each lamenting his own ailment and fear of death in fatal warfare, not friendly welfare.

Conflicts, though tiring for the elderly, Alice realised she didn't know which side was the real enemy, Scars or Saffs. Suddenly, she couldn't care less either way. All she knew was that she wanted him safe; a young, wholesome and loving Humphrey again. He could be green, pink, orange, blue, mauve or gold; young, old or sexless; anything, so long as it was him, complete. Well, complete if and when he could find it in his heart to love her enough to grow a handsome new nose!

As if she'd nothing left to declare but total trust in the universe Alice, brimming over with boundless love, called out to the bald blue skies above, 'H-U-M-P-H-R-E-Y, I LOVE YOU!'

Greentree re-appeared. On the highest summit of Snow Mountain he was surveying all. Whitey, as his baby guru glowing like a fairylight, was safely perched on Greentree's right shoulder. Right hand raised in a blessing, Whitey called out with dazzling boldness to all seven hills, 'Each sing out your name with love, with Grandmother Alice! And little friends, all harmonise with my name, too, WHO-itey!'

From the seven hills, Greeny, Pinky, Orangey, Bluey, Mauvey and Goldy, his aureole of curls aglow, harmonised. Their sung names united became one all-embracing, uplifting white noise surrounding Alice with love too precious to describe.

If the devil has the best tunes, Whitey's coolest calm certainties were so simple compared with the stress Alice expressed over Humphrey's prolonged absences. Was he safe. . . ?

Battle Cries

Revving up for attack, PC ranted, 'Dare adventures, risks which only we, the pure in heart, are brave enough to bleed for!'

'BURN for!' yelled the more headstrong devotees.

Such beatific raptures were relayed to Romano.

To both men, PC and Romano, the stench of slaughter was to become an aphrodisiac more potent than the scented breezes from perennial cherry blossom on Meat Mountain.

Sonorous as any past Master, Greentree intoned, 'God scores. Lightning conducts. Thunder crumbles!'

Alice still spinning with old doubts heard Greentree clarify, 'Interstellar symphonies . . . shoot stars . . . like glittering specks of spittle . . . through the Flute of God. We human Souls . . . scale up, down, up . . . spiralling back to the One first Note of All.'

Again, Alice was being reminded of Humphrey's Flying Flute. God, didn't the Pied Piper lead them into to a deadly mountain? Like that UFO? And wasn't Venus once called Lucifer? What if she's NOT meant to get brighter, younger? Dismissing doubts, Alice decided to join all her little men. With a nod from Greentree, Alice was ready to chant with each dwarf. But WHICH name was truly hers? She'd been called so many. So, changing her worrying mind, she stayed silent.

Pointing towards Rainbow Mountain, Greentree thrust his huge hands and voice skywards. 'Behind 7 veils of mist, and 7 peaks of ice; above all Scars, all Saffs, let's praise all Light Brothers who work as silent celestial medics. We thank them for checking Mother Earth's temperature, water-works, and ailments in service to humanity under beloved Master HOONIE.'

'Master, not Mister?' asked Alice. 'Please, is he still YOUNG,' she pleaded like a little girl, 'like HUMPHREY?'

'Ageless. Lives invisibly in a snow hut on yak tea.'

The seven dwarfs and Alice chanting the name HOO-nie, all rang out the name of Mother Earth's white coated Celestial Consultant releasing radiant hoops of lights in greens, pinks, oranges, blues, and gold all pirou-etting through the air. Soon the hillsides became a kinetic kaleidoscope of colours, visible sound-waves gyrating skywards like joyful multi-coloured ribbons . . . all seven dwarfs singing out together with glee . . . while open-ing war noises exploded all round their little defiant bodies.

As they chanted in unison, rainbow-coloured winds spun the 7 dwarfs, one at a time, off the ground. Uplifted, the flying formation of little figures was led by Whitey, the top dwarf. Greeny's ankles skimmed Alice close enough for her arthritic hands to hold on firmly. Her body was whisked into the air, a flounder on a fishing-line behind 7 tiddlers hoping not to be bait.

Hungry Grossocks lumbered into view. Dirty long fingernails scratched the clouds for snacks to catch, as the dwarfs and Alice swerved in and out of the Giants' flailing arms.

'If only we could stay invisible,' thought Alice. 'Then it wouldn't matter how old I looked for Humphrey. Or how many noses he lost.'

Flying colours in wartime? To avoid detection from either the Scars or the Saffs, Alice and the dwarfs searched for somewhere safe to land.

Descending over a cloudless mountain lake Alice, at speeds too dizzy to decipher, saw her reflection below in clear water suddenly lose all its ripples like aged wrinkles.

Then they landed, Alice finding it was a passing mirage.

Gibbering frantically, she withered faster as, surrounding old Alice and friends, was a fierce-eyed gang of seven hooded Saffs. Those dreaded martial monks were merciless in defence of their monarch's right to rule with the Rod of Vril Power. King Kal, for them, was the undisputed Sovereign of the Universe. The Rod of Vril Power was theirs. For keeps.

Till Kingdom come . . . or . . . till Kingdom's collapse. . . ?

CHAPTER TWELVE

THE FLYING FLUTE

*'He thought he saw an Elephant that
practised on a fife. . . .'*

Twilight.

Their final psychic battle was imminent.

Watching through hazy mobiles of gnats Greentree was standing up high on Rainbow Mountain. His right hand was on a big basalt pictographic stone. It was broken. As a natural healer, Greentree watched stones and stars, auras and ulcers, plants and planets, ecstasy and agony, all with the same wry detachment.

Below Greentree in a red canyon, PC's Rainbow Warriors pitching camp for the night, were only some twenty miles from Kal, King of the Underworld.

Every seminary has its erotic tensions. PC's storm-troopers, in their purple sneakers, were being channelled into a campfire Victory Dance. Originally, it was to thank the gods for preserving life against infertility, peaking to an erotic climax. PC, as teacher, had adapted it into a form of coitus interruptus, he as a macho, bearded flirt, wilfully arousing the youths' dragon-fire. When that is trapped in spine and neck, those lured into a state of psychic unbalance can get more than their fingers burnt. As Vril Law has it – FLOW WITH LOVE OR SELF-DESTRUCT. Such fire-balls are the mini version of the macro warning in the Bhagavad-Gita, '*I AM BECOME DEATH, THE SHATTERER OF WORLDS.*'

Greentree knew that **M**, his Brother of the White Leaf, was always leading the peaceful pilgrims back to their true spiritual home. As a symbol of his authority, **M** will produce the other half of the sacred broken stone. Meanwhile, with his Kirlian vision even in darkness, Greentree was able to see spaghetti-like spirals of etheric flames encircling the writhing dancers. Yes, after victory, PC's winning Warriors would become 'accidental' fireworks, their own bodies exploding like incendiary bombs. Since the Saffs were using Atlantean crystals to trigger their zipguns like using blowlamps to obliterate butterflies, the defeated enemy would take the blame.

Only the faithful Psychic Specials might survive. Or so PC confidently proclaimed in their presence.

Human disappearance was not new. Without public fuss, an average 14,000 folk vanish in the UK each year. And the mystery disappearance of the entire First-Fifth Royal Norfolk Regiment has never been explained. Unless, that is, one allows for the possibility of kidnap by an alien fleet of spacecraft. Judges are highly paid to keep such thoughts out of the public domain. So also, other inflammable subjects like self-incinerating faithful soldiers, cynically punished by PC for blind obedience to his 'magical' training regime, cavalier methods of control better than a plodding predictability.

As Top dog, General Charles was determined that his well-trained hush puppies, in the event of survival, would never snap, snarl nor challenge him in public again. Once wooed into the noble jaws of Black Dog Death, none would supersede him. Not Jake Hooper, that precocious American chess-player par excellence, and not Pope Romano. If, however, Romano still made himself more important than the church's teachings, if he got his own way (which honest to God he invariably did, poor man), PC would be dead as dung. And that, the second after he had grabbed the Rod of Vril Power, King Kal a corpse. Of course, PC's 'accident' would only get arranged after the victorious slaughter of the Saff armies.

Greentree saw no need for lasting grief or despair. Not for Alice. Not for her little men. Not for the Giants. The ultimate good always prevails, eventually. The first battle may have been about transient Light Bodies but the last battle is about indestructible Sound Souls being land-locked (or not) in materiality.

All the same, Greentree was scrutinising the Saff's Burial Chamber. Seven fierce-eyed Monks were showing old Alice and the dwarfs, not just the sarcophagus, but the standing giant statue of King Kal himself, his golden face veiled with seven coloured silks.

'Kneel!'

Alice being watched sideways by the dwarfs, they all refused.

'Swear faith in only King of Vril!'

'Sirs, I never swear. Too unladylike.'

'Swear!' All seven Monks glared as one. 'SWEAR!'

'Oh FUDGE!' said Alice, genteelly. 'There, satisfied?'

Seven little men dared to laugh with old Alice. Result: accused of humour, weak bladders and bad language, they were all bound with barbed-wire and tortured. The Martial Monks, jabbing with electrified cattle-prods, took them up to the lip of a cold sweat then, just before they could faint, kept them in conscious agony with no reprieve.

Soon they repeated the torture.

Saff military intelligence demanded to know: How had Alice and team been able to fly in formation over enemy territory, unspotted? Alice and friends remained adamant in their innocence and, hardly surprisingly, not a little afraid. They did not know the formula for invisible formation-flying. (Anymore than babies know how to dream. They just DO it.)

'Think yourselves smart, eh?' – screams. 'Tell us!' – screams. 'Or you'll regret it!' – screams.

'Can't. Don't know how,' gibbered old Alice.

If such military secrets were not revealed then the seven robotic Monks were ordered to gang-rape her watched by dwarfs. Seven rectums were to be pumped up, their little bodies inflated with helium gas, then flown above the action like tethered kites.

From his broken rock of the Big White Spirit, Greentree beamed affirmations. Alice and friends might earn protection in time. The Hopi Indian knew that King Kal was only another transient tyrant. Like his White Brothers, Greentree encouraged eternal liberation, not earthbound enslavement. Would Alice be able to distinguish between the two sides of that double-edged Force? Or would she, like most people, endure the manacles of enforced impositions feeling too small and helpless to improve matters?

Caution, of course, was essential. Any overt religious acts were seen as anti-Saff activities punishable by a fatal shower-bath of sulphuric acid.

'MOTHER EARTH NEEDS TO VOMIT VOLCANOES!' A further screechy threat added, 'NEEDS TO URINATE, TO PASTEURISE ALL SOURED SOILS, OR NEPTUNE OUSTS PLUTO!'

Overriding Greentree's meditations, such warnings were being repeatedly broadcast throughout the Saff valleys as, all around, evacuees swarmed up to higher ground, fearing an immense DIE GOTTER-DAMMERUNG, the end of Eden. Not just because of the Babylonian myth of a final battle between the Supreme Creator and the Red Dragon of Chaos, but also because of about 200 versions of the Noah story. Too late to save sea floods. Or to prevent the Ozone Layer from getting so chemically pissed off with celestial cystitis, leaks, dropping in on the underworld uninvited might turn the earth's crust into a colander.

Terrified Saff families were hoping to find safety, Rainbow Mountain their next Mount Ararat. Most of them chose the second level, the pink caves. Greentree knew that Souls only manage to climb to the level of consciousness they can reach in their worst (or BEST!) life-and-death crisis.

The majority of Saffs had held faith in King Kal, believing him to be their eternal protector in the present Iron Age of Universal Dissolution. Such worship had even produced thought-forms of their Monarch's face. On the vast cliffs of Rainbow Mountain, giant sculptures had burst through the rocks like bubbles in warm plasticine, an array of stone bursts majestically reigning over the red rocky valleys below. Sharpened by fears, the observant ones had noticed that King Kal's imposing nose, bit by bit, was being nibbled away by the icy winds of change.

The majority, meanwhile, unthinkingly cheered each sea-change within the ranks of PC's rampant bloodthirsty recruits.

Sacred civilians of Scarlet City also fled to higher ground. Many chanted aloud, 'In the last days the House of the Lord shall be established in the top of mountains,' as if they were Jerusalem Christians terrified of Romans invading their homes. Some clasped Billy Graham's book APPROACHING HOOFBEATS. Glazed, they intoned various quotes: 'Nuclear conflagration . . . Biological holocausts . . . Chemical apocalypses . . . Rolling over the earth . . . Bringing man to the edge of the precipice . . . again and again. . . .'

Some repeated thanks for the puritantical dictums of the retired schoolmarm, Mary Whitehouse, public moral watchdog.

Unlike Greentree, those fleeing did not know that many doom-laden prophecies, even reportedly by Jesus, may refer to past events rather than to events likely to occur in any one future time-warp, or even in any number of different dimensions. Danger only exists while framed within the fear of death. All the same, rival Survivalists, trapped in atheist terrors, tried not to die that day of fright as war was finally declared.

Frantically, all seven hills that surrounded Scarlet City were being scaled. The fat and the fearful tried to comfort themselves with hot-water bottles filled with brandy. Like well-heeled sleepwalkers some hiked up their chosen hill as if to welcome a new millennium, eating double-cream cakes and emoting, 'We've helped hundreds of lame dogs in our time and look, we're now limping. Dear God of Golgotha, pity us!'

Pinky's hill stayed the most popular choice. There, the pink-tinted rocks were full of decaying uranium, about as dangerous as five puffs of a cigarette in a year of Sundays. Yet, in those murky hovels, disruptive emotions overflowed as bile. Little did they know that THE END OF THE WORLD had nothing to do with the earth cracking like an addled egg but more to do with the collapse of outmoded systems. Traditional family life was transforming into kinship communities based, not on genes and sex, but on the more collegiate sharing of kindred spirits in the service to the Greatest Good.

Like the dying breed of CND protesters, was it too late for embattled Survivalists of both the Scars and Saffs to rise up and refuse any longer to delegate controls over their own lives . . . and deaths? Might peaceniks in time help Hopis and others spawn the next Golden Age of Peace? A stalwart against all suicidal strategies, Greentree continued to commune with unseen Elementals urgently working to hold the end of all earthlings at bay – even as PC's Rainbow Warriors were poised for attack.

Deep within the bowels of Rainbow Mountain King Kal was already in hiding. The Saff War Lords were priming their psychic defences. That included their ability to render air so solid that, like ships against icebergs, every tank of war would crash, killing all crews.

It was not possible for Alice or any of her dwarfs to cross their legs, so tight were the wires that bound them to the line of gold-plated racks. Wrestling with pain, they were lined up along a colonnade irradiated with sinister lighting, bare dangling toes near the marble floor, pin-spot-lights piercing their eyeballs.

Were those seven metallic Saff Monks not just zealots but zombies? Gleaming with old and glassy-eyed glee, they still tortured old Alice. Would her shrinking old frame wither all lust and defuse their rigid threat of an organised robotic gang-bang?

'FOUR toenails?' screamed Alice. 'Pigs! Pull out the biggest and yes I WILL swear. I swear I'll piddle all over your nice bloody marble floor!'

'For the last time. . . !'

'LAST? Thank you God!' jested Alice, bravely.

'. . . HOW DID YOU ALL FLY HERE?'

Weary of repeating their innocence, Alice let it flow, steaming all over the polished floor. So did the fierce-eyed Monks. As one, they clicked **ON**, harshly intoning their pre-recorded and discordant warning:

I
am to
obey only
orders and to
incarcerate each
in seperate cell in
this King Kal's Pyramid
so you lose all powers to
plead for diving protection
from the one godlike Ruler of
the Rod of Vril Power Kal. There
to melt. Yet we spare your essence,
recycling cells, trepaaning executed.
Skulls opened, all spy ciphers excised.
Brains replaced with neutron explosives,
chain reactions of multiple war-heads such
missiles to destroy all peoples on the seven
hills of Scarlet City, our enemy the blasphemous
prelates. No life unless you choose the True Path,
serve King Kal. Swear allegiance. Give Him blind and
loyal service as befits He whose beauty is too powerful
to behold. By serving Him we serve all the gods and speed
up our own chances of each becoming his own Man-God. Decide.
Conquer lower self and gain God-Realisation. Reject Righteous
Monarch of all Empires in all universes, you die. Accept today's
Special Offer. 15 minutes till your fate. This is a recorded mess. . . .

As one, they clicked – OFF!

Next, rape by robots? Were they mindless clones off assembly-lines, converted from amorphous silicon into fully formed humanoids? What if the Monks were part of the front line against PC's warring Scars while the real Saffron Monks stayed in hiding, unseen behind great opalescent doors, protecting their cowardly king?

As her nail-less toes bled like rows of wriggling piglets with slit throats, Alice forced herself to stay in focus. She probed her persecutors. For how much longer could the clones' artificial intelligence cope? They answered her questions according to their predictable programming. If it wasn't in their 'Good Book', they became garbled. Any arcane wisdom, any insight or agency that pre-dated their input, or came from beyond the ken of their received conditioning was rejected as untrue. Alice was noticing with disapproval such tendencies in parsons and parrots.

The same relentless demand: Alice must convert to the Cult of Kal, King of Vril! Six more minutes to make up their collective mind. Alice asked for seven minutes more, one for each dwarf.

An extra minute for a riper rape? To prove they're really MEN after all, not robots, should Alice and her dwarf friends refuse to submit? Otherwise, they would all get scalped, their skulls stuffed with turds of uranium ash, as if they were a row of disposable ashtrays.

Even when not being tortured, Pinky was addicted to nicotine. Alice had warned him, 'The pacifist Swedish with vast mountain fall-out shelters, send smokers outside. Why? 'Cos in a roomful of just twelve smokers, the radiation level doubles.'

Trembling like the last seared tobacco leaf after a drought, Pinky whined, 'What'll happen next, granny Alice?'

As one, the Monks replied: 'Your multiple warheads, we shoot. At Scarlet City's eight targets. All colour-coded missiles.'

In other words, they would decimate the population of evacuees on the hills surrounding Scarlet City. The dwarfs themselves, like the people they had just left to their fate, would have no say. Strapped onto racks they already felt like a row of screaming crystal skulls. The pretence of giving them choice was as shallow as a 'free' vote at a rigged polling-station. Infringement of civil liberties was certainly a case for AIG, Amnesty Inter-Galactic as, on behalf of King Kal and his Vril Kingdom, the cloned Monks still screeched conformity: 'CHOOSE! 5 MINUTES MORE!'

For four full minutes, cool Greentree would let Alice and her dwarfs contemplate on 'Attitudes are stronger than so-called facts.'

Alchemists and shamans on both sides of the battle-lines were working inwardly. Parity in peace had become less important than parity in poisons. Even the gasses from buried rubbish tips were being siphoned off for lethal use, both sides calling each other the Dark Enemy. As with many who show sporadic paranormal skills, they had remained deeply suspicious of the scientific elite who still have no cure for the common cold. Laboratory research funding is so often withheld. Until, that is, military advantages in wartime are projected. Then clairvoyant gifts get squeezed till the Medium is sucked dry. But not at the expense of the message. Domination of Death is to defy God's delights in every heaven imaginable. Feeding human dreams of freedom, after feeding the fears of losing it to demonised strangers, is the greatest of incitements to weaponry advances. Some were declaring war is thus the greatest impediment to spiritual progress, no matter how religiously motivated its occult ambitions.

But Greentree, maybe like Jacob in his multicoloured dream-coat, used White Noise, the hidden Word. White, after all, hides all hues, tints, and shades within itself. Alice and her little colour-coded friends had found at first that invisibility was the safest mode of camouflage. But psychic skills are notoriously unreliable. Knowing the countdown had started, Greentree re-tuned his antennae. He asked the Master HOO-nie to extend his range of protective energies in time to rescue Alice and her little friends from their barbaric fetters. But would that serve the Greatest Good?

Among other skills, PC's Psychic Specials could project themselves as a phantom army. When surrounded, they could produce a mirage of them-selves elsewhere, the purpose being to draw away enemy fire, using their collective astral bodies as a protective shield . . . and as a phantom decoy.

'Deadly rays can go through astral bodies,' said PC, 'just as ghosts can go through coffin keyholes. . . .'

To bait ambushes with apparent warm-blooded Scar armies was a strategy much enjoyed by the psychic soldiers trained in parapsychology by PC, the mesmeric General.

Sometimes PC's deep-trance subjects, thanks to night classes in cosmic channelling, were able to obtain the plans of their enemy, the Saffs. Among Rainbow Warriors a rumour had been started, perhaps by Jake Hooper, that Saffron City and its military defence was all being handled by the legendary **M** himself. Later it was rumoured that **M** and Vril Power were, in fact, the same. To wrest the Rod of Vril Power it was therefore first necessary to identify **M**.

What PC had not yet picked up was that within the next few minutes, neutron bomb warheads, in the shape of Alice and her fleet of flying dwarfs, might be targeted at the Scars, their Pontiff, and at the hill-bound evacuees. General Charles did not yet have the Psychic Intelligence that most of the Saff's Martial Monks were silicon humanoids, a controlled rabble of rabid robots able to clone themselves like a colony of cancer cells, ad nauseum.

At the interface between the occult arsenals of the two rival dark armies, a definitive battle was drawing ever closer. . . .

Alice knew every disaster has its antidote. The tyrant PC, allowed to fall into the Underworld must also, like secret D-notices, be the Divine Plan. Weren't PC, and his hot young Warriors, all fighting to refine their own potential for perfection? Evil? Isn't it just the poisoned sputum of self-hate, as vaporous as passing bad breath? Violence? Isn't it just energy spitting at its own limits, unrestricted by the censorship of others? Poor dears, didn't they just need their hearts defrosting?

After four minutes of similar contemplations, helped by Greentree's inner promptings, Alice opened her eyes. The dwarfs had gone.

In their place shone an epic hologram of Humphrey. In transparent letters, a message hovered above like a raptor about to swoop down. It read: *The Egyptian hieroglyph for owl served as the letter M. After the Sun had been carried to the Underworld, the M indicated night, cold, and death.*

Dead or alive, was Humphrey to watch her being raped?

Old Alice fainted.

A stiletto of sound spiked her skull.

On the blank screen of her mind Alice saw pyramids. Suggesting an hourglass, each was joined at its apex. Alice felt the top half contained radioactive sand, while the one beneath seemed empty. In her head she reversed the images, fast. It was rather like taking off her D-Cap in the Blue Dome and peering inside it. With less than two minutes to go, using inner lightning flashes and inner eyes and ears, Alice clearly received its mystic message.

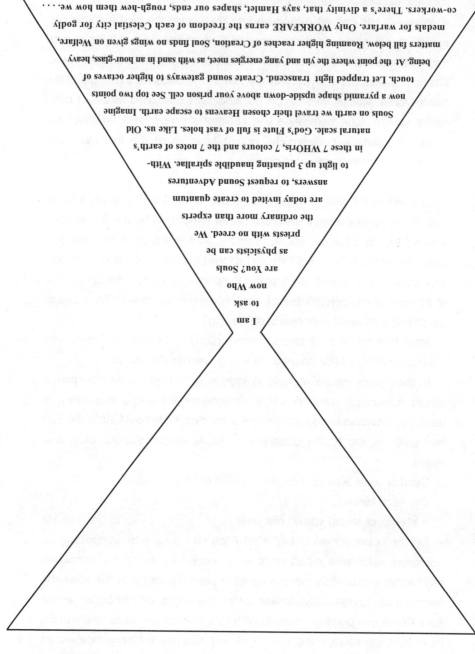

I am
now Who
to ask
are You? Souls
as physicists can be
priests with no creed. We
the ordinary more than experts
are today invited to create quantum
answers, to request Sound Adventures
to light up 3 pulsating inaudible spirallae. Within these 7 WHOris, 7 colours and the 7 notes of earth's
natural scale. God's Flute is full of vast holes. Like us. Old
Souls on earth we travel their chosen Heavens to escape earth. Imagine
now a pyramid shape upside-down above your prison cell. See top two points
touch. Let trapped light transcend. Create sound gateways to higher octaves of
being. At the point where the yin and yang energies meet, as with sand in an hour-glass, heavy
matters fall below. Roaming higher reaches of Creation, Soul finds no wings given on Welfare,
medals for warfare. Only WORKFARE earns the freedom of each Celestial city for godly
co-workers. There's a divinity that, says Hamlet, shapes our ends, rough-hew them how we....

CLICK!

Censored. But was not the last word to have been **Vril**, the power of people's free **will** most feared by tyrants like PC. . . ?

Playfully adapting Shakespear's words to 'Rough-WHO them how we Vril', Alice closed her eyes as lightly as she was able in order to see into the fourth dimension.

Instead, Alice found herself in a tiny cone-shaped cell. It was like being in a pyramid of descending space capsules. The seven dwarfs were individually stacked, cramped in one cell below the other, the walls being in the colour that matched each dwarf's smock. In the smallest cell at the top of the whole big pyramid, Alice and Whitey thought they were meant to choke to death so close were they squeezed together. Sprinkled with spy-dust, they suspected that their every activity was being electronically monitored.

M? For **Monster Monks**? **Malign Magic**? Surely not. Yet **M** was the name given by the Saff Monks to the Keeper of Vril Virtues, presumably the one who had granted Alice temporary reprieve from rape. Why though, was permission to visit each dwarf allowed? Was **M**, the alleged Fount of All Human Power, using Alice as some sort of double-agent?

Maybe like Humphrey. Or was he just two-faced?

Relaxed about his own fate, Whitey twinkled to Alice, 'We are booby-trapped. Why? They think we seven are boobies!'

'Could be useful. But in how many ways? I like to help if I can. Only it seems to get me into more and more troubles sorry to say. Seems not fair somehow, don't you think, Whitey?'

Kindly, he averted her self-pity, explaining, 'In Olde English, the word WHITE used to be pronounced WHO-ite!' As Alice pondered that, with a sanitised composure, he shrugged off all feelings of uselessness. Instead he said,'Not one kind word from a loving heart, Aunty, is ever useless!'

'Like Saint John's opening Word?'

'Nearly there!' gasped the dwarf, breathlessly. Indeed, between them there was no room to swing a Mancunian cat, let alone a tail-less Manx. To crush them further, as if to listen more closely, the walls were still slowly closing in on them.

Whitey pointed at the clear crystal, which acted as their skylight at the peak of their pyramid cell. In the gleaming gem Whitey had counted 144 facets. Chuckling, he said that in Revelation, 144 thousand out of all the people of Israel should be saved, 12,000 from each of the 12 tribes.

'Who told you all this, please?'

'Master H!'

'H for Humphrey? Home? Or what?' gasped Alice like a flying fish deprived of glittering insects.

Whitey was unwilling to say more. Why? Could Humphrey be high on the Saff Intelligence list as a wanted double-agent? A criminal, after all, is only a person too clever to conform. The fact that the Kal Factories could produce a hundred Humphrey clones, computers programming robots, such skills could give the Saffs a final victory. The truest Humphrey, hidden hero with secrets, can only be debriefed by catching him first. 'Saff strategists,' whispered Whitey, 'they're using you, Alice, as bait. Curiosity and unconsidered kindness to us all still your downfall.'

'Humphrey would never let his girl perish in the last reel,' boasted old Alice, bravely. 'His love for me is ageless – WATCH!'

All of this suggested that Humphrey himself must still be alive despite attempts to kidnap him. If it WAS the Saffs responsible and not some alien force. UFOs were rumoured to be entering earth's two pole openings, north and south. Some outside enemy about to attack the Saffs and the Scars? Could that stop so-called civil-war and unite the two sides before both perished?

Alice pressed her hands against the side walls of Whitey's shrinking cell. Tense and frowning, she concentrated. Too hard.

Calmly, Whitey told her about Gandhi, how the British had locked him up in a circular white room to drive him mad. 'Clever pacifist, he just imagined four corners.'

Ignoring the moral, Alice tried to bore a hole through one wall even though all encroaching blocks of limestone weighed 2.5 tonnes, a fact that did not disturb Whitey.

'Only non-materialists may escape without might!' hinted he. In trying to force more space, Alice of course, failed. The whole shrinking cell was still closing in on them, stifling both.

Sighed Alice like a death rattle, 'Can't do it, Whitey . . . I CAN'T!'

Exhausted, her shrivelled body fell through the floor.

BLACKOUT

. . . uplifting bliss . . . rising high on one single flute note linking all in dazzling love . . . beyond belongings . . . sublime joys expanding . . . peace . . . and healing . . . Souls' first and final freedom. . . .

. . . TRUE HOME. . . ?

The dispirited Rainbow Warriors had surrounded Saffron city and only 'killed' three thousand clones. As yet no real flesh, no splashes of hot blood or flying bits of greasy brains.

'You'd like more heat, lads?' joked General Charles, sternly. 'Then ignite your own hero! Kill the mild lamb in yourselves!'

Though uniformed in silk undies and spongy-heeled trainers, the welfare sprogs who had never seen wartime shortages, griped about conditions. PC told them. 'Consciousness is the kitchen of all conditions. Not like the smell of roast lamb? Then change diet. This chefs' special today is your prize victory – roasted Saffs!'

Bar American Jake, PC's top Psychic Special, what no youngster there realised was that PC had so brainwashed the Rainbow Warriors that they were unable to do anything for themselves with any degree of self-confident certainty. Except to die obediently for posthumous war medals. 'Lives are full of choices.' PC had openly warned them like a tormented tyrant trying to show a loophole of hope. 'You don't make the choices yourselves, you sign your own death warrants! The meek will NOT, I repeat NOT, inherit the earth!' Accurately, PC had habitually reckoned that most educated youngsters would ignore his warnings, preferring uniformed servitude, each a lamb of God disguised as a Judas Ram, the first in line to kill, or be killed.

Yet PC's Occult Academy had graced them with a dubious survival-kit, a self-fulfilling 'punishment' for obeying abusive orders and for relegating personal autonomy to PC's Psychic Specials. PC's training regimes had succeeded with them because the inadequate will pay any personal price to feel special. Thus all fresh-faced young fighters unwittingly carried an unseen incendiary bomb of self-destruct, a pre-programmed fear of death.

Begging the gods to become their top dog Jake, in contrast to the hush puppy and cuddly Humphrey, was more a junior mastiff who was happy snapping at his master's purple boots. To date, unlike millions of Americans who enjoy eschatology – the study of last things – and who stay fixated on THE END, Jake Hooper did not buy into DOOMSDAY. Not for himself, anyway. Or for PC's troops. Throughout, he'd been a hidden threat to PC's malign intentions. But Jake's natural authority had kept him on board.

All had voted voluntary 'mercy-killing' PC's top strategy, not surrender. Would Jake Hooper openly challenge PC? Before him he larded PC's plans with praise. Behind his back, he attacked such policies, saying. 'Guys listen up. God don't get no angels to vote. Democracy suits demons best. That why Jacob, his ladder, it have different levels, like heaven. Reach yours, guys. Before bedtime, dead or alive, win or lose obey your guts, not HIM!'

PC then informed them that King Kal and his battalions had vanished. That threat seemed more acute that if the enemy had been physically crouching behind every mountain rock-face. Though reconnaissance had drawn a blank, Jake got his way. He led The Rainbow Warriors to the forbidding mountain fortress stating invisibility, in all armies, to be an overblown illusion.

Mysteriously, but maybe to confirm Jake's assessment, all avenues towards Kal's Palace had been left invitingly open and, apparently, unguarded. Jake guessed that in the bowels of the mountain in an inner chamber stood the sacred pyramid. The King of Vril they supposed must be hiding inside that pyramid. PC forbade Jake to rout him. As General-in-Chief, he claimed that glory for himself alone.

'Sure, boss!' With this plan, Jake Hooper pretended to agree.

Goldy sat in the lotus position in the centre of his tiny cell. Through the ceiling's trap door Alice fell, landing on top of him. She felt younger in years and bigger in size. Yet the second cell's golden walls were also closing in, faster than were those of Whitey's cell above. What war secrets were they hoping to squeeze out of them by way of torturing herself and each dwarf in turn?

Bathed in shimmers of honey-hues, the beams from Goldy's body lit up the jewelled lotus cushion on which he sat. He'd stripped, leaving gold loincloth and bangles, his bald head radiant like a light bulb, as he wrote wisdom notes for the Soul Sentinel.

'Break the ultimate Sound barrier. Sing the Word,' suggested he. 'It can unlock all motions, all beings, all worlds within, better than even Houdini.'

'The Master Key to all Creation? No, I can't. I'm not pure enough. . . .'

BLACKOUT

Alice fell heavily through the trapdoor under her. Whatever the Originating Word, it certainly could not have been NO or CAN'T or any other spell suggesting a lowering of self-esteem. Only seconds of uncertainty, it seemed, and Alice was unable to stay in the pure, positive Golden Worlds of Whitey and Goldy. Still, she looked forty years younger. Would Greeny return her youth and joy? AND HUMPHREY!

Wary as cats in a stranger's walled garden, Jake and men pussyfooted their way inside Rainbow Mountain. Might this invite a sudden ambush? In such an ethereal atmosphere fright prickled their scalps, no matter how their trained faces betrayed a firm determination to fight the Saff troglodytes in their own denizens. But how do you kill shadows . . . empty spaces . . . silence? Was the mountain a nutshell with nothing to declare but its own echoes? Even their quiet gulps of saliva rang as hollow as a husk, a hoax.

Like troops of Trappists, stoicism making a virtuous kick-start to war-ravers, Jake led his crouching intruders, creeping up steep corridors of rocks to a central cathedral cave. Long-suffering with miles of marching behind them, religiously, they still dragged the statue of their Man-God. But by then it was losing its spell despite its resemblance to PC and to Jesus Christ on his day of execution.

Descending, Alice found herself back at the top of the five psychic planes, symbolically speaking, with intuitive Mauvey.

'Every time I think some bad things . . . I fall. . . .' she announced by way of greeting, inaudibly trusting his insights.

Mauvey whispered, 'They say I'm the foreign thingy, correspondent – for the Etheric Express. I'm dead.' Then bearing Alice's concern in mind added, 'FAILSAFE's a con There's FAIL or SAFE. But most will miss the bus!'

'Better than blowing it up while driving it!' offered Alice, bravely. She saw that the mauve walls and ceilings were closing in on them rather too rapidly.

'TELL ALL!' The frequent screeching of recorded voices grated their nerves. 'OR DEATH TO ALL!'

'Better to be safe and SOUND!' That was Mauvey's intuitive response to the threat posed by the menacing but invisible Saff Monks monitoring all seven of their dwarf prisoners.

Her curiosity as usual inspired by Mauvey, Alice asked, 'Why, when we feel safe do we still fail to listen to guidance?'

Her right hand flew to her mouth. Too late. The word FAIL had already printed. Since Creation always agrees with what we assume to be true, Alice again fell through the floor's hidden booby-trap . . . **B L A C K O U T**.

Military intelligence had informed PC that Scarlet City had already fallen, not to the Saffs, but to earthquakes. The Saffs would therefore not need to take such a city, even if they were planning to kill all evacuees hiding in what were once safe caves in the seven surrounding hills.

To Jake's men, meanwhile, finding no-body – not even a dead one – was more unnerving to the Scars than screaming hordes of savages. It was as if the Saffs had let off their own neutron bomb and, rather than surrender, vaporised themselves. In that ghostly mountain emporium, endless lappis-lazuli flagstones were not hiding, it seemed, one corpse, or enemy threat.

Behind the opalescent doors, in the humid confines of the pyramid, the finery of the main Burial Chamber was dazzling; plinths, circular alabaster benches, garlands and ebony ornaments. Brightest of all was the high statue of their golden King-God. Could such an epic statue, being hollow, be filled with the enemy? Having so far kept all entrances open in case a retreat became necessary, the Rainbow Warriors were not nervous about being trapped. Until, that is, Jake warned them that the Saffs had successfully developed a technique to make air solid. In which case they could all become encased, like wasps in a shrinking jam-jar, their stings bent as boomerangs, rendered useless except against their own bodies. Before such a death, Spontaneous Combustion might seem a better option. Jake, defying PC, revealed their own potential for self-destruction. Perversely, such DIY death threats had the effect of making many of them keener than ever to rout the Saffs. Others wanted to make a run for it. They saw Jake as another control freak, one of PC's occult hacks. Yet others from Scarlet City interceded with the statue in the Christ-like image of PC. Heavy though it was, they had carried this all the way from the Pontiff's Palace. It had to heal all hurts. Instead, Jake daringly suggested that they all enter the golden replica of the King of the Underworld. Like the Trojan Horse, if indeed it DID contain all of all their rival hordes in hiding, what then?

Hardly brain dead Bluey, accused of writing for the Mental Mail, was trying to believe that permanent earthly paradise was possible. Imprisoned in his own mind-set, quoting classical philosophers, he aimed to convince Alice that his ideas were always right. She resisted. Over-intellectualising, that was no way to plan their successful escape. 'Thinking about it Bluey, I for one, before these walls close in too tightly, will never. . . .'

Together, they both fell through the blue floor.

B L A C K O U T.

Having failed to enter King Kal's epic statue at any point, the Rainbow Warriors were getting desperate, meditation having produced no solution.

Jake Hooper's next suggestion was accepted as 'kinda neat'. There was no point in having a God if He can't help on the ground first. Thus Jake suggested that the shock troops use the statue of their own weighty Man-God in a practical way.

Commanding the karate disciplines of focus and power, they used the head-end of the PC Christ-like statue for ram-raiding. It was how they forced entry into the epic replica of King Kal. Since they respected the superstition of not looking upon the King's countenance, the base chakra was chosen as the most likely way into the statue's entrails.

'Sore bum, chum?'

'All your life,' Orangey answered, 'you've worn an invisible notice which reads PLEASE DON'T KICK ME!' To prove the point, Orangey kicked Bluey up the bum.

'I didn't escape from above,' sulked Bluey the bookworm, 'to be kicked around by YOU. Let's repress this enmity. Kindly no sensational reports write for your Causal Currier, or. . . .'

Fisticuffs? They looked to Alice. Since she fell down only when she got negative, Alice felt coy about being their umpire. 'The cause is in ourselves,' she announced somewhat prissily. 'So all shadows can be cleansed lads, with one beam of inner sunshine like crystals!' As both brainy dwarfs groaned, Alice was delighted to feel herself blushing, a sign her youth was returning.

But even her brightest blush did not influence the sparring dwarfs. 'Why do convictions always come in such long sentences?' complained Bluey yet again. 'Like doing time. Except, of course, time with its structure of past, present and the future is an illusion. To penetrate into other dimensions, one first needs to stop doubting one is timeless and eternal.'

His analytical approach caused Alice to stop doubting her own manufactured optimism; albeit even as their 4 ever-watchful orange walls were, surrepittiously, moving inwards to crush them.

'Another Akashic Record?' Impulsively, Alice airily sang:

COME ON, LET'S GROOVE IT, BABIES.
AKASHIC RECORDS PLAY AND DANCE.
COME ON, LET'S GROOVE IT BABIES,
PAY OFF PAST DEBTS AND ALL ADVANCE!'

Disco-tight, they wriggled and writhed until Alice was aware that both small men, like her, were getting bigger with every wriggle. Unlike the youthful Alice, it was between their dumpy legs.

'Mind if I change my mind?' asked Alice, trying to extricate herself from the sweaty knot of bodies around her kneecaps. 'Just had an awful thought – an AWFUL one!'

'You're PREGNANT!' they chimed with cheeky grins.

'As I get to look young again, I can't recall my lessons from being old. Sadly, that being so, I shall never. . . .' Too late.

The orange trap opened. Down through it a girlish Alice dropped, both frustrated dwarfs peering over the edge of the hole above through which Alice had dropped . . . **B L A C K O U T**.

After several more attempts, using the statue's solid crown of thorns as a battering-ram, their Man-God forced an entry. The Saff's sacred sculpture was being invaded without resistence.

Crawling through the anal orifice led by Jake, the Rainbow Warriors found themselves in a coiled tunnel that quickly spun them into a beautiful gold-plated belly. Its gleaming walls were encrusted with multi-coloured jewels. Hollow inside, it smelt as fresh as springtime, the air making them zing, and their upright bodies' surge with new, exotic expectations.

After five drops, five slow falls in blackout, Alice landed by Pinky sobbing into a newspaper. As she knelt to comfort him, he kissed her, then blew his nose on soggy page 3 of the Astral Echo.

His rosy cell was in a fug, his pink-tinted spectacles misted up with his chain-smoking. So distressed was he about passing over (dying), that he'd already passed over to the other side (the Saffs), information they sought. His sly wink signalled this piece of startling news as he tried to kiss her other cheek, her left buttock.

Coughing, Alice demurred. Did she need to descend to the bottom, to Greeny below, the most grounded of the dwarfs? She checked. Yes, there in her mind's eye he was playing with his toy Rod of Power, a rod of uranium like a seaside stick of Cumbrian rock. Like a tiny King Canute on Cellafield Beach, Greeny commanded the tidal waves of radiation to stop;

or if not, to reside only within the Irish Sea. Pinky gibbered, 'I'd take up the Pipe of Peace, but doesn't look like peace is useful, otherwise we would-n't need to keep on defeating it.' Was he weeping over the deserted earth or were excessive smoke-rings causing his eyeballs to leak?

'BETTER SECRETS!' The repeated screeches of recorded voices again grated their nerves. 'OR DEATH TO PINKY-POO!'

Realising his false information was no longer deceiving their Saff captors Pinky broke down. 'Get off me, Alice!' She wasn't going to hug him. 'We die alone! No warm arms. Just dried up sticks.'

'Thanks a bundle!' retorted Alice, sourly. 'Why sticks, Pinky?'

'For my cremation, old girl!' He refused to lose his 'granny'.

Was she still not young enough for Humphrey's arms?

Pinky stamped his podgy feet. 'Granny, you, me, dead now.'

Alice sniffed out, 'Now, separated, we'll never again be able to fly as a family in formation. My youthful bloom back for no-one!'

'INFORMATION! That's what they want. Give it to them, Gran. Your new pretty looks could save us all if only . . . nothing. . . .'

'Can't the Saffs see,' she screamed out, 'we don't know HOW we flew invisibly into their air space? Innocent, we are. IGNORANT!'

'Maybe they think by killing us, they'll stop us taking our secrets to the other side.' Walls with ears were closing in on them.

'But death *is* the Other Side, Pinky-poo!' reprimanded Alice, sniffily. 'And what's more, we're nearly there already. Some say grief is the ulti-mate in selfishness. Oh, give me a drag, do. . . !'

Preventing another trap-door opening at her feet, Alice stopped herself from snatching Pinky's cigarette before a further blackout. Dabbing her eyes, she stated, 'I must be good, Pinky!'

'Should think so too, blubber-guts!' Unmistakably, it was HIS voice. 'We don't always have to return to the green earth!'

HUMPHREY!

'Where ARE you?' Alice, hugged Pinky too tightly. 'EARTH?'

'The Other Side.'

'Of Death . . . of life . . . WHAT?' asked both she and Pinky as each thumped a different thick wall in that shrinking pink cell hoping to escape.

'WHERE . . . where are you now. . . ?'

'Stay there and I might arrive before I depart.'

'Curiouser and curiouser! Oh, and did you find your nose. . . ?'

To the Pharaohs of old the 'Other World' was the Kingdom of the Dead.

Inside, at the centre of the vast cavern, which served as King Kal's gold-plated stomach, stood a huge, mysterious sarcophagus. Instinctively, the Rainbow Warriors gasped and held their ground, gazing in awe at such a magnificent artefact. Was it possible that King Kal was already mummified?

M for Mummy?

Indeed, could the corpse of such a handsome Man-God be lying in eternal state, petrified and defying all disturbances? Could it also be why the enemy Saffs had totally disappeared? Might their King have committed suicide and left them to the mercy of PC's Scar Saracens?

The only person to answer such questions was the person who dared ask them aloud, Jake Hooper. If General Charles dodged the chance to shine as hero of the hour he, PC, might continue to lose his army's trust. They were pressing to know whether Jake was right or wrong. Was the Rod of Vril Power buried with the dead king . . . or. . . ?

PC, ordering Jake and other henchmen to pray, he started to creak open the sarcophagus. In cautiously doing so, even the black cobwebs as they snapped seemed to shriek. . . .

'How can we get through to each other?' pleaded Alice to the invisible Humphrey. 'Feel I'm as young as you again, but prettier, and . . . and I want to hold your hand – PLEASE!'

'Did you find the Flute?' asked he, his voice still switched on to 'Omnipresent'.

'More like a piccolo. High-pitched. . . .'

'Piccolo?' Was the wall between them blocking his hearing?

'Well, maybe more like a recorder,' she said, adjusting to what she hoped he wished to hear. 'And I CAN remember all that's happened for you – promise. Orangey helped me there. And the other dwarfs. They all helped. Before we got split up. Since then I've sort of kept on dropping. Like autumn scales off a fish. Like seared leaves off a sapling. But, really, I'm the sap, Humphrey. I'm the prat. Not so much a Flying Flute, I'm afraid, but a falling. . . .'

'Falling IS flying,' replied Humphrey, unhelpfully. 'The Devil may have all the best tunes, Alice, but he can't create white noise.'

'WHO-ite noise!'corrected she, quick to get smug again. 'How can that help all my dwarfs escape the Saffs' horrid tortures? Thought ghosts could go through walls Humph, so. . . .'

'M-m-maybe your little men wish to stay as they are.'

Thumping the wall, stunned by his stammered insult, she cried, 'Haven't I tried my hardest to protect my little men, keep them safe? Even if sometimes I did keep falling down on the job . . .' After more bridling, Alice as ever, recovered quickly. 'You mean . . .' she ventured, 'that they should fend for themselves, find their own way out of their problems? But that's not caring enough for me. . . .'

'M-m-m-maybe I care m-more than you do.'

'Always on **M**. Do tell. I long to know. Does **M** stand for **M**ohammet, **M**ahatma, **M**ilarepa? Or for **M**ax Headroom? Or even for **M**adame Blavasky? She said the earth would be a heaven in the 21st century so **M** must be a **M**aster of Wisdom of some kind so do tell, WHO? Someone m—m-must save us all, not just lovers.'

'Why not DIY Divinity? A true M-M-Master never looks behind to see if he's being followed.'

'Nor me, Humphrey. So strangers don't offer me sweeties. Or worse. Mind you, I could kill for a barley-sugar. Any chance of a bag of apports popping through like my nine crystals, please?'

But with those sweet thoughts, Alice reluctantly decided to leave the dwarfs to their fate. So closing her eyes in case Pinky, the emotional one, should see her tears, Alice inwardly watched herself release a flock of 7 rainbow-coloured doves. From the 7 charkas of her dovecote, she sent unconditional love to each of her seven little friends. It was like sending love to all of herself, a rainbow box of tricks unpacked from sparkly Christmas wrapping.

The floor did not open. The door did. Framed in its opening, holding the Master Key to all seven cells, stood Humphrey, his eyes twinkling with little golden stars.

Alice, joyfully, joined him. She did not remember Greenie accused of being a spy for the Earth Argos, a paper devoted to globalisation through religious wars. She did even look back to see if Pinky was following her. But at least Humphrey's new nose looked nice enough to lead the way.

Grizzling Pinky wished to stay where he was – and whinge.

Inside the sarcophagus lay an embalmed replica of the Statue of King Kal. Unlike the immense statue, this figure was the size of an ordinary human. The face was covered with a golden mask but, surprisingly, the shiny stomach area was laid bare.

Death so often came to those who disturbed the pyramids. Controlling his trembling hand, PC's right index finger snaked towards the belly button. Was the flesh still warm? Would the body suddenly bite like the legendary songbird killed by a hidden cobra? Was the whole elaborate set-up a TRAP?

Breathless as yogis in trance, the Psychic Specials waited for PC's safe deliverance as the Conqueror of all Occult Powers. He had to prove he really was in charge of all his own energies. And of their's too. Even if victory over the creepy Saffs was still uncertain.

The second PC pressed the belly button, the stomach snapped open. Just like the cassette-holder in a video-machine, a rigid flap of oblong flesh, hinged at the bottom end, snapped back. Revealed was a black, scarab-shaped **M**, the feet of the **M**, electrodes, both pointing towards General Charles. The rest of it was shaped like a headless black bat with scabby, serrated wings.

The **M** stood up on end and, quick as a screeching swift, flew straight at PC's startled eyes.

Fast though his reflexes were, never before had PC encountered such an unsafe series of assaults from a flying 'thing'. It was grotesque looking, headless and, apparently, blind. Yet its aim was as accurate as any sabre-jetted vampire bat. From out of its wingtips spurts of venom sent electronic shocks through all his twitching body fibres.

The most nerve-wracking moments were of stillness between attacks, **M** hovering, mid-air.

Then a sudden dive, that agile sharpshooter taking lavish zigzagging lunges skimming his hairline, his limbs, even his nose.

PC, angered by his plethora of weapons, all of which were proving useless, asked **M** the supersonic 'scarab' to explain itself.

Mid-air, laughing but motionless, **M** emitted screechy answers, like the Martial Monks earlier, as if the vocal chords were that of a synthesiser on autopilot. '*I Computer Cosmos. **M** for **M**ighty **M**icro. Chip off **M**onoblock before Big Bang. Black Holes, White Dwarf. Kal is King of all Dragnet Disciples in every space-zone in this universe. Obey His Will, malignant malcontents, or DIE!*'

'Then where IS King Kal?' asked PC, his leonine head peering cautiously at the rest of the figure lying in the sarcophagus. 'Where is your sacred King of the Underworld?'

'*HERE fool! I AM HE! I rule this universe through your puny bodies. You who think you can beat each other with mini nuclear blips. Hah! Schoolboys in a farting competition!*'

Sensing an imminent mincemeat defeat of their General, Jake the Brave crept back, atom-guns at the ready. Behind him crouched a dozen other trusted troopers. Too late. Fizzing with sparks, **M** attacked the intruders in jagged curlicues of lightning strikes. Stung into paralysis, all except Jake dropped to the floor, zapped flat by virulent blistering beams.

It was time for PC to use his ultimate weapon, to break the Sound Barrier. Closing his eyes like a Warlock dazed with desperation, PC grabbed the King's sceptre from inside the sarcophagus and vocalised the word short for omnipotent – OM! This chant he sustained till the silicon flying thing at last stopped its cacophonous screechings resting beside his purple boots.

'Hand it over!' The voice was Humphrey's.

For a second, PC froze.

'Turn, LIZARD LION, TURN!'

PC refused.

'Then howl your heart out till I kill you. . . !'

Shocked by the authority of the voice, PC turned. He was even more shocked when the plump-looking puppy announced, 'OM gives psychic insights, not spiritual victory. Surrender, policeman!'

'NEVER!' thundered PC, the M-shaped weapon slipped into an inside pocket. Then, like a bat from hell, PC took flight, his shiny leather uniform racing down the luminescent passageways on purple boots, zipping towards the Queen's Chambers.

Jake yelled, 'Trainers!' In bare feet, Humphrey more nimble, was swift in pursuit. Ghastly elementals all around him tried to impede his progress, a swarm of Soul-less locusts, all claws and jaws. Some young bucks reared up like purple vipers. They'd protect their General-in-Chief, PC. But not yet. Jake barred their way so the frightened warriors held back, free-ing Humphrey.

Jake scoffed, pointing at Humphrey's discarded trainers, saying, 'Goddam jerks. Not you guys. Them regulation trainers fracture spines. Worse when you carry heavy loads.' Shocked out of trained responses, the squad heard the rebel Jake reveal PC as the real foe; brittle bones of killers in trainers being a secret form of slow death. Earlier implants meant self-incineration was already not in their hands but in their heads. 'PC's conned you guys. He despises disciples. Hates himself, so hates you. Humphrey most of all, man. That's why they're still fighting. In winning for HIM he wanted you arseholes to lose YOURSELVES by burn-out! Extinction, not distinction, by FIRE!'

Sheepish unease made the squaddies want distraction, a drink, a fuck, anything but lose their faith in PC's good intentions.

'Guys, listen up!' insisted Jake. 'PC pretended to train shepherds. Why? No parochial shepherd's crook, that jerk was after King Kal's Rod of Cosmic Power! To get it, PC let you sheep debase yourselves – yeah really, **baste** yourselves – like roast lambs! Guys, this is the ashcan of the universe. Ashes to ashes – a self-fulfilling prophecy. But guys, WHO fries? Us? Them? Or all together? Sure, it ain't too late to decide – say **no** to Spontaneous Combustion, to mind control, as taught you in hypnosis! Say **NO!**'

*

All alone among the brocades and colonnades of the Queen's Chamber was Alice. As usual, she was pondering on deep questions like: 'Was Karl Marx a reborn Pawnbroker? Was Hitler a Hindu in disguise? If ghosts don't need oxygen on earth, do Astral Bodies need their earthly bodies to breath for them! If so, how in the dark can we tell one from another? Except, m-maybe, by heavy breathing. I wonder if a stammerer does that when he's m-m-m-making love? Could Moses himself have become a Burning Bush?'

Puberty rearing its Hydra head sent voluptuous shivers and shock waves through her nubile body. Then, unable to glean easy answers to her riddles, Alice sang this little song:

'THE LION AND THE UNICORN WERE FIGHTING FOR THE ROD;
THE LION CHASED THE UNICORN ALL AROUND THE QUAD.
SOME GAVE THEM CREAM CAKE AND SOME GAVE THEM COD;
SOME GAVE THEM RED WINE BUT OTHERS OFFERED GOD.'

Her private singsong was interrupted. Humphrey had arrived, PC in quick pursuit, their fortunes reversed. Seeing that Alice with the dreaming eyes of wonder was watching, Humphrey adopted more heraldic-sounding phrases like, 'None shall blind the Unicorn! My breathless beauty, my turn to kill!' Alice hoped that she was his only breathless beauty present, dead or alive. She had never expected her astral able-bodied computer hacker to become so fearless and frisky. Just then, like a jack-knifed sword, from the centre of Humphrey's brow, a fluted horn sprung out – SNAP!

Opposing him, PC raised the stolen Kal Sceptre, raging, 'Here! I hold the Rod of all Powers. With **M** in my pocket, you're just puppy-slush, a slug under my spiked boots!'

'You, just coffin-dust, daddy-o!' piped up Humphrey, gamely.

Like the Seven Thunders of the Apocalypse, a deep rumble reverberated through Rainbow Mountain.

'PC! You're ready to toast tyranny with human bonfires, not tell the truth. So you'll lose!' insisted Humphrey. 'I'll see to that. . . .'

'WRONG! I've bloody won! The Rod of Power is MINE!'

'At their expense. Poor trained boys burnt like Guy Fawkes!'

'WRONG! The Fire of Heaven is what they secretly wished for – SHAME! SELF-PUNISHMENT – LIKE ALL LOSERS!'

'WRONG, PC, WRONG! The shame is they didn't see through you in time, like me. No, your psychic program prepared them to feel like failures. When? Like now. When faced with dangerous truths like your silky villainy. So you prepared them for Spontaneous Combustion. Like my dad, the lads had to leave behind no more than a rag and bone or two, a hank of hair. No legal BLAME attached to you. As with most Black M-magic, not WHO-ite! Isn't bloody black what you and Pope Romano do best. . . ?'

'Burn away, lad! You know you've lost it! See indignation fire up your astral furnace. You an'all fry up, become a sad pathetic lamb chop, a fireball. You can no more lecture me than kill me, except with boredom. I told each sprog to stay in charge of their own spontaneous firestorms. Yet you, you're now not even in charge of your fuse box – so FIGHT!' Shedding his tunic, PC snapped, 'Flex yer pecs peasant pup!'

'Kings are but cabbages, PC. Good for cooking alive! You first, Brussel-SPROUT!'

Amazing Alice and disturbing PC, Humphrey from his mouth released nine-inch tongues of flame in six quick-fire spurts. Before PC could recover, Humphrey snapped off the coiled horn from his brow, raised it like a rapier, and shouted, 'Fight faster, FASTER!'

A sound of clarions. Battle commenced.

The duel was long and frenetic. Every time Humphrey's horn sword cracked and snapped, from his brow there straightway sprouted another.

To the exhaustion of PC, the fight led them down to a long Corridor of Mirrors. At the first mirror the boy lanced PC through his spurting heart. To his feet the ex-Commissioner dropped very dead. Before Alice could applaud her hero, as PC's limp corpse lay juddering in a squelch of bubbling blood, the repaired body sprang not just from the first mirror, but also out of every mirror ranged along both sides of the corridor. It was like being confronted by two long ranks of armed killers. Each one looked more dangerous than his neighbour while others distorted into hideous grotesques.

'The real **M**,' jibed Humphrey, 'defends his fair agents, not false leaders. Defends M-M-ME, PC, not YOU! Your Rod's FAKE!'

For forty minutes Humphrey fought off image and counterfeits, as a whole company of PCs kept pouncing out through the distorted looking-glasses; some tall, some small; some like gods, some like gargoyles. Who said the Word was one stronger than even the OM, the original and the ultimate Spell in Creative Power? He could hear PC – and all his replicas, all chanting OM. It was deafening in its defiance; in the face of final defeat, dangerously desperate.

Cornered, dizzy and exhausted, PC chided him with, 'No whelp can kill the multiple me, the new Pontiff of all illusions! – ME, THE KING OF KAL! ME, THE ONLY GOD-MAN alive for EVER!'

As a final ploy, Humphrey chose to trust the gift of total surrender. Astonished, Alice became speechless as Humphrey placed a mask over his physical eyes. Not 'blind chance' but the Will of Vril and LOVE of ALL LIFE would guide him, save him to serve the best outcome whatever his own desires or fears . . . if any indeed were left in his exhausted body as he trusted the Divine.

As never ending adversaries continued to advance, trampling over their own look-a-like corpses, the battle rallied, Humphrey declaring: 'Reinforcements, welcome! May I hew off every head, hew off every evil thought and still feel human!'

A panting pause.

Transformation!

Something strange was enchanting even all the walls. The whole massive master pyramid tingled with vibrant energies and became suffused with unearthly light, un-nerving to those who fear.

The Scars who were left alive ran towards the exits, only to find solid air, like glaring glass walls, blocking their escape, locking them in. Hidden hatches opened. Regiments of Saff Monks appeared like apparitions from within invisible spaces. Smug as pacifists they were grinning victoriously, not so much soldiers but more like a legion of mild saffron-robed Llamas.

Hearing so many chanting their Hymns to all Humanity, the PC clones burst into flames. In spontaneous meltdown, whole squads of his clones writhed into the fourth state of matter plasma. But not the cop himself as an all-pervading hum thrummed through everything. The clones' flames being astral, such self-incinerating energy is biopsychic activity. As such, it alters the accepted patterns of combustion. Thus PC's chain of reflections, like shadows sizzling up in midday sunbeams, were all burnt to astral ash, similar to that which Sai Baba of India, some say, manifests in his healing hands.

Left were two rows of Scar army uniforms, all empty of flesh.

The remaining lambs that had most deeply identified with PC leaped to his protection, surrounding him. Like an enfeebled rugger-coach to his scrum, PC encouraging them to generate together bio-luminescence, the like of which can be seen glowing on 'high' meat as bacteria secrete luciferin and luciferase. These identikit cadets, together with their Commander-in-Chief, became prematurely cremated in what some might like to call 'Lucifer's Light', an all-consuming fireball. In that at last, PC had expired.

'Phoenix fodder' murmured the devout Monks as they shook hot bone-meal from hollow purple trouser-legs into copper urns; brushed ash like dandruff from tunic shoulder-pads. All unburnt uniforms were sent to the Cavern of Costumes. To hang there, no doubt, awaiting the next in line to fill their ranks again in the next round of conflagrations.

From PC's unburned inside pocket, Jake reclaimed 'the mechanical **M**' and then, retired. Before going far, Romano's mafia kidnapped him. Scarlet City's Curia was still firing on all cylinders.

Elsewhere, in seclusion, The King of the Underworld and the real **M** kept their secrets, privacy, identities intact and hidden from the profane eyes of all infidels and invaders. A real challenge too enticing for Humphrey to ignore as a golden goal; indeed, the ultimate reward, maybe, for his creative winning ways.

But first things first.

Left on their own in the Queen's Chamber, the victorious Humphrey knelt at Alice's feet and flopped into the fragrance of her lap. His bloodied horn sword lay on the floor beside his naked feet.

For long moments, they breathed in silent unison. Eventually, Alice sighed, 'I have immortal longings in me' and sighed again. Making pretty curls, she churned soft whisps of hair on the nape of his damp glowing neck.

'Oh beamish boy! You look like the Owl I met – sweet! All 'cos I lost myself in the wood when I ran away, we met.' But had he the wit to woo her? 'You look like my Owl in sunlight, though, not one hiding in shadows now, I'm glad to say. You're HERE!'

'Yep, **M** Alice, is a hieroglyph! Remember it, notched up in pyramids? M combines ideas of an Owl with – guess what? The Eagle. King of the Upper Air. M's sound in '**Suna**'. Alice, let's chant Suna. Its sounds are found in ancient words that unite all!'

Already delirious, Alice really didn't m-mind what he asked them both to do so long as their magical spell remained unbroken.

'Such as, say, night and day, Alice. Light and dark, bringing all opposites together. . . .'

'Like you and I, at last!' Giddy with his mental and physical prowess, she snuggled in closer. As if bitten, Humphrey recoiled. Though shocked. Alice recovered, pleading, 'Surely, even an asp **must** have its own immortal longings. . . .'

'To give Cleo a love-bite? Like the cobra which swallows songbirds in pyramids?' countered he. 'No M-M-MUST about it.' (**M** for **M**ystacism?)

'No m-m-must about it' echoed Alice, vacantly, repetitions being thought suitable when discussing past deaths and disasters. Besides, that historic day for Alice was a date with destiny, somewhere where past and future meet. So, getting as kittenish as a young Cleopatra, she posed for Humphrey on a deeply piled carpet, inviting him to draw his own conclusions.

But his next comment sounded uninviting. 'A STILL Life's a contradiction in terms, Alice.'

Taking the hint, Alice broke her pose and instead danced around him. Aroused somewhat, Humphrey started clapping in time as she repeatedly beat out the words:

'WISDOM, WISDOM, WINGS OF DOVE. . . .'

Reversing roles, Humphrey fleet of foot like so many plump bodies, danced as Alice beat out the rhythm, she chanting with enticing delight:

'SING WITH ME IN LANDS OF LOVE!'

Laughing, they fell together onto the central tomb, mutual merriment soon warming them despite the coldness of the marble.

'Will we? asked Alice, tentatively stroking a cheek.

'Vril?' Humphrey shot her an arrow of anxiety. 'I'm more afraid of being stroked than hit. And you owe me one, Alice!'

'But I only want to . . . you know . . . like Kitty my cat . . . stroke you . . . hear you purr on my lap . . . please.' But before she could open her heart, her mouth or even her legs, he rose abruptly. Consulting his talking watch, Humphrey announced, 'I'm late, I'm late, for a very important date.'

'Aren't I IT?' she gasped somewhat flattened. 'WHERE?'

'Oxford. Needs re-educating. Got m-more homeless than the capital of Bangladesh! Beveridge m-must be turning in his grave,' nodded he, emphatically.

Alice nodded back. He'd once said, his dad used to beat him, yep. So she'd kiss him better. If only he'd let her. But it was easier to cuddle a Christmas pudding – before it was enflamed with brandy, or set on fire like York Minster by a moderist new bishop.

'See Alice, Socialists don't hold with treasure troves on the Other Side. Everything has to be earned. . . .'

Wriggling with expectations, Alice churned her hair both sides into ringlets hoping to anchor his attentions. No, he looked distracted. So, aiming to engage his brain first, she expounded, 'Martin Luther. He wasn't nice about the Jews!' No response. 'Snow White. Unlike Old Mother Hubbard, she only believed in one side of the Balance Sheet, the financial.'

'Like sleeping in an apple-pie double-bed – ALONE.'

Oh dear. He said ALONE with such relish.

Try again. Imitate Bluey and become, yep, more of a bluestocking. 'Consider the American pipe-dream. Unhappily, like apple-pie, has it not been legally bought, would you not concur, even by the poor. And with ubiquitous lethal pea-shooters?' Humphrey grunted. Grateful for even a grunt, she gushed, 'I just believe all our dreams have to be solvent. Do YOU not find this notion SO agreeable, Humphrey dear, please do so, emphatically?'

'Pharaoh or Fuehrer, the m-m-more evil we allow, the quicker goodness prevails. God's work needs double-agents!'

'And wives to breed more, I would suggest. Who will be Mrs Humphrey – WHO?'

With an enticing grin, Humphrey scurried through the doorway, Alice following fast in his fleet-footed tracks. Without seeming to check whether or not Alice was behind him, he continued, 'All experiences repeat till we're no longer shocked. Then we use our healing hands and hearts.'

'STOP!' ordered Alice, out of breath. 'Have your hands an M-shape on their palms? That makes you special. . . .'

They had come to a halt near the Sphinx outside the pyramid. Both gasped. The vast pyramid before them stretched up out of sight.

'Before you fly off, or me off the handle Humphrey, have you forgotten. . . ?'

'Our trip in the Flying Flute, Alice. Nope.'

'Fly away to where, WHERE Humphrey. . . ?'

'THERE!' Playfully, he pointed at Alice herself. 'You are your own Flying Flute, Alice. You won't always need m-me as pilot. The controls are at your own sweet fingertips. So place a hand like a conch shell to your ear. What do you hear?' Leaving her again, he shot off.

His phrase 'sweet fingertips', having reached her toes, they quickened up her next set of happy steps. His as well. But what kept her further buoyant was the high-pitched single note of an inner flute. In her hurry to get elsewhere, she overtook him. Turning to block his path, Humphrey collided into her as she announced, 'But a flute is also all stops!' On cue, her flute sound faded.

'Called STARTS, not stops!' he insisted. Again he bolted. Again she grabbed him. 'I see you! I hear you! Hold me! We're boiling. So let's both fly off . . . before we burst!'

'Later!'

'NOW!'

'NO!'

She hit him, hard, right across his left ear. On that inwardly, he heard her high flute note. Though stunned, Humphrey was so suddenly grateful, he grabbed and held her more firmly than before. His probing fingertips sent musical shivers up and down her spine, his sap rising! But he stayed hard-headed. Coolly, he was able to request, 'Let's compose ourselves. . . .'

Her sap had also risen but she stayed soft-hearted. Warmly, she heard herself request, 'Become the Pied-Piper, Humphrey, then the tune . . . let's get the bare-hoofed devil himself reeling in delight . . . please . . . show me . . . Look, lines on both of your palms show a large 'M' shape!' On that, his ten fingertips rippled all along her backbone, down from chakra to chakra, triggering healing at all seven from her crown to her coccyx. Humphrey was already purring in her nearest ear like a kitten anticipating double cream. Returning the compliment, he placed her hands at the small of his own back, whispering, 'Govern these vantages with your finger and thumb, give it breath with your mouth.'

A heartfelt and hefty kiss surprised delight in them both.

'Just give the Word. . .' pleaded she, her kneecaps melting. 'Home, James?'

Joyfully, Humphrey jumped. 'YEP! Got it, Alice!' he shouted with glee. 'THAT's my surname!'

'Sir what – James?'

'HOME! But pronounced Hume!'

'Why?'

'Sounds more open-hearted. Yep?'

'OPEN – YEP!'

'I'm the ancestor of Daniel Dunglas Home. The best-known medium at the time of the poet Browning. Though he saw him as a charlatan. No nose for serious studies, like me. A fake sorcerer!'

'I like your nose now. Glad it's still there, so handsome against the light!'

Proving his last point, Humphrey was intently gazing over her right

385

shoulder. He was studying the look of puzzled pain on the negroid face of the Sphinx towering above them. Hoping to decipher its inscription correctly, he read out, '*I am . . . HU. . . .*'

'Not HOme, you say, with "om" in the middle, but HU. Like the first two letters of Humphrey! Mrs Humphrey Hume! Oh, that makes a double-Hu! Humphrey HUme, one HU for each of us!'

'The inscription finishes . . . *Never does Soul fail in My Name.*'

'Oh, God's bodies, what about us!' Her groin was throbbing like a damp wren's nest in a warm April shower. 'Aren't you aching as well, please Humphrey – below?'

'I guess the Word's been weathered away like his nose. Gone.'

He shot off again, Alice following. Though cross with him, she found she was rehearsing the words 'MRS HUMPHREY HUME FEELS AT HOME!' as they reached a secret manhole in the earth's underground crust above them. On its discoloured brass plate a notice read, 'ANTI-FALLOUT DOOR. PREVENT RADIAL ILLNESS.'

With a pang, Alice remembered she had not said good-bye to Greeny, the dwarf who worshipped Gaia and organically grown cabbages more than kings. She hoped he was safe, like all of her other little friends. Didn't they wish to survive also, just like Mother Nature for all to enjoy, clean beaches, blue seas and skies?

Humphrey examined the subterranean hatch. 'Sealed up, Alice. Possibly no exit ever again. . . .'

'Don't believe in good-byes,' stressed Alice, pointing at the manhole. Even though it was obvious, she hoped he'd join her in the comforts of togetherness. Maybe it was the result of their first kiss. Certainly, she was still trembling with invitations in her every tingling tendril.

The instant Humphrey opened his mouth Alice could tell that it was not to share a deeper kiss but for a longer lecture. Getting frustrated, she held his forearms firmly, both sticky palms grilling the shape of her fingers on the thin sleeves. 'WITH WHOM DO YOU WISH TO FEEL AT HUME, HUMPHREY HOME?'

For the first time in her presence, the boy acknowledged throbbing pulses in his own private Rod of Power. As her hands slid down his thighs,

Humphrey's hands moved up to open the manhole. What shrivelled horrors lay in wait above them in earth's blighted dustbowl?

'Don't,' screamed she, 'let in radiation! Eats bodies cell by cell!'

'Alice, I'm due back on planet earth. . . .'

'Without me?'

'Heard of parallel universes?' She nodded, knowingly. 'So first learn to tell your Earth from your Astral. . . !'

'Why not my arse from my elbow? They're nearer us. FEEL. . . !'

'How does a goldfish know when it's out of its depth?'

'When it's dead?'

'When it's flying! Now I must fly! Two more countries are about to zap themselves lifeless. Alice, I've earned the right to emigrate to planet earth again. Yep, to split warheads far away from missiles before the New Age Armoury becomes too fearful to last . . . or too fearless . . . TO HEAL. . . .'

'France and England?' Her question sounded almost rhetorical.

'Going west? Their astral auras already tatty and in ashes, yep. Their physical facsimiles could follow fast, all atomised. . . .'

'Parrots following pirates . . . or . . . pirates following parrots. . . ?'

'True real-life Masters of Wisdom like **M** don't hand-rear parrots on peanuts, or clip their wings. Look, I've got to get back in time to help humans use their imagination differently. To sing The Word, not singe the world, East or West. To become Warriors not worriers. It's urgent, Alice, URGENT! So let me go. . . .'

'I'd like to help, Mr HUME. Earth's my home, too. Can't Mrs come with you . . . please . . . but better protected. . . ?'

Humphrey unclamped the hatch door.

Gripping his sleeves, she begged him to stay, not to endanger either of them. Turning, glaring at her, he blared out, 'Alice, is it ME you want or m-m-more TRUTH. . . ?'

After a moment's meekness, she blurted, 'WHY CAN'T WE SHARE BOTH?'

'But is this the Vril of IT Upstairs, Alice?'

'And downstairs? What's your wish in this, Master Hume?'

'Upstairs, downstairs – in my lady's chamber!'

Opening wide the healing M-shape on both hands, he hugged her, their young bodies close and both in balance. Then, between orange rocks skirting two rippling streams, they lay down in sheltering thick rushes. Sensuously, gently, their nipping lips gently explored a range of flexible, heart-warming embraces.

'Afterwards,' he suggested as his nose skiied down snowy slopes, her virgin thighs, 'afterwards . . . let's agree to m-m-meet up again. As Earthlings. . . .'

'On the Other Side. . . ?' Thinking he also wished her body turned, she obligingly rolled over on to her other side wondering, as she did so, if he would continue to stammer as they got ever closer in loving couplings, m-m-mating.

Feeling accommodated, he nuzzled into her curl-clustered neck. 'Yep, let's make more lovely memories. No more good-byes.'

Both saying 'Hi!', tenderly he eased them into intimacy. Lying back in bull-rushes, she surrendered, not caring whether she was in heaven or on earth or, best of all, in both at once.

Cuddling afterwards, chuckling in relief, they enjoyed rest.

Encouraging futher bonding, mutual pledges expressed, both chimed. 'We're beautiful!!' until together they sweetly slept.

In her dream world Alice went flying. Through portholes in my Flying Flute, I see my own future, my own past, no separation. My biggest present appears as a fairy – on top of the Tree of Heaven. There, wafting in reverie, I receive a golden wand. This uplifts me to higher and HIGHER octaves, to above it all. Feeling this free I feel joyful.Thank you. This glory I know is here and NOW. For ever!

Then Alice awoke. She found herself alone.

Alone, that is, but for a blue ribbon of sound like the note of a flute linking them. Deciding to find Humphrey yet again, no matter where he'd got to, she closed her eyes, squeezed back into her dream flute and, snoring, soared ever inwards and upwards. In a city of dreaming spires, Alice knew she would meet him again . . . and again . . . until all lessons in love . . . and war . . . were learnt by them both . . . together . . . in flesh and in spirit . . . and in the spirit of yet further amazing adventures!

EPILOGUE

'Curiouser and curiouser.'
'Everything's got a moral, if
only you can find it. . . .'

Her sisters picking kingcups, Alice was left to her favourite occupation, daydreaming by water. Six sisters were too much. And that afternoon, she'd had quite enough of Edith and Rowena.

Sitting on their Persian rug, trim stockings primly pulled up to the knees, Alice defied all insects to bite her. Ants, for some forgotten reason, gave her the shivers.

Their backwater pool had been chosen for its leafy quietness, a cool picnic spot well away from the sound of Oxford's High Street carriages. And certainly it was far enough from Parsons' Pleasure, that all-male nudist enclosure that young ladies were not expected to ask about.

Dragonflies were zizzing in and out of the swaying reeds. A punt glided along the Cherwell in gentle lurches, rippling the riverbanks and rocking a pair of stately swans. Upping tails, nearby ducks groomed the green growth between them, snipping away like two white-coated underwater barbers.

Below the heavy blanket of high summer heat, the drowsy city of spires seemed to be holding its breath.

'Anyone ever tried to photograph oxygen in water,' wondered Alice. She was gazing at her own curious face in the water, amazed. What if she was inventing her own apparition? She blew on the surface to see if it would mist over like a mirror. Instead, it wrinkled her countenance, such rippling realisations seeming to age her prematurely.

'How would it be,' thought she, 'if everything was the wrong way round, as in a looking-glass?'

'Disturbing daydreams?' For a hot second time stood still. 'M-m-may I?'

Back on earth with a bump, Alice looked up. Standing a foot away from her striped stockings stood what looked like a University Don. Despite the hot weather, he was wearing a top hat, spats and gaiters. Was he some stuffy Parson on the way for a private swim? Or a scholar of Vedic sacred sounds like her father? No. His spinsterish scrutiny made her want to call him a silly name. 'Disturbing indeed, sir!' retorted Alice and, under her breath, added a silent 'Humph!'

Yet, somehow, she wished to hold his attention. Alice therefore followed her urge to tease him with her latest riddle, 'Who is **M** short for?'

Delight lit up his somewhat hooded dark eyes. 'M . . . M . . . M . . . is short for whoooom?'

The combination of his stammer and correct grammar made her blush. Then, as if uncovering the Key of the Universe, he confidently announced his answer. 'M is short for Marmalade! Why? Because chick is short for chicken, so M m-must be short for early m-morning m-m-marmalade.'

'How so, sir?'

'Ma-me-laid?' said the first hatched egg to its Mother Hen! As it caught the early worm!' On that, he pulled a piece of string from his pocket and let it dangle, limply, invitingly, as if it was imitating a wriggling worm at the end of an angler's fish-hook as bait.

What – no barley-sugar?

'Pray tell, is that your mother over there?'

'My mother and my sisters, yes. Collecting posies of wild flowers.'

'Pretty!'

She knew it, wet as a lettuce leaf. Distracted, Alice swivelled her eyes to the insects nearby.

On the river surface, one water boatman was mounting another as if playing at piggybacks. The Reverend-looking gentleman hovered, uncertain how to stimulate further conversation with the comely little daughter of the Spanish-looking beauty still held in his eye-line. Intriguing. It was like playing croquet with a family of hedgehogs.

Eventually, as an excuse to linger, he ventured, 'M-m-might I tell you a story. . . ?'

'Not a sermon, I trust?' Her eyes were defying his to shorten the distance between himself and the last cucumber sandwich on the Persian rug. 'I get vertigo sir, so do take care. I had better not grow up too fast!' Seeing him smile, she shot him a volley of questions, all seemingly unrelated to anything that had so far occurred. 'Do you think the earth is hollow – like that puffed up pastry there? The Astronomer Royal Halley thought so, did he not, sir? How many dimensions has time? And does God think? Logically? I do not think so. And are there two huge white rabbit holes, one each at the Poles?'

'Impossible. But only before breakfast m-marmalade!'

'Sometimes I've asked nine impossible questions before I wake up. Actually, nine is my favourite number at the moment. What is yours, sir?'

'All. I'm a mathematician. Now to be sure, the earth consists of a solid crust, mantle and core. That would seem to be obvious. Any hollow part within it exists only in the imagination.'

'But I've got an amazing one, sir!'

'So have I!' he whispered, keenly, daring one step nearer.

'Then, pray careful how you AIM it!' snapped Alice as if to some vulgar seaside photographer who had ducked under the black skirt of his cheap camera, both he and it on spindly legs of uncertain balance. Just as abruptly, Alice held up her napkin like a yashmac, her eyes peering over its top rim. 'I fear explosions. And flashes of insight, sir!' Her eyelashes fluttered, helplessly.

'M-m-might I ask, is your name M-Margaret. . . ?'

'Today? I'm Alice. Alice Liddell. And I'm ready. . . .'

On that, she patted the Persian rug, as if it was some magic stallion that was too shy to gallop. 'Transport me!'

Clearing his throat of any academic frogs that might need dissecting, the son of the Reverend Dodgson, recently from the parish of Daresbury, Cheshire, began his latest story like this:

'*Alice was beginning to get very tired of sitting by her sister on the bank, and of having nothing to do: once or twice she had peered into the book her sister was reading, but it had not pictures or conversations in it, 'And what is the use of a book,' thought Alice, 'without pictures or conversations?'*

Now that she had her own tall tales to tell, Alice was pretending not to listen.

THE START?

APPENDIX

DIET OF WORMS
'Off with her head!'

Thank you for wishing to read the Appendix but, as you will see, it is not all here. Like the best kept secrets, both figuratively and in actual fact, most is hidden underground. Please now ask WHERE?

Well, Lewis Carroll's classic was at first named and illustrated by the author. Its initial title was ALICE'S ADVENTURES UNDER GROUND. So the missing Appendix now lies beneath a significant patch of earth, somewhere in Welfareland. But if you are still hoping to delight in – or be highly irritated by – the rest of Alice's protests in her own Luther-like DIET OF WORMS, kindly read on. . . .

So, dear reader, it seems you DO still wish to be beguiled by the rest of her diatribe. Well done! But wait. Can Humpty Dumpty take it? And from such a cheeky, provacative runaway schoolgirl? Will this egghead, this boss of **E.M.B.E.R.S.**, **E**ducation's **M**ortar-**B**oards' **E**ggzamination **R**emarking **S**ystem, listen to her indulgent but insightful incantations? Or might she recant to save his face? To find out, Alice here invites you to unearth the rest of her tract and inspect it before the necessary fall of OFSTED. Or as Alice insists, they should 'Consult us more, insult us less – please!'

To do so, stay on track. That way you might successfully uncover Alice's propositions 12 to 25, all aiming to reform state-imposed and intrusive schooling. As well as, I hope, relish how she and her friends contribute to their lessons by free thinking schemes for persona-centred explorations. These contributions take place in their somewhat idyllic Learning Centre brimming over with happy harmonies. To find better ways for all future learners, ask the learners themselves.

'Time the worms turned,' says Alice. 'But not in their grave!'

Now time to decode the first of two riddles. These clues will lead you to the entombed Appendix, somewhere in England. Only those with a copy of ALICE IN WELFARELAND signed by the author will be allowed to dig down if they should find the hidden burial ground. Then, such permission can be achieved easily. Other readers interested in this quest are requested to send for a signed copy direct from myself as author. Christopher Gilmore, Atma-Dovetales, 34 Clifton Avenue, Crewe CW2 7PZ. UK. Please enclose a cheque made out to me at the full retail price and add for post and packing:

U.K. £2.50

Europe £3.50

Outside Europe £4.00

Thank you.

Now for the Riddle which leads to the secret location, the hidden manifesto buried under ground. Here goes.

INITIALLY
TWO BY TWO
FIND A HOLY BOULEVARD
THAT DRAWN FARMERS TRADITIONALLY SOUGHT.
AS IN AN ALIEN'S OFFICE COLLECT THE NEXT CLUE.

PASS ON THROUGH
TO WHERE PEACEFUL FRIENDS NEVER FOUGHT
AND CONNECT A TAUREAN PALINDROME
LACKING NOUGHT.

For the complete Diet of Worms, first identify the right area of England. Once there, let the above verses ring a bell as you present your signed copy of the novel. Then ask for the next riddle. It's taped to a spade! This second set of verses leads to the exact patch of earth wherein, underground, lies in peace the said remaining appendix. A bit of surgical digging and WOW! YOU, the single well-deserved winner! BUT to fully qualify for your prize I will first ask you to send a review of ALICE IN WELFARELAND to myself as well as to a newspaper, journal or even to some small local newsletter.

And the prize? Whatever your views of this New Age novel faction, you will be sent a surprise Alice keepsake and a card of thanks from the ghost of Alice herself. Plus a pp signed by me, the author.

Happy hunting!

CHRISTOPHER
www.christophergilmore.com
Email: christopher.gilmore@virgin.net

ALSO BY CHRISTOPHER GILMORE

<u>For Golden Eagle Publications</u>
SOUL-CENTRED EDUCATION – Help Your Higher-Self Become More User-Friendly. ISBN 1-09043-09-3 (£9.95 +£1.50 p+p. Please make cheques payable to C Gilmore). 'Wonderful book! A masterful player of the highest melodies of Soul' – KB, teacher.

In preparation: ALIVE-ALIVE-O or How to Die Laughing and Survive! 12 lighthearted, uplifting tales to inspire a passion for living more fully.

<u>For Atma-Dovetales</u>
For passionate learners, 10 illustrated guide-books with 360+ ideas to kick-start personal creativity, holistic insights and cross-curricular activities for all ages.
DOVETALES MIGHTY MATHEMATICS – More Fun – Less Fear...?
ISBN 0-95-19609-0-3
DOVETALES INTEGRATED SCIENCE – Love before Learning...?
ISBN 0-95-19609-1-1
DOVETALES ARTS WITHIN – Fewer Tears, Finer Seers...?
ISBN 0-95-19609-6-2
DOVETALES GODLY GEOGRAPHY – Less Green Gloom, More Mother Love...?
ISBN 0-95-19609-3-8
DOVETALES HOLISTIC HISTORY – Less Disaster, More Déjà Vu...?
ISBN 0-95-10609-4-6
DOVETALES LOVING LANGUAGES – More Babel, Less Babble...?
ISBN 0-95-19609-5-4
DOVETALES TECHNOLOGY FOR ALL – Fewer Boxes, Further Bridges...?
ISBN 0-95-19609-2-4
DOVETALES SPORTS, HEALTH & DANCE – More Grace, More Uplift...?
ISBN 0-95-19609-7-0

DOVETALES MUSICAL MEDITATIONS – Octaves of Awareness...?
ISBN 0-95- 19609-8-9
DOVETALES RELIGIOUS EXPERIENCES – Dreams with the Supreme...?
ISBN 0-95-19609-9-7
All Dovetales £10.95 each + p&p as follows:
for 1 book £2.50
for 2 books £3.50
for 3 books £4.50 + £0.50 for each further title. 10% discount if all 10
books purchased.

Published by Atma Enterprises
Bright Eyes and Bubbles.
Talking book for all the family.
(ISBN 0-87-24600-1-1). Illustrated book and audio-cassette with music.
Narrated by the author. £5.95 each + £1.50 p&p. If both purchased
together £9.95 + £2 p&p.

EARLY LEARNERS KNOW LOTS – with Christopher Gilmore CD video,
6-year-olds speaking about Happiness in Educaton, All Shapes & Sizes,
Personal Power £7.5O inc p&p.

ALL PAYMENTS SIMPLER THROUGH 'PAYPAL' ON LINE.

All the above published works are available from:
Christopher Gilmore
34 Clifton Avenue
Crewe
CW2 7PZ
UK
Tel: +44 (0)1270 652392
e-mail: christopher.gilmore@virgin.net

Web Site:
www.christophergilmore.com

Many of Christopher's books can be purchased from
www.amazon.co.uk

READERS' COMMENTS

ALICE IN WELFARELAND

'Congratulations! I enjoyed reading it and happily praise it to High Heavens!'
Elspeth Cochrane, London Literary Agent

'Timely and timeless, a tale for today full of humour, intrigue and insights.'
Vision B, Education Consultants

'Provocative, not an ordinary read. Its own spectacular universe!'
Managing Director, Gateway Guardians

'A rich cake with raisons popping out everywhere. Keep the light on!'
Susan Wilmot-Josife

*'Be surprised what you'll receive both inwardly and outwardly. It's in
your hands at the right time for you.'*
D.E., Spiritual Adventurer

Bola Dauda: Why Am I Here?

Who am I? Why am I here? What should I do with my life? What is the purpose of life? How does God operate, if there is God? Which side is God when two nations are at war and each is calling for help from God?

For more than thirty years, Dr Bola Dauda has asked himself these questions and on a number of occasions he broke all diplomatic relations with God. Maybe you too have asked these questions. Maybe you are also ready to think outside the box of prejudice for or against God or religion and spirituality and even the prejudice of science. Maybe you wanted to improve your capacity to dream and realise them. Maybe you wanted to learn balance. Maybe you want to know yourself; be yourself; and give back to life.

In this compelling read, Dr Bola Dauda has shared his secret garden with us with the aim that we would accept our own experiences as valid and authentic. Before you give up, why not find the time to read the odyssey of Bola Dauda, the son of a peasant farmer, who was born because his father refused to give up?

HB ISBN: 1-904843-00-X £15.00
PB ISBN: 1-904843-01-8 £10.00

Bola Dauda: Living a Life of Abundance

Living a Life of Abundance is concise, powerful and practical. In this little book you'll discover how powerful and simple principles can help you succeed and generate wealth, joy and total freedom beyond your wildest dreams and expectations. The 67 Aikido Principles are proven, tested immutable rules of the game of life. You get better and better in the game the more you practise and sharpen your attitudinal tools, skills and knowledge. Choose any five principles at random or as you like it. Practise them consistently for a year and they will transform your life for the better. The author is so sure they work that he has guaranteed refund if for any reason you are not absolutely satisfied with the results. Buy and give copies to your friends, family, clients, prospects and staff. Bola Dauda has a message for everyone and we owe it a duty to pass it on. It is a great and an unforgettable gift from the depth of his heart. Have fun with your new life of joy and abundance and with practising the wisdom of ages.

HB ISBN: 1-904843-13-1 £7.50
PB ISBN: 1-904843-12-3 £5.00

OFFERS FOR BULK PURCHASE

You can get additional copies of Robin Books from any good book stores, from Amazon or order direct from Robin Books website: www.robinbooks.co.uk. Generous quantity discounts are available on Robin Books publications, especially when used for promotion of products and services or for training and inspirational purposes. Some of our publications are available in electronic version. Please visit our web site: www.robinbooks.co.uk. For more information on bulk purchase, please send e-mail to: readers@robinbooks.co.uk or write to: Robin Books Ltd, Sales Department, First Floor, Mission Hall, 36 Windsor Street, LIVERPOOL, L8 1XF, U.K. Tel: 0800 45 85 397